Simon Maginn
He was educated
Wallasey, and
studied music. After pursuing a doomed career as a pop
singer, and composing dozens of songs, he turned to
writing as a relief from his duties as a teacher of the organ.
He lives in a shared house in Hove, Sussex.

'The best debut novel I have read since *The Wasp Factory*.
Wonderful original writing glittering with savage imagery,
the pages breathe the tough, dark texture of a real world,
of real, inescapable fears, blurring the boundaries between nightmare and reality, mining the darkest seams of
terror imagined, and terror real'
Peter James

'*Sheep* is a novel that conveys a real sense of dread . . .
At times I was afraid to read on. As a first novel it's scary
in all sorts of ways, and Simon Maginn is certainly a name
to watch'
Ramsey Campbell

'What a fierce dark energetic imagination Simon Maginn
has. The book has everything for the aficionado – terror,
suspense, madness – but it also has style and vigour. I
think he's given the horror genre novel a badly-needed
blood transfusion'
Campbell Armstrong

'I was very impressed. Simon Maginn manages to create
and sustain a tense, eerie atmosphere which gains sub-
stantially from its isolation. Maginn develops his setting
and his characters with an authority which is compelling'
Guy Burt, author of *After the Hole*

SHEEP

Simon Maginn

CORGI BOOKS

SHEEP
A CORGI BOOK : 0 552 14122 4

First publication in Great Britain

PRINTING HISTORY
Corgi edition published 1994

Set in 10/12pt Linotype Times by Kestrel Data, Exeter

Corgi Books are published by Transworld Publishers Ltd,
61–63 Uxbridge Road, Ealing, London W5 5SA,
in Australia by Transworld Publishers (Australia) Pty Ltd,
15–25 Helles Avenue, Moorebank, NSW 2170,
and New Zealand by Transworld Publishers (NZ) Ltd,
3 William Pickering Drive, Albany, Auckland.

Reproduced, printed and bound in Great Britain by
Cox & Wyman Ltd, Reading, Berks.

Drink, yourselves, and stagger! . . .
The destruction of the beasts will terrify you!
The Book of Habbakuk 2:16

Let me sleep, and dream of sheep.
Kate Bush

For Craig A. Shieres III,
who died young and stayed pretty

Acknowledgements

I would like to thank everyone who helped with *Sheep*, particularly Michael Pompey; Sarah Jack, Jeanne Day and Hector Fraser for technical advice; Hugh Fisher for stationery, photocopying and moral support; and my editor Averil Ashfield.

1

Drowning

The word rolled round his head like a loose bearing. The child was drowning. He watched from the cliff top as the woman fought to keep herself and the child above the water. The sea, he noted, was quite calm. Surely she could manage to get the child back to the beach. Surely she can get that right, at least. They can hardly be out of their depth, he thought. The woman twisted herself round in the water, thrashing and writhing like a sea monster; the child was kicking and screaming and clawing at her. No way to behave towards your mother, I'll have to have a word. The woman opened her mouth and before the water could rush in screamed his name:

'James!'

The sound took a long time to reach him, and seemed to hang in the air. No, he thought, it's time she learned to stand on her own two feet; then he reflected that, of course, she could hardly stand in the water, and he laughed softly, indulgently. She could be so impractical sometimes, so emotional. She should stop all this screaming and just get the child out. If it was me, he said to himself, I'd get her across my shoulders and swim with one arm. Why doesn't she do that?

'James! For God's sake!'

Oh well, he thought as he watched the child come up for the last time, limp and quiet now, oh well, at least we've still got the other one, and turned to look at the little boy behind him, who was smiling and muttering, something about bones.

And then he was awake and the darkness was a shroud, and his pillow was wet and his heart was pounding, much too fast. He sat up, staring straight ahead, the tears running over his chin warm and sticky. He cleared his throat, but it turned into a sob in his mouth, and for a moment he was lost, his stomach heaving as if he were about to be sick. He got out of bed and went to the bathroom, the click of the cord loud, but also soothing. You pulled the cord, the light came on. Now why couldn't everything be like that? That way there'd be no dead daughters and no guilty fathers, no dreams. He splashed water on the face that stared at him in the mirror.

'Jesus,' he said out loud, 'I look a thousand years old.' He noticed more and more often, since Ruthie died, how he was aging. It's incredible, he thought, but I never really expected to get old. Not really. He had a fixed image of himself as he had been at twenty: it was an accidental glimpse in the reflective glass door of a shower stall in the university sports hall changing room. Wet, glossy, black-haired (all over) with *very* good eyes (really sexy eyes, he remembered thinking at the time, and blushed), and one of those light, lean muscular bodies that doesn't look too worked-on. And smiling, a smile that could start fires at two hundred paces (who was it who'd said that?) Now what was I smiling at? he thought, and the face in the bathroom mirror smiled back, ruefully, as he remembered. But this smile had creases round the eyes, below the eyes, little lines, Jesus! . . . How did that happen? How could I have let it happen? And in the cold, humming, desolate bathroom, a million miles from that steamy changing room, was a thirty-two-year-old man, who had

12

let his daughter die and whose son was growing up, growing *strange*.

Strange. Like a stranger. Like someone else's child, like one of his son's friends, polite, observant, already starting to compile the dossier that would one day condemn him, utterly, beyond hope.

Strange. Eerie, humming, secret. He no longer knew everything in Sam's head, probably not even half. Ten per cent? Five? There was no way of guessing. Sam had suddenly stopped eating meat, no sausages, no bacon (no bacon! he thought, and was incredulous), fish-paste instead of meat-paste sandwiches in the Bart Simpson lunch box. Why? James had no idea. James would come across him, in his room or on the stairs, or sitting on the low wall round the swings, *humming*. James was bewildered by his fear of this humming, was astonished that he could feel fear of his own son at all. But it was so. One day Sam's class teacher had been waiting when James came to pick up the boy. Sam had been crying, his face was puffy, his expression sullen. What's it about, Miss Bryant? Well, it's a little hard to explain, Mr Tullian, but Sam has started teaching the children rhymes. *Rhymes*? Oh God you can't mean *dirty* . . . He couldn't complete the thought and felt unable to breathe. For Jesus' sake what are you talking about?

'Now she's sinking like a stone
Now the Devil's got his bone.'

What?

Alone, in the middle of the night, James met the eyes in the mirror and admitted silently to himself that he no longer knew his son. And Adèle, said a small detached voice, do you know her either? and he felt his pulse slip

13

for a second. He wasn't at all sure that he did. Those landscapes she painted, so utterly devoid, so *blank*. The shoulders in the mirror were slumped, and James felt a shudder run through his muscles as he formulated the word 'death', and the neon strip buzzed as if it was on the moon. He splashed more water on his face, waiting for the buzzing feeling behind his eyes to clear. Then he blew his nose several times, very conscious of the noise he was making in the silent house. He clicked off the light and went along the darkened hallway to Sam's room.

James could tell that Sam was not asleep. Sam had recently developed the secretive habit of pretending to be asleep when he didn't want to be talked to, but James had learned how to spot this. What the child didn't know, and had no way of knowing, was that when he was really asleep he drooled. His mouth would hang a little open and a line of saliva would form, like a line of glue, between him and the pillow. James hugged this knowledge to himself like a charm: it was secret information, power, power over his polite son. And besides, who knew what it might do to Sam's self-esteem to be told that he dribbled like a baby? James had to pretend that he didn't know when Sam was pretending, and just wait for Sam to 'wake up' when his curiosity became overwhelming. He waited, leaning in the doorway. After about thirty seconds Sam's eyes flickered open, and James smiled.

'How's it hanging, chief?' This was a line from a film they'd gone to see, just Sam and him. It was an American comedy, with a real jive-talking main actor, and that was how he had said hello to people. Sam had squealed with delight when he heard it and for days afterwards would say little else. James said it to him now meaning everything's OK, it's just your dad come in to make sure you haven't died in your sleep. Nothing to get excited about. Sam smiled and yawned.

14

'What timesit?'

'I don't know. Late. Much too late for being awake. You go back to sleep. I'll see you tomorrow.' James came over to the bed by the window and ruffled Sam's hair. His forehead was a bit dewy; it was a warm night.

'You want the window open?'

'No. Stick it up your face.' (This was from the same film.)

'OK.' James slid away, trying to make no noise. Sam was OK. Everything was OK. He tried not to notice how big the room was without Ruthie's bed in it.

Sam counted to twenty, slowly, then said a four-line rhyme in his head (Now there's stones around her feet/Now the Devil's got his meat/When the sun comes up again/He'll slip away and go to bed). Then he heaved himself up and sat against the headboard. On the table by his bed there was a small glass jar. Inside it there was a tiny diver, with oxygen tanks on his back and blue flippers, and a mask over his face. By turning the jar over he could make the diver float down to the bottom, so slowly that you could look away and say your name ten times and look back and he'd only have moved the littlest bit. Sam turned the jar over, then immediately looked away and nerved himself not to glance back until just the last moment before the diver touched the bottom. He could see a street light through the gap in the curtains and he concentrated on this, screwing up his face, squinting like a cop.

To fill up the time he tried to think what it was his dad was so upset about. He'd heard him muttering in his sleep, then he'd heard a gasp and then, after a short pause, steps into the bathroom and water splashing. Dad hadn't used the toilet or pulled the chain, but he had washed his hands. And he'd blown his nose three times, which Sam had never heard him do before, unless he had a cold. His eyes

15

had looked a bit red, but that could be just because he was awake in the middle of the night. Also his dad wouldn't come right up to him if he had a cold, like that time he'd had the flu and had forbidden Sam even to come into the room. Sam had cried – he was too little then to know why he couldn't see his daddy. Of course, right after Ruthie had died (Sam knew all about that, in fact he knew more than they did, because they didn't know that Ruthie would come back) Mum and Dad had cried a lot, and Dad had always been blowing his nose and looking red-eyed. But that was *ages* ago. Sam jerked himself round, but the diver was still nowhere near the bottom.

Sam admitted defeat and lay down again. His mum had told him that if he couldn't sleep he could try counting sheep, and he began to do this. He imagined a great heap of sheep, an enormous pile, reaching up into the sky. They were in a big field, and there was someone throwing new sheep on all the time; their heads hung limply because they were dead. Sam only counted these new sheep. He didn't even try to count the ones that were there already because there were far too many, he just did the sheep that the man threw on with his stick. Twenty-one, twenty-two. Sam could get up to about eighty-something, but after that it all got too much and he was frightened to carry on because the numbers were so big. Fortunately by fifty-nine he was drooling contentedly.

The diver sat at the bottom of the jar, perfect with his oxygen cylinder and his mask and goggles, waiting expectantly to find himself at the top again and begin once more his endlessly, breathlessly slow descent through the immeasurably deep water. Downstairs in the cramped disorderly kitchen, the dog complained in his sleep as a fly brushed his nose, his hind legs twitching, dreaming of attackers at his rear. His ears lifted at the sound of

16

footsteps from upstairs, and his eyes flickered. Then he sighed heavily, pulled in his hind legs and, turning his head, slumped back into the warm ooze of animal oblivion, leaving just the pointed ears operating to guard himself and his house. The fly buzzed softly away, and absorbed itself in the momentous task of depositing thousands of microscopic eggs into the chicken that was defrosting on the draining board. The fly twitched its front legs as it performed this orderly, insectile act of contamination, its brilliant, subtle eyes processing the jumble of lines and planes in the dark room, scanning, canny, alert. The eggs slid effortlessly down the sharp tube, finer than a hair, and spread out under the skin of the chicken, settling into the firmly packed muscle of the wing. The fly pulled the tube back and stood motionless for a second, then buzzed away, a miracle of miniature design and unwitting agent of corruption.

The next day, mid-morning, Adèle stood, frozen, at her easel. The room, at the top of the house, was perfect for painting, with a big picture window and a skylight. She knew it was north light you were supposed to have but she liked this light better. Just going up the stairs to the room gave her a thrill – her heart jumped about like a fish in a river. When she opened the door and saw her table covered with tubes and glass jars of brushes and knives, and the stacks of canvases leaning against the wall, and the shabby blue leather couch that James had spotted at the Sunday market up at the station, and had insisted that they get a taxi for and install in her studio *right now*, she got a feeling that was important, mysterious, precious. This was where she lived. There was nowhere else in the world that was so much hers. Her heart trembled to think that something might come and change it. She was almost frightened to give herself up to the feeling too completely

17

in case God was watching and thought, hm, looks like this girl's forgotten life's a vale of tears already.

Indeed she had not. When Ruthie died in her arms, in the terrible glittering water, too small and weak to withstand its repacious demands, Adèle had thought that she'd finally stepped over into the real world, that everything before had been merely a nasty, deceitful trick to make her think that the world was all right. This was the real world, the dead child and the feeling that nothing could ever be done to make it right again, and that although nothing could ever be that bad again, events like it could happen, at any time, without any warning, just when you were smiling and thinking things were fine. Nothing could ever be fine now because Ruthie had died.

She sometimes looked away from Sam, suddenly frightened that he was going to be taken from her too. Some days she would wake up thinking, one day it's going to happen, you might as well just get used to the idea, and would be cool and distant with him, not wanting to be involved. Sam called these her please and thank you days, because she became very polite and correct in her dealings with him. He would be equally correct back, watching her closely until she melted a bit and was herself again.

Adèle thought, my own child, my only child, and her eyes became unfocused. She knew that Sam found her odd sometimes, but also knew that he didn't judge her. He was, in many ways, a remarkable child. But then, she reflected, weren't most children his age like that? They only began to judge their parents when they were older, say thirteen. And then, watch out! She would be tried in the balance and found embarrassing, this she knew. No more stolen kisses in public, no more damp little fingers reaching for her hand when they crossed the road, no more fingernails digging into her palm when the big trucks

18

went past. Her eyes filled up as she contemplated her fate. She would be the one who made him look stupid in front of his friends (his girlfriends? she thought, and couldn't believe it would ever happen), the one who made him shrivel in shame when she told him that his friends would have to go home now and he would have to go to bed. She sighed, an immense long-drawn intake, hold and breathe out. She looked again at the canvas on the easel.

It was a landscape. In fact she thought it was more like a cloudscape: there was very little land in it. The sky was a vertiginously deep azure, shading down as it reached the horizon to a colour just above eggshell. The grading was invisible, and there were a few streaks of thin white cloud near the top. The land was brown and dark greens. The ground, in contrast to the realistic sky, was a simple geometric arrangement of fields, with a harsh, angular tree near the middle. She looked closely at the picture, screwing up her face and twisting her head. She tried her hardest to think critically, sternly, just as her agent would, but she couldn't really manage it. It was her painting and who else was there to judge it? It was beautiful. And then she thought, it's completely empty. No houses, no roads, no cars and, of course, no people. Not even any animals. She went over to her table and rummaged about for a tube of zinc white. Sheep, she was thinking. Sheep.

Uncle Sebastian put his arm round James's shoulders.

'Thanks for coming in, James. Glad you could make it. Burger?' James politely declined, but asked the cowboy behind the counter for coffee, white, two sugars. The restaurant – was restaurant the right word for a place where they gave you a beefburger and then kicked you out again in an average of twelve minutes, James wondered – was done out like a cowboy joint, with big (plastic) cattle horns mounted on the walls and (plastic) cowhide chair-covers. There were a number of alcoves, which were supposed to resemble pens in a cattle shed, but which succeeded in looking rather too grimly functional, suggesting, James thought, an abattoir. Nor were these the only gimmicks. You could get beefburgers with names like Cowpoke's Pleasure and Hungry Heifer, and you could get them in different shapes: cow-shaped (of course), sheep-shaped (for the Woollyback Burger), shaped like a map of Texas, like a ten-gallon hat, and best of all, like a woman's bust: Saucy Sue's Bust Burger. Uncle Sebastian had an ingenious though depraved imagination.

'You'd be amazed the people who come in here,' he was telling James as they waited for the coffee. 'Little fellas in business suits, with their little cases, ordering the biggest thing they can see as if they're trying to impress the man behind the counter. Makes them feel big, you see, like a cowboy in a film. They enjoy that. London is a really prosaic place,' (Sebastian gave the word 'prosaic' a long, multisyllabic going-over, to make sure that James didn't miss it) 'and this joint makes them feel like they've stepped into *High Noon* or something. You get the idea?'

'Ingenious,' said James, without thinking what he was saying.

'It certainly is,' Sebastian said, leaning forward as he spoke. 'What it amounts to is a completely new way of selling beefburgers. I don't mind admitting, it's an operation I feel proud to own. And this,' he gestured widely, 'this is just the flagship: soon, in two, maybe five years, there are going to be Cowboy Joes all over London. All over Britain. Franchise them out like a Pizza Express. The only thing to do in a recession is the opposite of what everyone else is doing. Expand. I have to say it, James, I'm optimistic.'

'I can see that,' James said, sipping the coffee, then

grimacing and stirring it vigorously. Sebastian made him feel – well, he couldn't say exactly what Sebastian made him feel. Perhaps like the worm that the early bird got. Pulled?

'So. Why am I here, Sebastian?' Sebastian laughed, a £50,000-plus-per-year laugh, redolent of clubhouse and lodge, and slapped him on the arm, then patted him playfully on the cheek. Tactile bastard, aren't you, James thought. He managed a smile.

'Right to the point, eh Jim? You know, when Adèle first introduced me to you, I thought to myself, she's got herself a good one here.' Sebastian had a slightly Midlands cast to his voice, nothing as definite as an accent, certainly nothing you could call Brum, but unmistakably north of the golf-club belt. A deeper u, a shorter, harder a. The kind of voice that might at any moment announce itself as a plain-speaking man who grew up in a council house and had felt the rough side of his father's belt. A voice that, after a few brandies, might well start to expatiate on the possibilities open to a fellow of vision and determination in this once-great country; and having started, might have difficulty stopping. Not, James felt, the kind of voice that gets straight to the point.

'Well, I'll get straight to the point too. You're a good, big, strong lad, eh? Good pair of shoulders. Good pair of legs.' James received the bewildering impression that Uncle Sebastian was about to make an improper proposition. What say you and I just strip off here and now and have a good wrestle. Nothing like it for relieving the tension.

'But that's just the start of it. You've got a head on those shoulders. And you've got something between those legs, eh? You can manage. People. I'm talking about people, James. There's not many that know how to manage people, men. Now I look at you, and I see, you

21

know what I see, Jim? I see potential. OK, your own business is going down the chute. Sorry, but let's stay in the real world here. Building trades always suffer first in any recession. Small, one-man operation like yours, no-one could be surprised you're going under. No-one could say you're at fault. I honestly think – and I'm being totally open with you now, Jim – that *you*,' and here he paused to poke James in the collarbone, 'have got a long way to go. Who knows how far? That's up to you. All I can do, all I want to do, is just point you in the right direction. Maybe just push the door open for you a little bit. It's a tough world, Jim, now more than ever, competitive. And I like that. But it never did a young fellow a bit of harm to have a little push to get him going again.'

James swallowed hard and said nothing. Sebastian made him sound like a cross between a car with a faulty distributor and a dog frightened of the road. His coffee was thick and cool at the bottom of the mug (authentic chipped enamel). Was this smug bastard ever going to spit it out, or was this conversation going to go on until one of the cowboys came and shot him like a cur? James had a vision of a hip-holster and a fat Uncle Seb backing away from him, wide-eyed and sweating.

'So, Mr Jarrett – sorry, sorry, Uncle Sebastian—' the words tasted like shit in his mouth. 'Am I to understand that you're making me some kind of, erm, offer?'

'OK.'

Finally Sebastian settled down and outlined his idea. It took shape as James listened, and by the time Sebastian had finished James knew that he'd accept, at once, unconditionally, without even consulting Adèle. It was a great idea.

Sebastian had been visiting his brother who lived in Fishguard, west Wales. On an impulse he'd decided to

22

get himself lost. It was something he liked to do from time to time: it gave him a feeling of freedom and exhilaration, emotions hard to come by for a hard-driven, self-made man. He took lefts and rights at random, letting his hands do the deciding. At a business seminar once he'd heard someone say that there are two parts of the brain, and that one side is responsible for all the serious, logical manoeuvring, and the other side does all the imaginative, funny stuff. Something like that, he couldn't remember the details, but whatever side it was that was driving the car that day, it wasn't the one that had built up a fast-food empire almost from nothing.

He'd finally found himself completely lost, about two miles down a road that seemed to be leading from nowhere to nowhere else. He stopped the car and got out. It was a misty autumn day, warm and clammy. Sebastian saw a small hill at the other end of the field to his right and climbed it. And there it was. Later Sebastian would elaborate the story and say that he'd been drawn there by some kind of force, magnetism or something. Ley lines maybe. Sebastian, for all his worldliness, was a sucker for the inexplicable.

It was a large, sprawling farmhouse, Victorian, built of local stone, the pieces small and irregular, held together with cement. Although clearly abandoned, derelict and in places open to the elements, it nevertheless looked immensely strong, like a once-impregnable fortress. The windows were deeply inset, and the walls were obviously very thick. It stood in a field; the field ended in a cliff, then there was the sea. The Atlantic. Next stop America. Whatever part of Sebastian's mind was in the driving seat that day, it responded at once to this Emily Brontë location, wild and deserted, perched on a cliff top. Having decided that he wanted it, he was not surprised to see a For Sale sign propped up against one corner. There was about the house a kind of stoical indifference. People, it seemed to suggest, might indulge their meaningless passions and dramas in it, but generation after generation could rise and fall and the house would remain.

Sebastian was deeply impressed with the property, even before he looked at it close up. Something he didn't admit to feeling was a sense of apprehension, which bit at him like a cold draught in a hallway. A house could be neither good nor bad, but it could certainly be indifferent, and maybe it could be just a little hostile. This one would certainly do no-one any favours, and might just conceivably decide to trip you up if you weren't careful. The apprehension translated itself into excitement in Sebastian's mind. The old commercial spirit rose up, and he was already making the arrangements. The house would be his. It was already: he could feel it stretching out to him, pulling him into it. The house would be his.

Having bought it, at least in his own mind, he walked over to it and strolled around. It was surprisingly big, on three floors with irregular bits sticking out at the sides and round the back. The windows had a primitive quality to them, as if they were just holes clawed out of the dry stone. The front door, which was out of sight from the direction of the road, had two great stone slabs as steps. One of these was unmistakably a tombstone, though there was only the faintest memory of a trace of carving on it. It looked unbelievably old. The front door itself was a huge thing, a great lump of oak that seemed as if it could have been part of the hulk of a slaving ship. The iron knocker, indeed, did recall the kind of fitting that a leg-iron might be attached to, as if to remind the visitor that the great wealth it had taken to build the house and buy the farmland had come from the darkest, cruellest aspect of the great nineteenth-century trading endeavour, the side that was not sugar. Bristol's influence could be felt even here.

He could see at once that it had been, not a grand house, but better than that, an important house, a house for powerful and influential people. Something between the baronial squire and the gentleman farmer/landlord. The people who had lived in this house were people of stature, whose whims were attended to as matters of serious import, and whose instructions were law. They were also people who liked a good time. One of the perks of being a rich man – Sebastian thought of himself as rich, not wealthy – was that you could buy yourself pleasant company. The house expected its residents to live. Parties. Dancing. Sebastian had a vision of a throng of people, music playing. There were people dancing on the grass on the field, near the cliff, glasses clinking. Girls. Sebastian's mind finally reached the goal it had been skirting round, and he knew what he wanted to do in this house. He was going to have what the Americans might call a *ball*, and what he described to himself as fun. Innocent, healthy fun.

The house had clearly been deserted for quite some time. There were a couple of windows missing and boarded up and the roof was sagging rather badly over the south-western corner: from what he could make out by peering through a ground-floor window, the interior had been gutted by a fire and would have to be completely refurbished. A big job, he thought seriously. And then, he said, he thought: Jim Tullian. Who better? Family. Well, as good as family. Or perhaps soon-to-be-family. Eh? (James and Adèle had never married. Her parents were waiting hopefully. His had intimated that they would not attend the ceremony if it ever took place.) With the market depressed, now was the time to buy. He made a note of the estate agent's number on the weatherbeaten

25

sign, and an hour later was ensconced in a padded chair in Haverfordwest, negotiating. The estate agent had worn the look of a man for whom Christmas had come early.

'James. Now when that terrible, terrible thing happened with Ruth,' and James felt himself shrink away from the name on the lips of this person, this Uncle Sebastian, 'I felt as if it was my daughter that had died, I couldn't have felt any worse. I mean that, James.' You don't know what you're saying, James thought, or you wouldn't be saying this. 'And I thought wouldn't it be a good idea if you and Adèle and little Sam could all get away from here, right away, somewhere where you could all be together and just, you know, maybe start trying to get over it all. A break. Recharge your batteries. You know what I mean.'

'Sebastian . . .'

'Now don't say anything just yet, Jamie,' (*Jamie?*) 'just let me finish. I understand that little Sam' (he's seven years old, for Christ's sake) 'is having a bit of bother at that school you send him to. I heard something about bad behaviour, playing up, is that right? Something like that. All very upsetting. And then there's Adèle, now she, I understand, has got a show coming up, an exhibition. An important one. She's been shortlisted for a prize of some kind.'

'No, but the Turner Prize Committee have expressed . . .'

'And the show's in May of next year.'

'April.'

'April. All right. Could be an important time for her.'

'Important. Yes.' James was acutely aware of how important the exhibition was going to be. He knew every detail of what she had done, all the work, the perseverance, the swallowing of setbacks, the fighting of

26

indifference and criticism, the cultivating of friends and contacts, to get herself into the position she was in now, where her agent was getting calls from the likes of the Turner Prize Committee. Right from her first-year show at art school she'd shown promise. That was the word they used. He remembered the day she first showed him some of her paintings. Hm, he'd said, shows promise, and she'd hit him, hard enough to leave a bruise which later she kissed better at inordinate length . . .

'James? Are you with me? Now what I say is this: you, Adèle and little Sammy all go and . . .'

'Wait. Let me tell you,' James broke in, just to make himself feel like he had a role to play in the conversation (conversation, he thought, or briefing?). Sebastian behaved like an occupying army sometimes.

'Your idea is this: we, that is to say Del, Sam and me, go to stay at your little place in Wales. Over the winter, let's say the six months October to March. I take Sam out of that school we send him to and teach him myself. I dare say I can prove my educational competence. Del has a place to work that's calm and where she won't be interrupted every ten minutes by kind friends and neighbours bearing gifts and pitying looks. Meanwhile, old Dobbin the talking carthorse here buckles down and clears the place up, ready for the proud owner to move in in the spring. He might, for instance, be thinking of a party to mark the occasion. Everybody has a great time, time waves her mysterious wand and old wounds start healing over. And at the end of all this idyllic bliss, assuming that Unc's happy with the work of course, Dobbin gets himself promoted to Foreman Fred, supervising the chirpy chippies at work on a vast and growing empire of theme beefburger restaurants. Is that about the shape of it?'

James was aware that his voice had been rising as he

27

spoke. Despite himself, the indignity of this situation was working on him, making him sound somewhat like an actress meeting her first bishop.

'Now James . . .' said Sebastian, holding a hand up in front of him, as if to stem what he obviously thought was going to be a floodtide of unfortunate, unretractable statements, made in the heat of the moment, which no-one would ever remember to James's detriment. But if they could be stopped now before they started . . .

'I'll take it.' James heard himself speaking like a person who's just been talked into buying the thing he most wanted in the whole world anyway. 'Thanks Sebastian, I mean it,' he said and smiled. He stuck his hand out in that gesture of masculine solidarity and business done; Sebastian took it, and then pulled James to him, his other arm going back around James's neck, his winey breath in James's ear.

'Good boy,' he was saying, and 'good lad.'

2

The Sturdie Posts

The sheep cropped listlessly, ears down, shuffling forward as they ate, occasionally lifting their heads to scan the desolate field. Their almost full-grown winter coats made of them shapeless blobs, like a child's drawing, except for the delicate legs and feet and the watchful, mournful faces. White with irregular black blotches, they meandered over the cold, stony field, their movements slow, measured and arbitrary. Their jaws worked without pause.

From the farmhouse, Lewyn Bulmer watched them as the light faded. He had cleaned the place up as well as he could, though there were areas where the damage was so extensive that nothing could be done. The rain had been getting in where the roof had collapsed, and there was a great deal of water penetration, rotten timbers and sagging, discoloured plaster. Still, he'd done his best, swept out the mice-droppings and the brittle bodies of dead insects, opened doors and windows to clear the smell of neglect. He'd checked the electricity and the water and the flush on the toilet. He'd made up beds with his own sheets and pillowcases. He'd even put some asphodel in a glass jar and left them on the kitchen table, along with milk, eggs and a small jar of coffee. There was a pan of stew on the cooker. They should be arriving by nine, Dilys had told him, a man, a woman, a child, and a dog. A family. Neighbours for you again, Dilys had said, and stroked his face.

Dilys had brought him up while his mother was – away. His father had run the farm, silently, brooding over his wife's desertion. She was just a girl, Dilys had explained to Lewyn, aged thirteen, when he asked her, so young, not much older than you are now. You mustn't blame her. It doesn't mean she didn't love you, of course she loved you. Would she come back again? Dilys had looked at the serious thirteen-year-old and hugged him, hard. No, she said, and cried, the first adult tears Lewyn had ever seen. It was Dilys who taught him the songs that he now sometimes sang to the sheep when they were lambing in the shed, their ears flattened against their heads and their eyes wild. Dilys had shown him how to wash his clothes, how to cook, how to pray. Brought him up with the unspoken assent of his father. By fourteen he was fully grown, and sombre. By sixteen he knew what he wanted to do, and on his eighteenth birthday he signed up for ten years with the First Glamorgan Fusiliers.

Two years later when Lewyn's father became ill, Lewyn was given a compassionate discharge from the army, the only family he knew. The letter came one day when he was on exercises in Salisbury. He had sat on his hard bed in barracks and cried, his head in his hands, rocking back and forth, and Private Delaware had sat with him. Later that night he slipped a scrap of paper into Delaware's sleeping hand; it had written on it his address and I love you. Delaware hadn't woken up and Lewyn had kissed him goodbye, once, very chastely on the mouth, his tags jingling clearly in the silent room, and squeezed Delaware's arm, hard enough to mark it.

As Lewyn sat in the darkening house watching the sheep in the next field, he felt again that kiss, and his hand on Delaware's arm, and blushed. What a long way away all that was, he thought, and yet his body tingled with the recollection as if to say, no, it was here and now, this is the same warm body. Lewyn had lived long enough on his own to come to an understanding of himself, and even a wan liking. His own company, which in the long years of nursing his bedridden father – washing him, putting him on his pot, cleaning his teeth, spooning in the porridge and the mashed potato, while his father's stern cold blue eyes bored into him with the malevolence of the helpless – which then had been a burden, a pressing weight like the sixty-pound pack he'd carried in basic training, was now light as air.

The rigorous, monotonous life on the small farm suited him well, the routine governed by the cycles of tupping, lambing, shearing and slaughter. Each day, when he'd finished the many small chores that his solitary existence required of him, he would go up to the large attic room at the top of the house, where the bench and the weights were. He would strip to his army vest and shorts and push himself through a strenuous routine that left him dripping with sweat, muscles tight and aching, his head thumping and the blood fast and churning through his veins. At the age of thirty-eight he still had the hard, bulky physique he'd inherited from his father, the same body he'd had at fourteen.

These daily workouts, the feeling of strained flesh, the trembling of muscles as he clenched his teeth and tried for one more repetition, but most of all the lightness in the head and the fluttering in the stomach when the bar clanked into the grooved rest for the last time; the sensation of floating, of dreamlike weightlessness, coupled with a faint and not unpleasant nausea; this was when Lewyn felt most alive. Felt most himself.

Later, in the chipped white bath in the cold bathroom, he would succumb to the heat of the water and the

31

lubrication of the soap and, eyes closed, allow the stark and often brutal pictures to flood his mind as his hand worked, slowly and then faster. The final image, before he shouted out and came, would be violent, cruel, horrible, and he would immediately disown it. That was not really me, he would say to himself, not really. That was the only part of himself that Lewyn had not grown to like, but, he knew, it was a big part. The obscene images, although they seemed to come from outside, from somewhere else, came from him, from his own mind, from his own body. Lewyn knew all this, and yet he felt that something exterior was working on him, that he was taken over by something else, something – well, Dilys would call it something evil.

Lewyn no longer prayed. When his father died, in terrible pain, the unyielding blue eyes locked on to the crucifix on the wall, Lewyn realized that he could no longer pray to any God that allowed such suffering into the world. If there was a God then he was perverse, sadistic, insane. In fact a God like that would not be a God, but would be a Devil. Lewyn believed in the Devil. And he believed that the source of the vicious scenes of torture and humiliation was the Devil, a Devil that had no God to restrain him or punish him or condemn him. A Devil triumphant and grinning. There were times when Lewyn awoke in the blackness of the night as the wind raged round the house, and feared for his soul.

One of the sheep strayed to the fence at the edge of the cliff. It nuzzled the salty, wiry grass, seemingly oblivious of the long, long drop to the sea just a dainty step away. It was Lewyn's father who had put up the sturdie posts, and uncoiled the barbed wire and fastened it, three strands, all along the cliff edge, the length of four fields.

Lewyn could remember the hammering and sawing,

and the excitement of this unusual job. His father had let him hold the posts as he raised the sledgehammer and slammed it down. Lewyn had felt no fear that his father might miss, that the iron hammer might land instead on his hand or head. He trusted his father completely then.

In the twelve months before the fence went up they had lost forty sheep over the cliff; the beasts had seemed to become reckless and foolish, they meandered along the edge, taking curious dancing steps, unable to maintain a straight line. They held their heads in stilted, awkward positions. They wobbled, danced, fell. Some of them seemed simply to walk to the edge, sniff the air, and step over. And in the incident that had prompted the erecting of the fence, fifteen sheep had panicked and run headlong over the cliff, a frenzy that Lewyn's father had witnessed and had never forgotten. While he lay dying he would sometimes call Lewyn to him to tell him the story. The day after that incident, Lewyn's father had driven to the vet in Haverfordwest, something that usually only happened at lambing, if a lamb got into a difficult birth position, or when, very infrequently, there were triplets.

His father arrived back with the vet in the early afternoon. The vet took his case of instruments and followed Lewyn's father down the cliffside to the rocky beach. Lewyn had trailed behind, fascinated by the vet with his black jacket and shiny little shoes, and his case with brass finishings on the corners.

'Can't use this one,' the vet had said when they came to the first carcass. 'The head's all bashed in, see?'

Lewyn had seen the creature, sprawled lazily over a flat rock, its head a mess of red and mushy white, with splinters of bone mixed in. Already there were flies crawling over the mess. The sheep's eyes were glazed over, open, staring out to sea. It looks surprised, little Lewyn thought, it wasn't expecting this at all.

'Better drag it up a bit, out of the way of the water. It'll have to be burned. They all will. Will you give me a hand, Mr Bulmer?' The vet had an alert and mobile face, and seemed always to be on the verge of laughing but seldom did.

'Little thing,' Lewyn's father had said, staring at the ruined animal; Lewyn looked at him, astonished. Lewyn was ten: never before could he remember hearing that voice from his father, a deep and rumbling voice full of tenderness and pity.

'Little thing, there now.'

Between them, the vet and Lewyn's father wrestled the wet, inert carcass, pulling at the hind legs. It was surprisingly heavy for all its daintiness. Lewyn took hold of a foot and helped them, strong even at ten. They hauled the sheep over the rocks until they reached a hollow under the cliff, almost a cave.

'What would make them do it, Mr Astley? I've never known them to do anything like it before, why would they?' Lewyn's father had asked in a voice that was bewildered. Lewyn had been momentarily shocked by this evidence of helplessness in his father, almost ashamed. The vet sensed that Lewyn had better be got out of the way.

'Hey Lewyn, do you think you can get back up to the house by yourself?' he asked challengingly, his eyes shining.

'Yup.'

'And do you think you could come back down again, with a big two-gallon can of petrol?'

'Reckon so, aye.'

'What do you think, Mr Bulmer? Can he do it?'

'Aye, he's a strong lad, a good lad.'

Lewyn could still recall the pride swelling his whole body at these words, a rush of delight. He determined that he would perform this task perfectly, quickly. This new feeling completely wiped away the unease and anxiety his father's odd behaviour had brought on. He dashed away, excited, happy. Have I ever been so happy since, Lewyn Bulmer, thirty-eight, asked himself as the house grew black and dismal around him.

The path doubled back on itself a number of times. At the first turning Lewyn heard voices and stopped.

'Hold the head still now, Owen, will you? Steady as you can.'

'Like this?'

'That's . . . the . . . way . . .'

Lewyn crept away from the path and crawled over to the edge. He poked his head over, and directly below him he saw the bald patch on the crown of the vet's head. His father was straddling a dead sheep, both hands holding its head. The vet's case was open beside him. The instruments and needles and bottles twinkled in the flat afternoon light. The vet had put on a pair of glasses, his neat jacket was on the rock next to the bag, and over his left hand and arm he had a long black rubber glove. In his right hand he held a small saw.

Lewyn watched, goggled, as the saw bit through the top of the sheep's head, the bone grinding against the steel. The vet was cutting off the top of the sheep's head at the widest point, below the ears and above the eyes. Like cutting off the top of your egg, Lewyn thought, and smiled weakly.

The vet sawed slowly and mechanically for about three minutes, pausing occasionally to wipe his forehead with his shirtsleeve. The blade dug in and out, in and out, smeared with blood and tissue, until finally the vet pulled it out and placed it on the rock. Gently and with the utmost care he took hold of one of the sheep's ears with his gloved left hand, and pulled away the top of its head.

Lewyn heard a sound, a little slithering, slurping sound, and felt his stomach roll over as the brain of the sheep, with the meningeal fluid like milk and the rich red blood, flopped over the side of the skull and spread itself across the rock. What a lot of brain, Lewyn thought, maybe they're not so stupid after all. Lewyn looked at his father; his jaws were clamped together and his eyes were narrowed to slits as he grasped the lower half of the sheep's head.

The vet went to his bag, whistling, and took out a long pointed instrument with a wooden handle, like a meat skewer, only with a curved hook on the end. He brought it over and, grasping the semi-solid mass of the brain with his gloved hand, he dug the skewer into the greyish slimy tissue, twisting it round and then pulling it up, slowly. He did this four, five, six times, until, pulling it up, he stopped and looked at Lewyn's father, his eyes twinkling.

'I believe we've got one, Owen.'

He drew the skewer out, slowly, slowly, an inch at a time, while the brain made its sucking and slurring sounds, and then drew it clear. And then kept on pulling, for on the hook at the end of the skewer was a flat grey ribbon, narrow and ridged along its length, as if in sections. Lewyn put his hands to his head but could still hear the slippery, gurgly noises. He repeated to himself, 'The Devil, the Devil,' though he didn't know why. When the ribbon was over two feet long and the vet was standing above the sheep, his arm outstretched with the – thing – wriggling and turning on the end of his skewer, its other end free of the brain after the vet had given a final tug, Lewyn stood up and shouted aloud:

'The Devil! The Devil!'

He screamed, a tiny child again, utterly terrified and appalled, and staring, staring at the grey ribbon turning lazily this way and that, unable to look away. His father had run up the path and got him, got hold of him, turning his head away and holding him flat to his body. There were flecks of brain on his trousers.

'There now, there now,' his father murmured, stroking his head. Lewyn had wept, with fear but also shame at his weakness, crying like a baby.

Lewyn had been given a spoonful of whisky and put to bed, and all that afternoon his father and the vet had collected the sheep from their resting places on the rocks and in the shingle, and had dragged and carried them to the hollow under the cliff. Where there were separated limbs or loose tissue the vet had scooped them up with his gloved hand, whistling, and dropped them on to the pile.

By five o'clock there was a heap of bodies, a rough pyramid, the off-white wool matted and stained with blood. Lewyn's father left the vet to finish off and went to the house to collect the petrol and some loose lumber. Back at the beach, dumping the can and the wood, he dug into his pocket and produced a small flask. He and the vet drank in turn, the vet smacking his lips in appreciation. The vet stacked wood at the bottom of the heap, while Lewyn's father sprayed the pitiful mound of wool and hoof and surprised faces with petrol.

The vet lit a sliver of wood with his cigar lighter, and, gingerly, put it to the wool of the nearest sheep. Almost at once the wool blackened and charred and the smell rose up, acrid. But the fire's progress was slow and it soon went out.

'I think we may need some more petrol, Owen, I wonder if you wouldn't mind?' the vet said. Lewyn's father brought down two more cans and this time Lewyn followed him, chastened and white, but composed, carrying more wood.

The bodies burned, but without enthusiasm and unevenly, until Lewyn's father, with no regard for safety, threw on more and more petrol, climbing up on to the heap of corpses, trampling over their heads and backs and dainty hooves. When both cans were empty the vet again lit the fire and this time it took, its grip steady and bright. The day was windless and the choking, stinking black smoke rose straight up in a thick pillar, up to heaven, thought Lewyn. Again they fetched more wood and petrol and by six-thirty the pile had settled into a great heap of cinders and glowing fragments, giving out an intense heat and a rich, savoury smell. Lewyn found himself salivating. The pile burnt steady and hot, settling and crackling. The air above it shuddered. The tide started to turn at seven, and the light began to fade.

Breaking a silence that had lasted for fifteen or so minutes, the vet said brightly, 'Well, I think that's that, Owen. I'm sorry for your trouble, I truly am.'

'Aye,' said Owen Bulmer, and sighed.

'I'll have to order some spray from Swansea, it'll take probably a week or ten days. As soon as I get it I'll be back. Also I'll write to the Veterinary Investigation Service, and the Ministry of course.'

'Ministry,' said Lewyn's father blankly.

'Of Agriculture, Fisheries and Food.' He announced this mouthful with great solemnity.

'You have to do that, do you?' Owen Bulmer had enquired defiantly. He didn't want strangers knowing his business, nor any trouble with any Ministry neither, thank you.

'Well, no I don't have to, this isn't what they call a notifiable disease, but generally speaking . . .'

'Then I'd much rather you didn't, Mr Astley, and obliged to you. If it's all the same.'

'As you wish, Owen. Well, until I get the spray, there's not much you and your boy can do but wait and pray to God that it hasn't spread to the whole flock. And watch out for foxes, they can spread it. If I were in your position I would put up a fence, a good strong one, right the way along, just in case there are any more afflicted animals. Much easier to contain it up there than down here, I'm sure you'll agree.' He ruffled Lewyn's hair and beamed at him.

'And of course we want to stop them chasing each other when one of them gets it into his head to jump over.' The vet laughed, and Lewyn laughed back, though he wasn't sure how funny this really was.

'Now don't you worry, your dad'll take care of it all, you'll see,' said the vet. 'Nothing to upset yourself over. Just a little worm, that's all it is.'

When they'd had their tea that evening, Lewyn's father had given his son a garbled version of what the vet had told him about the life cycle of *Taenia Multiceps*, and its sinister transformation into *Coenurus Cerebralis*.

'He calls it sturdie. It's a disease sheep get from the soil. What happens, see, is that there are little, little eggs sometimes in the ground, and the sheep eat the eggs. They're so small these eggs you can't even see 'em, see, they're tiny, but when they get into the sheep's stomach they start to turn into worms. Like the worms in the soil, but flatter than that. These worms, they're like threads to start off with, but they eat the food that the sheep eats, cos they're in its stomach, and when they're big enough they come out of its stomach and go along its spine. Then what happens, they go into its brain. They – they kind of eat away at its brain, and the sheep don't know what's

39

happening, but it makes them go dizzy, they get vertigo. What that means is that they come over funny when they're high up, and they can't stand straight and they can't even walk straight, and they fall over. So it's nothing to worry over, Mr Astley says, it's just a worm, and you can kill it with spray on the ground and keeping dogs and foxes away. It needn't kill them if you treat 'em soon enough, Mr Astley says. Sometimes it's in droppings of foxes and wild dogs, but Mr Astley he thinks sometimes it's just there in the ground, all the time, and it just comes out every so often, not for any reason at all.'

Lewyn looked at his hands as his father spoke. His father was trying hard to make his voice convey re-assurance and control. Nothing to worry over, just a worm. A worm that lives in an egg in the ground and eats the brains of animals while they're still alive and makes them dance and run over the edge of the cliff and smash themselves to pieces. That's all.

'Mr Astley, he says people can't get it, this worm it can't live in people, only in sheep. So you got nothing to worry over.' His father looked at him, appealing to him to believe him, to trust him, to have faith in him. Lewyn thought of his father's voice a few hours earlier, querulous, asking the vet, 'What would make them do it, Mr Astley?' Then he put the thought away, though it would return later.

'OK,' he said.

'And tomorrow we can go and get some wood and put up the posts.'

'OK.'

Lewyn had felt pleased that his father had spoken to him for so long, and so seriously. And it would be good helping him with the sturdie posts, working alongside him. He tried to dismiss the vile, lazily turning worm from his mind, and think about other things. But in the night he'd cried again, trying to stifle the sound of the gulps and sniffles by covering his head with the pillow.

Dilys had come over the next day. Lewyn's dad told her about the vet's visit and the worm, but omitted the part about Lewyn's panic. Lewyn glowed with pleasure and complicity, and when Dilys had come to him all sympathy and soothing, he'd fought shy of her and said he had to help his dad with the fence. She'd held him at arm's length and looked hard at him.

'Lewyn. Is everything all right?'

' 'Course it is,' he'd said, avoiding her searching eye. He'd been crying, she could see that. But she couldn't make him talk to her. She smiled, and patted him on the behind.

'OK my beauty.'

Lewyn sat on, on the cold stone ledge under the window in the farmhouse, gazing out at what was now impenetrable darkness. Not like me, he thought, to be just sitting here. Woolgathering. He was startled by a banging noise from upstairs; his beefy body froze with fright, and then he thought, shit, loose window.

He stood up, stiff, and went to the stairs. The staircase turned through ninety degrees halfway up, and the deep, velvety blackness at that first landing sent a thrill of horror through him. Lewyn, long inured to solitude, darkness and silence, found that, even now, he could be scared of the dark. He laughed, softly, at the thought, but it was true. In the army he'd been on a tour in Northern Ireland, three months, and once he'd been caught in a firefight at a border crossing; he'd kept his head and managed to get himself and the men with him out safely, without any injury. He'd been commended: at nineteen it was quite an accomplishment. And then, two weeks later, he'd been involved in the defusing of a suspected car-bomb outside a pub in Newry, and had had to stand guard, at what was in theory a safe distance, until the experts arrived. Seven minutes, and every second could have been his last. He'd sweated it out, and his CO had shaken his hand and praised his courage. The big, brave soldier. Now here he was at the foot of a stairwell in a deserted farmhouse, his bladder turned to jelly at the thought of going up the stairs.

'Wish I'd thought to put a light in,' he said, and grinned with fear at the sound of his voice.

The only working lights were in the kitchen and scullery and in the attics. There were no lights at all on the first floor. The wind had sprung up and the loose window was creaking and thudding. He could smell the cold air streaming down the stairwell. He licked his lips and rubbed his hands down his trousers. He put one foot on the first stair, and the blackness on the landing came forward to meet him; he backed down again.

Involuntarily he clutched his penis as he fought with the implacable, irrational and incapacitating fear. Then he was up and moving, walking fast and heavily, stamping on the bare wooden stairs. Now he was turning and could see the doorway facing the top of the staircase, stamp, stamp, grinning like a fool, glancing nervously behind, his hand clutching his cock. A few steps more and he was at the top of the stairs, his heart thumping as if he were deadlifting a hundred and twenty. He rested his back against the wall, and the nightmarish terror that something might be behind him left him, like cold water draining out of a tank. The corridor stretched in both directions, but the banging of the window was coming from the right-hand side, and Lewyn immediately knew which room it was. Of course, it had to be that one. He stood in the dark corridor with the cold air streaming round his legs, and felt the flesh on his scrotum crawl. Suddenly he wanted to urinate, very urgently.

they-think-me-mad-I-am-not-mad-please-jesus

He dashed the words away from his mind, shaking his head. Unknowingly he had adopted a hunter's crouch, knees slightly bent, buttocks pulled in, neck and head drawn down, fists clenched. His powerful body was responding to instructions laid down millions of years ago, moulding itself to a shape that had served it well in forests and jungles, when it was faced with an enemy. Minute muscles were responding to infinitesimally subtle commands and pulling up the hairs on his legs and forearms and neck, to make him look bigger, more ferocious. He noted with surprise that he was erect, and formulated the thought 'fear is like desire'; they certainly felt very alike. Except that fear froze you, made you immobile, presumably a defence designed to minimalize any noise you might make in a forest or jungle, while you were hiding from the tiger or the bear. Or the demon. Only people, he thought, have ever been menaced by demons, and he grinned at the idea, displaying teeth. Only people fear the dead; animals simply eat them. I'd better go and shut that window, he thought, and laughed aloud. With a conscious effort he relaxed the muscles of his body, one by one, a technique he had learnt from Dilys.

He turned to the right and walked down the corridor, past two doors, turned left and there it was. Two low steps led up to it. Unlike the other doors this one was of solid oak, three inches thick. There was a bolt at top and bottom, a deadlock, and a big iron handle. The surround was also of oak, and the impression was one of tremendous strength. Lewyn stood outside and the window slammed shut, then creaked open again. He mounted the steps, one two, pulled the bolt from the top and then from the bottom, turned the deadlock with the key that was in

43

it (it was as cold as petrol on his fingers) and then took the handle in both hands and pulled.

At first nothing happened; then there was a moan and a great gush of damp air as the wind pushed the door open from inside. He stepped back and stumbled slightly as the door swung wider, silently and smoothly, and the window slammed again, *bang*!

I-will-watch-he-will-not-have-me

He strode into the room, the blood singing in his ears. In three paces he was at the window, which had swung open again. He grasped the handle and slammed it shut, secured the lock. As he looked out he saw the lights of a car, then the car itself rounding the bend leading to the house. He tried to penetrate the blackness to see inside the car, and for a moment met the eyes of a woman. She looked terrified, as if she were riding a deserted ghost train which had gone out of control, and he thought: Edith, she's come back.

He stood motionless for a long moment, then turned on his heel and advanced out of the room, looking neither left nor right but only directly ahead so that he would not see the iron rings in the wall and the crudely carved inscriptions. There's no handle on this side of the door he thought, and then he was out, was pushing the heavy, awkward door shut, was bolting and locking it, and was in flight down the corridor, *as I was walking up the stair*, on to the landing, *I met a man who wasn't there*, his boots rattling against the bare wooden stairs, ratatatat, in full ignominious retreat, his bladder bursting. He reached the front door at the foot of the stairs and, flinging it open, stood outside and leaned on the wall, gasping at the freezing air and the wind off the sea, his big chest heaving up and down like the waves. He put his hands on his hips and bent down like a runner after a long race, and breathed the air and blew it out again in great blasts. Then

44

he could hold it no longer and, turning to the wall, unzipped his trousers with trembling hands, pulled out his cock and, one hand braced against the wall and the other holding his cock, his legs spread and his head tilted up, pissed. He closed his eyes as his aching bladder emptied, and the pulse in the great vein in his neck slowed a little. He opened his mouth and unknowingly emitted a long soft moan, as his water steamed and foamed at his feet, and he grinned at his foolishness.

He heard the car approaching, in low gear, then idling, then cutting out. A door opened and he heard a dog bark, then the other door opened and there was a great deal of shuffling and rattling and quiet voices. The dog barked repeatedly, a musical low-pitched wo wo wo, and then there was a child's fluting voice: 'Dad?'

The family, Lewyn thought, and smiled.

'Hello!' he called out. 'You're welcome!'

They were seated round the kitchen table, as Lewyn heated up the stew and made coffee and put down some milk for the dog.

'I won't stay,' he said over his shoulder as he stirred the stew. 'I should be getting back anyway, I just thought I'd see that you were all right and say hello.'

'Well . . .' said Adèle, at a loss, glancing over at James, 'we weren't expecting a welcome.'

'Dilys told me you were coming,' Lewyn said, then, 'but of course you don't know Dilys yet. Anyway, your Uncle Sebastian he rang her to tell her, see, and she come over to tell me. I had a key from, from last time. Which reminds me.' He pulled a bunch of keys out of his pocket and removed the right one, put it down on the table. 'I've kind of been looking after the place a bit. Not that it's anything to do with me, not really.'

'Were you upstairs, just now? About five minutes ago?'

Adèle asked, her voice sounding strange to her; somehow it seemed like an accusation.

'Yes, I was . . .'

'Oh then it must have been you I saw,' she rushed on, 'at the window at the back. I swore I saw someone as we were driving up, but Jamie wouldn't have it.' She smiled across at James, who gave her a tense grin in return. 'It really gave me a fright.'

'That's funny, cos you gave me a fright an' all, don't know why,' Lewyn said, and they laughed.

'I thought you looked like you'd seen a ghost,' Adèle said, still laughing.

'Right, well I'll be off now. Stew's all ready. I hope it's all right.' (I hope *you'll* be all right.) 'Sorry about the lights upstairs, I just didn't think of them, stupid really. I'll call in tomorrow for the pan.' He picked up his jacket from the window seat in the bare living room adjoining the kitchen, and opened the front door.

'Mr Bulmer.' It was Adèle, coming out from the kitchen.

'Lewyn.' He smiled.

'Oh yes. Lewyn.' She smiled back. 'Thanks for doing all this. Really. You can't imagine how worried I've been about it, we all have.'

'Oh I'm sure. Take a bit of getting used to, I dare say.' He looked down as he spoke, as if, she thought, he was unused to talking to people. Then he looked up.

'Oh I, stupid, I forgot to say, I've made up beds for you, I'll show you. How could I forget to say that?' He went to the stairs and without the smallest hesitation started up them, with Adèle following. He turned left at the top and went to the furthest door.

'This is the biggest room, the nicest I think, with the double bed, I hope that's not . . .' he stopped, embarrassed. Dilys and Dave he knew slept in single beds, but then people from the city, he'd thought, and they young . . . Adèle sensed his difficulty.

'That's just perfect. White sheets. And you've put flowers . . .' She beamed at him, and he blushed and turned away.

'And then for the boy, I've made one up here,' he said, opening the door to the next bedroom. There was a single bed on high metal legs, and on top of the pillow sat a grizzled-looking toy monkey.

'I thought he might like it, but then I suppose he's a bit old for teddies and suchlike,' he said, embarrassed again and sure he'd done the wrong thing. Adèle wanted to kiss him, but instead patted his shoulder.

'Well, if he doesn't want it I'll have it,' she said.

'Right. I'm away now,' he said and rattled down the stairs, calling out goodnight as he passed through the living room; then he stopped. The child (what was his name?) was standing at the open front door, and turned to look at him. Bright little eyes, Lewyn thought, and then heard, discerned, a faint humming sound that the boy was making, as his eyes flickered over Lewyn's face and body. Then the child smiled, and Lewyn said, 'Well bye then,' and brushed past him out of the heavy front door.

Hope that dog's not going to be a nuisance, he thought, as he walked up the path across the fields to his house. You could never tell with dogs. Better be sure they've got him wormed. Quiet, the man of the house was. Good-looking fellow. He smiled. Neighbours again, he thought. Got to be better than the last lot, anyway. Can't be no worse.

'Jamie,' Adèle said as they lay in the unfamiliar bed, which felt as if it was miles up in the sky on its stark iron legs.

'Hmmmm,' said James reluctantly. He assumed she wanted him to go and do something, and he was so *warm*.

'I just thought. That stew.'

'Hmmm,' he said and wriggled.

'Sam ate it, didn't he?'

What was she talking about? She'd seen him eat it. He'd gulped it down, even had more.

'I didn't think at the time, but that means there wasn't any meat in it. Now I think about it I can remember. There wasn't.'

'Hmmmm,' James said again, and wriggled his head into a good position to nuzzle her neck.

'Well, don't you think that's odd? I mean on a *sheep* farm?'

'Very odd,' he murmured, 'extremely sinister,' and his warm wet tongue entered her ear and she was gone.

3

Talking to Strangers

James, Sam and Elvis the dog had driven into Fishguard to buy food and some of the endless small things they'd discovered they'd forgotten (corkscrew, coathangers, tea-towels, alarm clock . . .), and to get James some of the tools he was going to need. Uncle Seb had put a largish cheque into James and Adèle's joint account, and there was suddenly money! a phenomenon long departed from their lives. It was beautiful warm October, and the trees dotted along the roadside, oddly individual and ancient-looking, were changing colour, something that fascinated Sam who was at that moment demanding a complete explanation.

Alone in the farmhouse, Adèle was pottering about. Pottering about was, she thought, probably the thing she liked doing most in the world. Well, apart from sex of course. And painting. And watching Sam paint. Well all right, *one* of her favourite things. She sang the words aloud as she sat at the kitchen table, having one of several post-breakfast Silk Cuts. She'd continued smoking even when pregnant, though she'd cut right down. Guilt, guilt, but ah what a guilty pleasure, what a pleasurable guilt! All of Adèle's set at boarding school had smoked, it was only the odd and the friendless who didn't. She'd never given up, even after just about everyone she knew (or at least kept in touch with) had stopped. James had never smoked, unusual for a man his age and (say it) class. She suspected that he found it beguiling in her, despite his professed horror of it, in the same way that he was beguiled by her indefinably lofty manner, her (only somewhat) privileged background, and the *grave* accent on the middle vowel in her Christian name. Adèle. A-d-e-*grave*-l-e. He was, she knew, surprised rather than beguiled by her success as an artist. He would acknowledge that the paintings were good, some he thought very good; underneath his words, however, she sensed the unspoken thought, 'but anyone can do *that*.'

She herself was surprised by her success. At art school she had gone about awed by the seemingly effortless style and confidence of her fellow students, amazed at their abilities and their faith in those abilities. Their work was amusing, brilliant, original; hers always seemed to her to be cramped and anxious, which was more or less how she'd felt. She'd gone through her three years in a state of ill-defined dread, of her fellows, her tutors, of just about everybody, come to think of it. She'd been prey to a wide array of intestinal disorders, which had conspired to make her life miserable for much of the time. And that was what she thought her canvases looked like. But it was she, and not they, her brilliant friends, who had got on, progressing from group shows in anarchic squat galleries to solo shows in art centres and those horrible trendy cafés, through a brief profile in a new-names-to-watch article in *Marie Claire* (a publication she was, she freely admitted, besotted with) to her first contact with a real London agent, and then the delicious, tantalizingly slow blooming of her success.

She stood up, stretched, and wandered through the ground floor. Everything, she reflected, was livable in, but damaged. It reminded her of her early days in Brighton, when she had lived for a brief but unforgettable three months in a squat. Slumming, she thought, and smiled. Not even one of those well-managed middle-class squats with electricity and working sanitation, but a condemned carpet warehouse. Calor gas and stolen showers in the nearby sports centre. This place had much the same feel, both crumblingly dry and unpleasingly damp, scorched timbers poking out like broken bones, gaping window holes like blind eyes, dangerous floors.

Dangerous.

She continued her rendition from *The Sound of Music*, warbling out of a glassless window, and was startled, shocked, to see scores of little black and white faces watching her. Christ, she thought, the hills *are* alive. She put her hand to her breast where her heart had just kicked her. Bloody creepy *sheep*.

'Gw'an, eat your fucking grass, you morons!' she yelled at them, discountenanced by their blank, unblinking stares. The one nearest her glanced away, then back, then clumsily turned itself round and moved away.

'Mint sauce! Mint sauce!' she bellowed out after it. 'Ha fucking ha! And carrots and peas and gra-vy,' she sang, and threw her cigarette end out of the window. Ruthie, she knew, would have been frightened of the sheep. Perhaps not frightened exactly, but timid, cautious. When Uncle Daniel had bought her, aged four, a huge stuffed giraffe (from Hamley's, God knew how much it had cost!) and they'd brought her into the sitting room to receive it, she'd just stared and stared. She wouldn't go near it. Adèle had pushed her towards it, but Ruthie had backed away with a nervous little smile, which had turned into tears. Buried her face in her mother's legs. Adèle had been mortified, and Uncle Daniel, single his whole life and not used to the ways of children, had laughed it off, but was clearly offended and, to Adèle's anguish, a little disdainful. And, God save her soul, Adèle had been ashamed. Of her own child! But she could be so *annoying*. No, *used* to be so annoying. Was so annoying no longer. Tense, thought Adèle, mimicking her old Classics mistress, Miss Grealis, attend to the tense if you want to make sense.

The giraffe had been adopted by Sam, aged two, who would topple it over and try to break its legs off. For a while that had been his only mission, his real work. And where had all of Ruthie's caution got her? It was almost funny. Well, perhaps funny was the wrong word, in the circumstances . . . Adèle felt tears at the back of her eyes and in her sinuses, and returned to the kitchen.

Wash the dishes, isn't that what housewives are supposed to do? She dutifully ran hot water and as always fell into a kind of trance state until everything was piled up on the draining board. She rinsed it all by slinging cold water on it from the bowl, breaking a glass. She didn't care. You had to rinse them or the washing-up liquid gave you cancer. Something like that. She'd read it somewhere.

'Well, here we are on holiday,' she said, and stood up to do a little dance. 'Holiday,' she sang, doing her best karaoke Madonna. Sam thought they were on holiday here. And in a way they were. After Ruthie, Adèle had kept on painting; she'd painted on the day of the funeral, that ghastly suburban cremation, where she hadn't been able to cry. James had cried, no stopping *him*, and he hadn't worked for weeks, had cancelled a dormer window he was scheduled to put in along with dozens of other smaller jobs.

For a while it had looked as if he was going to be one of the lucky builders who would ride out the recession, accumulating all the work that the other, unlucky, liquidated builders had had to cancel. Mostly small things, repairs and minor renovations, fixing banisters and even

52

mending leaking taps. He took what he could get, with good grace. She had to give him that. They'd even had a week's holiday, a real holiday in Cornwall at a guesthouse. (Sam had been terribly impressed that they had their own lavatory and their own bathroom, and even a kettle in their room with cups and sachets of coffee. And the pictures on the walls were real pictures.) And then *bloody* Ruthie . . .

Now Adèle did cry, simultaneously glad she hadn't got round to doing her make-up yet. James had spent his days after Ruthie's death at their disgracefully abandoned allotment, which just happened to be up near the crematorium. He didn't plant anything, he just dug it. Turned it over. Then home, beer, television, crying. Adèle supposed you could call it a kind of breakdown. Not, she thought, a particularly stylish one.

And then Sam had said the Odd Thing. Quite out of the blue, while Adèle was reading a seed catalogue (it was *she* who was the gardener), and James was sitting in front of *Taggart*, red-eyed, tipsy, maudlin.

'So isn't Ruthie coming back any more?'

He had seemed genuinely puzzled. Adèle had felt a slow shock, like the prickly kind of sweat you get with the flu. They didn't know how much Sam had understood; he'd accepted everything, had looked appropriately solemn, and clearly knew that what had happened was serious. He'd been told that Ruthie was dead. When you were dead you didn't live at home any more. Your body got burned (God it sounded brutal) and your spirit went up to the sky, where you were happy for ever. Your clothes went to the poor children. Neither she nor James wanted Sam to get any funny notions about religion and God and the fucking Baby Jesus. He got enough of that garbage at school. They wanted to tell him honestly what it was about, as far as they knew or believed. Presents at

Christmas had never been from Santa Claus, but had been bought by Mum and Dad because they loved him. They thought he deserved, or rather needed, to be given the truth.

Adèle turned the television off (this was serious), earning a baleful look from both Sam and (maddeningly!) James.

'Ruthie's dead. The water killed her and she died. So she can't ever come back,' Adèle had said, almost angrily. Sam stiffened, sensing her mood.

'I'm not angry with you,' she said quickly, and sat beside him on the arm of the two-seater.

'But can't you make her come back?' Sam had asked earnestly. 'Can't you make her?'

' 'Fraid not,' Adèle said, carefully, softly. 'Sorry, matey. No-one can make her come back now. If we could we would, because we still love her. We'll always love her, just like we'll always love you. But dead is dead, pumpkin.' She stroked his head.

'But you haven't even *tried*,' Sam said. 'Why don't you try?'

Adèle had begun to get a very peculiar feeling, a kind of light-headed, singing feeling, as she stared down at her son's short black hair. What was going on under that neat little haircut?

'*How?*' she whispered, and then James was on his feet.

'Bed!' he'd shouted, 'bed, right now!'

Sam had burst into tears and stomped up to his room.

'Sam,' Adèle had called after him, 'I'll be up in a minute.'

When Sam's door had clicked shut, James had stared hard at Adèle, both of them on their feet, both furious. A familiar posture, thought Adèle wearily.

'He's seven years old!' she'd shouted abruptly. 'Did you have to scream at him like that?'

'What in God's holy name did you think you were doing there?' James had flung back. 'I mean, what *exactly* did you mean, "how?" '

'I didn't mean anything! I was just trying to explain . . .'

'No, no that's not it at all!' he yelled, and she could hear his father in his voice. That and the beer.

'You were practically, practically encouraging him to think . . .'

'Think what, James? Jesus! What are *you* thinking?'

He said nothing for a second, then quite carefully:

'I wish she hadn't died.'

Adèle had felt her whole body trembling as she held on to the back of the sofa.

'I couldn't help it! I couldn't help it, James, I swear to God . . .' This burst out of her before she could stop it. She hadn't known that her guilt about Ruthie's death was so close to the surface. James stared: the tears, never far away, were running down his face.

'Oh God, Del, that's not what I meant,' he'd said, and they both sat down, as if they had rehearsed it.

'James, I don't think it's any good talking about it right now,' she'd said, weary beyond belief, and reached for the television knob. She'd left him looking hopelessly at an advert for lager, and gone up to Sam's room.

She'd sat down outside his door, to collect herself.

You haven't even tried. Why don't you try?

Seven years old, she'd told herself. Nothing weirder on this planet than a seven-year-old. Her question – how? – had just been an attempt to explore his mind a little, so she could reassure him that everything that could be done had been. Nothing more. She'd knocked, then gone in, her heart full of dread and something the consistency of diesel oil. There'd been a little furtive scuffling sound that made her smile. Who knew what a seven-year-old boy did in bed?

'Sam, your dad's sorry he shouted at you. He didn't mean to. He's upset, but it's not your fault.' God, she felt tired.

'OK,' Sam said, fiddling with a small blue slime ball James had bought him in a joke shop. Adèle hugged him, but he was made of wood.

'Do you miss Ruthie?'

'Yes,' said Sam, but somehow mechanically: yes was the right answer, that was all. Sam was very good at right answers.

'So do I, baby. Every day.'

'Mum?'

'What?'

'Don't tell Dad, but I think one day Ruthie will come back.'

And Adèle could think of nothing to say. Nothing in the world.

Why don't you try?

There was a knock on the door, and she jumped, completely disorientated.

'Mrs Tullian?'

Adèle sank back; Lewyn.

'Coming!'

It took no more than three minutes for Adèle to become completely ensnared in a complicated discussion with Lewyn about his grazing and hay rights in the fields. He didn't have a lease, but he had understandings and it was customary, and besides if he didn't use the fields they'd get overgrown and have to be ploughed over, which would cost them and they'd lose the revenue from the hay . . .

'Stop!' Adèle called out, laughing, tears banished. 'Mr Bulmer, please . . .'

'Lewyn.'

'Lewyn. Look, you can graze water buffalo for all I care. We're just here for the winter. Really, we don't want to change anything.'

'Yes, but the income from the hay from last year . . . '

'Lewyn. I really don't give a fuck about the hay. Really.' The word 'fuck' struck him hard, and he glanced at his hands. And what big hands they are, she thought.

He smiled.

'Oh. Well that's all right then. I just thought I should bring it up. I haven't discussed it at all with Sebastian Jarrett yet. Been on my mind a bit. It'd finish me, to be honest, if I lost the grazing. I've always had it, and me dad had it. Sorry. Didn't mean to bother you with it. I suppose you've got enough to think about, what with – everything . . .' He trailed off.

'I want to thank you for being here last night. First night in a strange place, it really made a difference.'

'Oh that was, that was nothing . . .' he said, and blushed. And what lovely eyes you've got, she thought, lovely real deep blue. And something else, some little impression tickling her like a stray hair . . . it eluded her.

'I suppose we're going to get to know each other pretty well, stuck here all winter. Sorry, I don't mean *stuck*, you know what I mean.' She scratched absently at her cheek, brushing the imaginary hair away. What was it?

'So what I thought would be nice would be if you came over to dinner one night. And Dilys, was it? The woman you mentioned last night?'

'Dilys. And Dave, her husband. Well, thank you very much. I'll ask Dilys. They're much more for going out than me, really.'

And what about Mrs Lewyn Bulmer, she was about to say, and then thought oh, so *that's* it. No Mrs Bulmer. And not just single. What was that horrible phrase, a bum bandit? How had she picked that up, that sudden knowledge? She just knew.

'And of course anyone you might care to invite, Lewyn,' she said casually.

'Oh, no, there's no-one like that,' he said, and smiled in a way she found oddly conspiratorial. Our little secret. But what a handsome man, she thought abruptly, and what a good physique too, real rugby player's build, short, thick, heavy, solid like old furniture, a mahogany dresser with all the drawers locked tight. She found herself suddenly at a loss again. She, with her cheap finishing-school upbringing, the perfect hostess.

'Oh where are my *manners*!' she called out brightly, if rather startlingly.

'Tea, Lewyn, or coffee? Let me guess . . . Strong tea, no sugar. Right?'

'Well, coffee if you've got it. And two sugars. Black. Actually,' he said, and they both laughed. Oh, she *liked* him. She buzzed about with kettle and teaspoons.

'Our first night! Sam slept like an angel, I was sure he'd be up the whole night but he went straight off. And me! I'm usually unbearable in strange beds, tossing and turning, but as soon as I hit that pillow . . . !' Actually she'd had a long, difficult night, with James (maddeningly!) like a corpse beside her: she'd been listening to all the secret, tiny sounds that occur on quiet nights in the country. It had begun to sound curiously orchestrated after a while: *organized*. It all meant something, but she with her city ears couldn't even begin to decode it. And then there was the house as well, doing all the things that any ordinary house does on a quiet night, so many almost imperceptible sounds. And then Sam . . .

'Must be very quiet for you,' said Lewyn, 'boring I'd imagine, after the city.' She tried to picture what ideas Lewyn had about 'the city', and came up with the image of Piccadilly Circus at midnight, great flashing signs for Coke and Fuji Film and streams of people, drunk, busy. Young boys hanging around outside the Burger King . . .

'Have you ever lived in London, Lewyn?' she asked.

'Me? No, never even visited. Can you imagine it!' He seemed ashamed.

'Well, let me tell you, you're not missing anything. I love it here,' she declared emphatically, determined that it be true.

'Right. Must be getting back,' he said, standing so suddenly that Adèle was momentarily sure she must have offended him.

'OK. Well, any time you're passing . . .'

'Oh, and I'll take that pan back if it's no trouble.'

'Yes, of course.' What could she have said? She dug the pan out from the pile of dishes on the draining board.

'The stew was lovely,' she said appeasingly. (You *must* give me the recipe . . .)

'Oh, I'm glad you enjoyed him. Grow most of the stuff meself. Cheaper that way. The herbs too.'

'Well, that's marvellous,' she twittered, wincing at the banality of her words. She was lost, completely unsure of herself. She couldn't have offended him, surely. She handed him the pan and he smiled, radiantly, charmingly. Then he grasped her hand, in the clumsiest handshake she'd ever felt, clumsier than the most gawky sixth-former from St Dunstan's at a too-brightly-lit, alcohol-free disco.

'I hope you're going to like it here,' he said, terribly earnest.

'I'm sure we will,' she replied seriously, and then couldn't help herself, and laughed.

'Sorry, sorry, you just took me by surprise. I can't remember the last time anyone shook my hand. Sorry.'

'Don't be sorry. It's good to have a laugh. Not much to laugh at, not round here.'

She felt confident again, and dared to say, 'Lewyn, would you mind if I came up to your house with you? To tell you the truth, I could do with getting out for a bit. And I'd love to see it. Would you mind?'

'Well, he's nothing much to see, not really. Bit of a mess, what with just me there.'

'What, worse than this?' she said, gesturing widely around her. He grunted.

'All right then. If you like.'

'Wait here. I'll just change my shoes and put my coat on . . .' She ran up the stairs, relishing the rattle of her feet on the bare wood.

'Dad, why does that lady talk funny?' Sam stage-whispered as they left the tiny Spar supermarket. James sssssshed him, suppressing his laughter till they got outside.

'That's just her accent, chief. People talk differently round here. It's you and me that talk funny to them.'

'Really?' Sam was wide-eyed with the wonder of it. The labels on all the tins were different, old-fashioned looking. And there weren't any trains, seriously. No tube . . . It was baffling. How did they get about? He helped his dad load the bags into the boot and back seat, while Elvis, joyously released from his mournful vigil at the rear window, lolloped about barking and getting in the way. Sam glanced nervously around him. It was like being in another country where all the words were different, like in France where you had to say 'Pardon' when you meant excuse me, and 'Mercy' when you meant thank you. How, he wondered, could they possibly remember it all?

Adèle followed Lewyn up through the field and on to the road, then off the road on to a path, rutted and overgrown, that led up between low hedges to his house. The air was wonderfully soft, misty. Autumn was her favourite season. Lewyn tramped on, oblivious, as she trailed behind, breaking off twigs and pulling at the ferns. It's so *rural*, she kept thinking idiotically, and smiling, smiling.

'These are my fields,' he said, pausing at a gate in the hedge, and she marvelled at the great green expanses and the grey dry-stone walls. And the sheep. Everywhere you looked, each one a near-perfect replica of the others, all stepping neatly through the short grass, just eating. All right for them, she reflected, they didn't have to worry about cholesterol and fucking size twelve jeans. What do they think about, she wondered, but came up with a blank. Just nothing. Baa.

Beside her Lewyn was gazing out absently, worrying (she guessed) about his grazing rights on her fields. *Her* fields, indeed. But he seemed to have more than enough room of his own. Why would he need the other fields as well? She decided not to ask. She didn't want to start all that up again. He could have them if he wanted them.

'All look the same, don't they?' he said, as if catching a delayed echo of her thoughts. 'But they're not. Every so often there's one that's a bit different. Seems to have a mind of his own.' (His, she thought? Surely they were all females? Then she remembered: sheep, like pans and houses and any other 'countable noun' as Miss Grealis would have said, were masculine around these parts.) 'You'll get one, he'll come up to you and have a sniff. Won't be scared of you. Or he'll wander off on his own and keep trying to knock the gate open. And he'll be the one that they'll all follow. He can get 'em panicking, they'll follow him anywhere. And then you'll get one as won't take the tup, not anyhow.'

'Tup,' she echoed blankly.

'Aye, you know. Ram you'd probably call him. You'll get a sheep that'll just kick him off, no matter how many times you try. Got a mind of his own, see.' (She was struck with sudden hilarity at the thought that ewes and rams were all 'him' for Lewyn. Now might that be an explanation for . . .)

'And we had one, back when me dad was alive, I swear to God he'd try and talk to you. He'd come right up and stand there, bold as you like, and he'd shout at you, and then when you talked back at him he'd shout again. Used to crease me up he did. I'd talk to him most every day. Missed him when he'd gone. Sounds stupid I know.'

Before the winter was out, Adèle was sure that she too would be reduced to talking to the sheep. A girl needed *some* intelligent company after all, and neither of her males was much of a talker. Only way to stay sane, she thought, and then shuddered violently at a picture of herself running through the fields at night, sheep scattering round her in all directions. She was shouting, 'I only want to talk to you! Please!'

'What, cold are you?' Lewyn asked.

'No I'm fine. Someone just walked over my grave.'

'Oh yes,' said Lewyn politely. City talk, he thought wisely.

'Mind you, they'll do a bit of shouting once the truck comes for 'em. They know something's up, see. Don't ask me how, but they know all right. They'll all get on, but they makes a hell of a racket. Funny, but once they're inside they quiet down again. I think they just forget. And they like the ride. I used to go with 'em a few times, me and me dad. Big double-decker truck with planks in the side, and they all just stand there looking round with their heads poking out. Like they're going on holiday. Day trippers. But then when they get the other end . . . Well anyway.' He clammed up again, abruptly. Adèle was getting used to his mood changes now. And if he had once had a sheep that he was on chatting terms with, she guessed that the whole business of slaughter was probably something he preferred not to dwell on. They stood in silence for a while. Then, without knowing she was going to, Adèle asked, 'Lewyn? There was no meat in that stew, was there?'

'Meat? No.'

'Are you vegetarian?'

'Aye. All my life, just about, and me dad.'

'Do you mind if I ask why?'

'Mind? No I don't mind. I seen 'em, see, I seen 'em in the truck and then I've seen 'em being done. Processed they call it, but it's just slaughtering, like any other kind. I've seen 'em rolling their eyes and stamping, and shouting. Trying to run. Trying to kick their way out. Biting each other, trampling. I seen one bite another one's ear clean off it was so scared. Shitting themselves, begging your pardon. The ramp down from the truck at the other end gets so slippery with the shit and the blood from them biting that they can't walk down him. So they fall over, break their legs, then the ones behind panic and trample 'em, and they're screaming and screaming. They got just enough sense to be shit-scared. They know what's coming. Processing plant, abattoir, whatever you want to call it, it's got a smell, not just the blood and that, but it's the fear, you can smell it and they can smell it an' all. Slaughterhouse stinks of fear. No I won't touch no meat, no thank you if it's all the same.' His voice was ferocious.

'And that's not all. Cos sometimes he don't work like he should, see, the stun gun. So they gets slit open and hung up, and they're still kicking, still screaming. Then they're headed for the machine that rips the skin off 'em. I used to get dreams . . .' He stopped, and then spat very deliberately, as if he had a bad taste in his mouth.

And there's something else, Adèle thought, I'm sure. Something you're not saying.

63

'Anyway, you don't want to get me started on that!' he said, and gave a hard bark of a laugh.

'You'll find a lot of 'em round here don't eat no meat. Not just me.'

'Sam's just become a vegetarian,' she remarked after a short pause, 'though he never said why.'

'Oh yes. Well, we should get up to the house if we're going. Don't want to stand around in a field all day. Don't want you to get foot rot!'

Elvis sat very erect, his head tilted up arrogantly, as he was bounced about on the back seat with Sam amongst the carrier bags. He knew how to behave in a chauffeur-driven limo. He would periodically lean forward and pant down James's neck, as if discreetly issuing instructions: just pull over to the kerb here, driver; and on the corners his feet would scratch at the battered plastic seats, as he maintained his dignified posture. A large dog of no clear pedigree.

It was only a three-mile trip, and only that because of the serpentine twisting of the road. Direct, it was no more than a mile and a half. James was in no hurry and they ambled along at thirty or so, enjoying the sights. Sam had already grown blasé about sheep, cows and horses (on the way there he'd been issuing 'more cows!' bulletins every thirty seconds or so) and now only commented on such exotica as barns, tractors and hay bales being thrown into lorries.

James kept his eyes on the road, but his thoughts were elsewhere. Twice in the night he thought he'd heard Sam muttering, quite loud but muffled, as if he was shouting through plate glass. Once he thought he'd caught the word 'Ruthie'. He still hadn't spoken to Sam about the accident: the months after it had seen all three of them running to their own corners, time out, dazed, punch-drunk. Apart from the time when Sam had said the Odd Thing, they had hardly talked about it at all, and that hadn't been talking, that had been raw panic. For James it wasn't Sam's question that had been disturbing, though, it had been that little whispered word from Adèle: *how?* In that moment he'd realized that he knew even less about Adèle than he thought. He'd felt a wave of helplessness crashing over him, one of those infrequent, true revelations of how totally alone people are beneath their skulls.

He pulled off the road at the crest of a deep decline, where the road widened out enough for two cars to pass. He could see the stones standing on the tip of the hill just above Fishguard Bay: eight gods who had fallen out of the sky one apocalyptic day, and been turned to stone by the wickedness of the Welsh. The fields were mostly for grazing, but there was some harvesting going on and some hay-baling. The colours were faded, nostalgic and seductive, like a fifties children's picture book, *Ten Little Chickens*. The high smell of sprayed manure and cut grass filled up the entire scene, and the sun was strong enough to bring out all the intricate mouldings and ripplings of the land. You could even see a twinkle of sea, just about.

Now that the time had come, James found himself at a loss as to how to open the conversation. Sam did it for him.

'Dad, are you sad?'

'Yes. Yes I am.'

'Why?'

'I'm sad because of Ruthie,' he said, and didn't realize till he said it how true it was. It was the complete truth about his life at this moment.

'Oh that,' Sam said. He'd thought it was because of the house, all messed-up. Cautiously he added; 'But it wasn't anyone's fault was it? Mum said it was a naccident and it wasn't anyone's fault, just bad luck.'

Just bad luck. How could she possibly be so bloodless about it? Just bad luck was a flat battery on a cold morning, or having every screwdriver except the particular one you needed. He felt a little nudge of anger, and bit it down.

'That's right. It wasn't anyone's fault. Not mine, not your mum's, not yours. Not Ruthie's.'

'And Mum tried everything she could to save her, didn't she?'

'Of course she did. The waves were too big and she couldn't keep Ruthie out of the water.'

'Yes. It was the water that killed her. But it wasn't the water's fault either.'

'No. Not the water's fault.' Thus far had been agreed already. The water just couldn't help doing it. Sam thought for a moment.

'And you were with me, up on the hill, with the Frisbee. So you couldn't see, and you couldn't hear Mum shouting.'

' 'Fraid so.'

'And I was on the hill with you. So I couldn't hear either.'

'Yup.' God, seven-year-olds could be tedious, James thought weakly. So literal. The dog was (very unhappily) in kennels, so he was in the clear, thank God.

'And Mum couldn't have known before that the water was going to do it, could she?'

Ah but *there*, you see . . . The red flag indicating danger to swimmers hadn't been up, true. True. But had it been entirely wise of Mum to go out in such a heavy tide? Adèle had medals for four-hundred and eight-hundred metres, breaststroke and crawl, from her posh school. Real alloy gongs with blue ribbons on a pin. But that was in an Olympic-size swimming pool, built with old girls' money after a particularly shameless tin-rattling campaign. Not in a strong tide off the Cornish coast. With a young child. Who couldn't (wouldn't was more like it) swim. Ruthie was, surprise surprise, frightened of the water. She didn't like to get her ears wet, or her beautiful long black hair. She didn't even like splashing in the kiddy pool at the sports centre. Just the kind of challenge that Del would feel obliged to rise to.

'No, couldn't have known.'

'Though you didn't want me to swim earlier on, did you?' Which was true. James had forgotten.

'But I'm not as good a swimmer as your mum, so I didn't want to risk it.'

'But you thought the water was too big.'

'Too big for you, yes. And for me, for that matter.'

'But you would have saved her if you'd been there.' Now there was a question. How many million times had he asked himself that, through the endless sitcoms and wildlife documentaries?

'I'd have done anything I could.' But unspoken: yes, probably, because I'm stronger. And I would never have let her go out there in the first place.

Birds that James couldn't identify twittered past, low; Elvis growled absently at them.

'And Ruthie, she didn't even want to go in the sea, did she? She *cried*.' This came out almost triumphantly: Ruthie had always been crying. Not like Sam.

'Ruthie was a bit scared of the water.' Adèle would relate how Ruthie had screamed them out of swimming pools, off beaches, off reservoirs. Ruthie had never trusted the water; she'd never really trusted anything. And she'd been right, right, right.

'So Mum was being silly, wasn't she?'

A slow fog crept over James. The child was cross-examining him. Your honour, where was this line of questioning tending? I fail to see the relevance . . . except that James could see very clearly the relevance. Sam was echoing his own most abjectly dishonourable, disloyal thoughts: if it hadn't been for Del's obstinacy!

'No, no.'

'But you just said . . .'

'Sam! That's enough of that!' *Damn!* No matter how he tried he always seemed to be shouting at Sam to shut up. He tried to be calm.

'Your mum did everything she could, Sam. That's all there is to it.'

'And I couldn't see, I was playing with the Frisbee, so it wasn't me,' Sam sang out in a nursery-rhyme voice. James was suddenly toying with the tiniest little bite of a memory . . . *playing with the Frisbee, yes, and Sam had been flinging it harder and harder, and hadn't he been shouting 'down, down'* . . . ? James couldn't be sure if this was a real recollection or a dream, like the dream where Sam stood behind him, chanting. Down? or *drown*?

James started the car.

'No-one's fault,' he said again, but distantly. What was there in the world that wasn't ultimately someone's fault?

Lewyn's house, thought Adèle, was nothing whatsoever like the farmhouse of her imaginings. She'd visualized copper warming pans, well-kept knick-knacks, a great kitchen table and roaring fires, maybe even the odd corn dolly. Lewyn's house was rather, well, suburban was the word. Adèle had the city-dweller's distaste for the suburban, as well as the snob's. Built of brick, tidily curtained windows, ugly floral carpets, mantelpiece with clock. Despite herself she was looking for clues: a framed picture perhaps of a handsome moustached man, an old valentine card with Love Always Roger x. Of course she was disappointed. There was just an untidy, single man's house, no more. Gym (upstairs), workroom (cellar), and living quarters in between. The kitchen was grimy and neglected, the 1960s cooker grease-bound and the working surfaces smeared, imperfectly cleaned. Bet you new Flash does it in half the time of your old cream cleaner! she thought and smiled grimly. Inadequate housewife as she was ('you're a tramp and a lush and an unfit mother,' as James used to say to her in their old flat – he'd got the line from *Dallas*) she could smell the depth of Lewyn's domestic ineptitude in every corner of the place. What is it about women like me, she wondered, that we can't see a cooker without wishing it scoured and gleaming? Inveterate lavatory-scrubbers the lot of us, she thought. Guilt probably.

Lewyn was an efficient if uninspired host.

'This is the bathroom,' he'd say, showing her the bathroom. 'And this is the bedroom . . .'

His bedroom was neither spartan nor sybaritic, certainly no bachelor's passion pit, but no monk's cell either. It was just messy. And he had a single bed, at item of furniture for which Adèle had only the profoundest contempt. You could sleep in a single bed, maybe. But you certainly couldn't do anything much else in it. Except of course . . . She caught herself looking for wrinkled, stiffened handkerchiefs or crumpled tissues, and chided herself. Nosy bitch! (*But what did he have under his mattress?*)

He showed her the weights and pulleys in the gym (she casually demonstrated her competence with York machines by inserting and twisting the key to change the weight. And she, oh, very matter of factly, curled four of the black iron plates. Lewyn watched, impassive.)

In the course of showing her how the lat extension pull-down pulley worked, he stripped off his shirt (she hated to admit it, but she was impressed) and as he lifted his arms she saw a large, untidy scar running down from his armpit and under his Hanes Beefy-T Athletic.

'How'd you get that scar, Lewyn?' she asked, and was shocked as the weights abruptly crashed home, the pulley banging against the frame. Lewyn stood facing the machine, his arms back at his sides. Then he reached for his shirt.

'Oh that? Had that a good few years now.'

'War wound, huh? Or were you gored by marauding sheep?' She kept her tone light, but she had been more than startled by his reaction. He buttoned his shirt, looking away from her.

'I'd completely forgotten I had him, tell you the truth.' Adèle said nothing. Waited.

'Well, I'll tell you if you've got a few days to spare!' He sat on the bench, and she sat on the floor against the wall.

'Nothing much to it really. It was just an accident I suppose you'd call it, though it wasn't no accident either, not really. It was Edith.' He paused and looked at Adèle. 'Edith Charpentier. Oh well, I suppose you was going to find out anyway. She was the woman who lived up Ty-Gwyneth before your Uncle Sebastian bought it. Her and her husband Raoul. He was French, 'parently. She had a bit of trouble, see. Truth of it is she went a bit mad. Went round saying all kinds of things about Raoul. You wouldn't believe the half of it! Said he was the devil, he'd murdered the children, all this.' Lewyn paused and glanced over at Adèle, as if, she thought, he's checking my response. He's being very careful what he says.

'Well anyway, she came up here one night. Banging on the door, middle of the night, in her nightie an' all, no shoes on her and it was winter. So I got up and let her in, gave her a cup of tea, and she started all that "He's the devil" business. Said he had her locked up in a room

70

in the house and she'd only 'scaped by going for his eyes with a nail or summat. She wanted me to get the police, cos he was planning to kill her, 'parently. She was begging me. I wasn't going to do anything of the kind of course, and I told her so; then she starts screaming and crying, all confused stuff, bits out of the Bible an' all sorts.' Lewyn swallowed hard. Adèle believed this part.

'And then, I was just trying to quieten her down a bit, and she started to – you know – she started to stroke my hair and she was *touching* me. So I got her off me, and then she was going, "You're in it as well!" and she pulled out this nail. Big six-inch masonry thing. From the pocket in her nightie. And she said, "But I've got it all written down. On the wall." That's what she said, then she, kind of *slashed* at me with this nail, and she caught me under the arm, as you saw. Bled terrible, and I was up the hospital for tet'nus, cos the nail was all rusted. Never healed right for months. Had to have stitches and all sorts.' He sighed.

'And that's that really. Years ago this was.'

Adèle waited, but that seemed to be it. As an explanation she felt it ranked alongside 'ship sinks' as an explanation of the *Titanic*. But she wasn't going to start asking a lot of questions. Lewyn clearly thought that he'd told her enough, and would probably evade any deeper probing, at least for now. And there was also some small part of her that was flashing a warning sign saying 'You really don't want to know the rest.' Caution, submerged structure. Dangerous.

Dangerous.

'Shocking, isn't it? All these rural goings-on?' said Lewyn, and laughed. They stood up and went downstairs.

After Adèle had left Lewyn went back up to the gym and again took off his shirt. He raised his left arm and ran his finger down the scar, regarding himself in the full-length mirror bolted to the wall. He hoped he hadn't said too much. And he felt the injustice he'd done to Edith in his account. Yes, she was mad at the end. Who wouldn't be, after what had happened? After what had been done. What she'd seen. Her madness had been, in a curious way, entirely sane: it was the only thing she could do that made sense. And Lewyn knew that, disordered though her accounts had been, they had contained truth.

All written down. On the wall. With a rusty six-inch masonry nail.

4

Blue

Adèle worked fast, applying the paint with a palette knife. She was merely blocking in, great swathes of pure colour, allowing the form to emerge from her hands. She found she worked best when she wasn't conscious of doing it; somehow the paint got thick and sticky when she was trying too hard and the lines didn't flow, the shapes were too rigid. She allowed her mind to travel freely when she was painting, and sometimes it was like flying. She would feel her senses going out, one by one, like stars being covered over by night clouds, until only the colours remained, vast luminous fields of colour; then she would come to, and a painting would be there, like a surprise birthday present. She would leave it for a while, a day or a month, and then add the finishing details; only at that stage would she be aware of using her skill and technique.

Sometimes it was like flying: today, however, she was thinking about what she would cook that evening for Lewyn and Dilys and Dave. Her range of vegetarian meals was not very extensive, and most of her first ideas struck her as rather dull: vegetable lasagne, pizza (without any *salami*?), lentil croquettes in tomato sauce. She wanted the meal to be a success. She had realized that in a situation as isolated as this (there was no phone, even) neighbours would be a lifeline. They had the car but Fishguard was at least fifteen minutes away in good conditions, and Lewyn's phone was their only immediate contact with the outside world. In London everything had seemed almost limitless in scope – there was a twenty-four-hour 7-Eleven five minutes away (seven days a week, three hundred and sixty-five days a year, as they proudly proclaimed on the matchboxes), and every conceivable emergency service only a phone call and a few minutes away. Friends. Company, that you sometimes had to work hard to escape. She would look forward to an afternoon alone as a treat, and a weekend with just James and Sam was something that had to be planned long ahead. But here! It would be possible (hell, it would be inevitable) that she might go for a whole day without a *conversation*! Of any kind! With anyone! If Lewyn didn't come round, or if she could find no excuse to visit him (and she'd already 'run out' of tea, pepper and eggs) then she was doomed to spend the whole day with only James and Sam for company.

She blushed at the tone of the thought – it seemed uncharitable – but, all the same, her relationship with James had never been based on talking. The blush deepened at the thought of what the relationship *was* based on.

Their first week together had been spent almost entirely in bed. On Tuesday, she had staggered out for milk and cigarettes; on Thursday he'd gone to get satay chicken and special rice; and on Saturday they'd gone to the pub. They'd stayed there exactly one hour and fifteen minutes. Then back to bed. God, it had been heavenly. They were both astonished and even abashed, afterwards, by the pleasure they got from each other. It had seemed endless, and by the end of the first week they were both bruised and tender and stiff from their exertions. Say one thing for him, she thought lewdly, he's got staying power. He was what, at her (only moderately) expensive boarding school would have been called an ever-ready eddy. A five times a night man. A-1 shag. And *big* . . . Of course size doesn't matter, she added dutifully, but Christ it made a difference! The very first time she had been frankly and openly incredulous at the size of him, the girth, the length. She'd even believed she'd never be able to get him in, but of course they'd managed somehow.

Vegetable curry and fried rice? Nut loaf with cranberries and mushroom sauce?

(Getting him in her mouth had been a different matter, but once they'd got the angle right . . .)

On Sunday she'd gone back to her flat. She didn't see him on Monday, or Monday night. She moved in on Tuesday, and they'd spent twenty-six nights apart since. Nearly ten years. She could hardly believe it. And in all that time they'd had only a handful of extended conversations.

And Sam (bless him) ran mostly to 'what's inside the dog?' and 'what would happen if you ate wood?' type discussions, entertaining but not a conversation. In a conversation you talked about God, food, little black dresses reduced from £27 to £15, your work, the horrors of breast-feeding. Families. That sort of thing. Adèle had been delighted (if somewhat taken aback) by Lewyn's description of the slaughterhouse: it had been a real conversation with a real person. His nostalgia for the talking sheep had chilled her slightly (she was reminded of a car-window sticker she'd seen as they were driving through Heathrow: 'A Virgin Sheep Is One That Can Outrun A Welshman!') but then all it really showed was that Lewyn too was someone who needed to talk. Even if it was only to a sheep . . .

Three of the twenty-six nights she hadn't spent with James had been right after Ruthie had died, when his inability/refusal to talk to her had led to rage and violence.

75

On one occasion she'd shoved him so hard that he'd lost his balance and cracked his head open against the door jamb. Even then he hadn't responded, he'd just retreated, sulked, cried, while she rubbed the blood off the door, viciously.

Lamb casserole with rich dark gravy and soft stewed root vegetables . . .

She shook the thought from her head. All right then, just the stewed bloody root vegetables. She wanted something nice but not too fancy. Didn't want them to run away with the idea that she was some kind of little rich girl, patronizing them with her sophisticated urban ways. (First Year Etiquette and Comportment. Rule Number One: Always make your guests feel at home.) Frozen veggyburger and Smash (Sam's current favourite). Egg and chips.

'La-di-da,' she sighed, and stood back from the canvas.

There was a problem in the composition. Or rather, more specifically, it was a pile of shit. She needed a large object of some kind in the bottom left foreground. Something very close-up and detailed to balance out the misty autumn landscape. It would come to her. She lit a cigarette and went down to make a cup of tea.

After he'd got to 'hold the string very tight and don't move' while James knocked a small wooden peg into the ground to tie it to, Sam had got bored and wandered off.

'Stay where I can see you!' James called after him. 'And don't go in the house. Your mum's painting!' Sam decided to make a hole in the dry-stone wall.

James could see the problem in its entirety.

The house was built practically on a stream; the ground on the far side of it banked up, so that water drained down into the fields surrounding it. The house wasn't just damp, it was all but running. So: a trench all the way round it, like a moat, perforated clay pipes in the trench, then a covered pipe right across the field like a culvert to the septic tank near the cliff. It would put an additional burden on the tank, which would mean emptying it more often (and watching it carefully in wet weather, unless you wanted the end of the field to become an open sewer). But it was the only real solution. Then renew the damp course, or replace it completely lower down. Spray everything with silicone. And hope for the best. It ought to work.

I'll bet there's no record of the plumbing and electric lines, he thought grimly. And I'll *bet* there's no map of the drainage lines already in place. So no JCB. It'd be a pickaxe and shovel job. He was looking at two weeks' work, and that was before anything could be done actually in the house. And he'd have to go very carefully: digging down into God knew what, he'd be lucky to avoid slamming the pickaxe into an underground power cable or pipe. Softly softly catchee monkey.

The string was stretched between two pegs, one near the house, the other near the septic tank. He walked the distance; close to two hundred feet, he estimated. And not level either, slightly hilly. To get a proper gradient on the pipe he'd have to dig deep, then lay shingle, rake it all down. Long strips of wood and a spirit level. Christ. He got his spade and went back along the stretched string, turning over the turf. The ground was soft, and, he feared, rather more clayey than might have been wished for. Clay was a swine to dig, and when it got wet it was a complete *bastard*. It was at least double the work of dry soil. The spade would immediately become clogged and heavy, his boots would be caked, and after an hour his dodgy back would start complaining. And then all the stones . . . Bloody Sebastian was certainly going to get his money's

77

worth. Still, better working than thinking. He started to dig in earnest, beginning near the septic tank.

Within ten minutes he was sweating, despite the cold. He pulled off his anorak and jumper, and felt the wind bite. He could see Sam at the far end of the field, methodically damaging the wall. He started to shout at him, then stopped himself. The poor kid had to do *something*. And they could rebuild the wall together some time. A nice little job for a fine day, dry-stone walling. His shovel turned up something white. Chalk? No, it was more like bone. He picked it up and cleaned the clay off it. A bone of some kind. Hardly surprising on farmland. He glanced along the barbed-wire fence running the length of the cliff edge. There were tufts of wool on the barbs. Sheep had been meandering about in this field for scores of years, maybe hundreds. Bound to leave the odd bone behind. Lewyn had agreed to put the sheep into the adjoining field while James was digging, the field on the other side of the low wall that Sam was at this moment patiently dismantling. James flung the bone out over the cliff, and shouted at Sam to leave the wall alone.

'Go and ask your mum to make me a cup of tea,' he called; Sam plodded off obediently. He was a good child. Not perhaps the little bruiser that James had had in mind; he was more introvert, more intricate than that. He didn't want to be a footballer, he wanted to be an *architect* for God's sake. But he was a good 'un. Intelligent, sensitive, perhaps a bit secretive, but not a milksop. James turned up another bone.

In the house Adèle paused as she squeezed out a tea bag: she felt a shiver run over her. Draught probably. James had done emergency work, what he called first aid, on the house, boarding up the gaping windows and getting the electrics to work. But it was still barely habitable. Everywhere you went there were draughts, coming up through the floorboards and down the chimneys. Lewyn had lent them a Calor-gas heater which Adèle had put in her makeshift studio on the second floor. Or rather James had put it there, complaining that she *would* want it up two flights of bloody stairs. But he'd do anything for her, she knew that. She wished he'd decided to do a bit more inside the house before he started on the drainage problem, but she accepted his reasoning. Get as much as possible done outside before the wet came, and the frost. Once the ground froze you could forget about digging. And so what if you had to wear two jumpers inside and you couldn't take your shoes off? She shivered again. It was still only late October; God help them come February. *If we're still here*, she thought, and was immediately puzzled by the notion. Where else would they be?

Elvis lolloped into the kitchen and came to her, and she buried her hands in his warm glossy fur, crouching down to him. He breathed his unspeakably bad breath on her enthusiastically and she pushed his face away. She stroked his belly. He was getting to be a stocky, older dog, with little touches of grey round the muzzle. A phlegmatic, serene animal, and so gentle with Sam. Never so much as bared his teeth at him, even when Sam was the most terrible of twos and believed that Elvis's tail was detachable if he could only pull hard enough.

There was a knock on the door, and Elvis woofed and padded off to see. Adèle followed, surprised by a feeling of unease, almost alarm. But it was only Sam, looking frozen and dejected.

'Hiya Sammy! Sammy Davis Junior,' she said, and rubbed his cold little ears.

'Whatcha been doing? Helping your dad?'

'I held the string. Then he had to do digging, and I

can't hold the spade right,' said Sam, 'and then I couldn't play with the wall.' He sounds *way* off, thought Adèle. Poor little frozen mite.

'He says will you make him a cup of tea, please?' The 'please', she reflected, was Sam's addition. James had never been one for common courtesy.

'Well that's funny, cos I was just this minute making one. Isn't that funny?'

'Yes,' said Sam correctly, looking as if he would never find anything funny again.

'Oh baby, you're frozen stiff. Do you want some hot milk? I believe there's some chocolate Nesquik lying about somewhere that might interest you.'

'Yes please,' he said and followed her, tragically, into the kitchen. Elvis came along as well, treading respectfully behind.

Adèle got out some large sheets of sugar paper and his paints and brushes and the plastic water jar with the magic lid which didn't leak when you knocked it over. Even at seven, Sam was becoming a connoisseur of good design. She left him at the kitchen table with his hot chocolate in the Can You See The Lions? mug. (The lions were at the bottom.)

She put her padded jacket on and took James's tea out to him. As she neared him she stopped, and the shiver walked over her again: lying around his feet were some largish white objects which, even from a distance, were unmistakably bones. And he was holding another one in his hand, cleaning it off.

Don't touch it! she screamed inwardly. He looked up (guilty, she thought: why are you looking so guilty?) and waved the bone at her.

'Jamie?' she said as she handed him the tea. 'What are all these doing here?'

'Don't know. But there's enough of them.'

'Are they . . .'

'Sheep. They're sheep bones.'

'Are you sure?'

'Well, either that or midget bones.'

Or children's bones, she thought, and felt a surge of vertigo.

'Curiouser and curiouser,' she said. 'What they wanna go buryin' the midgets for, Jiiiiiim?' she drawled in her country-bumpkin Bristol accent. His parents' accent.

'Well, you know country folk,' he drawled back. She regarded the scattered white objects.

'Highly irregular. Elvis'll be pleased.'

She hugged him and he gave her a warm wet kiss on the ear.

'Come in and have something to eat,' she suggested.

'I'll give it another hour. My curiosity, as you posh folk say, is piqued.'

'OK.'

She went back to the house and watched Sam painting. He was humming.

James dug on. The bones were everywhere, and he found himself digging down deep rather than along the neat line of turned-over turf. The sheep in the next field had gathered at the dent Sam had made in the wall. They were watching.

Sheep bones, he told himself. Just sheep bones.

Why?

Too small for human bones (unless they were children's). Too small. Have to be a midget. Why would anyone bury midgets? His mind feverishly circled round the problem as he dug faster, slamming the spade into the glutinous, slimy clay. The sheep stared at him with their dead eyes, innumerable pairs of flat, black little eyes. They were starting to jostle each other; he glanced over at them and saw that their ears were up, their heads stuck forward.

He threw down the spade and picked up one of the bones. It was blackened halfway along its length. Barbecue. That was it. There was a barbecue, and they buried the bones afterwards.

Sam was painting a house. There was smoke coming out of the chimney. Adèle watched him, puzzled. There seemed to be rather a lot of smoke.

More blackened bones, some of them ending in crumbling, charred fragments. Some of them broken cleanly. The sheep were making small sounds as they jostled and pushed at the wall, that strange, banal sheep sound, baaaa: really it was more like maaa. Ma. The sound a young child might make. If it was in trouble. If, just for instance, someone was trying to harm it. *Burn* it . . .

He shook his head, and picked up the spade again. Sam dipped his brush; the water in the magic jar was becoming very cloudy. He reached for the black again. More smoke, and now not from the chimney but from one of the upper rooms. His humming was louder, and Adèle again felt giddy.

Don't touch it!

Maaaa!

James plunged the spade and turned over something more worrying than the white of the bones. Something blue. Bright sky blue. He lifted it clear of the ground: it was wool. Knitted wool. Charred.

Maaaa!

He held it in his hand, all time frozen, a clear still point. Blue.

Adèle watched as Sam dropped his brush, splashing more smoke into the ever blacker sky, and ran out of the kitchen, threw open the door, ran across the field.

James flung the piece of cloth over the cliff, into the

sea, and then Sam was there, scrabbling in the loose soil.

'Sam?' James was suddenly confused. Why was Sam here?

Adèle watched from the doorway, her mind full of black smoke.

'He was frightened of them,' Sam was saying, 'he thought they were devils. But they were frightened of him. They screamed. Like this.'

And Sam opened his mouth, a bone in either hand, and screamed, a high shrill mad shriek of terror, on and on; he drew breath, and then it came again, wild, unmodulated, inhuman, a ferocious, primal sound. James grabbed at him, and Sam went limp, falling awkwardly amongst the bones.

Spare ribs. Chilli sauce.

Adèle wrenched herself forward, dimly aware of the audience of alert little black and white faces gathered at the wall.

James came towards her carrying the slack bundle in his arms.

'Go and phone the doctor, he's had some kind of a . . .'

'There's no phone! There's no phone! Oh God!'

'Adèle.' James spoke loudly, not exactly shouting. 'Go up to Lewyn's and phone a doctor.'

'But shouldn't I stay here with Sam? Oh God what's the matter with him? Why was he making that noise?'

'No. I'll stay with Sam. Go and phone.'

Adèle stared at Sam for a moment, went to touch his head, then James pushed past her. She started to run up the field; the sheep, she noted, were dispersing. Nothing to see here. It's all over.

James carried Sam into the house, and realized at once that there was nowhere to put him. No couch, no armchair. The front room was devoid of any kind of furniture. He went into the kitchen and, clearing a space among the paints and brushes, laid him on the table, feeling that he was doing something very wrong. The child was completely limp: in fact he appeared to be fast asleep. Half remembered words floated into James's head, epilepsy, narcolepsy, hysterical paralysis. Or maybe Sam had just fainted dead away, as Victorian women were wont to do, fainted with terror. He'd been muttering something about being frightened before he started screaming, making that noise. Could people really just faint with fear?

James regarded his son, curled up on the kitchen table, and tried to make himself think. In the time it would take a doctor or an ambulance to get out here, he could drive the boy into Fishguard. If any treatment was needed straight away then that would save time, rather than have someone come all the way out and then have to go back. And it seemed dreadfully wrong to be just standing here, watching the child asleep on the kitchen table. He would leave a note for Adèle. He cast around for a pen and paper and saw Sam's painting on the floor. Smoke. He picked up the still-wet brush and wrote on the back of the painting, in big splashy black letters:

'Taken him to F'gd. Stay with Lewyn will ring.'

He felt for his car keys: in his jacket. Where was his fucking jacket? You took it off down by the septic tank. By the hole. He sprinted out and ran down his line of turned-over earth. The brown and green anorak was right there, on the edge of the hole he'd dug. The bones gleamed dully all around it. He grabbed for it and ran back.

Sam was sitting up, rubbing his eyes.

'Sam?'

'What?' Sam had that cross, bleary look he always had when he was waking up.

'Are you all right?'

'Got a sore throat. I was painting and then I fell down the hole. Got a sore throat.'

From all the screaming. Did he remember?

'Apart from that.' James approached him, feeling inexplicably reluctant to get too close.

'Do you feel all right apart from your throat?'

'Yeah but who was out by the hole?'

What?

'What do you mean?' James went to the table and sat down, swinging Sam's legs round and holding them.

'There was a man by the hole. Had a stick thing.' Sam's eyelids were drooping, as if he wanted to go back to sleep. James watched him narrowly.

'Sam, I was by the hole. I was digging. Remember?'

'No, it wasn't you,' said Sam, shaking his head crossly. 'He was different. Had a stick thing. Why am I on the *table*?'

'I'm going to take you into town. Do you feel like a drive?'

'OK, but I feel a bit sleepy. Is it late?'

'Come on, chief.'

James helped him off the table, and the boy stood shakily, as if coming round from an anaesthetic.

'Aren't we taking Elvis?'

'No. Can you walk OK? Want me to carry you?'

'Legs feel funny.' But he managed to stagger out to the car, climbed in, and was asleep on the back seat before James had turned the key.

Adèle stared at James's note, not able to read it clearly. She didn't understand for a minute. Then she thought, bastard, why couldn't he wait for me? It was almost as if he wanted me out of the way, sending me off like that. Bastard! Now she'd have to wait for hours, assuming he remembered to ring at all. She found her cigarettes and lit one up, fuming.

Lewyn had looked considerably startled when she'd found him in the garage, tinkering with a motor of some kind. No, he'd looked horrified. She'd been shouting 'Doctor! Need a doctor!' and he'd actually backed away from her, with a wrench in his hand. She laughed harshly. Just another crazy woman coming after him with a rusty nail, she thought.

It would be at least half an hour before James could ring, and he'd probably have to wait at the doctor's for a while. An hour, probably. She glanced at her watch: still only 1.15! She felt she'd been awake for days. She walked out into the field, and it seemed natural to follow the line James had dug. Follow the yellow brick road. And at the end of it, a pit.

She peered in. Dark, moist-looking ground. A few bones. What was there here to bring on Sam's fit of screaming? What had he seen? When he was a baby she'd come across him a few times staring hard at absolutely nothing, staring out of his cot at about the level a person's head would be. Once he'd held out his hands and said, 'Da! Da!' delightedly, gurgling. Children are always seeing ghosts, she reflected. Elvis was the same. He'd suddenly stiffen, put his ears back, growl. Nothing there. But then Elvis also growled at people wearing hats and (to her perpetual shame) black people. Racist dog. Where had he got that from?

And then she thought, where's Elvis now? After a few brief, formal, inconclusive meetings with the sheep, he had taken to keeping well clear of them. He just didn't like the way they looked at him, she guessed: a few seconds of meaningful eye contact and he was backing down, licking his lips, lowering his head. He certainly felt no ancestral urge to go rounding them up. She wandered round behind the septic tank, and there he was, shame-faced, grinning up at her, a bone between his paws. She laughed. To a dog, the world and everything in it is just food, she thought. Just meat.

She went back to the house to get his lead, and then returned, picked up his bone (he looked reproachful but that was all) and clipped on the lead.

She felt strangely carefree as she walked up the field and on to the road; just taking the dog out. Her son was (for all she knew) lying in a coma in a doctor's consulting room in Fishguard (oh, and her daughter was dead) but begone dull care! She had always known that one day something would happen to Sam. And now it had. And she was relieved. She couldn't wait to see Lewyn's face when she appeared yet again! She should wear a Halloween mask and a green wig: *that'd* give him something to think about.

James parked the car outside the chemist (Renfrew and Sons, Dispensing Pharmaceuticals, as the sign rather inexpertly put it) and went in. He was out again within minutes, and followed the directions the assistant (Mrs Renfrew, he wondered, or a Son in drag?) had given him: down to the square (except it was a triangle), then right up New Church Road, then left.

A woman answered the door: no, The Doctor was on his rounds. Was it an emergency? It seemed awkward for James to say that it was, when the patient was sleeping soundly on the back seat, dribbling, not bleeding, not even bruised, in fact not in any way distressed. Apart from a sore throat.

'I don't know,' James said lamely. 'But we're pretty worried about him.'

The woman, who had probably seen several thousand anxious parents in her time, looked sympathetic.

'He had a kind of fit,' James added, after it became clear that the woman in the neat wool suit and the perm from Alyson's Coiffures was waiting for a bit more to go on.

'Oh I see. Well, The Doctor' (and James could hear the capital letters in her tone) 'will be back at around two o'clock for his dinner. If it was an emergency, you could call an ambulance and get him to the hospital in Haverfordwest.' She paused; then, cautiously—

'If you like, I could take a look at him. I'm a qualified nurse. Not a Doctor, you understand, but I could take a look.' James couldn't help detecting the hopefulness in her voice.

'Oh, would you?' he said, relieved, but still uncertain. He was sure there was no call for an ambulance. Ambulances were for gushing wounds and heart attacks and broken legs. Not for little boys with sore throats who'd had a funny turn. Anxiety tempered by embarrassment. And the dread of making a fuss.

James picked Sam up from the back seat with some difficulty (he was a big seven, and dead weight) and carried him inside. The woman who was not a Doctor led him into the consulting room, and James laid Sam down on the brown vinyl adjustable couch with the disposable paper cover. He hovered as she did all the things nurses are trained to do (temperature, blood presssure, pulse) without disturbing Sam in the slightest. He noticed a big, fancy framed certificate on the wall and alongside it a smaller, less ostentatious one: Sylvia Anne Castle, SRN.

'How long has he been asleep?' she asked as she ripped the Velcro tabs apart on the blood pressure cuff.

'How long? About half an hour. Well, he passed out, and then he woke up again, and then he went to sleep again. In the car.'

'With your permission I'll wake him up.'

'Yes, of course.'

'What's his name?'

'Sam.'

She leaned over the little boy and stroked his (perfectly dry) forehead.

'Sa-am,' she sang out, 'Sa-am,' so gently that James was amazed at how readily Sam opened his eyes and blinked. Usually it took the equivalent of a plane crash on the roof to waken him.

'Now don't you fret. You just fell asleep. I'm going to take your jumper off. OK? Can you lift your arms for me? That's my lovely, there.'

She stripped Sam to the waist, he co-operating solemnly. She sat him up and tapped his back, all over. Then she went to a cabinet and came back with an object like a pencil which she shone into his eyes, holding his eyelids back.

'I'm only doing what any casualty doctor would do first,' she said calmly. She put the ophthalmoscope back in the cabinet, and came back, sat on the couch beside him.

'How'd you feel? Any pains? Headache?' She stroked his forehead as she spoke, and Sam watched her in awe, his little white chest painfully thin-looking next to this large, heavy woman.

'No. But I've got a sore throat,' he reported accurately, though trying to imbue the fact with a little drama.

'Let's have a look then. Open wide now.'

She switched on an adjustable lamp and swung it over, then took her glasses from her breast pocket, put them on, and peered down Sam's mouth.

'OK. You can get dressed again now.'

James hung about, helplessly.

'Is he all right?' he burst out, embarrassed.

Sylvia Castle turned to look at him.

'He's certainly in no immediate danger. You say he had a seizure of some kind?'

How to *begin* . . .

'He screamed and then he passed out. Only it wasn't just screaming, it was . . .'

'Has he ever done it before?'

'No. Nothing like this.'

'Excuse me asking, did he excuse himself?' It took James a second to understand the question.

'Oh. No, no he didn't.'

'Any disturbance in his breathing? Did he bite his tongue? Any convulsions, twitching?'

'Well no I don't think so but . . .'

'Did he hurt his head?'

'No.'

'Anything else you can tell me?' She was looking very directly at James.

'No,' he said finally. 'Just this screaming.'

'OK. Thank you.' She turned back to Sam. 'Sam? Do you remember what happened?'

'I was painting. And then I think I fell in a hole or something. And then I was on the *table*.'

'That's right, he fell into a hole I was digging. He was saying something . . .'

'Just a moment, if you please,' she silenced him.

'Now Sam. Did you feel funny before you fell in the hole? Did you feel, oh I don't know, kind of dreamy?'

'No but there was someone there and he was telling me something, he had a stick.'

'That was me. My spade.'

She gazed at Sam for a while; he gazed back sorrowfully, blinking.

'Right then. If you want to wait for The Doctor he won't be long. You'll want The Doctor to look at him. The

90

Doctor will recommend what to do.' She went to the sink and washed her hands.

'I'll get you a cup of tea. Would you like to sit in the waiting room? And would you like some orange juice, Sam?'

Sam nodded, mournful, and now also somewhat disappointed.

'Yes please.' It wasn't like on *Casualty*. There weren't enough machines.

They sat in the waiting room, where there was an electric fire (one bar) and tattered copies of *Punch* and *The Lady*. Sam looked at the cartoons in *Punch*; he'd read the caption, then ponder it for a moment; then, 'Dad . . .'

Sylvia Castle came back in, bearing tea, orange juice and a disapproving look.

'Is it your car, the one by the gate?' she asked, as she handed James the tea. James admitted that it was.

'I must ask you to move it, I'm afraid, Mr . . . ?'

'Tullian. James Tullian.'

'Mr Tullian. You see that's where The Doctor leaves his car. You can park further up.'

'Oh. Yes of course.' James responded at once to the authority in Nurse Castle's voice, as he supposed many thousands of people had done before him. He ruffled Sam's hair.

'Back in a minute, chief.'

Sam watched him go, then carried on puzzling over the cartoons. Sylvia regarded the solemn little child for a few seconds; something troubled her about him, she couldn't say what. She left the room, frowning, then paused outside the door. Now she couldn't see him she realized what it was.

Humming. A slow, unmusical drone, like a honey bee. She listened hard; he only stopped to breathe. He was humming continuously. Humming, screaming, fainting. Quite a busy lad, she thought. No wonder his father looked half out of his mind. And where was his mother? She sighed and went back to the consulting room to open a new file in the name of Sam Tullian. It wouldn't surprise her one bit if it wasn't soon to become quite a thick one. And it would only be a matter of time before Mr and Mrs were needing files as well.

This time, Lewyn had merely looked annoyed as she came up the path to the garage, with the dog lurking behind her, snuffling. He saw at once that she had a bone in her hand, and found that he wasn't at all surprised. He had begun to get the impression that her elevator didn't go to the top floor, as Dave, a voracious reader of American literature, would put it (usually about Dilys).

'It's only me!' she called and waved. Lewyn stood up from the shearer motor and smiled politely, as Adèle explained what had happened. She hated to be such a nuisance, but if he wouldn't mind if she waited for James's phone call . . .

'He's got my number then, has he?' Lewyn asked, eyebrows raised.

'Oh shit! Pardon me. I don't know if he has. Are you in the book?'

'No.'

'Shit!' *Damn* these suspicious, ridiculous people! Why the fuck *not*? she wanted to yell at him, but restrained herself. Neighbours.

Lewyn sighed.

'I could run you into town if you like. Won't take but quarter of an hour.'

Adèle really did hate to be a nuisance. She'd always been her own woman. She never let James do any of those things (as she called them) in the house, like changing fuses and unscrewing jars of pickle. And now here she was interrupting a working man, being chauffeured around. Still, she really had no choice. James had seen to *that*, haring off in that absurd way. Overreacting. He was probably in a phone box in Fishguard right now arguing with an operator who wouldn't give him an ex-directory number. And would he even know the address? (Come to think of it, did she know the address?)

She accepted, and Lewyn went in to get the oil off his hands. As she was waiting she looked down at her hand and realized she was still carrying the bone. What on earth did she think she was doing, wandering around the Welsh countryside with a bone (*sheep* bone, she told herself carefully) in her hand? Like Lady Macbeth, she thought vaguely; no, that was blood. Still, where there were bones there must be blood. Sheep blood. She remembered Lewyn's horror of the slaughterhouse. He, she thought, must really think I'm mad. He's humouring a madwoman. She felt cold at the thought, and angry at James. It was his bloody doing, the whole business. He should never have started all that digging. God knew what was down there.

Sam's painting floated into her head; she flung the bone away from her, as far as she could, and called Elvis.

And then she thought: tortillas with spiced cheese and salad. She could pick it all up while she was in town. And guacamole. And exotic fruit salad.

5

Puzzling Evidence

'Da-daaaa!'

She entered the room, plates in each hand and balanced on her arms, and sailed to the table where Dilys, Dave, Lewyn and James were waiting obediently, smiling at each other. Lewyn was wearing the slate-grey polo shirt Dilys had bought him last Christmas. Dilys was gorgeous in paisley silk blouse and pearls ('Real!' she'd hissed at James when he'd complimented her on them. 'You can bite them!'). Dave grinned nervously from a good wool sweater of indeterminate design, and James was his handsome finest, starched white shirt and slicked-back hair.

'Da-daaaa!'

There was a moment of silence as she expertly laid the plates before her guests. It was the kind of moment she sometimes had nightmares about. Their eyes flickered anxiously from the plates to each other. Lewyn gazed off into the distance. It was a disaster.

'My, aren't these pretty?' Dilys murmured finally, smiling conspiratorially at her husband. 'I don't believe I've ever had *these* before! What do you call them?'

Adèle summoned up a smile from the bottom of the pit she'd just crawled into.

'Tortillas. They're Mexican.'

Gamely, bravely, Dilys sliced off a corner of one of the

94

folded cardboard things on her plate and, eyes shining, bit deeply into it.

'Oh!' She was shaking her head. 'Oh, but . . .' She looked round at the ring of faces watching her.

'Oh, these are *lovely*. Just lovely.'

James glanced at Adèle and started to eat, followed by Dave and finally Lewyn.

'Really, you don't need the cutlery! Just grab 'em up!' exclaimed Adèle, leading by example, and the men reluctantly put down their knives and forks and ate.

'And there's the salad, just help yourselves, and guaca . . . avocado dip. And corn bread.' Adèle piled things on to her plate. She felt like a slave at the court of Nero, proving that nothing was poisoned. Mexican food, she thought, and sighed. She'd practically had to force her burritos into James the first time; he'd just sat there, gazing at them, looking obscurely resentful.

She poured wine (really it should have been bottled lager, but tracking down the tortilla shells alone had been more than enough trouble, not to mention the cayenne pepper), and laughed and babbled about her hunt for these exotic rarities.

'So I'd completely given up. And then there they were. Spar, it would seem, had a South American promotion about two years ago, and they were still there in the stockroom! A whole case of them. The manager nearly kissed me! Oh, they keep *for ever* in the tin,' she reassured them hastily, 'and the manager, he was so sweet, he *knew* he had some somewhere, so I invited him along for next time. He said he'd always wondered what they were . . .'

James gave her his patented just-take-it-easy-now look and she subsided, still smiling though. Dilys needed to know how you made them, and Adèle was happy, happy, happy to tell her. Dave rolled his eyes at Lewyn, who was chewing away dutifully, if cautiously.

Dave spoke up when Dilys had run out of wonderment. 'Ten o'clock he starts.'

Lewyn murmured agreement.

'Oh now David . . .' said Dilys, but he was not to be shamed.

'Bruno and Tyson. Can't miss that.'

'That's tonight, is it? I thought it was weeks away. Losing track of time already,' said James, and Adèle was reminded of his long sessions in front of the screen. She looked tenderly at him and touched his arm.

'No telly here, lover.'

'Well actually I was thinking we could go up to mine,' said Lewyn. 'Only up the way a bit. Shame to miss him.'

'Del?'

She felt her tenderness dissolve as he looked coolly at her, challenging her to stop him breaking up her first dinner party so he could go and gawp at two men beating the . . .

'Well I won't join you, if you don't mind. I never really cared for the sight of blood.'

'Nor I neither,' said Dilys emphatically, and drained her glass.

'Two grown men trying to kill each other. For money.'

Dave glanced at her glass: she reached for the bottle.

'Well tha's all it come to, when you look at it,' she finished stoutly, to Adèle's silent applause.

'How can you hit someone, when you don't even hate him, don't even know him? Stupid I call it.'

This was clearly an old argument and the seam was nearly exhausted. There was a short silence. It was 8.30 now. If they were going to get through the tortillas and the guacamole *and* the exotic fruit salad then they'd have to eat up. The men attacked the alien food with noticeably greater determination, and Adèle hated them for it. Particularly James. Bastard, she thought. You bastard.

She smiled brilliantly at him as he fought with the food. Bastard. You'll get yours.

Sam was lying on the floor at the top of the stairs, just out of sight, listening. All his life he'd been listening, listening to Ruthie cry (*always* crying), to his mum shouting, to his dad trying to explain, giving up. Mum loved Dad, and Dad loved Mum, but the words didn't mean the same things. And he knew about 'bedtime' when they loved each other, ferociously. He knew when he was being sent out of the way, so they could love each other. And they said things that meant more than the words, he knew that as well. They were doing that now. He shifted a bit nearer the newel post, attending, buzzing.

By 9.40 all the food had gone. Coffee? (Real filter coffee, made with the percolator that James had chosen to regard as some kind of instrument of class oppression. He thought coffee should come out of a jar.) Not for me. No, nor me, thank you.

'Well, I would *love* some coffee,' said Dilys, and then, 'that was just lovely, Adèle. I wish I could cook like that. Dave and me, it's mostly just bean stew and curry and, well, God knows what you call it!'

Adèle smiled serenely at her. The plates were collected by Lewyn and stacked in the kitchen. She followed him in to put the percolator on.

'Oh, I wish you didn't have to go!' she said, 'just when we were getting to know each other,' and heard Dilys cackle.

'Suppose you'll have to be getting away, if it's a ten o'clock start.'

Lewyn nodded and, hesitating by the door (God, what a *handsome* man), he thanked her, politely but fully, for the dinner.

He went out to mobilize the men, and Dilys came into the kitchen.

'How will you get home?' Adèle asked her.

'Oh I can walk it, he's not far. Or I could stay over. Long time since I had a slumber party!' Adèle gave her a smile, and Dilys breathed in her ear, 'I've got a teensy-weensy bit of grass. Eh?' and they laughed, mocking their pathetic shadowy men.

Lewyn had beer in the fridge. Beer and telly, the old firm. James had never been much for sports of any kind, though he'd played football at school and later university. Second, third elevens. He'd once, briefly, been in the fifth eleven, when he was working at the Greater London Council. He'd never been much of a team man. But he took an interest, could hold his own in barbershop conversation, and was secretly fiercely proud of his prowess. Or ex-prowess. He hadn't kicked a ball in, what, five years? (Couldn't be). And he was proud of his body (ex-body? he reflected darkly, unconsciously pulling in his stomach). Thighs like a – what was it Del had said? Thighs like a thunderstorm. What the fuck did that mean, he wondered, and smiled. He felt, to be frank, drunk and randy and lonely. Sprawled in front of Lewyn's thirty-two-inch colour television, Dave and Lewyn on the couch, watching the between-rounds adverts. Dave said something to Lewyn, and Lewyn murmured something back, none of which he heard. He smiled.

'How's your boy?' Dave said, turning to face him. 'I heard he had a fall.'

'Oh, yes, no he's fine. It wasn't anything,' James said.

'Dilys was dying to get her hands on him, I can tell you,' said Dave. 'Fancies herself as a bit of a healer, she does. Never healed me of anything though. Just the opposite, as a matter of fact.' They laughed.

'Del thinks she can sense things. Says she can sense something in the field. Doesn't like me digging it up,' said James, and sensed immediately a stiffening, thickening in the air, as if Dave and Lewyn had frozen solid on the couch. Bruno and Tyson were suddenly back, filling the screen with bloodied, closing eyes and gaudy shorts, circling each other. Intent. James stood up and went to the bathroom, not entirely steady to be honest, weaving slightly. Worse for wear, he thought. But it was good to be in another house, no child upstairs, deep soft chairs, central heating, colour telly. He hadn't realized how much he was missing those things. To get comfortable in the farmhouse you had to go to bed. And it was never really warm. And he didn't feel right bringing beer home with him. Adèle drank maybe three-quarters of a can in an evening. He was always finishing her drinks off for her. Not that she'd ever said anything, just as he never said anything about her bloody cigarettes. Chacun à son bleeding.

He came back into the room, and Lewyn was saying:

'. . . not knowing, that's all I mean.'

'Not knowing what?' he called out cheerfully, and was suddenly chilled. Dave and Lewyn did nothing as obvious as look at each other or avert their eyes, but somehow their whole posture was yelling something at him, like a distant car-alarm going off late at night. Neural alert. Sam, he thought, a hard, brittle thought like a fragment of fibreglass in the neck of his shirt. Sam drooling in the back of the car. There was a roar from the screen as Bruno stumbled, gloves up to his face, one eye completely closed and starting to colour.

'Good to see someone looking after the old place,' said Dave, not entirely convincingly. 'Bit of a mess he is, no mistake.'

'Yup. Someone did a thorough job on it, I'd reckon.

It's more than just age and the fire. Some of it looks deliberate. Do they know how the fire got started?'

All three men stared at the screen. Then James heard Lewyn's voice, low and hesitant.

'James. There's a couple of things I want to say about that, if that's all right.'

Dave swigged from his can and glanced across to Lewyn.

'I was telling Mrs Tullian just before, the other day. I don't know if she mentioned anything to you?'

Adèle? She hadn't said anything. What with Sam, and then worrying about the dinner party, they hadn't really spoken much at all. (Well, come on, hadn't actually spoken at any length for years, he corrected himself.)

'No.'

'Well it's like this, see. There were people living there a few years back. Didn't go too well for them. They ran into some trouble.'

Dave looked sympathetically at Lewyn; he was finding it difficult to get started.

'Yeah, they had a few problems, you see, and . . .'

'Raoul and Edith Charpentier. Shar-pent-ee-ay. French. On his side.' Dave took over, and Lewyn, relieved, sank back and nursed his can, eyes fixed on the gory battle on the screen.

'They arrived in 1966, nice young couple and two little girls, a year between them. Pretty as anything. Raoul, he was quite a fellow. He'd been an architect for a while, done very nicely by the sound of it. He worked from home. I had a look at some pictures he had of things he'd built. Funny-looking things I thought they were, but he was successful: made a fair amount of money at it by all accounts. Ty-Gwyneth, it was their dream. Well, his dream I suppose anyway. He thought he was going to get planning permission to build on the land, he wanted to put up a new house, then knock the farmhouse down. He showed me some of the plans and drawings and that, you wouldn't believe it. Had an observatory, and a kind of platform that was going to stick out over the cliff, sort of like a deck. He was going to build gardens out over the cliffs, so they hung down. Bloody weird thing in my opinion, but there you are. He didn't get no planning permission though, council don't let you so much as put up a hay barn on those cliffs. And the house is listed, 'parently. I suppose he should have known that but he seemed to think, because he was a big-deal architect and all, they'd roll over for him. But they didn't. A big blow for him that was.

'Anyway they'd just come down for weekends to start with, then they moved in. He did a few alterations, but not very much. I think he lost heart a bit after all that council business.

'Then they started having these parties. What would happen, all day Friday cars would be arriving, big bloody flash things, he used one of the fields for parking. He'd rigged up lights along the cliffs and down the path to the beach. He had a music system with speakers all over the place. Hell of a racket. I'd come over sometimes to Lewyn's and you'd be able to hear it, thumping and blasting away like God knows what. Don't ask me what kind of music it was, I haven't got much of an ear, but *loud*? I should say. Wa'n't it, Lewyn?'

'Aye.'

'This'd go on all Friday night, all Saturday night, then all the cars'd screech off again. This'd be in the summer.

'One time, Lewyn and me, we went down there to have a look. Felt like kiddies, sneaking round in the bushes 'n' that. Funny it was. Anyway we saw them, they was all out on the grass, front of the house, all lights on and this music going, *dancing*. All drinking their heads off. God knows

101

what else they were doing. Lewyn he found a – what do you call it? Lewyn?'

'Syringe.'

'Aye, syringe, down on the rocks below. They were just off their heads. These were all friends of Raoul's. From London.' He tried not to make it sound accusatory, but London was clearly the sink of human depravity for Dave.

'Saw someone off the telly there, didn't we Lewyn?'

'Aye.'

'Off one of those chat shows, actor or summat. And all these women, well I say women, weren't much more than girls some of 'em. Wearing next to nothing. He didn't never invite us though, did he?'

'No.'

'No.' Dave laughed. 'Can't say I'm surprised, what with celebrities there and all. Wouldn't have fitted in, I dare say. Wouldn't have gone, anyway.'

'Nor me.'

'Dilys, she wanted to go, but that's just what she's like. Likes a bit of a party does Dilys. You should hear the state of her singing!'

Lewyn went to the kitchen for more beer.

'So this was all going on anyway. All over one summer, he'd have a party once a fortnight or so. Got so we was used to it.'

Lewyn had never got used to it. Living as he did, the nearness of so much ostentatious fun, pleasure and company unsettled him, deeply. Being alone was one thing: being alone with parties going on next door was quite another. He remembered lying in bed, listening to the thump of the music and the occasional screams of laughter and surprise. Excluded. Even though he didn't want to be included, not with that lot. And even though he hated drunkenness. He had been surprised by how much it rankled. Never got used to it.

'Then one night, Lewyn, he heard all this screaming going on. Di'n't you Lewyn?'

'Aye.' Lewyn declined to tell this part either.

'Yeah he heard screaming, so he went over to have a look. Everyone running around in a panic. Then all the police and ambulance and that, from out Haverfordwest. I came over and all when I heard that, must have been three o'clock or so. Woman had fallen off, 'parently. Killed herself. Accident though. Police took a lot of them away to question them, Raoul included. Took hours to get everyone sorted out, and they had to fix up a winch to get the woman up from the beach before the tide came in, lot of running about going on. Wa'n't it Lewyn?'

'Aye.'

'So that was that. Di'n't hear anything more about it for a while, and he stopped the parties and all. You'd see him in Fishguard with Edith, she was wearing sunglasses by then, wouldn't look you in the eye. Wouldn't talk to you. But Raoul was the same as always, very – very charming he was, wa'n't he?'

'Aye.'

'And full of plans and ideas and that. Interesting man. Very tall and good-looking, tanned, held himself very straight, like he was ex-military or something, with Edith holding his arm. Like they were out of a film, her in her sunglasses. Can't explain it really.

'Then we stopped seeing Edith. Raoul said she wasn't well and needed rest. She was looking after the children, they were about nine and ten by then. Never saw them neither.'

'Didn't occur to us at first, though, did it? Didn't think anything about it, did we?' said Lewyn tentatively. He was still apparently transfixed by the spectacle of two grown men knocking the crap out of each other, though James got the distinct impression that if you

103

asked him what was going on he wouldn't be able to tell you.

'Though Dilys reckons she thought something was up. Trust her.'

'Aye.'

'So then we started getting visits from the police. They'd had an inquest, the coroner said it was death by mis-adventure, but police weren't happy about it. They asked all about Raoul and that, but we couldn't really tell them much. Dilys wanted to tell them all about this dream she'd had, about the kiddies and all, but I don't think they were taking her too seriously. Laughing up their sleeves I reckon, but they were very polite, wrote it all down.'

James had yet to become accustomed to this loping, elliptical delivery, and realized that his mind was wander-ing. Dave was clearly leading up to something, but so far all he'd got hold of was Lewyn's phrase 'ran into some trouble'. It sounded like Adèle's 'just bad luck'. He saw himself on the cliff top with a piece of blue knitted wool in his hand.

'Next time I saw Raoul he told me that Edith wasn't getting any better and they'd had to send the girls away to boarding school, cos Edith couldn't look after them any more. I asked him what was the matter with her, and he said it was her nerves. He'd got in some doctor from London, Harley Street is it? and she had to just rest. She couldn't see anybody. Lewyn, he called round there one time, didn't you?'

'Aye aye.'

'Raoul wouldn't let him in. Said Edith got upset if anyone came in the house.'

'Upset. Aye.'

'It was all I could do to keep Dilys away. I told her she'd get into trouble if she started going round there. Had a few rows about it, I can tell you! I told her it wasn't none of our business, but she kept on saying we should do something, get the police round again. But she didn't do anything. Anyway, nothing much happened for a bit. I thought it had all blown over.'

There was an outburst of commotion from the television as a boxer crashed to the floor, bouncing off the ropes, and the commentator said, 'Well, he looks like he's in trouble with that eye.'

'Then Lewyn got a visit from her. From Edith. She was in a bit of a state, weren't she Lewyn?'

Lewyn merely grunted.

' 'Parently she said to Lewyn that Raoul had turned funny. Reckoned that he'd killed that woman who fell off the cliff, threatened her with a knife and then pushed her over. Reckoned he'd been taking drugs of some kind.'

(*Raoul Charpentier, high on the cliff top, his arm tingling from the tourniquet, which minutes earlier had caused the veins in his forearm to pop out like wax running down a candle, while he aspirated the syringe, injected, then let it fall through the air on to the beach far below. Holding this beautiful, musky creature in his arms, dancing to the music, Charlie Parker, Dizzy Gillespie. He has a stiletto. His hand plays with it, the carving on the ivory handle. A beautiful, ornamental thing, the blade tapered and sharp. They dance along the cliff, other couples are dancing closer to the house, the lights have been dimmed. Edith is watching from her bedroom window, she has a headache. The air is cool after a hot windless day, there is a breeze floating in off the sea. She is dreadfully unhappy. Watching.*

The woman has her head against Raoul's chest. He has both hands free now, he is stroking the blade behind her back as they shuffle lazily, languidly. Then she jerks her head up, smiling, puzzled. Surprised. Then she stumbles back, she says 'Oh!', then she is falling, Raoul yells, 'Watch out!' then goes to the edge, and everyone is running to him.

He shouts, 'She's gone over!' Edith is motionless, shocked by the fact that she is not shocked, that she always knew, that she did nothing. Let it happen. She ducks back, too late, Raoul has seen her. She locks her bedroom door. She brushes her hair. The face in the mirror is hideous. She must protect the girls. She doesn't know how to.)

'Reckoned he was going to kill her and the kiddies. See, she thought he was the devil. Edith thought he'd killed the woman as kind of a sacrifice. And she said that the people at the parties were in it as well.'

'Everyone was in it. Everyone,' said Lewyn firmly.

'Tha's right. Dilys says you call it paranoia, though what she knows about it 'scapes me I must say. You know anything about paranoia, James?'

'I'd have to ask Del, she's the one with the education,' James said, surprised at the way the sentence came out. Blurred somewhat. Pissed again, he thought. Del *will* be pleased.

Dilys flatly refused to wash any dishes. 'Get that good-looking young man of yours to do it,' she said. 'Or isn't he house-trained yet?'

' 'Fraid not,' Adèle said and smiled.

'But you don't care.'

'Well—'

When she'd first met James, she'd thought he was the sexiest man she had ever seen. And that was it, really. She'd grown to like him, got used to him, whatever, more or less on the strength of that. No, there was more to it, obviously . . . She found her thoughts expanding and gave up.

'No. I don't care. Not really.'

'By the way, I'm making these *extremely* weak,' Dilys said, looking up from her work. She was manipulating cigarette papers and very small pieces of dried-up vegetable matter from a plastic bag. Thai Grass. Adèle was of just the wrong generation to have any really extensive knowledge of drugs. Too young for acid, too old for Ecstasy. But Thai Grass she knew of old. She'd baby-sat people having 'heart attacks', paranoid delusions, fits of depression so severe that they never seemed truly light-hearted again afterwards, fits of laughter that bruised and exhausted them, fits of yawning that turned into inability to breathe, that made the face ache for days. She and James had once had some that had made him *so randy* that . . . well. It was an entirely different experience from the little blocks of waxy, crumbly cannabis resin. All she usually got, though, was a particularly heightened sense of alertness, acuity. Perception. And a sense of freedom. She loved it.

'You should have seen your faces when I put that food out,' she said, and Dilys laughed along with her, but was straight away frowning again.

'I suppose we're just not very used to – novelty.'

'Something else.'

'I'm sorry?'

'There was more to it than that. Lewyn looked actually frightened.'

'Lewyn, Lewyn. He's a beautiful boy, wouldn't you say?'

'Well, yes. Oh yes, he's gorgeous.' (Though hardly a boy, by anyone's reckoning.)

'Not for me to say it, I suppose, being practically his mother.'

'Yes, I think he mentioned that, you brought him up.'

'Well, you see, I *had* to. She was nothing but a little girl herself, his mother.'

'Yes. Yes.' Adèle noted that she had been sidestepped, conversationally.

'Dilys. About the food?'

'My, how direct you are. To the point. A real city girl, eh?'

'Dilys . . .'

'All right. I'm going to tell you in just a minute. Don't be all in a rush now.'

'Sorry, I don't mean to be pushy or anything.' Adèle was surprised, in fact, at how pushy she was being. And surprised too that such an innocent little fishing expedition should actually yield a fish. She hadn't really meant anything about the food. Had she?

'Lewyn, he's told you about Edith?'

'Well, he told me *something*.'

'Yes, I can imagine. "Well, she 'ad a bit of trouble, see, and then she went mad." Something like that? I thought so. Never one for the fine details, my Lewyn. Never uses a word where a raised eyebrow will do. Not a big talker.'

'No.'

'Not even to me. Never has been. Comes to me one day, he says, "Well, tha's it." His dad had died in the night. End of story. I think with Lewyn it's a kind of tactfulness: he doesn't want to embarrass anyone with anything. Wants to spare you. He's always had to be very strong, see, from a very young age. He knows how chaotic things can get when people aren't strong. It frightens him. So he leads by example. Should have been a soldier, that was the real life for him.

'See, that's why he maybe looked a bit tense over dinner. 'Cos Edith, after a while she more or less stopped eating. After he sent the girls away, after that woman died. She'd have us all round for dinner, and she'd just push it around her plate, talking, talking, not eating. Some of the food it was – well, it was quite novel. Sometimes it didn't taste quite right, 'cos she never tasted it herself. Sometimes you didn't really know what you were eating, but you had to eat it anyway. She cooked a lot of French stuff, lots of herbs and garlic. I'd say to her, my, lovely this is, what on earth is it? Kind of like a joke. She'd say, "Ah, old Provençal recipe, family secret." Raoul's family was French, see. After a few of these dinners, Lewyn got it into his head that the food was – what shall I say? – that it wasn't what you'd normally call food. One time he excused himself and sicked it all up in the toilet. It got so he was truly frightened of eating it. But he didn't want to admit it because it seemed so foolish. Like being 'fraid of the dark. Did you know that? Terrified he is. But he won't admit it.'

'Dilys, why did Edith go mad?'

'Because she was a silly, spoiled girl who had no-one to talk to.' Adèle was startled by the bitterness in Dilys's voice.

'Too much on her own, too much imagination in her, too much life really, too much for her to handle. I think she just got so bored down here, she had to invent something to interest her. Once Lewyn had turned her down. He did, you know. Didn't want no part of her.' There was fierceness in her voice, pride, triumph.

'So she came up with all this monkey business. Devils, sacrifices, all that silly stuff. I mean, I think she thought she was in one of those films. She was the heroine, locked up in her room, waiting to be rescued.'

'Locked up?'

Dilys paused.

'Yes. Raoul locked her up. He had no choice, after a while, she wasn't safe. He wouldn't hear of her going away, he looked after her himself. He did all he could.'

'Locked up *here*?'

'Raoul made a nice room for her.'

'*Here?*'

' 'Fraid so, my lovely. So he could keep an eye on her.'

Adèle felt a rush of blood in her face.

'Dilys, what are all those bones in the field?'

'Bones? What, sheep bones are they?'

'I don't know.'

'My dear, are you feeling all right?'

'I don't know.'

'Just sit quiet now. Here, better pass that over to me. Hope I didn't make him too strong.'

'What happened to Edith?'

'Well, I'm sorry to say Edith died. She threw herself out of the window. Well, jumped anyway. Doctor was giving her all kinds of pills apparently. Should have let me have a look at her, but Dave wouldn't hear of it.' Dilys sighed. 'So. She jumped. They buried her at her family's place, out Stafford way.'

'Dilys, why . . . ?'

'Oh now, why why why, you're just getting yourself upset now.' Dilys took her hand, held it very tight, looked hard at her.

'You're all right. It's just a bit of a shock, bound to be, but you're all right. There's nothing to hurt you here. I know. I know.' Adèle found that she was crying, and Dilys was saying, 'Oh now, oh now, there then,' gripping her hand, frowning.

Dave had given up trying to get Lewyn to help him out. Lewyn had just withdrawn, beer can in hand, watching the post-fight analysis, slow-motion shots of the strangely stylized savagery, the sprays of blood and sweat forming perfect parabolic traces, like a scientific demonstration.

'Funny really. Cos he was all set to leave, he'd all packed up and everything. And then it just burnt down in the night. Lewyn it was who called the fire brigade. They had to come out from Haverfordwest way, so it was well burnt by the time they got here.

'Raoul was outside shouting "The children! Get the

children!" Cos of course they were back living there by then. He'd had them back after Edith died, said he wanted them near him. They were up in their room. "Get the children!" But no-one could get in. Raoul was trying to, but they held him back. He'd never have made it. A lot of old wood in there, dry as a bone. Next day the police and the fire went in, didn't find anything, but in the kiddies' room they found some bones. Just the bones. Ah God.'

Dave dried up. Lewyn was motionless. James was shaking his head, unable to believe what he was hearing.

'It's unbelievable,' he said finally.

'So anyway. Raoul just took off after that.'

(*Raoul Charpentier, arranging the bones in the children's empty beds, approximately the right number and size, no skulls of course, no hands or feet, but enough. Bones he'd been collecting for some time. Sheep bones. He arranges them neatly, then gently lays the girls' pyjamas over them, then the bedclothes.*

He knows how buildings burn, knows where to put the materials, reels of old film from an auction sale in London, to burn hot and leave no trace. Raoul Charpentier walking through the silent, darkened, empty house, checking everything is in place. Nerving himself up, cracking his knuckles. Only one chance to get it right, better not have forgotten anything. Check it again. Again.)

'And then the house was just deserted, for a long time. Must be, what, fifteen year now? Lewyn had the spare key that Edith had given him, in case she ever locked herself out. Ironic that, I suppose. Is that the right word?'

Lewyn gazed at the screen, blind, remembering how he'd gone into the house after Raoul had left. The police had taken everything remaining away, to be examined. Not that they seemed particularly suspicious. Raoul had apparently given them a forwarding address in France,

Châtellerault. He would have to come back for the inquest on the children. Yet another inquest. The woman at the party, then Edith, then the children. He was seeing a psychiatrist, he told the police, and they were sympathetic. There was something about him they liked, and he'd been through a lot. He'd broken down for them, said he blamed himself, cried. They'd looked away, embarrassed, and he'd pulled himself together. They gave him a cigarette. He'd kept his dignity, his film-star bearing. They liked that. Christ, if it had been *their* kids . . . They shook their heads. Quite a fellow.

Lewyn had cleaned up some of the mess, carting away heaps of soaking plaster and carpet and wet, scorched wood. He'd marched about, stamping, whistling. Brought in his little portable radio, put it on LOUD. He'd forced himself into the girls' room, flung the debris out of the window, took no more than half an hour but it was a long time. Then he'd pulled back the bolts on the secure room, glanced in. It had already been cleared before the fire, no particular damage: he'd tried not to look at the walls

just-a-game-he-said-what-we'll-do-is-play-a-little-game

not to look at the walls, and not to think, go straight back out. He'd felt sick from the soot and the burnt, wet smell. His hands were sticky. He'd run home and had a bath, then another one, biting down hard on the panic. He'd been sick around midnight. He'd kept the radio on all night, and the light, forcing sleep away. Please God I don't want to dream, not tonight. Please.

'It's just unbelievable,' James said again, stupidly, dimly aware that his speech was impaired.

'Aye, I can hardly believe it myself,' said Dave. 'Any road, tha's what happened. Tha's why the house is such a state.' James wanted to ask, and what about the field? but felt suddenly too weak. He didn't want to hear any more.

'So. Is there any more?' Adèle asked, and laughed. Dilys had sat with her in the bathroom while she composed herself, breathed deeply, washed her face. Dilys sat on the edge of the bath and Adèle removed her smeared make-up with a pad. She smiled at how she'd felt when she was putting it on earlier that evening. At how she felt now.

Dilys laughed too.

'What, more grass? Haven't you had enough yet?'

'You know what I mean.'

'Oh that. I'd have thought you'd've had enough of that and all.'

'What happened to the girls?'

'Funny but I can't even remember what their names were. It'll come to me in a minute. Oh they were lovely, those two. Did everything together, always playing little games. My Lewyn, he used to spend hours with them, larking about. He's not normally much for children, but you should 'a seen him with these two, he couldn't resist them. So pretty. Briony and Jonquil. That was it.

'Well, when Edith got sick Raoul packed them off to some school or other. He couldn't really cope with them, and Edith couldn't do much. Could have got someone in, I suppose, cos money was no problem. But he sent them off. He said it was a lovely school, lots of fields and things. Horse-riding and swimming and ballet lessons. He said they loved it.

'Then Edith died, as I say, and he brought them back again. I think they must have been pretty shocked about their mum, cos I never saw them playing or anything like before. Few days later, you won't believe this, there was a fire in the house.'

'You mean here?'

'Yes. Raoul was out for a stroll, late, and came back

and the house was burning. Couldn't get them out. He was beside himself, but it wasn't no-one's fault. It was the third thing, you see. First that woman at the party, next Edith, next the kiddies. Just terrible. Like it was supposed to happen, for some reason. As if God was punishing him for something, or maybe testing him. Like Job. Just terrible.'

Adèle was watching Dilys's reflection in the mirror. She got the same feeling she'd had when Lewyn had given her his rather terse account of things. As if Dilys was checking how much she believed. Ship sinks, because it is struck by iceberg. All drowned. Or as if she was going to say, 'Nah, I'm just pulling your leg, as if . . . !' Adèle found that she didn't know what to say. Somewhat absently, working moisturizer into her cheeks, she asked, 'The woman? At the party. You didn't explain that.'

'Oh. Well, she just went and fell off the bloody cliff, tha's all. Wandering about in a daze, evidently. Drunk. Just fell off, tha's all.'

'Oh.' Adèle imagined Dilys thinking, 'Would that do?' Yes. It would do. *Just bad luck*, you see.

'Well. Quite a colourful history then, this house. I wonder what Uncle Seb saw in it?' *Parties, dancing. Girls. A ball*, came the reply. Wasn't that what he'd said? Have a ball.

'My dear, I've known this house just about all my life. Lewyn's grandma used to own it, did he tell you? I got a picture of her standing in the garden here, all stiff and formal she looks, with this funny hat on her head. Her best, probably. I love this house. I always loved him, first time I ever saw him I loved him. You don't need to go worrying over him. Bit of a mess right now, but that young man of yours'll put it all straight in no time. Handsome fellow, isn't he? And does he love you? I could see that

114

straight off. You're just what this house needs. A bit of loving. Shall we go back down?'

And Adèle was thinking fields, riding, swimming, ballet lessons. It sounded like heaven.

The television had now moved on to something else, as if the drama of the fight had never happened, the hundreds of thousands of pounds not won or lost, the eye not damaged, the blood and sweat not spilled, in parabolas perfect or otherwise. Pity we don't all live in the telly, James was thinking, so we could just move on when things didn't work out. Have a break for adverts, then return in a different programme.

Dave suggested they go back.

'I don't like leaving Dilys too long case she has any fun without me,' he said. Lewyn stirred himself sufficiently to say goodnight, but he was clearly lost in his own world.

'See you again Lewyn,' Dave called, and James shouted, 'Bye then.'

James was having a few small problems with his cerebellum, fine motor control. He fumbled his jacket on, spilled keys out of the pocket, grabbed for them and missed, grabbed again, stumbled. Shit. Shit-faced again. Well not exactly *shit*-faced, but not exactly clean and sober either. Dave discreetly led him back to the house: it seemed like a long, arduous journey, full of pitfalls and adventures. His feet seemed to have gone a bit stupid. The darkness was full of darker forms, great lumbering things, unknown, unseen. A shape flitted past him, then another; bats, he thought after a moment's panic, just bats. It was incredibly dark. It never got that dark in London.

More fumbling at his front door. Now his fingers were messing him about: Dave watched, decently making no comment.

Adèle met them as they entered: she instantly knew

James was drunk, he immediately knew she'd been crying. They had one of their few rare moments of mutual understanding. No man's land. Pax. They stood by the door while Dilys got her coat. Did Dave want to come in for a moment? Have a cup of tea? No, better be off really, past his bedtime. Dilys thanked Adèle for the dinner, squeezing her arm as she went past. Lovely night. Our turn now. See you again.

Adèle shut the door and bolted it. She went into the kitchen where James was making a cup of tea. He came over to her and hugged her, and she found tears welling up again. He held her harder as she sobbed silently, her whole body shaking. He kissed her hair, her neck. They separated, smiling awkwardly at each other, and sat with their tea. Adèle broke the silence.

'Dilys was telling me about the people that lived here before.'

'So were Dave and Lewyn.'

They fell silent again. Adèle lit a cigarette.

'Dilys said she was locked up here, Edith Whatshername. Her husband locked her up. Here.'

'I didn't hear that bit.'

'She said there was a special room.'

'No.'

'I want to look at it.'

'*No.* What's the point? You'll only get upset.'

'Did you know about it?'

Hard question that: he'd known there was a room that had deadlocks, he knew he hadn't been in it, had always so far found reasons not to go in it. He'd been intermittently aware of how strange it was for there to be a room in the house that neither of them had ever entered. He'd blanked the thought out, evaded it. They'd been here over a week, and the room had been there too. He'd known that much.

116

'No. I didn't.'

'Well, I'm going to have a look,' said Adèle brightly. 'Coming?'

Afterwards, James had put it down to his being drunk, to Adèle having smoked funny tobacco, to both of them being disturbed, jangled, by the stories they'd been hearing. Nerves, hysteria, hallucination.

They were in the room. Longer than it was wide, with the window opposite the door. They'd left the door open. The light wasn't working (no bulb) so they'd kept the landing light on: it lit up a small triangle on the floor and part of one wall. James stood in the lit area. He found himself glancing over his shoulder periodically.

Adèle was at the wall. It was covered, from ceiling to floor, end to end, with scratches in the plaster, writing. The letters were clumsily drawn, angular, esses like backward zeds, upper and lower case promiscuously mixed, giving it a runic quality. Adèle was reading it with her hand, like Braille.

'Adèle, come on, what's the point? Leave it.'

'–though-he-says-theyre-not-his-how-can-he-say-that–'

Adèle was sensing the extraordinary determination that had gone into this account, the tenacity of the woman. It would take her days to read it: God alone knew how long it had taken to write, character by painful character. How long had Edith been incarcerated in this room, and on whose authority? Adèle kept coming back to Raoul, with his film-star bearing. He'd made a nice room for her. He'd sent the children to the school of their dreams. At every point he was in there, organizing people, managing their affairs. And then explaining himself.

'–you-wont-help-me-I-will-find-someone-who-will-youll-not-get-out-of-here–'

Adèle was getting snatches of Edith's record: the writing was not in lines, from end to end of the room, but

117

in columns like a newspaper. In the darkness she couldn't quite grasp the layout.

'Del look, let's come back tomorrow.' James's voice was almost pleading. Still slightly slurred.

'You go if you want, James. I'm just going to read some of this.'

'Come on, Del,' he urged. There was something worrying him, something he couldn't place. He thought: lawnmower bluebottle powersaw, not knowing what he was thinking.

'–they-said-no-we-dont-like-that-game-he-said-heres-a-new-one-then-youll-like–'

refrigerator generator amplifier

'–its-called-sheep-you-put-on-the-blindfolds–'

Because they don't know the words.

'–out-on-the-cliff-he-had-his-bayonet-he-must-have-seen–'

Why do bees

Hum

James called out, 'Sam!' then the door slammed. Complete darkness. Adèle shouted, 'James! James!'; he was at the door but it wouldn't open. Adèle ran to the window: it was immovable. She shouted, 'James! I can't breathe! James, open the door!' He shoved at it stupidly; it was stuck, why was it stuck? She ran to him, pushed him aside, she kicked at the door, she beat on it with both fists. He tried to stop her and she turned on him, flailing in the darkness while he tried to cover his face. 'You bastard! You bastard!' He cowered away from her and she turned back to the door.

'I can't *breathe*!' she screamed with a great lungful of air, 'I can't breathe in here, let me out, please, I only want to talk to you, please, *pleeeeeeeease!*'

The door swung open: Sam was standing there in his Count Duckula pyjamas, rubbing his eyes.

118

'I thought somebody was shouting.'

'Did you lock the door?' Adèle bellowed at him. He looked at her blearily.

'What?'

'Del . . .'

'Why did you lock the *door*?'

'I was asleep, then I thought someone was shouting,' he repeated, looking cross and sleepy, 'so I came out and then the door shut.'

'Del, the door wasn't locked, it just jammed.'

'I couldn't breathe! James!'

He took hold of her and led her off to the bedroom.

'I'll tuck you in in a minute, Sam, you go back to bed,' he said, and shut the bedroom door. Adèle seemed to be in shock, she was trembling, her eyes were glazed; she was breathing very deeply. Hyperventilating. Her colour wasn't good. One hand was bleeding from her assault on the door. He tore off the blankets and wrapped her in them, sitting her and then lying her down. She had become, not rigid, but passive, absent. He didn't like the look of her. He left her lying on the bed, swathed in the tangled blankets. He padded softly to the secure room. He swung the heavy oak door a few times: it moved easily. He glanced inside, then pulled the door to, bolted it top and bottom and locked it. He withdrew the key and dropped it into his trouser pocket.

'James!' Adèle was calling. He went back to her, closing the bedroom door quietly.

Sam got back into bed. He was very tired, he'd had a busy day. First there'd been the hole, then the nurse, then the doctor – though the doctor had just asked him a lot of questions and stared at him. Not a real doctor. Then a long night listening, after he'd been put to bed. He catalogued it all neatly in his mind.

The lady who lived here before lived in the room and

wrote on the wall. That was a bad thing to do, you were supposed to write on paper (as Sam had found to his cost when he'd decided to decorate the wall by the stairs at home, aged five. Now he wrote everything down on paper). Then she jumped out of the window. Also bad, you weren't supposed to play with windows. Cos if you fell they'd have to scrape you up and take you away in a bucket, his dad said. So the lady must have been put in a bucket. She deserved it really, doing all those bad things.

The man played games on the cliff. Now that was bad, but it was also fun. Sam was interested in games. He'd heard his mum in the lady's room saying something about a game. Sheep. You put on a blindfold.

The little girls had been very good, though they sounded a bit boring. After the lady went to live in the room, the man sent the girls away. So maybe they were bad really, but pretending to be good. But he sent them somewhere nice, like Beaver Camp. Hard to decide about those two.

But the best thing was the lady who fell off the cliff. Sam had had to duck back into his room to hear this, when his mum and the other lady went to the bathroom. The tap had been running, so he couldn't hear properly, but she'd definitely said 'Fell off the cliff'. She was drunk which was OK as long as you knew when to stop like his dad did. She mustn't have known when to stop, just gone straight over.

The little girls had come back, then they'd been in the fire and burnt, like Ruthie. So they were probably no good.

One other thing: his mum had used a word he didn't know. Sam was always interested in unfamiliar words. She'd said it when she was in the lady's room, before she'd started being silly and shouting. Bay-net. He'd have to look it up. Tomorrow.

His dad was coming to look at him. He clicked off his Bart Simpson night-light and closed his eyes.

James glanced in at the boy, a huddled form under the blankets. He was too distracted to notice that he wasn't dribbling.

James went back to Adèle. He'd remade the bed and she was lying beside him, eyes wide open. She breathed deeply, slowly, taking each breath with conscious effort. For a moment she thought she was going to die in there. Never get out. Blind terror. Was that how Edith had felt? She tried to stop thinking in case James could hear it: it seemed awfully loud, a high, strong, angry sound. The wind came up, and she rolled over and slept.

Dilys and Dave strode arm in arm along the cliff-top path, singing, as the waves crashed and thundered below. They alternated lines, coming together for the refrains, and Dave improvised a lower descant part.

> 'Thou God of Harmony and love
> Whose name transports the saints above
>   And lulls the ravish'd spheres
>   And lulls the ravish'd spheres.
> On thee in feeble strains I call
> And mix my humble voice with all
>   Thy heavenly choristers
>   Thy heavenly choristers!'

6

The Destruction of the Beasts

Lewyn was in the slaughterhouse. The great machines were thudding and grinding around him. He was lost, looking for something. He had to find it before someone else did. He went from room to room, pushing his way through the racks of hanging carcasses which seemed strangely unstill. In one room he'd find a heap of hooves and ears, in another a pile of entrails with the blood running down a gutter into a drain. All stirring, slithering. There was a room where a man was standing in the far corner with his back to Lewyn, doing something with an immense slab of meat, which again did not appear to be entirely dead, flopping about. He looked round and Lewyn apologized and closed the door: it was private.

Lewyn walked alongside a conveyor belt. Parts of animals were coming along it. Some of them he could identify, many of them he couldn't. He picked one up: it was warm, the fur matted and sticky. He put it down again when it twitched in his hand. At the end of the conveyor belt a little girl was standing, with a white cap and gloves, collecting the pieces and pushing them down a steep chute. She smiled.

'Where's the other one?' Lewyn asked her. The girl shrugged.

'She went off somewhere.'

Lewyn nodded and walked on. That was what it was.

He had to find the other girl before anything happened to her. He descended a staircase and came out into a dark cavernous hall. He walked across it, trampling over things he couldn't see, careful not to lose his footing in the seething, grisly stuff underfoot. Then he caught sight of her: she was running from him.

'It's all right!' he shouted. 'Come back!' but she kept running until she tripped and fell into the mess of cartilage and fur and tissue.

'Hold on!' he shouted, but he couldn't reach her, and she quickly became covered in the restless slime until she was indistinguishable from it, had become part of it. He found a door and emerged into daylight, carrying a bloody hunk of something, where James was waiting for him.

'We'll go in the barn,' Lewyn said, 'where no-one can see.'

'What about the beast?' James asked.

'It's all right,' said Lewyn, 'I killed him,' and awoke. The television was still on, adverts. Lewyn stared at it for a while, then unplugged it and went to bed. He left the light on.

7

Still Life

Lewyn had come down to help James for the day. There was a concrete path round the house which had to be taken up. Lewyn was going round softening it up with a sledgehammer; James followed him with a crowbar and pickaxe, prising open the cracks, then hammering the crowbar in to get leverage, then smashing the pieces. It was slow, heavy work, and they stopped frequently. Elvis was suspicious of Lewyn, running round him and barking, getting in the way, until Lewyn lay down on the ground and rolled over. Elvis approached him, sniffing, and Lewyn grabbed him and wrestled him over, rubbing his stomach and scuffing his ears, to which indignity Elvis submitted with good grace. Then he stood up and shook himself and trotted off.

It was November now, but the first frost hadn't come yet and the sky was clear. Still autumn. The sheep were at their mundane, incessant work, heads down, completely undismayed by the colossal noises ringing out, as if they remembered a time when giants had worked Wagnerian anvils and the earth had trembled.

James had cleared the bones away before Lewyn came, throwing them over the cliff, obscurely ashamed of them. He kept meaning to ask Lewyn about them, and kept shying away from it. He wasn't entirely sure he wanted to know. While he was working he was worrying about what might be under the concrete. Every part of the house seemed to harbour some secret. He was expecting at any moment some new thing to burst out. But it was just rubble, hardcore. Good quality too. But wet.

They stopped at twelve for a cup of coffee. James dragged out a pair of deck chairs he'd found, and they sat in the bright, cold sun.

'How's your boy?' Lewyn asked.

'He's fine.' Sam was with Adèle. She was supervising his school activites – they might be on holiday but that didn't mean he got off free. They'd both had to go to a small office in north London to establish their fitness to teach Sam. They'd sat opposite a stern-looking woman who'd scrutinized their O-level Certificates and had given them a stack of syllabuses to follow. Sam was coping well with the new arrangement: he was fascinated by books, and was beginning to get a feel for maths: he would manipulate his little coloured Cuisenaire rods with a dexterity that surprised Adèle. He had a problem book with sums and the answers at the back: he never, ever, cheated. He was puzzled but excited by the division questions: if Mary has twelve oranges to share equally between Harry, Bob and Bill, how many would each boy receive? The division of numbers intrigued him, the curious, relentless reductions, but so did the original premises: why did Mary have twelve oranges, and why was she giving them away?

'Mrs Tullian all right is she?' Lewyn never called her Adèle. Nor did he say 'the missus' or 'the wife' or any of the other innumerable joky appellations that women are heir to.

'Yeah, she's OK.' Though she didn't seem to have quite got over the incident in the secure room. She was just a touch distracted, inclined to periods of withdrawal and abstraction. She wasn't sleeping very well either: she'd read late into the night, and sometimes James would wake to hear her moving about the house. She wasn't herself. But the painting was going well. She was experimenting with a different style, working on a series of still-life studies, as well as the landscapes. Sheep, not surprisingly, had begun to figure quite largely in the landscapes. There was one that James particularly liked: it was a big picture, with a lot of impressionistic background, and taking up much of the left foreground was a sheep's face, very close up, blurred on the near side, stark black and white, with another close behind. The sheep looked surprised, almost amused, its ears up. James liked it because in real life you never got that close to a sheep; they kept a meticulously cautious distance from you, though he had been surprised by how calm they were. They didn't startle easily. He'd thought of them as mindless panicky creatures, and was impressed by their impassive, almost nonchalant, demeanour. He'd asked Adèle if they could hang this one in the front room (now equipped with a couch and a few other bits and pieces from a second-hand place in Haverfordwest), and to his surprise she'd consented. She was normally very secretive about her paintings. There was a strong wooden peg driven into the cement above the fireplace, and he hung the painting there. She would get them all framed when she knew what was going to go into the exhibition.

He was less enthusiastic about the still lives she'd shown him, though he could admire the technical achievement. Damaged fruit, dead flowers and meat; half-empty milk bottle, snail, broken shower attachment and meat. His Adidas trainers, over-full ashtray. And meat. He found the subject matter, to be frank, disturbing in a way he couldn't express. He just didn't know what she was getting at, nor could she offer any explanation.

James tried to rouse himself: he was being rather a torpid conversational partner.

'So how are the sheep, Lewyn?' It wasn't much of an opening, admittedly, but it was something.

'Why do you ask?'

Why did he ask?

'Oh, no reason. Just wondering.'

'Well, as it happens, I found one of them in the lower field, down by the cliff path. He was in a fair state, looked like he'd been got at by something.' Lewyn's tone gave nothing away, but he'd been shocked by the savagery of the mutilation. Head hanging off, rear right leg missing. Could have been the work of an animal, dog perhaps. But that wasn't what it looked like. The beast, he'd told himself. The beast in the barn, woken up by his dream. The recollection of the dream, particularly the latter part with James, troubled him and he looked away, out to sea. He'd had problems with the sheep before, in the days of the Charpentiers. He'd never reached any kind of conclusion about it. Sometimes he thought he remembered doing it himself: in the dream he'd been holding something, a leg perhaps?

'Well, it happens. A dog could have done it. You'd be surprised how nasty they can be. But apart from that they're fine. They don't get up to too much, as you may have noticed. Keep themselves to themselves.'

Was there a rebuke there, for James's inquisitiveness? He cast about for something to say, and found nothing. Lewyn stood up.

'I'll just use the toilet a minute,' he said.

On the stairs he encountered Sam, who was writing in an exercise book. He closed the book as Lewyn came up.

'Hello piglet,' said Lewyn and Sam smiled politely. 'What you writing?'

'Oh, just a story,' said Sam modestly.

'Oh yes.' Sam had a dictionary open beside him. 'Bathe' to 'beach'.

'What's the word then?'

'Bayonet. It's a blade that goes on the end of a rifle. What's a rifle?'

'Rifle? It's a gun. Big long gun. You know what a gun is?'

'Oh yes. To shoot people with.'

'Tha's it.' Lewyn was taken aback by the boy's coolness. He supposed children didn't understand what violence meant, maybe they thought it was like a cartoon where no-one really got hurt and the coyote rolled out flat by the steamroller always popped back into shape again.

'Hope you're not going to have people getting shot in your story,' he said, and Sam smiled.

'Oh no. I just wanted to know what it meant. Any word you don't know, you can look in the dictionary and it'll tell you. It's got all the words there are. I know lots of them already. Not all of them though.'

But a dictionary couldn't tell you what a gun felt like, smelled like. It couldn't tell you about the fear and the sick exhilaration the thing produced, the weight of it in your hands, the smell of the cartridges. As for a bayonet, no definition could express the feeling of fixing it to the muzzle, a twist and then a snap, and then the horror of imagining a situation so desperate that you would stick it into someone, a warm living man, make him scream and bleed, make him writhe, make him cold. The gun was an impersonal thing, your target was a faceless form a long way away. But to use a bayonet you had to chase your enemy, see his face, smell his breath. Watch him fall. A bayonet was intimate, bodily, almost private.

'Nasty thing a bayonet is. Very nasty.'

'Have you seen one?'

'Aye aye. When I was in the army. Long time ago now.'

'Did you kill people?'

'Of course I didn't!' Lewyn was momentarily outraged, until he recalled that the person he was talking to was a little boy, seven years old.

'No. I never used one on anyone. Don't know if I really could, if it came to it.'

'Why, is it very hard?'

'Hard? No he's easy enough. Nothing to him as far as that goes. You just clip him on, level your gun as if you were going to shoot, but a bit lower down. You bend your knees. Like this.' Lewyn got into position, weight well balanced, head forward.

'Then you run at your target. In the army we had people made out of bags of straw, hanging up off a pole.' Lewyn blinked rapidly as the memory returned. A hot, dry field, the sun blazing down. A company of men, tired and heavy in the middle of the afternoon. The sergeant demonstrating the procedure patiently, as if he were addressing a group of mental defectives. The drill was straightforward enough, and within half an hour the company was presenting, fitting, removing and stowing the bayonets in the proper jerky, mechanical way. So far so good.

Next, running and screaming. Four at a time. The straw men were hanging from a structure like that used for children's swings, attached by chains. They wore jackets, but had no limbs or heads. Nothing to strike with or scream with. No eyes. You ran, screaming, at them, rammed the blade in, twisted it (quarter turn, clockwise), jerked it out. If the scream was less than full-throated you were sent back to do it again. Lewyn had never screamed before, not in adult life, and found it extremely difficult, as did several of the others. He had three attempts before he achieved the right voice, and it was a liberation. He remembered the lightness in his head as he ran across the dry grass, the scream streaming back behind him, a dizzy, exhilarating feeling. Then the sudden stop and the release of the thrust as the blade tore the canvas and the straw man swung away. It was a powerful, dramatic thing to be doing, once the earlier feeling of being ridiculous had evaporated. The scream cleared his head of everything, all fear, all embarrassment, all uncertainty. It was only funny afterwards. And only disturbing much later, as his throat remembered the screams and his arms trembled from the thrusts into the closely packed straw, more solid than he'd imagined.

The child was listening hard, and Lewyn was horrified by himself. What was he doing, telling all this to a young kiddy? What had got into him?

'Anyway, tha's enough of that. You don't want to go thinking about guns and bayonets. Not at your age. Shouldn't have told you all that, not really.'

Sam understood. There were some things he wasn't supposed to know. His dad would tell him them all when he was twenty-one. There were quite a few of them by now, and the list was growing all the time. He imagined the conversation they would have, his dad perhaps consulting a notebook and ticking them off one by one as he dealt with them. But what if he needed to know before then? Maybe his dad would make an exception. He turned to p. Pyre.

Lewyn said, 'Right better get on,' and went to the bathroom. He passed the room where Adèle was painting, and his nostrils flared. A thick, oily smell, and turps, and something else. He couldn't place it.

He locked the bathroom door. As his water splashed into the bowl, he pondered over what he should tell James. Dave's account of the Charpentiers had been accurate as far as Dave knew, but there were gaps, omissions, and one major inaccuracy. A rather important one. Dave only knew what Raoul had wanted him to know, planting his information in a calculatedly off-hand manner, disarming and laced with charm. Lewyn knew more, much more, and had been able to untangle the truth from Edith's chaotic outpourings. He'd held his knowledge to himself, wearing it like a hair shirt. He'd never disclosed it to anyone, not Dilys, no-one. To do so now would be like exposing himself, for the information was indecent, shocking, somehow shaming to the one who knew it. He should have told the police. He hadn't. It was too late now to regret it, but regret it he did. His knowledge involved him in what had been done, made of him a witness, with a witness's share of the guilt and responsibility. He flushed the thought away and went back down to smash some more concrete.

Adèle was having a few problems with the meat. Now that it was starting to decay, the lines and colours were becoming far less clear cut, were engaged in a subtle and complicated negotiation between solid form and fluidity. She found she was looking more and painting less, finding her hands blocked by the difficulty of the task. The meat also seemed to be growing something like a crust or a skin, so that the surface, in contrast to what was beneath, was hardening, thickening, drying out. There were patches where the colours were just on the verge of turning, from umber to green and vermilion and even saffron, but somehow that was something she only knew to be latently there but couldn't yet see. It was all very tricky: unless you were scrupulous about it, you ended up either with a sort of cartoon T-bone steak, or a formless brown smear. It was a matter of seeing perfectly and then holding the image in your head long enough to portray it. And you had to do it fast, or the paint, like the meat, started to thicken and coarsen and dry out. She sighed and lit a cigarette.

The exhibition was beginning to take shape in her mind. Two contrasting sets of paintings: landscapes with more and more sheep in them, and the still lives with the meat. They would counterpoint each other, formally as well as thematically. Of the three canvases that had been completed so far, there were two landscapes and one still life. She would make her final selection when they were all finished, take slides of them and send them to her agent. He would undoubtedly have a few comments to make, so she needed to leave herself at least a month for alterations and reworkings. She was nervous about his response to the still lives. She'd never tried anything like them before, apart from a few hesitant technical exercises at college, and it was quite possible that he would reject them. It was, of course, her choice as to what went in and what didn't, but for an exhibition as important as this she would trust his judgement more than her own. If he did reject the still lives she would have to have a pool of 'spare' paintings to make up the number. There was a lot of work to be done before April came around.

She looked again at her subject. It was too crowded, too busy. Folded curtains and pillowcases, each with its own floral design, screwdriver, plastic carrier bag and meat. Abruptly she took away the curtains and the carrier bag. That was more like it. She'd only sketched in the other objects in grey crayon, so she could keep most of the painting. It put the meat into greater prominence in the composition, balanced nicely by the red plastic handle of the screwdriver. It flashed through her mind that this was really quite an odd painting, quite a *strange* painting, but the technical improvement was undeniable. Good. Good.

* * *

James and Lewyn worked on into the afternoon, reducing the neat concrete path to a neat line of bags of concrete rubble. James was secretly relieved that there was just concrete in the bags. He and Lewyn sat in the deck chairs again as the low sun set behind the trees. There was a silence between them, but James was less troubled by it now. Lewyn was clearly a man of few words, and that was fine by James. It was a good silence. All his life James had been worried by silences. His father and mother had had some terrifying periods of wordlessness, periods of such extreme tension that James had sometimes felt like screaming. James had talked a great deal as a child, but as he'd got older he'd begun to gain a clearer understanding of the deadly quiet he was speaking into, and the terrible fear of it that had made him want to talk so much. Aged eleven he'd clammed up, afraid that the desert of non-communication around him would just absorb him, leaving him dried out, a husk. There was something almost predatory about it: it was a trap. He'd shut up and stayed shut up, contributing his own dune to the desert. By adolescence he was habitually quiet, very shy, very inarticulate. All desire to explain or describe or express gone. He was what he'd feared he would become: barren.

And then, much later, he'd met Adèle and she'd talked and talked and *talked*, but easily, without fear or panic, effortlessly throwing out her impressions and feelings. She expressed. And James stayed quiet, soaked it up. Now he was afraid that she would come to see his quietness as a trap also, that she too would dry up, turn to sand. He wanted to talk to her, before this happened. He kept meaning to. But the fear was growing in his mind that it was already too late, and this feeling got into his mouth and gummed it up, dried it out. He was well aware that she often now talked simply from her fear of his

133

secretness, and that there was creeping into her voice an edge of panic. Fear begetting fear.

Lewyn, however, just kept his own counsel; if there was something on his mind he'd say it, if not, not. So between him and Lewyn he sensed the growth, not of a desert, but of a quiet, orderly garden. He smiled across at Lewyn, pleased with his solidity and self-containment.

'All right, Lewyn?'

'Aye aye.'

'Stay for something to eat?'

'Very good of you.'

James felt a tremendous peacefulness: it was partly the cessation of work, his body tingling from the day's exertions, partly the beautiful clear cold air. Bats twittered past and he could hear Adèle and Sam in the kitchen, the clanking and rattling of plates. He should go and give Adèle a hand, but it was so luxurious to sit, quietly, in a deck chair as the sun went down.

'James, before we go in there's something I want to tell you. Been on my mind.' James smiled; not the grazing rights again, surely! Adèle had regaled him with the story of Lewyn's worries about taking hay and grazing on the fields.

'About the field.'

'Look Lewyn really, you don't have to worry about that. We're just happy that the fields are being used for something. It'd be terrible to let them get wild. We really don't mind.'

'No, no I don't think you understand me right. I don't mean about the sheep and that.'

'Oh.' James waited, trying to look encouraging in the half light.

'See, it's something that happened a long time back, when the Charpentiers were here. What Dave told you the other time, I don't know if that was right or not. I

134

don't know how to say it really. But after that last party, when the woman got killed, couple of weeks after, he had a fire. Raoul did. Bonfire. I was out in the top field and I saw a lot of smoke. So I come down to have a look. Hid behind that wall over there. Wrong of me to do it I know, snooping around, but this was late summer, and people usually don't start having bonfires till autumn, when there's leaves to burn. Or they're cutting trees back. So I was thinking what's he got to burn this time of year? So I came down. He had a big fire going, lots of timber, and he had a stick, he was poking at it. Obviously I couldn't see what he was doing cos of the smoke and that, and the heat. But that was it, you see. The smoke.' He paused, and James saw himself tossing a tiny fragment of charred blue wool over the cliff.

'That was what'd made me suspicious, see. That smoke. Cos I've smelled him before.'

(*A thick column of smoke rising up, straight to heaven. The devil! The devil!*)

'There's no mistaking him once ever you've smelled him. He was burning meat.'

(*A barbecue that's all it was a barbecue grilled leg of lamb on the bone baked potatoes corn relish please*)

'He gets right into your nose, that smell, and you don't ever forget him.'

(*all-right-then-lets-play-another-one-its-called-sheep-youll-like*)

'Then he put the fire out and he started digging. Just over where you've been digging, matter of fact, where that septic tank is.'

(*what they wanna go a-buryin' the midgets for Jiiiiiim?*)

'And he put all the ashes into the hole.'

No!

'And then after that the children went off to boarding school. 'Parently. Never saw them again.'

James felt an overpoweringly strong wish to be in the kitchen with Adèle and Sam, chopping onions or even peeling potatoes. Anything rather than having this eerie conversation with this intensely serious man as the bats flitted by.

'I don't understand,' he said at last. 'Dave said the children died in the fire in the house. After Edith had died.'

'Maybe they did. I'm just saying what I saw, tha's all.'

'But what you're suggesting . . .'

'All I'm saying, all I'm *saying*, is what I saw. I'm not making no accusations. But I was kind of wondering if, maybe when you were digging in the field, maybe you found anything.'

'What like?'

'I don't know.'

'I didn't find anything.'

'Please, don't take me wrong or anything . . .'

'I didn't find *anything*!' James shouted, and flinched back from the sound. He desperately wanted to be back in the calm, reflective silence they'd had before, but Lewyn had broken it, broken it badly.

'Jesus Christ, Lewyn!'

'Aye, well . . .'

'I found sheep bones. That's all.'

'Sheep. Aye.'

'Jesus Christ!'

'I just wanted to tell you. What I saw.'

James sat, stunned. He was frightened of them, he thought they were devils, but they were frightened of him, they screamed, like this. He had a stick-thing.

'I found a piece of wool.'

'Oh aye.'

'Not sheep wool, knitted wool.'

'Aye, I thought perhaps you'd found something.'

'Oh Christ. I don't believe it.'

'No, dare say.'

They sat on in a new silence, a complicit, guilty, hard silence, like plate glass.

'Don't say anything to Del,' James said.

'Of course not.'

'She's got enough on her plate as it is.'

'OK.'

'Please.'

'I won't.' Lewyn had expected to feel relieved, but instead he found that he felt ashamed, as if he'd done something improper towards James. But the urge to speak out had been so strong, he just couldn't help himself. He was mistrustful of any feeling as strong as that: he didn't like the idea that he was housing things he couldn't understand or control. The beast was supposed to be in the barn, not in him.

Lewyn had known about the beast all his life. As a young child he'd avoided the barn, and when he had to go in he'd carefully avert his eyes from the pile of lumber under which the beast hid. The beast ate rabbits; they would be found stretched out on the stone floor, not damaged in any way, but dead, as if they'd had the life sucked out of them. But he was harmless, Lewyn knew, as long as you didn't look at him. In his dreams Lewyn had sometimes already killed him, but he was never really dead. You couldn't truly kill him, no-one could. He was a fact of life, almost a companion. And if one day he should rouse himself and shake off the lumber, and go looking for food other than unfortunate rabbits – well, Lewyn would face that when it happened. But as long as he did nothing to disturb him he was safe enough.

'Maybe we should go in?' he said, as James showed no signs of moving. James sighed.

'Yup.'

Dinner was a very different affair from the dinner party of a few weeks ago. This was just the family feeding itself, with a guest. No table settings or South American delicacies this time; Sam had his usual Smash and veggy-burger, with some salad on the side that he dutifully despatched first, to get it over with. For the rest of them, Adèle had made chilli with kidney beans, and rice. (Even so, there was enough of the hostess left in her from Westdene to ensure that each plate was garnished with chopped herbs and the rice was mixed with poppy seeds. Presentation.) And this time she was amused rather than offended by Lewyn's ill-disguised reluctance to put any of it into his mouth. Elvis hung about with his optimism-in-the-face-of-all-odds expression: he never got anything from the table, not even from Sam, and he knew it. The triumph of hope over experience, however, kept him at the table, watching the movement of fork to face and back again. Maybe this time.

Lewyn chewed slowly, methodically, subjecting the food to every test his nostrils and palate could devise, then forcing the bolus of matter down. Swallowing food, other than what he prepared for himself, was a thing that he did only with deliberate effort; it was a matter of determination. First you scooped something up on the fork, having searched the plate for unfamiliar material. Then you raised the fork, now trying not to look at it too closely (Lewyn had found that no food looked entirely, convincingly, innocent close to). Your nose sucked up the aromas, alert for the telltale scents of anything amiss: the dry, crumbly, secret smell of fungus, the urinous tang of flesh, the rich, febrile whiff of the over-ripe, any odour hiding behind a stronger one, or an unfamiliar edge to a familiar smell. The high, giddy reek of strong acid, or the singing, soapy flash of petrol.

Then you raise the fork further, closer to your mouth. Despite yourself you have to grab a look at it before it touches your tongue and lips, in case it is the tidily folded wing case of an insect, for instance, or a clot of human hair, or— Disguising the movement as a blink you shut your eyes as the tines of the fork touch your tongue and whatever it is is deposited into your mouth. The fork tastes sour, metallic, bloody, and you get it away from you fast, back to the plate. Meanwhile every nerve in your mouth is frantically filing reports, OK so far, this may *just* be all right, and you chew, squeezing out every particle in case there is something hidden inside, some putrid, insane thing . . . You can delay no longer, and in any case you have got to get this obscene gob of filth *out* of your mouth, quick for God's sake swallow it, your epiglottis obeys you and you push the thing down, push it down, your throat convulsing, your mouth slimy with saliva, your pulse hard and fast. And all the time you must appear relaxed, genial even, and above all else you *must not* spit it back out. There is a whole plateful of it to go. You ration your gulps of water. You try to remember to smile.

Adèle observed this stubborn, dogged fight with admiration and respect. She could only guess at the difficulties Lewyn faced, but she could see clearly enough the rigidity, the jerkiness of his movements, and the frequent short pauses as he gathered up his will. What grim battles we all have to fight sometimes, she thought, just to get through half an hour of a day.

Lewyn finally swallowed the last forkful and pushed the plate away, aware that he did it rather too forcefully. He smiled up at Adèle, who smiled back sympathetically.

'Thank you Mrs Tullian. That was very nice.'

*　　*　　*

For sweet (James wouldn't tolerate the use of the word 'dessert', and gave a nasty, ironic twang to 'afters') there was ice-cream and blackberries. Adèle loved blackberries because they were free! and because the fruit was so unpredictable, some sweet and fragrant, some bitter. And she loved the grittiness, the realness of them. She'd shown Sam how to select the right ones to pick – and had got the unmistakable impression that he was humouring her. He couldn't disguise the fact that he just did not believe you could eat the things that grew in hedges. Until she popped one into his mouth, and he raised his eyebrows. After that he ate more than he dropped into the cleaned-out Flora tub, despite her warnings, and later paid the price of not listening to his mother. It had been a lovely afternoon, cold but so clear you could see everything, and they meandered along the hedges, listening to the birds. Sam had seen a frog (his first), and then she'd spotted the sloe bush, laden with dusty, velvety black drops, astonishingly generous. She polished one for Sam and, warning him that these weren't like the blackberries, dropped the cold black bead on to his tongue. He chewed it thoughtfully, said 'Hm . . .' and went back to the blackberries. Possibly a bit of an acquired taste, she agreed.

To show respect for Sam's stomach trouble later that evening, she'd washed them and put them into the big chest freezer in the basement. They'd go sloppy, she knew, when they defrosted, but they'd be none the worse for that. Sam would probably need about a week to get over his feeling of being betrayed by the natural world.

And she'd forgotten about them! She'd been digging around for the ice-cream and there they were. One of the tubs had tipped over and she'd had to scoop them up off the bottom. She'd been struck by a thought, but had been distracted (Sam had been shouting that the kettle was boiling for his Smash) and it had just flitted away, evaporated. She'd stood for a moment, perplexed, and then, balancing the tubs on the cardboard ice-cream box, gone back up, clicking off the light with some difficulty. She'd had the dishes all served out and ready to go before they started eating. Sam's helping contained more ice-cream and less fruit.

With the main course finished Lewyn was visibly more at ease, and the silky, runny, brilliantly coloured pudding was quickly eaten, Adèle as always savouring the sound of spoons scraping bowls as the last traces were scooped up. Sam licked his dish, though he left the blackberries on the side, and she was happy for him to do it. Goddamned little housewife-and-mother, she chided herself, but she did like to feed her menfolk. James did cook (though much less frequently than he believed he did), but he took no pleasure in it and it generally put him into a sulk, so she didn't enjoy it. He'd once smashed three plates serving out rice that hadn't been rinsed and thus wouldn't readily come off the spoon. And she always felt that she had to exaggerate her gratitude for it, and make lots of those idiotic slurping, appreciative sounds, while he gracelessly shovelled the food down. Not a natural cook.

James stood up to make the coffee, and Adèle lit a cigarette, using her dish as the ashtray. Pushing her luck really, she knew, but James would just have to put up with it. It made her feel free, spontaneous. Well dammit she *was* supposed to be an artist, she could get away with it.

Lewyn was manoeuvring his tongue round his mouth, dislodging the tiny gritty seeds that were stuck between his teeth. He looked distracted, she thought, almost tormented.

'Hard day, Lewyn?'

'Aye. I'll sleep tonight and no mistake.'

'What, haven't you been sleeping then?'

Wrong, she thought immediately. Intrusive, clumsy, nosy. Sniffing round for wrinkled handkerchiefs again.

'Well I have a bit of trouble sometimes. Dreams, you know.' He seemed disinclined to pursue it, but she felt that if she could get him on his own he'd open up. Come to think of it, he did look tired.

'Can I go upstairs and read please?' Sam asked, and Adèle gravely assented.

'Yes you may.'

'Thank you.'

'That's all right.'

Sam said goodnight to Lewyn and went up. Elvis, reluctantly accepting that this was the end of whatever remote possibility there might have been of getting anything, padded away after him.

'Painting going well is it?'

'Yes I think so. Hard for me to tell really.'

'That one of yours is he?' Lewyn turned to look at the sheep portrait.

'Well, yes. I don't know if it's really finished yet . . .'

'Now don't you put yourself down. I think he's marvellous.'

Adèle blushed (not often that *that* happened these days) and stared with Lewyn at the painting. Yes. It looked all right.

'Bit startled he is, isn't he? Got his ears up.'

'Yes I suppose so.'

'Frightened even. Maybe.'

Adèle laughed.

'I suppose it's not every day he has some strange woman peering at him from behind a bush! He probably thought I was after him.' She noticed that she'd picked up Lewyn's gendered noun, but it sounded natural

142

enough. 'It' would have been too cold, and 'she' would be artificial, she felt.

'They have the strangest way of looking at you, don't you think?' she said. 'It's as if they go dead for a moment, they just freeze'

(*just flitted away, just*)

'and their eyes don't even flicker. And then they kind of dismiss you, stop seeing you; as if you're invisible.' She was making heavy weather of this, she knew, but she had been astonished at the alienness of the sturdy, compact creature she'd spied on from behind the blackthorn. It had made her feel, not invisible perhaps, but worse than that, irrelevant, of no conceivable importance, not even worthy of fear. Merely another item, like a wall or a hay-feeder. If she'd dropped dead on the spot the sheep would have just stepped fastidiously over her. There could never be any sort of communication between them, not of any kind. Wholly alien. It was this quality that she'd tried to paint, but what had come across was fear. The sheep's, she wondered, or her own?

James stood at the sink with cold water running over his hands, rinsing the cups. (He could never be quite sure that Adèle had done it properly.) They were certainly getting a thorough rinsing now, because James was miles away.

He was crouching where Lewyn must have crouched, watching the smoke and the haze from the fire, getting glimpses of someone moving about on the other side of it. The smell was dense and suffocating.

James watched through Lewyn's eyes as the figure behind the fire reached into it with a stick, poking, prodding, drawing back as the wind shifted and he was engulfed in smoke. He doubled up, coughing, his eyes burning.

James shook his head. He refused to believe it, any of it. Maybe it was a joke, maybe the Welsh were playing a game with the tourists, tell them a few stories, get them going. He tried to picture Lewyn and Dave huddled over their beer glasses, inventing further and further outrages: I know we'll tell 'em that Raoul killed, partially ate and then burned the children, no how about if Raoul is really the devil see and we're the only ones that know, no I've got it the devil comes out of the sea on to the cliffs at high tide and drags people down. Reckon they'll go for that?

Not a likely scenario, he thought, as he remembered Lewyn saying 'I'm just telling you what I saw,' his face creased with the seriousness of it. He didn't believe Lewyn was joking. So Lewyn must therefore be serious; thus Lewyn was either correct or incorrect. Raoul had either killed and incinerated the girls, then somehow fooled the police into believing it was an accident, or he hadn't. If he had, then what about the woman at the party; what about Edith, kept a prisoner in her room all that time? Had he killed them too? He'd have to have been some kind of psycho, a mass killer, planning and executing each death, covering his traces, planting false information with his neighbours, convincing the police. A fucking psycho.

Or Lewyn had simply got it wrong. Seen a perfectly innocent bonfire. Maybe Raoul was burning tyres, that would explain the stench and the smoke, then he'd buried the residue because it was unsightly, and he was after all an architect, deeply concerned with issues of aesthetics and visual beauty. And the piece of wool? Well, maybe he just wanted to burn some old clothes. And the bones? He could have found a dead sheep in the field and decided this was the best way to get rid of it. Surely that was more likely than – than all that other stuff.

had a stick thing

Lewyn had said sheep sometimes got attacked. By dogs.

What else could you do with them but burn them and bury the bones?

had a

James shut off the tap, briskly, then turned it on again and drank from it. He had a peculiar taste in his mouth.

This could be such a beautiful room, Adèle was thinking, as they had their coffee. Stone walls and thick, dark beams, and a stone ledge round three sides of it faced with wood where you could sit and gaze out of the windows. She would have to see if she could get the fire going properly – her first attempts had resulted in the smoke going anywhere except up the chimney. A wood fire on a cold winter afternoon, everything brushed and clean, Elvis growling as the logs crackled and spat, and the wind outside flinging the dead leaves around in gusts. If they could sort out some of the draughts she could even pull the couch up to the fire and bring down blankets and a pillow. She and James could drink whisky and make difficult uncomfortable love, in front of a log fire. That's what the house needs, Dilys had said, loving. She pictured the firelight on their naked flesh as James touched her, stroked her; the baby oil would be brilliantly cold for a second, then James would cover her, working against her.

She caught Lewyn's eye and blushed again. Well, he could join in too. She wondered what ideas Lewyn had about log fires and baby oil. She could watch him and James together, a heavy, thickly muscled body and a lighter, leaner one. Like that film with Oliver Reed and Alan Bates. Would James go along with it? She looked over at him speculatively; he was saying something to Lewyn about repointing, particularly that west face. Just you wait till I get you upstairs, she thought, and her stomach tightened, turned over.

145

Lewyn stood up to leave and James went to fetch his coat.

'I'll walk you halfway,' he said. 'I could do with a blow.'

Lewyn, after thanking Adèle and receiving her assurance that it was nothing, a pleasure to have him, stood awkwardly, looking at the painting. She started to collect the plates and bowls and he assisted; she had a strong impression that he wanted to say something to her but was unable to. It crossed her mind that she was perhaps wrong about him and that he wanted to let her know that he fancied her, maybe whisper that she should try to get away tomorrow, he'd be waiting in the barn. Would she turn him down? she wondered idly. Of course she would. But if he were to persist . . . Hm. There was certainly something about him, aside from the directness of his blue eyes and the undeniable attractiveness of his hard, strong physique.

She had to admit it, she was a pushover for silent, difficult men, men with a shadow. It had taken her years to discover that what she had thought to be hidden depths in James was merely something missing from him, not still water so much as a stagnant pond. The only times now that she felt again the original fascination for him was when they set sail on the tempestuous tides of torrid abandonment (as she liked to think of it). And that particular boat hadn't been pushed out for, let's call it ten days though it could well be more like three weeks. What with the upheaval of moving and the worries about Sam, not to mention the sheer bloody noise the charmingly antiquated bedsprings made and the way that one or other or both of them always seemed to manage to get the mood broken by an obliging draught up the – well, it just hadn't been happening much.

And apart from the troubling question of, if they weren't having sex then what exactly *were* they doing together, and the inevitable anxieties about their relationship (a word she always thought of in an American accent) and was it her fault, was it his fault, was she getting too old to arouse him, was he bored with her – apart from all that, she was becoming good and randy. She mentally stripped Lewyn and found a big, capable, potent man who'd been living alone (as far as she knew) all his life and who was probably ready for a bit. She smiled at the crassness of her thoughts, but there they were. Would she be able to navigate the boat with a different crew? Only one way to find out.

James returned with the coats; she realized that she'd been that close to flirting with Lewyn, in so far as flirting was on the menu with such a dank, dark cellar of a man. Well, a girl had to amuse herself *somehow*, and if the boat had sprung a leak— She smiled and shook the proffered hand.

'Lovely to see you, Lewyn. Thanks for all your help. Sleep well.'

'See you again, Mrs Tullian.'

'I'll just be a few minutes, Del.'

As soon as the cold black air hit him, Lewyn knew he was going to be sick. The feeling had been rolling round in him for the last half-hour, unidentified, just another strand in his internal background noise. But now he could feel his abdomen clenching, and he tried hard to relax the muscles, breathing slowly, not fighting it but willing it down. James walked beside him, not speaking. His head was full of tangled thoughts, he couldn't pull any single one out and speak it aloud. He'd hoped the night air might clear his head, but it seemed to be having the opposite effect, clouding further the murky water. They reached the point where the path to Lewyn's house joined the road, and stopped.

'Lewyn, look. What you were saying earlier on. About the fire.' James didn't know how this was going to come out: it was just the handiest loose end hanging off the ball of confusion in his mind.

'It could have been all sorts of things. Couldn't it? It needn't have been what you think it was. I mean it's all a bit hard to believe, wouldn't you say?'

Lewyn shrugged, grunted.

'I saw what I saw. Believe what you want.'

'I'm not questioning what you *saw*, but surely there must be other explanations.'

'Raoul Charpentier was not a good man. If I had to say what I truly believe, I'd say he was a bad man. An evil man. I don't know what he did or didn't do. I didn't see him actually do anything, that's why I didn't go to the police about it. I wish I had, I really do, if I could go back and have the chance again I would. Those parties, they weren't just people having fun; Dave didn't tell you, but he saw it same as me. People wearing masks and things on their heads, playing games. One time I saw them, Raoul was chasing them round with a stick, and they were falling about they were so drunk. On the cliff edge. In the dark. They'd go coupling in the fields. It's a miracle that more of them didn't go over. Maybe they did and no-one found out. Maybe that woman wasn't the only one. Edith said she saw him dancing with her just before she fell, she said he had a knife. Who knows what else she saw? Raoul said she was mad, well she certainly acted mad, she said the things mad people say. But what made her mad? Doesn't mean that everything she said was wrong. I think she was mad because she was shit-scared, if you'll pardon me. Of Raoul.

'And she told me, she *told* me, that Raoul wanted to kill her and the kiddies. Then the kiddies disappeared off to some fancy school somewhere, after he had a big fire

148

in the middle of summer and buried the ashes. No-one ever saw them again. Edith fell out of the window. Who knew what happened except Raoul, who was going round telling everyone she was so mad she had to be locked up like an animal? Harley Street doctor. Who ever saw him, 'cept Raoul? Then the house just burned down while he was out for a walk. Just burned clean away! Then off he goes back to France or wherever it was. Well you might find it hard to believe, but you never met him, you never met Edith. Those children. Dear God help us all. I'll go to my grave wishing I'd said something to someone, *helped* her when she asked me to. I could maybe have stopped him, I could have said *something* . . .'

Lewyn fell silent and felt the bile rising in his throat, hot and choking. James regarded him, amazed: he'd had no idea that Lewyn was capable of such passion, or of putting it into words. He didn't know what to say, and when Lewyn reached for his hand and shook it, and then maladroitly pulled him to him, he hugged him back, patting his shoulder. Lewyn held him for a moment with his eyes squeezed hard shut. Then he released him and walked across the road to his path.

'See you again James.'

'Goodnight Lewyn.'

Adèle had gone up to bed. Somehow the idea of washing dishes had become a dim, distant labour to be performed sometime in the future, tomorrow possibly or next week. She had to lie down. Her stomach was churning. What she had taken for lust was forming into a hard, tender lump in her groin. The prospect of scraping the remains of food off the plates was nauseating. Come to think of it, the whole idea of food was itself distinctly unpleasant. Any food. Steak pie or chicken chasseur or a big plate of greasy fried bread and beans and sausage. Stilton and liqueurs. *Stop this* she instructed herself as some sphincter low down clamped shut.

She felt hot and irritable; she kicked the blankets off, exposing her leg, which immediately froze. She rolled over on to her stomach and bitter, scalding fluids trickled into her mouth. She swallowed, swallowed again, but the taste wouldn't go away. Her stomach felt as if it was about to boil over, like a pan of rice, and she retched and coughed. She lay still for a moment, then sat up. The nausea receded: she sat gasping and swallowing, calculating the distance to the bathroom, and then a wave of burning, acidic vileness rose up irresistibly into her mouth, and she struggled out of bed, holding her hand to her mouth. The taste was rich, fermented, juicy.

She ran to the bathroom, and, with her head over the lavatory bowl, waited. Again it receded; then suddenly her whole interior reached up into her throat and gouged its way out, bolt after bolt, she saw lightning streaks as she retched and heaved, and the smell bloomed up around her, the sweet, tangy smell of vomit. She was aware of the sounds she was making, dimly, then her mouth was flooded again and she coughed and choked. There was a line hanging from her mouth, she reached for the toilet roll and wiped it away. She crouched on the floor, knowing it wasn't over, panting. It came again, hotter, harder, juicier, pumping out of her mouth in waves. She cried out in distress, and her teeth locked as the acids raged in her mouth; another bolt, but there wasn't much to come up now; another, the muscles of her abdomen clenching on nothing. She spluttered, her whole upper body in spasm. Dear God! It was almost funny! *Gaaaaaaa!*

She let her head rest against her hand, which was braced on the lavatory seat. She closed her eyes and a kind of bliss came upon her, the bliss of not feeling sick, of having her body free of the rotten, clawing nausea that had possessed it. She raised her head. Was there more? She felt giddy, exhilarated, elated. She laughed aloud. Dear God let me die now, for I am in Paradise! Her legs were extremely wobbly, her stomach felt bruised, trampled on, and her throat was etched with lines of trauma drawn in acid. But the cessation of nausea was transcendentally exquisite. She got herself back to her bed and lay down in a transport of physical well-being. Her head was singing. Was there more? Yes probably, but later, later, for now she would just lie here, for a week or two maybe. She remembered that she hadn't flushed the lavatory. Ah well, she would go and do it in a minute. In a day or two.

Lewyn had got as far as the barn when his body erupted, a violent, unbearable horror of sickness prostrating him. Oh no, he moaned, hugging himself, oh no.

James smelled it as soon as he shut the door behind him.
 'Adèle?'
He ran up the stairs, and her white, damp face smiled sweetly, sadly at him as he entered the room.
 'James, do you feel the teeniest bit unwell?' she asked, and he smelled the vomit on her breath and ran for the bathroom. They were both sick again, later in the night. As he staggered back to the bedroom James looked in on Sam: he was out for the count, dribbling innocently. James got into bed where Adèle was now sufficiently recovered to want a cigarette. She was even hungry again. James felt strong enough to go downstairs and get her a glass of milk and a piece of bread.
 Whatever it had been, he reflected, standing in the cold bright kitchen, it must have been something that Sam hadn't had. Coffee perhaps? But coffee didn't make you sick, not in his experience, and he'd rinsed the cups himself. Then he remembered: Sam hadn't had the chilli.

Wise child that he was, he'd stuck to veggyburger. He examined the pan, his nose wrinkling in distaste as he pushed the remains around with a fork. It all looked OK. What was in it anyway: tomato, onion, kidney beans, tomato purée. Chilli powder of course, and garlic. Del had made it a thousand times. And rice was just rice, surely? If the onions had been off Del would have spotted it, you knew the moment you cut into them.

He went to the bin and found the onion skin and the empty tins. It all looked and smelled like it was supposed to. He cut a piece of bread and debated whether to butter it. He decided not to. No good pushing your luck. He rinsed a glass, and his eye fell on the pudding dishes. There were blackberries in the top one. Sam hadn't eaten them. James felt saliva squirt into his mouth, and his jaw tightened. Blackberries. From the freezer. He put down the glass.

He opened the door to the basement and clicked on the light. The chest freezer, along with everything else in the basement and the basement itself, had been undamaged by the fire which had mostly been confined to the top floor of the house. It hadn't got down this far. Adèle had spent half a morning swilling it out, though it had looked clean enough. She'd made him open it the first time, admitting that she couldn't bear the thought of what might be inside. She'd screamed when he jerked back as he opened the lid, then kicked him on the thigh as he laughed. It wasn't just empty, it was clean. Gleaming white.

The light hummed as he approached the freezer. He touched the handle on the lid, then pulled his hand away. He stood looking at it. He didn't want to open it.

Why not.

He just didn't, that was all. He'd go back upstairs and Adèle would drink the milk and eat the bread, probably getting hiccups as she usually did with dry bread, and he'd lie down in the warm bed and sleep. That would be nice. He shifted his weight, looked away, looked back again.

Why not.

No reason, just that there might be dead children in it or live rats or a seething, crawling mass of plump white maggots or just something waiting in there, waiting for him to open the lid so it could slither out. Touch his face. Flop on to the floor and crawl round his feet, slimy, hissing.

He touched the handle again. He looked away, opened up the lid. He peered in.

Plastic bags of frozen vegetables, peas, green beans. Some sealed Tupperware containers. Pastry. He reached down and rummaged beneath them, and his eye caught something that was instantly familiar, but unplaceable.

Something blue.

He pushed aside a large bag of oven chips. A blue patch. On something dirty white. Furry. He stood, not moving, not breathing, and his ears began to sing. It was part of the hindquarters of a sheep. The blue patch was the dye the farmers used to mark them. It sat awkwardly on the bottom of the freezer, a large irregular piece of flesh, not cut, not sliced. Torn. He blinked. He slammed the lid down again, stood back, his heart pounding. He rubbed his hands against his trousers; then he turned his back on the freezer and went up the stairs, turning off the light. He shut the basement door and walked to the sink, poured washing-up liquid on to his hands and washed them, once, twice.

And then he thought: it's not working. It's not even cold. And by the look of the – meat? – in there, it hadn't been working for days, weeks even.

He filled the glass, took the plate of bread, went up to

the bedroom. He lay quietly while Adèle ate and drank. Then he turned off the light and rolled over, away from her. His last thought before he slept was: the woman beside me must be insane.

8

The Smile of Death

Adèle woke to find James gone, the sheets cold beside her. She yawned and stretched and her abdominal muscles complained: it took her a few seconds to remember why. But she felt marvellous, ready for anything. Purged, renewed.

She found James in the cellar, with a bucket of water and a sponge. He had the freezer on its side, so that the open lid was flush with the tiled floor; he was kneeling on the lid, his bum sticking out as he leaned in. She contemplated giving him a good hard kick but thought better of it, and boiled water for tea.

The table had been put back in the kitchen from the front room, all the dishes had been done and there was a general air of clean wet surfaces and good order. She was impressed. She sat at the table and had a cigarette. She used an ashtray this time.

James came up from the basement and poured the contents of the bucket down the sink, then filled it up again. She noticed that he was using bleach in the water. Funny kind of time for spring cleaning, she thought, but then who was complaining? If it was left to her spring would never come. He went back down.

'Hello Adèle, my you're looking lovelier than ever this morning. I hope you slept well and woke refreshed? Why yes, thank you James, and may I add that it's a joy and delight to renew our acquaintance after hours of cruel separation,' she said as he departed, though perhaps not loudly enough for him to hear. When James started cleaning, she knew, he took a pretty dim view of anyone who was just sitting around enjoying themselves, and was even less receptive than usual to any kind of pleasantry or badinage. She dropped the tea bags into mugs. James was inclined to the view that tea should come out of a pot, whereas she was not. In the early days, this kind of difference of outlook had worried her terribly – and there had been so many of them: in her years at college she had had thousands of conversations about such things as class, gender and race. She'd been able on a good day to get herself worked up into a frenzy of guilt about her privileged background. She'd dropped countless numbers of her habits, many of them around the preparation, serving and consuming of food and drink. By the time she met James she was able to flick ash on the floor, drink from mugs that weren't clean, use a fork without a knife, even eat without a plate, straight off the table, if the food came pre-wrapped.

And James had been horrified. For him, it was something akin to an insult not to use what he called a coaster under a cup, he flinched when she put a milk bottle on to the table (he favoured a jug) and he was profoundly disturbed by her newly, joyfully acquired habit of filling the kettle down the spout rather than taking off the lid. James' food-related behaviour was tighter, more rigid, more formal than hers had ever been. And he was the genuine article, a working-class man.

Adèle had had a short period of confusion, which had culminated in her coming to a standstill in front of a shop, gazing at a set of cork table mats decorated with thatched cottages and rosebuds. And she'd never looked back. She'd rather lose James than use table mats. That was what it came down to. His weapon was something she called the smile of death, a face he would use when a profound outrage was perpetrated on him, such as a knife being used for both margarine and jam. Adèle, the smile would say, you are beyond belief. Lurking behind the smile she sometimes thought she saw his mother, but she didn't want to speculate too much about that. He never spoke about his parents. She had never met them, at his insistence. It wasn't always clear to her who he was ashamed of.

She took James's tea to him; he looked up over his shoulder, then returned to his work.

'How're you feeling, Jamie?' she asked, determined to get *something* out of him, even if he was sulking. He grunted, and she cursed him: bastard!

'Jamie? Is there something wrong?' She knew how he hated talking about what went on between them, but she also knew she could make him do it if she persevered. Usually she didn't.

'Jamie?'

He backed out of the freezer and stood up, facing her. The daylight from the kitchen cast him into strong silhouette – she couldn't see his face.

'Well what do you think?'

This was a predictable response, his first line of defence.

'I don't know, maybe you'd better tell me.'

He stood before her, furious, she could tell by the set of his head, the way his hands rubbed against his trousers, like a fast bowler getting ready to throw.

'How long has it been like this?'

'James. Please. How long has what been like what exactly?' She was aware of the snotty-bitch tone that had crept into her voice, her outraged-consumer voice. She couldn't help it.

'Del, this freezer hasn't been working, for weeks by the

look of what was in it. I've had a look at the plug. The fuse has gone. You've been using it just about every day. You apparently didn't notice.'

it just flitted away, flitter flutter

She frowned. What was he saying?

'I emptied everything out. Everything.'

He waited for her to respond, but she was frowning, looking distracted.

'Del?'

'Flitter flutter, bread and butter.'

'What?'

'What?' She couldn't concentrate. She was suddenly unsure of the identity of the person facing her. She couldn't make out his features.

'I put everything into a bin bag. Here. Would you like to have a look?'

Why would she want to look at what was in the black plastic bin bag? She had a flicker of memory, dark branches waving in a strong wind, running fast, alongside a wall . . .

'You had something in there that shouldn't have been. Didn't you.'

What did he mean? Ruthie was dead, buried, burned rather, it couldn't be her.

He picked up the bin bag, heavy, swollen like a pregnant animal.

'Here!' He put his hand in, rummaged about.

Don't touch it! James!

He pulled something out.

'No!'

'How did this get here, Del?'

'I don't know!'

'I think you do.'

'No.' She dropped the mug of tea, heard it shatter and splash, steaming liquid and fragments of pottery skittering

158

over the tiles. He shook his head and smiled at her, that dreadful, condemning smile . . .

'Flitter flutter, bread and butter, bite your tongue and make you stutter!' she yelled at him.

'What are you *talking* about!'

'I don't know!'

He approached her, the hunk of rotting meat in his hand.

'Please. Put it down. Don't touch it.'

He glanced down at the ragged, stinking lump in his hand and dropped it on the floor. It landed with a heavy wet smack. It was leaking.

'Adèle? It's all right. I'm not going to hurt you.' He came closer, cautiously, and she backed away until her foot touched the bottom of the stairs. She turned and ran.

James stood, shocked by the scene. He hadn't meant to frighten her. He'd woken up early and the image of the freezer had smacked him in the face. He was genuinely unsure if what he remembered had actually happened. He'd felt the warmth of Adèle's body beside him, and couldn't in any way reconcile it with the repulsive, sloppy, stinking mess at the bottom of the freezer, the freezer that their food had been coming out of, for weeks. He'd padded downstairs, the sun shining strongly through the landing window, and had gone to look. Yes. It was still there. A kind of rage had come over him, rage at the goddamned bloody inexcusable *messiness* of this bloody woman; and then he'd been brandishing the stump of meat and fur at her, and she'd run, terrified. Of him.

I should go after her, he thought. The floor was slippery, tea and animal tissue strewn about. He stepped carefully through it and ascended the stairs; then he thought no, I'll leave her for a bit. She's in no fit state to talk. He went to find Sam, who was writing in his room, and called Elvis.

The three of them walked up to Lewyn's house. Elvis snuffled along, aware that he was off the leash and therefore on trust.

'You and Mum were sick, weren't you?' Sam asked.

'Yup.'

'I wasn't though and Elvis wasn't.'

'No. That's right.'

'So why were you and Mum? Did you eat something dirty?' Sam knew that if you picked dirty things up off the floor and ate them you'd be sick. Elvis was allowed to do it because he had a constitution of cast iron, and it just went straight through him. But people were different.

'Did you eat something off the floor?' Sam persisted, ever keen to pinpoint a misdemeanour.

'No. There was something wrong with the food.'

'Oh.' Sam sounded disappointed.

'Sam? You haven't been . . .' What exactly. Dismembering sheep? Taking fuses out of plugs? Hoarding decaying parts of animals?

'Sam.' He tried again. 'You haven't been playing in the basement, have you?' He wasn't supposed to go down there, because he might hurt himself and not be able to get out and they might never, ever, find him.

'No.'

'Seriously now. Have you?'

'No.'

'OK.' One thing about Sam, James thought, he gave you a straight answer to a straight question.

They reached Lewyn's house. Elvis went directly for the barn, snuffling and scratching at the door. Lewyn's door was open and James called in.

'Lewyn? Are you decent?'

Lewyn appeared at the doorway from the gloom of the interior. He looked terrible.

'Are you all right? Del and me had a spot of stomach

trouble last night, and I was wondering if – you'd had – anything . . .' He trailed off. He really didn't need to ask.

'Aye, I wasn't feeling too clever. Something we ate, I dare say?'

'Yeah. I think so. The freezer's on the blink.'

'Oh yes.'

Lewyn watched Elvis snuffling round the door of the barn, where he'd stood, then squatted, finally lain down, wishing to die, moaning, crying, abject.

'I'm really sorry.'

'So what was it?'

James heard hardness, anger in Lewyn's voice.

'The blackberries.'

'Blackberries. Really. I thought it had been that, what do you call it? Spicy stuff.'

'Chilli. No, we think it was those bloody berries!' He tried to make it sound like an innocent misadventure, just one of those things.

'Anyway, we're both really sorry.'

'Mrs Tullian all right is she?'

'Del? Oh yes, yes she's fine now.'

'Are you sure?'

James met his eye and couldn't pretend to misunderstand the question.

'She's still a bit upset.'

'Aye. 'Spect so.' Lewyn looked away and back again. 'Well must get on.'

'Yes. Sorry Lewyn. I hope it won't put you off coming over.'

'Aye well . . .' Lewyn winked and nodded at Sam. 'You all right, piglet?'

'Yes, cos I didn't eat any of the blackberries. Neither did Elvis. So he's all right. Elvis was only sick once, when he was a puppy. He ate a dead bird, and it had worms in it.'

'Sam.'

'*Living* in it!'

'Sam. That'll do.'

Sam looked annoyed, but left it at that. He'd wanted to tell Lewyn about how the worms ate the bird, so the bird didn't really die it just turned into worms and then they turned into flies, so his dad said, and then birds ate the flies, and then . . .

'OK Lewyn. Come over any time. We won't make you eat anything. Promise.'

Lewyn looked away, smiled.

'OK.' He watched them as they left.

'Tell Mrs Tullian I hope she's feeling better soon,' he called after them.

9

Being Silly

Adèle squinted at the painting. There was something in the background, behind a leafless tree. At first she'd taken it for part of the tree, but the closer she looked the more she became convinced that it was a human figure.

It was a big, wide landscape, intended as one of the centrepieces of the exhibition, great rolling fields and a hard whitish-blue sky. Sheep were roaming about all over it, small white blobs on the hills, and a group of them close up in the front, gawping directly out of the canvas with their knowing, beady black eyes. She'd differentiated them as far as she could, varying their positions and angles, but their expressions troubled her – no matter what she intended they came out the same, neither blank nor animated but some curious thing in between, alert, avid, watchful, but oddly disinterested, as if whatever happened wouldn't matter much to them one way or another.

But yes, they looked frightened. Their ears were up, their noses sampling the air for danger. One of them had a foreleg lifted off the ground, as if it were about to stamp. She'd spread the close-ups along the whole length of the painting, and their eyes were focused on the viewer from a wide semi-circle. All except one, towards the back of the foregound group, which was looking away from the viewer, towards the tree at the end of the field. It was this

163

one which had attracted Adèle's attention to the tree.

She stood back and looked again. Definitely. Someone was hiding behind that tree, she could see the top of a head and part of an upper body. What was he doing there?

Adèle had never painted human figures. She didn't know why, but she was deeply reluctant to bring people on to the canvas, it would make her responsible for them somehow. And in any case, what business would anyone have in one of her inimical, desolate landscapes? She remembered seeing the films of the Apollo landings, those comic balloon-men swimming about on that terrible, dead infinity of dust and rock. It had chilled her to the marrow. People weren't supposed to be there, and she felt much the same about her landscapes. They just couldn't support human life. They could only barely sustain sheep, she thought. And yet here, beyond any doubt, was someone. The first man, lurking behind a tree. There was a painting she'd seen on a trip to the V and A, of Adam hiding from the wrath of God in the Garden of Eden. Was that what she was thinking of? But the artist in that painting had portrayed Adam as a pathetic, cowed, cringing creature. Her man was hiding, but not from fear. He was up to something.

She lit a cigarette. She was more or less chain-smoking as she painted now, as much to keep the smell at bay as anything. She looked over at her new still-life group: syringe and meat. The meat was beyond gamey, beyond high, it had gone over into that other world of decay and decomposition. It was rotten. She prodded it with a brush and something slithered away, out of sight. The smell, she conceded, was not good. She had taken to locking her studio when she left it: otherwise, she was sure James would have been in there with his bloody bin bags and bleach. All that silly fuss about a bit of rotten meat. How was she to know the freezer was out of action? What was she, a fucking mechanic? He was supposed to be Harry the Handyman.

But of course she had known really, though she'd swear on a stack of Bibles that she hadn't taken the fuse out. Had she? She thought of the screwdriver in the previous still-life, and for a moment was assailed by one of those baffling flashes of something like memory: the click of the light and the chill of the basement air on her bare legs. The fuse like a lost earring in the palm of her hand . . .

But she would *swear*, she'd swear on Sam's life, she'd never seen that torn hunk of sheep before. Oh no, definitely *not* (but where had her still-life model come from, she wondered; and found that she didn't quite know, it was just there, wasn't it, like the screwdriver and the syringe.

climbing down the cliff steps, the handrail a particularly intense shade of pink in the black air, clambering about on the freezing slippery dark rocks, and there it was, no needle, but the barrel and plunger intact, Medispose)

She wheeled around but there was no-one. The door was safely locked. She dropped the cigarette on to the floor and ground it out with her foot. She picked up her brush.

James's gravel had arrived, twenty bags of it and twelve sixteen-foot lengths of pipe, four-inch polypipe, yellow flexible stuff, and the collars. Unloading it from the truck had taken the better part of the morning, principally because the driver, a polite, nondescript man with sandy hair, had been in no particular hurry. James was beginning to get used to this way the west Welsh had, as if the rolling, convoluted roads had got into their heads, making the shortest distance a long trip. There really was nothing for it but to stand and talk to them.

James, never much of a conversationalist at the best of times, found himself mostly confined to nodding and smiling as the driver's rapid, rather staccato voice rattled on, quick-fire bursts of heavily inflected speech, slightly nasal, with a singsong quality to it which James found distracting.

'Had to come over the top, cos Fishguard's out, widening him for all the lorries, hell of a job by the look of him. Been out for months, still that's the way it is I suppose.'

'Yup.'

'Then they're going to put in a new bridge, did you hear that? Cut right through Lower Town, and the Sailor's Return coming down to make way for him, though the necessity of him I can't see, I'd have to say, lovely old pub that, been in have you?'

'No. No . . .'

'Oh yes, lovely old pub. Keep banging your head on things, but it seems a pity to knock him down so they can build a bypass. Still the amount of heavy traffic through Lower Town, you wouldn't believe, and there's some tight corners, dangerous he is really I suppose. Nothing like a bit of progress eh? No end to it sometimes. Why they can't leave things alone a bit escapes me, but then I s'pose you can't have things all the same for ever, not with things the way they are, can you? Bloody vandalism though, when it comes to knocking things down just cos they're in the way. I was saying they should take him up higher, cut through by the old Brynhelwyn road, and bring him out by Dinas Cross, save them building a bridge and they wouldn't have to touch Lower Town at all. Don't you think?'

'Er . . .'

'Made a film in Lower Town, did you hear that? Aye, they made that *Under Milk Wood* there, never saw him myself but he was supposed to be very good. Not much for cinemas me, though I'd be curious to see that one, just to see it all on film; they had that Richard Burton in the Sailor's evidently, when they were all here for the filming, Neil's got a picture of him up, signed his name and everything . . .'

James was exhausted by the time the lorry negotiated its way out of the gate and round the dog-leg corner. But the driver's calm, self-assured voice had soothed him, driven from his mind the picture he'd been carrying of Adèle shrinking back from him as he came towards her with a piece of rotting meat in his hands. He didn't like that picture, not at all.

He went inside; he stood outside Adèle's studio, listening to her quiet noises.

'Del? Do you want something to eat?'

'No, James! I'll get something later.' Then, almost as an afterthought; 'Thank you.'

'You all right in there, Del?'

'I'm fine James, really. I'll talk to you later.'

'OK.'

Sam was sitting at the kitchen table. He was playing with a farmyard set they'd found in the basement: cows and sheep and pigs made of garishly painted, brittle 1970s plastic, and a farmyard like a model of a film set, house, barn, milking parlour, a pig shed. A ruddy-faced farmer with side whiskers, waistcoat, floppy hat and stick, and a dog.

'Hi chief. Want some beans on toast?'

'Yes please.' Sam didn't look up, he was busy. James looked over his shoulder: Sam was balancing one cow on top of another, the one behind with its rear legs on the floor. James saw that there were other pairs of animals dotted round the farmyard in similar positions. He deliberated briefly whether to say anything, decided not to. But sometime soon he'd have to have one of those chats with Sam, and he couldn't think of anything he was less anxious to do. Most seven-year-olds would have friends to misinform and alarm them about such delicate matters; Sam was, by necessity now, but also by inclination, a solitary child. He would have to grope his own way towards an understanding of the joys of sex, at least until James could no longer decently avoid the subject. He trod on a pig, and returned it to the table.

'No, that one's finished,' Sam said, and dropped it back on the floor.

'Whatever you say chief. You's da boss man,' said James in his *Beverly Hills Cop* voice, and Sam giggled.

'I thought you were supposed to be doing your maths anyway, fatboy? Isn't that what we agreed?'

'I did it already.'

'I've *done* it already. Is that perhaps what you mean? Let me see.' Sam showed him his maths problem book and a piece of paper. James glanced over the answers: all correct.

'Top of the class. Again,' he said and Sam giggled again.

'But there's only me in it!'

'That's right. You're top *and* bottom. How does it feel to be so talented?'

'And I didn't look at the back, in case that's what you're thinking.'

'The thought never crossed my mind. I trust you totally.'

'Can I have HP sauce in the beans?'

'No. Absolutely not. Unthinkable.'

'Please. Please can I?'

'Hm. What's fifteen thousand four hundred and fifty-eight divided by ninety-three?'

'That's not fair!'

'Come on. Ten seconds.' He opened the tin.

'*Dad.*'

'Eight, seven . . .'

'*You* don't even know that one.'

'Oh no?'

'Do you?'

'Five-four-three-two-one,' he said and put the bread under the grill.

'That was too fast!'

'Life's like that, ratface. Take it or leave it.'

'*Dad!*'

After dinner (the word 'lunch' was like the word 'cunt' for James: he would neither say it nor think it and disapproved strongly of those who did) Sam helped him with the gravel. The problem was making sure that the pipe was laid at a gradient, and a reasonably even gradient at that, so it would drain properly. Sam watched, puzzled and impatient, as James again tapped in posts at either end of the trench, higher ones this time, and stretched a string between them, loosely knotted at the far end. Sam wanted a blow-by-blow explanation, but all he got was:

'Wait. Watch. Attend.'

Sam was left down by the septic tank end and instructed to raise or lower the string as directed. James got the spirit level, the stick with three bubbles in it, vertical, horizontal and forty-five degrees. Slanty, as he'd explained to Sam. (Why anyone would want a stick with a slanty bubble in it was beyond Sam, but he'd patiently forborne from mentioning its obvious uselessness.) James held the level against the stretched string and called out 'Higher. Lower,' until Sam got it to exactly the right place, then James knotted it tight. He started lugging the dead-weight bags of gravel around and Sam helped him, grunting and panting. He slit them open and poured them out into the trench, along half the length.

Sam fidgeted and hopped about while James delayed things further by selecting two long battens and joining them together with a prop. He took, to Sam's way of thinking, quite unnecessary pains to ensure that the join was also completely level. Shouldn't they just get on and start messing about with the gravel?

And then it started to rain. James sent Sam inside, though he intended to carry on, rain or no bloody rain. Sam returned to his animals, disgruntled. He *knew* they should have got straight to the gravel. When he'd finished the animals he went upstairs to his book.

It rained steadily all afternoon, thick, dripping rain. Adèle came down at four o'clock and started making dinner (tea, for James). She was pleased with the painting – sometimes she surprised even herself. James had said he'd cook that evening, but she found that she wanted to do it. After last night's fiasco, she felt she had her reputation at stake. She decided to go for safety: baked potatoes and salad and cheese.

She sang 'Didn't we almost have it all?' as she cut up the tomatoes and cucumber she'd paid an arm and a leg for in Fishguard. It was her kind of music, a big, emotion-saturated ballad, and she sang *loud*, really giving it some.

James hated her singing, but then he would, wouldn't he? He hated anyone expressing themselves. He found it embarrassing.

While she was singing, she was suddenly struck by the strength of her voice and stopped in mid-line. God, she sounded like some wounded animal! James came running in, soaked.

'Del? What's the matter?'

'Oh I was just *singing* for *Christ's bloody sake*,' she yelled at him, and flung the knife into the sink.

'Singing?'

'Yes, bloody singing. You know? Like this,' and she sang at him, 'Didn't we almost have it all?' as hard and loud and high as she could; her voice cracked at the end of the line, and she listened, dismayed. James watched her, completely at a loss. He muttered something, she thought it was 'need your head looking at', but she couldn't be sure, and went back into the rain.

She poured dressing into the salad bowl and tasted it. Hm. Something missing. She held her head on one side, pondering, then went out of the side door into the garden.

'Del. What's this.'

James' voice was controlled, but only just. He had had about enough.

'I would have thought a man of even your modest capabilities . . .' she began in her hoity-toity voice, and jerked back as he picked up his plate and banged it down again. Sam watched, all eyes.

'Del don't – don't start talking like that.'

'James James James, my darling boy, it's *baked* potato and *grated* cheese and *green* salad, with *garlic* dressing. What did you think it was?' She thought she detected the traces of the smile of death lurking: and what a mean little mouth you've got, she thought. Why didn't I ever notice that before?

'OK. So what's in the salad? Exactly.'

'Well, let's see. Tomato, cucumber, green pepper, lettuce, apple, grated carrot. Parsley.'

'So what's this?' He picked out a strand of something with the end of his knife, where it dangled wetly.

'Oh.'

'Yes. Oh.'

'James please, don't start shouting . . .'

'What is it? You tell me.'

'I don't know!'

171

'Well you put it there didn't you?'

'No!'

'No?'

'I don't know! James, please . . .'

'What is it, Del?'

She stood up, banging her knee against the table.

'It's grass, isn't it?'

'Really, this is too ridiculous.'

'You put grass in it didn't you?'

'Of course I didn't, people don't eat grass!'

'No. Sheep eat grass.'

The logic was unassailable. She walked away, determined to escape his vulgar, hectoring voice. Sam sat, keeping very still. James put the knife down, stood up, put on his coat, went out into the dark, wet night.

He had to think. Adèle seemed to be having some kind of breakdown. Ever since that night in the secure room she'd been strange; maybe even before that? He tried to think back, but could remember nothing out of the ordinary.

Christ, as if he didn't have enough to worry about! Here he was, right in the middle of a long, difficult job, maybe his last chance to keep his business afloat. Sebastian was dangling carrots in front of him, but he had to get this job out of the way first. He'd pulled Sam out of school, cancelled contracts; there was a nice young couple renting the flat in London, with a six-month shorthold tenancy agreement in their kitchen drawer, so there was no house to go back to. Christ! She certainly chose her moments.

When Ruthie was born, Adèle had gone into a deep depression. Nothing unusual about that, the doctor had said, women often suffered terribly with their hormones after childbirth. But that had been another choice moment: he struggling to establish himself in the grip of the first Tory recession, in an unfamiliar part of north

172

London. He would come back to a flat, the curtains still drawn, the post uncollected, the heating on in the middle of bloody *July*, Adèle lying on the couch, undressed, smoking, and Ruthie crawling about in soiled nappies, running wild. I'm a bit tired, she'd say, what time is it? Why are you back? Because it's the evening now, Adèle. Is it?

He'd never got angry. He'd clamped his teeth and seen to things. She couldn't help it and he'd never held it against her (though he'd never exactly forgiven or forgotten it either).

And over the years there'd been a few—

Well. Once.

She'd taken it into her head that the man in the flat downstairs was trying to get at her. She'd claimed that he kept her awake, playing the piano: James had stayed up all one night listening. There, did you hear it? Hear what? Oh, he's stopped now. She claimed she'd seen him sitting in the ground-floor window with a Ouija board. She said she'd found a mark chalked on the front step, a star in a circle. She'd gone out and scrubbed it off. He'd wake up in the night and Adèle would be taking off her shoes, getting back into bed. Del? Where've you been? She'd mutter something, but he was sure she was still asleep.

Then he'd been woken up one night by a commotion from below, shouting and thumping. He'd run down and there she was, wrestling with the disbelieving Mr Raphael. She'd got him up and accused him of trying to drive her mad. His English wasn't quite perfect in any case, but he'd certainly been unable to make any sense of her shouting. James had grabbed at her, and she'd allowed herself to be taken back to bed.

She wouldn't go to the doctor. It had passed, and he put it down to strain and 'women's troubles' (his mother's coy phrase). Then Sam had come along and she'd been so happy, so delighted and relaxed; she could be such a lovely woman, he reminded himself sternly. Her eccentricities were just part of it, he'd thought, part of her intense, playful engagement with the world.

Of course, that had all ended with Ruthie in the sparkling Cornwall water. Her work had become successful by then, and she'd painted her way through that unendurable, deadening period – painted herself out of a corner, he thought.

But this new business was different. He was fairly certain she was sleepwalking again. She'd complained that she could hear the sheep at night, trampling about and bleating. He'd noticed mud on her feet one morning; she couldn't explain it.

Well it happens. Could have been a dog

Since she'd started locking her studio he hadn't seen any of the new paintings, but the ones he'd seen so far were troubling him in ways he didn't like to think about too closely. And now the *food* . . .

He stood on the cliff top, the rain drumming around him and on him, and finally allowed himself to formulate the question that had been working away at him since that night in the secure room:

Is she dangerous?

He felt a great surge of relief wash over him as the words hung in his mind. All the confusion and worry and guilt were pushed aside leaving just this one, eminently practical, consideration. Never mind how she'd got to be this way, never mind if he was contributing to her distress, or if there were things he should be doing to alleviate it. What was essential was to consider whether or not she constituted a menace, to him, to Sam or to herself, and if so what actions he should take to make her safe.

Clearly she could not be allowed to prepare any more food. Whether or not grass was harmful to eat (had she washed it first, he wondered, and was presented with the perplexing image of her with a colander full of grass at the sink) it certainly wasn't *right*. Nor was it right to take food from a freezer that had stopped freezing and that had a piece of sheep carcass in it. He remembered the peculiar taste he'd had in his mouth after eating the blackberries and ice-cream, and his body shuddered again at the thought of the food in his mouth being in intimate, juicy contact with that damp, furry *thing* . . . For a moment the nausea returned, then receded again, but his mouth was sour and acidic. She must have blanked the thing out of her mind, in some way not really seen it. Or maybe she'd somehow got used to the idea that it was in there, decaying quietly; accepted it. Liked it? His jaw was clamped shut and he relaxed the muscles, swallowing repeatedly.

Was she dangerous? He knew, with all the certainty there was in the world, that she would never knowingly hurt him, or Sam. It was simply not conceivable that she would do that. She might be neglectful, erratic, sloppy; she might even be slipping over the increasingly thin ice of sanity towards a point where she would abruptly drop into the frigid, murky water of madness. But he was unable to think that she might hurt them, whatever happened. She would sooner hurt herself, he was sure.

So was that a possibility? He knew that a depressed woman was perfectly capable of self-harm: he'd heard of women who felt compelled to cut themselves with razor blades or burn their hands and arms with cigarette ends, in a desperate attempt to find peace and release from their inner torments. He thought of hiding his Bic disposables, and then developed this into hiding cutlery, taking her matches away, disconnecting the cooker, decommissioning the iron, checking her drawers for nail files or paper clips or . . . It was ridiculous. It would be simpler

175

just to lock her up (like Edith Charpentier.) No-one could live that way. He ran an imaginary eye over her body, checking for scars or bruises, and found none. He would have noticed. Of course she could always swallow bleach or hang herself from a beam or drop her hairdryer into the bath. There were dozens of ways a resourceful person could (he forced the words into focus) *kill themselves*. (She could, for instance, jump out of a window. Like Edith.)

But she would never do that either. She would know how much it would damage Sam and him if she did; and it would in any case be undignified and ugly. No, he was sure that wasn't a real possibility.

He watched the Rosslare night ferry pulling out of Goodwick harbour, lit up like a floating Christmas tree. How lovely to be on that ferry, in the brightly lit saloon with a plastic glass of lager in front of you, just to sail away and in a few hours' time you could be in a smoky Irish pub, one more solitary drinker brooding into your glass, striking up some kind of meaningless, impassioned conversation with somebody as drunk as yourself. You could probably find work in Dublin, find a room to rent. Would it be raining there?

He sighed. His place was here, with Sam and Adèle, he was connected to them in a million ways, more ties than he could ever cut. He loved them. Adèle needed him terribly right now, she would certainly go mad if he were to leave, he knew that. But it wasn't a matter of obligation or guilt or duty: it was love, it was his life, his identity. What would *he* become without them? He pictured a James Tullian coming home to an empty room, beer cans and fast-food trays and dirty clothes, and the phone number of a woman met in a pub; no, that was someone else's life, someone with no Adèle and no Sam, and James pitied him from the bottom of his heart.

He was soaked (again!) by the time the ferry

disappeared into the loneliness of its passengers' futures, and he turned round and went back to the house. It was a beautiful house, or it would be when he'd finished with it.

Adèle was reading in bed. It was a book about a teenage drug addict in America, her diary, and the girl's experiences had brought tears to her eyes. The girl was good, desperately wanted to be good, but felt separated from her family, was dreadfully alone and frightened. She'd started smoking cannabis, but was tricked into taking heroin by a girl in her class and liked it, and had quickly found that she couldn't stop. She'd ended up in a town she didn't know the name of, giving someone a blow-job in return for heroin. Adèle closed the book and howled, the bed shaking and creaking with the force of her anguish. She gave herself up to the storm and was rocked and buffeted by it, shaken, thrown all over the bed. She was beyond worrying about Sam's possible reactions to the noise she was making, as the storm crashed and shrieked around and in and through her.

Some period of time later, minutes or hours, she came to and sat up. Whatever had been happening to her in the last few weeks, whatever it was that had been taking hold of her, had drawn back a little, and left her enough of herself to see it. How close had she been to losing herself completely?

(*dark branches waving, and she was running along a low wall*)

She was unable to make any sense of her behaviour. It was as if someone else were doing it and she was remembering their actions. She felt confusion mounting again and thumped the mattress with both fists:

'No!'

She was strong, she was determined. It had to stop, all

177

of it. She would go into her studio tomorrow and clear it out, all those sinister pictures, those gruesome still lives, that *meat*! How could she have stood it for so long? If only she could vomit it all out, like the tainted black-berries, throw it all up and flush it away and be done with it (but it would still be there in the septic tank, until that got emptied and then it would be dumped out at sea somewhere, floating around in the unspeakable, mon-strous black sea, the sea that had come in and claimed Ruthie's life).

(*down by the septic tank where they bury the midgets*)

'No!'

She would go in tomorrow and take the pictures and the meat downstairs and burn them, bugger the wasted canvases; and she'd start again, paint things that were wholesome and good and beautiful. Wasn't art supposed to be beautiful?

She heard James come in and listened to his footsteps on the stairs. She scrubbed at her face with a corner of the sheet. He knocked on the door (his own bedroom door!) and she croaked 'Come in,' then cleared her throat and said loudly, clearly, sanely:

'Come in, Jamie!'

He came over to her, literally dripping, and she hugged him, pulling at his wet hair and kissing his neck and throat.

Sam waited for the sounds from next door to subside. First Mum had been being silly, shouting and crying and carrying on, then Dad had come up and those other noises had started. Sam knew the sequence well, low voices and a long period of silence, then the bed creaking rhyth-mically (Sam tapped along with it), more silence, more creaking, then sounds like they were playing farmyards, grunting and moaning, finally his dad saying 'Easy, easy,' a burst of creaking, and that was that. His mum scratching

178

a match for her cigarette, low voices and laughing. They would be asleep soon. Sam fingered the key under his pillow. He had nearly read it all now.

'Easy, easy . . .'

James levered himself up off her, holding his weight on his elbows, and she pulled his nipples and chest hair, running her hands down to his belly where she kneaded and grabbed at him; he sat up and lifted her hips and she gripped the muscles of his arms as he thrust faster, deeper. She reached for his hand and put it to her mouth, gnawing at his fist, and he covered her again, gasping and muttering in her ear. She pushed her fists up into his armpits and he jerked and splashed and ran into and over her, his mouth locked on her neck.

'So. Did you come yet?' she asked him after a few breathless moments, and they laughed. She reached for her cigarettes and he rested wetly, heavily on her while she stroked his back. By the time she'd finished the cigarette he'd be ready to bring her off (his term; she preferred 'pleasure her'). If he managed to stay awake that long.

Lewyn sat, staring out of his bedroom window. He could see nothing but the traces of the rain on the glass and his own reflection. The dream was fading, all except one scene where he and James were shaking hands in the barn. Lewyn had given him a sheep as payment; James had it slung over his shoulder. It's OK, he'd said, you'll never see it again, I promise. I'll take care of it. And then he'd *smiled* . . .

It was the smile that Lewyn woke up with, his hand working at his achingly hard cock. He was glad the dream had finished before anything further had happened with the handsome, smiling James. And he was sorry. He didn't want to think about it, but that wasn't true either because he wanted to think about nothing else, just at the moment.

He looked over at his bed, and was filled with revulsion and something like horror. He turned back to the window.

10

4.38 a.m.

James fumbled into his wet, obstructive clothes, fighting
with the laces of his trainers. He couldn't find his watch
and the bedside clock had stopped at 4.38, a completely
impossible time for anyone to be outside shouting. The
clock flipped on to 4.39. He felt as if he was in someone's
dream. Where was Adèle? He thought he heard a door
closing quietly, but it was only a tiny clicking sound, and
all hell seemed to have broken loose outside.

He ran down the stairs and out into the boggy field.
The noise was coming from the next field along, two
voices, oh Christ he knew one of them, it was a voice he'd
lived in dread of for many years, ever since the incident
with Mr Raphael in the north London flat. A high,
cracked voice, screaming, arguing, pleading. Adèle.

He found them at the cliff edge. The ground was
sodden, and there was freshly turned earth scattered
around. Adèle was in her dressing gown, barefoot; she
was being held by Lewyn Bulmer. James thought: he's
trying to rape her, the slimy *bastard*, and then realized
that Lewyn was restraining her, as she yelled and
struggled, attempting to attack him.

'James!' Lewyn shouted, and stumbled as Adèle
hooked a foot behind him and pulled his leg away. In the
marshy grass it was difficult for him to get a proper
footing. James watched, astonished, almost amused, as

they wrestled. She could be bloody strong, he knew. He came forward and his foot struck something. It was warm.

The sheep had been ripped open – his foot had connected with part of the entrails. He regarded it: he could feel the warmth of its fluids and tissues rising up to him through the damp, clean air. He saw the exquisitely detailed formations of its blood supply and organs. Heart and lungs he could identify, the rest of it he wasn't sure about. He wasn't quite certain it had the correct number of limbs, and he knelt down to check it properly.

'James! For God's sake man!' Lewyn's voice pulled him away from the ruined animal, and he found one of Adèle's flailing arms and pulled it behind her back, as she screamed and threatened.

'You bastards! You'll be sorry, you cock-suckers!'

'Adèle.' He spoke loudly but calmly, bringing his head to her ear.

'Adèle, I want you to be quiet now.'

'Fucking bum-sucking shit-lickers!'

'Adèle. This is James. I'd like you to shut up now.'

'James?' She stopped struggling and fell silent. Everything suddenly seemed terribly quiet. James could hear the cautious sounds of sheep around him as they manoeuvred themselves out of the way.

'James?' She sounded surprised.

'It's OK, Del. Just be quiet now.'

'It wasn't me!'

'No, that's all right Del, be still now.'

'It wasn't me!'

'Lewyn, er . . .' He didn't know how to put it. Lewyn let go of her and she relaxed, her back against James, as he held her arms to her sides. Lewyn stepped back.

'I heard shouting and, well, singing I thought it was, so I came out. She was digging.' He pointed to the spade:

the handle was smeared with something James didn't like the look of, even in the dark.

'I asked her what she was doing and she went for me, she just went wild! Jesus!' Lewyn was beginning to react to the situation.

'I saw the sheep on the ground, and she tried to go and get it, she said she had to bury it, and when I wouldn't let her she started screaming again.'

'Lewyn, I'll take her back to the house now.'

'Shall I come with you?' Lewyn sounded hesitant.

'No, she'll be fine, really. I'll talk to you tomorrow.'

'I hope I didn't hurt her, but I . . .'

'She's all right now, I'll take her back.'

Adèle was standing, quite relaxed, leaning against James. She was swaying gently. James spoke into her ear.

'Del? Shall we go in now?'

She allowed James to navigate her round the disturbed soil, past the rich, copper-smelling mess, and towards the house: he held both her arms with his, and walked her away, as if he were pushing some kind of ingeniously constructed robot. Lewyn watched them, both hands on his head, blinking. They almost looked as if they were dancing.

James gazed at the little glowing numbers on the bedside clock: they had become meaningless, like a readout from the cockpit of an alien spaceship. Dots and dashes. Beside him Adèle slept soundly, even going as far as to snore occasionally. He remembered the last time he'd been up all night on her account, listening out for the ghostly, imperceptible piano music from downstairs.

Daylight began to work its way into the window, bringing faint, elusive detail to the looming forms of wardrobe and dressing table.

He was finding it very difficult to believe that the scene

he'd witnessed just hours before had actually taken place. It seemed, on the face of it, far more likely that it hadn't. Adèle's dressing gown caught his eye, smears and streaks of something on the white background dimly visible in the slyly growing light. It had happened. Tomorrow he'd have to do something about it. He was dreadfully tired.

11

Miss Laker's Condition

Sylvia Castle opened the door in a full-length dressing gown and oddly inappropriate pink fluffy slippers. Inappropriate, James thought, for a woman of her size. And age. He found himself so distracted by the slippers that he couldn't remember for a moment what he was doing there.

'Mr Tullian, isn't it?' she said, and looked enquiringly at Adèle.

'It's my wife, that is – it's Adèle.'

'Oh yes?' said Sylvia Castle, scanning Adèle's face and realizing at once that something was amiss. Sam sat in the car, watching.

'Come inside please. I'll get The Doctor up.'

Dr Castle listened as James recounted the events of the last weeks, ending with Adèle's adventure on the cliff the night before. Adèle sat beside him, miles away. The doctor listened very closely to everything James had to say, then asked to speak to Adèle alone. James felt treacherous and guilty as he closed the door of the consulting room.

Nurse Castle settled him in the waiting room and fetched Sam from the car to join him. She'd been expecting something like this.

'Mrs Tullian?' Dr Castle spoke firmly, trying to engage

185

Adèle's attention: she was awake but completely unresponsive, and wouldn't look directly at him.

'Mrs Tullian. Is what your husband says true?'

'There is no Mrs Tullian.'

'Excuse me?'

'We're not married. My name is Adèle Laker.'

'I see.' He waited.

'I didn't do it.'

'Have you been experiencing any headaches or dizziness of late?'

'What?'

'I said, have you . . .'

'Where's James?'

'He's waiting outside for you. Do you know where you are?'

She shrugged. What difference did it make where she was?

'Miss Laker, I'd be very grateful if you'd answer a few questions. Just a few. Then . . .'

'Where's James?'

Dr Castle watched her, excitement growing in him. Either a neurological dysfunction or something much rarer, much more subtle.

'How have you been feeling lately, Miss Laker? Have you been depressed or worried about anything?'

'I'm worried about – you know who.'

'Who's that, Miss Laker?'

'*You* know.' She smiled, startlingly.

'I'm afraid I don't.'

'He's hiding behind a tree, I can't see him yet.'

'Behind a tree?'

'He'll come out though, sooner or later.'

'Please go on.'

'I can't quite see his face yet, he's too far away.'

'Yes?'

'When I know who he is I can stop him.'

She fiddled with the cuff of her coat, eyes directed up and to one side.

He watched.

Fifteen minutes later, he emerged, calling Nurse Castle. She went into the consulting room, now fully and properly attired, without slippers, and they conferred.

She came out and James's anxious, bloodshot eyes met hers as she opened the waiting-room door.

'The Doctor is just going to make a few phone calls,' she said, 'and we may have to ask you to wait for a while. Would you like a cup of tea?'

'Has he found – anything—?'

'It's too early for a definite diagnosis. There may have to be some tests.'

'Where?'

'The nearest facility is Cardiff.'

'What kind of facility?'

'Please be patient, Mr Tullian. We'll let you know as soon as we know anything. I'll get the tea.'

Half an hour passed. Someone arrived at the front door, a smartly dressed youngish woman. Sylvia Castle showed her into the consulting room. James sat, feeling dead inside, with Sam wriggling on the hard wooden seat beside him.

'Dad?' Sam whispered, as if they were in church. 'Elvis hasn't had his walk.'

'He'll have to wait,' James answered, flatly. He couldn't think about the bloody dog right now. Elvis was in the kitchen at home, shut in. Well, he'd just have to wait.

Twenty minutes. James looked at his watch: still only a quarter to eight. He yawned.

The smart young woman came out, and was shown to the door by Nurse Castle.

'Excuse me,' James said, intercepting her on the way back, 'who was that?' The feeling of having abandoned Adèle to an army of strangers was eating away at him.

'Judith Colquett. She's a social worker. Approved social worker I should say,' she told him, giving 'approved' a very particular inflection as if to say, 'though not necessarily by me'.

'Sylvia?' the doctor called.

'Excuse me,' said Nurse Castle, and hurried into the consulting room.

James stood up.

'Wait here, Sam,' he said and followed her.

As he entered the room Adèle was standing, awk-wardly, oddly, in the middle of the floor. Sylvia and Dr Castle were in a huddle at the doctor's desk. They looked up at him.

'Mr Tullian, please could I ask you to wait outside. We'll call you in in a . . .'

'What's wrong with her?'

'Far too early to say, Mr Tullian,' Dr Castle replied in a bedside-manner voice, and James said:

'Tell me.'

The doctor assessed him, took in the bleary, desperate eyes and the weariness of his posture, the rumpled, still-damp clothes.

'All right. My preliminary diagnosis is that Miss Laker is in the early stages of a possibly severe psychological disorder.' James struggled to understand. Who the fuck was Miss Laker? Adèle? He went to her; she seemed not to see him.

'Adèle?' He turned back to the doctor. Between Adèle's frozen, unseeing demeanour and the profession-ally formal manner of the doctor, James was beginning to feel invisible.

'She'll need to have some tests. I think it's best that she

be admitted immediately to the Acute Psychiatric Ward at Cardiff Royal Infirmary.'

James felt, simultaneously, a wave of relief and a gust of shame at the feeling. He realized that other people were now involved, and the dismal, helpless feeling of betrayal surged up in him.

'It's OK, I can look after her. Really. There's no need,' he said: Dr Castle looked at him questioningly.

'I'm not sure you understand me, Mr Tullian. I regret to say that, having conferred with my colleague Miss Colquett, it is my belief that Miss Laker should be admitted under Section Four of the Mental Health Act.'

'What?'

'For her own protection and the protection of others. And so she can be given the appropriate tests.'

'Protection?' Surely it was *his* job to protect her; hadn't he always protected her in the past?

'No. Please. Look, I can look after her, I know what she's like, she's just been under a lot of strain recently. She'd never hurt anyone, never, she's not like that.'

'You mentioned food poisoning? And animal mutilations? We have to consider the welfare of everyone involved in this, Mr Tullian. There's a child.'

James got a picture of an immense machine grinding into life, a machine that would take Adèle away from him: a machine that he had activated, turned the key.

'Section Four is a seventy-two-hour order, for tests and initial examinations. After that a further order may be necessary.'

'Tell me what's wrong with her. Please.'

'I'm really not qualified to say, Mr Tullian. She'll have to be examined by properly qualified . . .'

'Tell me.'

'Schizophrenia.'

189

The word flew round the room like a splinter of glass. Adèle watched it out of the corner of her eye.

Sam slept in the ambulance, his head on James's knee, adding his own small pool of dampness to James's already damp trousers. James held Adèle's hand for a while, but there was no response: it fell like a lump of wood when he released it. She sat upright, frowning, looking away at nothing. The paramedic travelling with them made a few attempts at conversation, then read his *Mirror*.

More waiting at Cardiff: this time the seats were moulded plastic with thin foam cushions, orange and green. Sam dozed off again. Ten thirty-five, Tuesday. People walked about, getting through their daily routines, doing their jobs or being ill: everyone knew exactly what was expected of them, whatever their function. Even Sam seemed to know the right thing to do in the circumstances. James sat, wishing he'd thought to change his clothes before he came out, wishing he felt more ready to deal with it. Wishing he knew what to do.

'Mr Tullian?'

A good-looking middle-aged woman was approaching him. He stood up, ashamed of his shoddy, wrinkled clothes in the face of what was clearly a well-tailored and expensive black and jade suit.

'Would you come with me please?'

James woke Sam, and they followed the woman to a small room equipped with chairs and a coffee table. Sam promptly fell asleep again.

'My name is Sheila Kavanagh,' said the woman. 'I'm the consultant psychiatrist here. I've just been talking to Adèle.' James was relieved that the troublingly unfamiliar Miss Laker had been banished again.

'She's resting now. We're going to need some blood and urine samples, and she may have to have an EEG.

At the moment we're looking for anything at all unusual; it'd help me if you could answer some questions?'

'Of course.'

'Does your wife take any kind of drugs, either prescription or street drugs?'

'No.'

'You're quite sure?'

'Yes.' Adèle was reluctant to swallow even a Nurofen. He debated whether to mention the grass, but he didn't want to get her into any more trouble than she was in already. He felt as if he'd told enough tales for one day.

'Would you describe to me what led you to refer her to, er . . .' she opened a cardboard folder, 'Dr Castle.'

James, bleary and buzzing, went through the story again, automatically, the events sounding both incredible and also strangely ordinary to him now. Dr Kavanagh listened, noting down a few things as he spoke.

'This must have been a hard time for you,' she said when he'd finished. He nodded, smiling bleakly.

'We're going to do everything we can. Your wife is in good, experienced hands here.' She gave him a brilliant, flashing smile, then put it away again.

'Dr Castle said she had schizophrenia,' James said, miserably, his voice sounding in his ears like a child disappointed with its Christmas presents. Dr Kavanagh snorted through her nose.

'I'd be grateful if you'd keep this just between us, Mr Tullian, but he had absolutely no business to tell you that. We *could* be looking at schizophrenia: on the other hand we could have a simple case of LSD or mescaline-induced behaviour. Or an atypical brain tumour. Or hydrocephalus. Or a number of other things. All possible. All treatable.' She produced the smile again, leaning forward.

'And if Dr Castle turns out to be right in his diagnosis and Adèle is indeed suffering from schizophrenia, then we can treat that too. Believe it or not. Contrary to what you see in the films, Mr Tullian, most schizophrenics are perfectly peaceful, non-violent individuals, who are capable of benefiting enormously from drugs *and* psychotherapy, both of which, I'm proud to say, we're able to offer here. Unfortunately in many hospitals psychotherapy doesn't get much of a look-in.'

She patted his knee: James felt her control and optimism, and her faith.

'Please, don't look so worried!' she said. 'Many of my patients go on to a full recovery and a resumption of their normal lives. I won't lie to you: many do not. But Adèle is a strong, intelligent, creative, loving woman. Her chances are good. Believe me.'

'How long will it take?' James asked, and Dr Kavanagh smiled again.

'Ah, what a question! I've had cases where the patient has recovered in forty-eight hours. I have other patients in their nineties who have been receiving treatment all their lives, and who will never recover. We must hope, Mr Tullian. I must also say that there are degrees of recovery, and that there is a strong likelihood of relapses. But we must hope. There's nothing else to do. And there's nothing more effective. Believe me!'

He tried.

12

Heaven and Hell

Dilys was happy to do it, she really was. She felt flattered that James had asked her: after all, she'd only met Sam once, and that briefly. But then, she corrected herself firmly, he really didn't have any other option. It wasn't as if he'd selected her from a list of dozens. Dave had pointed this out to her at the time. You could always rely on Dave to bring you down.

They'd gone out with Sam and Elvis, who had stuck close to Sam most of the time, panting up nervously at her and Dave. Funny name for a dog that. Sam said it had been his choice: his mum had wanted Foo-Foo, Sam explained solemnly, and his dad couldn't decide between Killer and Shit-breath. But he was his dog, Sam stated, so he'd named him. Dilys was shocked at James's choices, but Dave laughed and ruffled Sam's hair.

It was like being a grandmother, Dilys thought. It had been God's will not to bless them with children; she and Dave had sat in Dr Castle's office while he'd explained it all to them, the monstrous, damning polysyllables falling heavily on to the worn carpet. She was fertile, Dave was not: that was what it all came to. Orchitis, after adult mumps. She'd had Dr Castle write it down for her. She still had the piece of paper, with 'Lustral' and a smiling face at the top. She kept it in the drawer where she might otherwise have kept the photo albums. But whatever words Dr Castle might have scribbled down, Dilys knew that the reason didn't lie within them. It lay, quite simply, in God's plan for them.

Then Catherine Bulmer had disappeared, and Owen Bulmer had walked up the path with the struggling red-faced two-year-old Lewyn in his arms. He'd been a difficult, unhappy, desolate child, but he was living, screaming proof for Dilys of the love and mercy of God and the efficacy of prayer. Dave accepted the fact that nothing on earth was going to stop her bringing him up. She'd return him at night to Owen's empty house (Owen had insisted that the boy sleep under his roof, wherever he spent his days). Lewyn had been God's intervention in Dilys's life, like Naomi with Ruth's child.

And now here she was with another unknowable, secretive, oh delightful child, walking through the winter fields. He was wearing his England shell suit (James's choice again, she thought dourly) and he was carrying a quarter-sized baseball cap, though he didn't seem inclined to put it on.

She knew now that Lewyn was never going to marry. He just wasn't made that way. She'd smiled and waved when his train pulled out at Fishguard station to take him away to his new life in the army, Owen stony and aching beside him. Then she'd gone home and cried. She hadn't believed he'd ever come back. What was there for him to come back for? But she knew it was for the best.

She'd hated herself as she'd written the letter that she knew would bring him home, detailing the sudden deterioration in his father's condition, his growing helplessness. More long words, more inadequate explanations. She'd felt as if she were to blame, but what else could she do? Owen needed his boy back. She'd prayed for forgiveness for the joy, the joy! when he'd stepped out of the taxi wearing the same clothes he'd gone away in. She'd cried again, this time all over him, tears of gratitude and relief and shame. He'd shaken his head when she'd tried to tell him about God's plan and His mysterious ways, and it had hurt her, but she knew that God had brought him back to her just as surely as He'd entrusted him to her in the first place.

But there would be no child of Lewyn's for her to sing to sleep; God apparently didn't wish Lewyn to wish it. This realization had brought her as close as she'd ever come to doubting God's wisdom, as close as was possible for her. To be unable to have a child – well that was unarguable, a simple, hard fact built into Dave's body, a body built, after all, in God's image. But to *choose* not to! She'd accepted it, but it had shaded over part of a sunlit field for her, for ever. Her God became more complex and baffling as she grew older.

She held Sam's little hand as he climbed over a stile, and she knew she had been wrong ever to doubt, ever to question. He was a funny, serious child, intensely interested in everything and capable of extraordinary concentration. He was fascinated by the plants growing in the stone walls, one in particular that produced thick waxy circular green plates detaining him for several minutes. How could it grow out of the *rock*? Neither Dave's nor her explanations satisfied him. He would just look perplexed and say 'Oh'. He was to stay for his tea and sleep overnight, so that James could have some time to himself. (Lewyn had suggested that they go into Fishguard and have a drink, and James had been grateful. He was shell-shocked.)

Elvis had to go back on his lead when they returned through the fields with sheep in: despite Adèle's (appallingly, all too literally) being caught red-handed, he was still a suspect for the previous sheep death, and Lewyn had insisted on it. He'd also insisted that Elvis be wormed, though Adèle had done him just before leaving London. He was taking no chances: he just couldn't afford to lose any more sheep.

Lewyn, resting between two sets of upright rows, regarded himself in the full-length mirror. His arms rested heavily at his sides, and he admired the blood vessels and the clean, precise definition of the muscle groups. It had never occurred to him that he was, deep down, profoundly narcissistic: even if he'd known the word he wouldn't have applied it to himself. Ever since he could remember he'd been aware of his body, interested in it, pleased with it, and looking at it was as much a part of his daily routine as feeding or washing it. He was carrying his years pretty well, he thought, probably better than most. He was just the right side of heavy, the weight packed into tidy, well-articulated slabs.

'Not bad,' he said, and smiled. Yes, he fancied himself, the smile acknowledged, but with good reason.

He soaped himself more than usually thoroughly in the bath, and even dug out an ancient bottle of aftershave. He combed and Brylcreemed his hair and tweaked at his ears and nose with a pair of tweezers. He would wear the grey chinos and the dark green cotton polo shirt. The only good shoes he had were his formal black brogues, his funeral/christening/wedding shoes. They hadn't seen much wear. But it was a jacket he was really stuck for: if not the denim and not the black with the too-wide lapels, then what? He had a good waxed cotton Barbour, but it wouldn't be right with the shoes. He toyed with the idea of driving down to H.E. Edwardes in Fishguard, he could just make it before they closed, then he thought, no, Dave had a brown suede one that would be just right, vegetarian or no vegetarian. He scrutinized his teeth. Not bad. He smiled again.

*   *   *

Sam waited politely while Dilys said grace. He even closed his eyes when he saw that she and Dave did so.

'Who were you talking to?' he asked when she'd finished, and she glanced over at Dave as if to say 'I told you as much.'

'We were thanking God for giving us food to eat,' she told him, and he frowned.

'Oh.' Why, he was wondering, did they get their food from god: couldn't they afford to buy any?

'What's the difference between Neil's wife and the *Titanic*?' the overweight man with the beard called out hilariously. He was in a knot of youngish men, on the far side of the bar from where James and Lewyn sat in the Dinas Cross Hotel bar. Lewyn looked over at them: there was a lad there he'd seen before, T-shirt and cropped hair.

'Doesn't look like we're going to get a game,' Lewyn said, 'they'll have the table booked right up till closing time.' Not that there really was a closing time: out of season Martin kept pretty much whatever hours he liked, something that was necessary if he was to make any kind of a living through the long winters. One or other of the lads would sometimes ring the bell at eleven, but it was strictly a joke.

Lewyn thought of other nights he'd spent in here. He recalled the feeling of leaving the bright, yeasty place, leaving a gang of men, uproarious at the bar, just settling in for a long session. Lewyn usually had to be up at 5.30, so he could rarely stay late. And besides, what was the point of staying, sitting in a corner, talking to nobody except for a few words with Martin the owner? Excluded. He'd been in the habit of making a great fuss of Martin's dog Shaun, mostly to mask his feeling of aloneness, awkwardness. The lads on the other side of the bar might

197

as well have been in Cardiff for all the contact he had with them. Long, long evenings punctuated by trips to the bar and the toilet. Scrupulously indifferent glances at the men (he'd never, he realized, seen any woman set foot in the place apart from Martin's wife Carol) and the awareness of half-amused looks back. Prolonged study of beer mats, wallpaper, the imitation coal fire.

But tonight was different, he had company! Not, admittedly, that James was being exactly companionable, but he was there, Lewyn was not alone. He could order two pints of beer, he could even be put out that the pool table was so busy. He felt vindicated, almost triumphant. This is James, my friend, he wanted to announce. You see? Shaun trotted over and Lewyn tricked him (easily) into giving him his paw. The dog gave James a wide berth: he'd had a lot of trouble over the years with drunks, and James was already halfway to being one of them.

James stirred.

'Sorry Lewyn. I'm not usually quite this boring. It's just, you know . . .'

Lewyn nodded.

'I thought it was going to be the right thing, us coming out here. Like a holiday, you know? We all of us needed to get away, and it was a chance of six months' work, put us back on our feet again. I can't believe this has all happened. I don't know what we're going to do now. Christ!'

'Aye.'

'Something must have just triggered it off, I suppose. The doctor said it can lie there for years, and then some little thing will bring it out.'

(like the beast, Lewyn thought)

'She says it usually strikes much younger, but it can happen any time. To anyone. I mean, Del's always been, I don't know, unusual I suppose you'd say. That was what attracted me to her in the first place, she wasn't like anyone I'd ever met before. *Wasn't.* Jesus. She's terribly bright, you know. And she sees things differently, she's got her own—' James clucked his tongue against the roof of his mouth, shook his head. How could you explain the astonishing, unpredictable uniqueness of this woman?

'She gets excited about things. She notices things, I don't even see them. And she can talk to people, anybody. We'd go out and she'd spend the whole time talking to some drunk at the bar. By the time she left she'd know everything about him. She kind of collected people. She was always writing letters to people she hadn't seen for years.'

He didn't say, in fact that's partly why I never let her meet my parents. He had tried to picture Adèle sitting in the bare concrete and turf garden on a plastic chair, balancing a cup and saucer, talking about current affairs with his mother, letting slip something wrong, peculiar, eccentric. He had never risked it, not that his mother had ever pressed him. Even if he'd been properly married to Adèle, his mother would not have accepted her. James didn't think he could have stood her disapproval, disdain. Adèle had sent her pictures of the children; she'd sent polite thank-you letters back. That was the extent of it. Adèle, he knew, had been first amused, then angry, then contemptuous. She thought he should be free of the need for his mother's approval by his age. It was ridiculous, unbecoming: not brave. Adèle believed passionately in being brave.

'She's a lovely woman,' Lewyn said, and James was surprised, not at the sentiment, but that Lewyn should voice it. Though of course, in the few short weeks they'd been here it had been Adèle who had befriended Lewyn, got to know him, chipped away at his solitariness and suspicion.

'So how long do you think she'll be gone?'

'The doctor said at least six months. She's on a treatment order.'

'And after that?'

James shook his head.

'She didn't know. She said she could make a complete recovery in six months or she might never recover. She said sometimes it's just a matter of a few days. It can just hit and run. Or it can be permanent.'

Schizophrenia. Terrifying, icy, alien word. Like someone being encased in crystal, aloof, alone, cut off. Blank. Dead. But not quite dead. Her symptoms were apparently not unusual: the belief that someone else was controlling your thoughts and actions, the belief that someone was trying to get you. The certainty that things were being arranged, planned by someone. She had stopped short of saying she heard voices, but claimed she was acting on someone else's behalf, doing what they wanted: she hadn't said who it was that was controlling her in this way. The doctor told him that her speech was disordered: she'd said she'd been losing sheep, instead of losing sleep, for instance, and that she was paining, instead of painting. She'd said she killed Ruthie deliberately, because someone else wanted her to, as an experiment. Who? She wouldn't say, she'd just smiled. She'd said someone was in her paintings, changing them, making her paint things she didn't want to. There was someone hiding in them. The sheep were trying to warn her about something, some dreadful thing that was going to happen. But they were also involved in it in some way. They could hear her thoughts. She'd said one of them had laughed at her.

'She's going to be on medication for a while, until she's more stable. But people get better, the doctor said, it isn't like it used to be. They can stop it getting as far as it used to. She said there are lots of people living ordinary lives who've had it and recovered. She said the important thing was not to give up hope.'

James stared bleakly at his glass. Hope. The doctor had also said there were ninety-year-olds who'd had it all their lives. Unreachable. Frozen.

Lewyn was recalling the first glimpse he'd had of her, as he was closing the window in the secure room, her white, strained face in the car as it rounded the corner. Edith. She's come back.

'Poor woman. It must be terrifying for her.' Again James was surprised, this time by Lewyn's insight. He hadn't thought of that. He realized that he'd been thinking of himself, of the – well damn it the *inconvenience* of it all, the bad timing, the extra burden it would put on him. He hated himself.

'It was only four thousand that went down on the *Titanic*,' came the voice again. James looked up and, this time surprising himself, laughed aloud.

'But how can Jesus love me when he hasn't even *met* me?' Sam was demanding earnestly.

'He loves everyone, everyone that's ever been and everyone that ever will be,' said Dilys, leaning forward.

'But what about bad people?'

'He loves them too, but they don't love him.'

'Oh.' Sam frowned. He hadn't heard any of this before.

'You never married then, Lewyn?' James asked, breaking the silence.

'Me? No.'

'Never found the right woman, eh?'

'Oh I don't know. Never had the time I suppose really.' He looked away, as another roar broke out on the far side of the bar: 'Confucius he say man who puts prick in fire fucking grate.'

'Well, that's not true. I just never thought about it. Bit late now I 'spect. And there's not many women that'd want to live out here, it's not exactly much of a life. Different for me, see, cos I was born to it. I never did anything else, 'cept the army.'

'You were in the army?'

'Oh yes. Long time ago.'

'Did you like it?'

'Like it?' He thought of the terrible food, the lack of freedom and privacy, the endless fiddly routines of cleaning and drilling. 'It was what I always wanted, since I was a kid. Soldier. I never wanted anything else. But I had to leave, cos of my dad and all, and that was that. Been here ever since. I don't expect I'll ever leave now. I don't mind it. It's not a bad life.'

'Confucius say: man who put prick in biscuits fucking crackers.'

Lewyn sighed.

'Well, one more and we'd better be away. I thought maybe we could walk back along the cliffs. Beautiful at night it is.'

Sam lay in bed, mulling it over. Jesus died because everyone in the world was so bad. It wasn't his fault, but he took the blame for it anyway. But then he came alive again. He was *really* dead and then he was *really* alive. It was true, then. Jesus had made an old man come back. And someone called Elijah who was a prophet had done it as well. It used to happen all the time, so it seemed. And Dilys said that one day everyone would come back, everyone who'd ever died. Even Ruthie? he'd asked. Yes, even Ruthie. But not just yet, though it might be soon. The good people would go to heaven, and the bad ones to hell. It was all very straightforward. Jesus could do it because he was God as well, and God could do anything he felt like. Dilys hadn't been sure about Elvis, but she said that if he was a good dog then he'd probably go to heaven, and he'd live for ever. Was Elvis a good dog, Sam wondered? He never bit people and he didn't bark much. That would probably do.

Dilys had given him a Bible, a small thick book with tiny writing, in columns. That had the whole story in it, and it was all true because God had said it. God never told lies. The paper was rattly and some of the words were spelled wrong, but that was because it was written such a long time ago, before people knew how to spell properly. Dilys had said he should read it, or some bits of it anyway, and anything he didn't understand he could ask her. He liked Dilys, she was nice. He'd be seeing more of her, she said, now that his mum was in the hospital. She wasn't ill though, she was just upset and had to go away and rest. She was tired. Sam was aware there was a bit more to it than that, and that his dad knew his mum had been being silly and had to stop it. She had gone too far. Still, he thought he could probably manage without her for a while.

Dave was unhappy about it.

Of course it was wrong that the boy should have been brought up without any instruction. What were the teachers thinking of? It could never have happened when he was at school. He'd had it every day then, till he was sick and tired of it. It hadn't been until he was about sixteen that he'd really believed it. He remembered sitting in the bare, frigid chapel; the minister had stopped in the middle of a sentence and looked right at him, and he'd suddenly felt it, it had tingled and flickered all over him. It was true, he knew. For a moment he'd forgotten that his bum was aching from the wooden bench and that the woman two rows ahead was picking her nose and that he wanted to go to the toilet: his body had become warm and soft and his head had started to buzz. It was true! Actually true! He was saved!

The moment had passed and his faith had flickered on and off like a faulty light switch ever since, but he always held on to that long-gone moment, that instant of warmth and excitement and complete happiness.

But (and here was where he differed from Dilys, differed often and not always amicably) he knew that there were some people for whom it wasn't true. Were they wrong? Dilys of course would say yes, but Dave wasn't totally convinced. He refused to believe that God couldn't see the good in people, even if they didn't know it. Jesus had died for everyone, hadn't he? Dave was disturbed and secretly deeply uneasy about much of the Old Testament. Dilys's favourite, Elijah, for instance, staging a competition with the priests, seeing whose God could burn the sacrificial bull, even when it was doused in water; Ba'al, not surprisingly, had failed and Elijah had ordered the execution of the priests. Four hundred and fifty. And so it went on. Couldn't people be different but still good?

And Sam's parents, however ignorant or misguided they might be (or even actually mad, in Adèle's unfortunate case), didn't they have the right to do what they thought was best for him? Sam would find God in his own time and his own way.

'It's our duty, David,' Dilys said firmly. 'We can't just abandon him to damnation. It would be a terrible, terrible sin.'

Sin. Damnation. Dave gritted his teeth and said nothing. What kind of God would throw a little boy into everlasting torment because he didn't know his Bible? No God he wanted to know, certainly not the God who'd breathed on him that dim, distant day in chapel.

204

But Dilys would have her way. As usual. Perhaps she was right.

Adèle lay perfectly still under the much-too-bright light while the nurse injected her with the poison that would eventually make her so weak that she'd go back. She had a television in the room, but it was just full of their nonsense. It wasn't real. The nurse was very nice, but if she really was nice why would she want to poison people? Someone must be making her do it, Adèle decided, and smiled warmly at her.

'You as well?' she said, sweetly, sadly, and someone called out in the corridor, 'Hey! What the *fuck's* wrong with this *fucking* drinks machine?' Adèle thought, he means me, he thinks I'm not working properly. Did they all know, then? They must. She had become a machine and everyone knew it.

'It's not me,' she said, 'I'd never do anything like that.' The nurse smiled and stroked her forehead. Adèle felt she deserved a better explanation.

'You see, it's more of a metal-fistical problem,' she said, and stopped because her voice was far too loud and in any case the nurse could hear her thoughts perfectly well. The nurse went away, promising to come back in a while.

'Just try and relax now, lovely. Do you want the television on?'

Adèle turned away from her. It wasn't her fault, but she was as bad as the rest of them. Television indeed! The light was buzzing: it would probably blow up at any minute, and she'd get covered in glass. She pulled the sheet up over her head, but she could still see everything. Even with her eyes closed.

The sky was so beautiful!

James and Lewyn lay on their backs, side by side, on

the wintry grass. The cliff-top path wound away out of sight on either side, leaving them on a small promontory.

It had been Lewyn's idea to lie down for a moment as they were walking back from Fishguard. There were two cows in the field; they'd stood up when Lewyn and James approached, like well-behaved children rising when a teacher came into a classroom. They stared at the men, not in the least surprised, almost as if they were expecting them; their great sturdy warm bodies moved in and out as they breathed the freezing air and turned it into steam.

'If you go into a field of cows and lie down, do you know what they do?' Lewyn said. 'They watch you for a few minutes, then they start to come over to you. Very slowly they do it. You have to lie dead still. Eventually they'll come right up, surround you. You get a whole ring of cows around you. And they breathe on you: trying to keep you warm I suppose they are. Fine creatures, cows. Lovely breath they've got, lovely warm sweet breath.'

The sea was crashing and thumping far below them, sending huge concussion impacts through the rock: you could almost feel the vibrations. There was a tiny sliver of a moon, just a fingernail, and James thought, if Del was here she'd wish on it. She was always wishing on things, birthday-cake candles, midnight on New Year's Eve, the times when they said the same thing at the same moment; sometimes she'd just close her eyes and cross her fingers and wish for something with no pretext at all, screwing her face up with the effort. Lucky pebbles. Lucky pictures. He'd never known what it was she was wishing for so fervently, though he guessed it was something to do with him and Sam. And Ruthie of course, before the accident. Had she stopped wishing things for Ruthie, he wondered, or had she carried on anyway?

Heaven, he thought. Up past the stars, where everyone would be happy for ever and ever. Was that where Ruthie had gone? Or had she vanished totally, completely, leaving no trace at all except the smoke from the crematorium chimney? He wished that he could believe in something.

'You see that star, in between those two bright ones, straight overhead,' he said, and Lewyn followed his pointed finger. 'Watch it carefully.'

'Christ he's moving!' Lewyn said, after a few moments.

'Yup. It's a satellite.'

The house seemed very different when Lewyn shut the door behind him and flicked on the light. Bloody messy, really, come to look at him! He'd have to clean it all up.

He put a record on the scratchy Dansette as he made himself a cup of coffee, and tried a few dance steps in the greasy, unwholesome-looking kitchen, manoeuvring round the chairs and table.

'Da-da, da-dee, three steps to heaven,' he sang, and realized that he had neither sung nor danced for a very long time.

It was after ten when James woke up.

Christ! Where's Sam?

Then he remembered: Sam was over at Dilys and Dave's. Because Adèle had gone mad and been hospitalized, and he couldn't cope. Quite something to wake up to, apart from a hangover. He splashed his face and brushed the sour, gritty taste out of his mouth. Adèle gone, Sam gone, even Elvis gone. He'd been abandoned. He rummaged around for clean things, but ended up in his usual work clothes, check shirt and V-neck pullover, and those ugly green corduroy trousers he'd bought in the Spastics shop in Highgate. Bought specifically for working in, but no more acceptable for all that. He found his anorak and went out into the overcast morning.

It was a five-minute walk to Dilys's house, along a quiet narrow road with fields on either side. Sheep glanced up as he passed, incuriously. Incurious as to Adèle's mental state, to his reactions, to the possible future effects on Sam. Life went on. Eat grass.

Six months. Forty-eight hours. Ninety years. What would life be like after Adèle? The only image that came to mind was one from his young days, drunk in a club, lights and music going crazy, a girl in a short plaid skirt, she was with a group of people, all glancing around. He was leaning carelessly up against a ledge near the dance floor. Did you still get girls in plaid skirts in clubs? He remembered brushing up against her, clumsily, and she'd said, 'You're drunk.'

He'd smiled.

'Yes. I don't think I can plausibly deny that.' Loquacious when in his cups, always.

'And you're gorgeous.'

'Well yes, I don't think I could plausibly deny that either.' He'd been amazed at his audacity, and delighted at hers.

'What are you doing later?'

Later? Oh, going home, having a kebab maybe, perhaps a joint cadged off his flatmate Gary. Nothing too much.

'Nothing too much. What are you doing?'

'I'm going home with you. What did you think?'

'Oh. Right.' A pick-up in a club, and then ten years later here he was trying to contemplate life without her, one child dead, one child strange, her in a bin with the rest of the loonies. Life can be hard, oh yes indeedy.

He stopped and leant on a gate, watching the sheep.

Adèle had been his life. Her odd, aggressive, almost predatory personality had been something he'd been

208

living with, adapting to, for most of his adult years. After Ruthie had been born he'd gone out one night with Madeleine and Steve. Steve had felt sick and gone home, and Madeleine had wanted him. And he'd wanted her, repulsed by Adèle's distant, exhausted demeanour and her dismissal of him. But he hadn't. He never had. Ten years.

And now *she'd* left *him*. Left him for her own imaginary landscape, her imaginary terrors and delights. Would she even know now if he left her? Would she care? Forty-eight hours. Ninety years.

Dilys answered the door, surprised to see him.

'I took him home, about an hour ago. Isn't he about?'

'No, he isn't.'

'Well, he let himself in. I thought he'd be with you.'

'I'll go straight back.'

'I'm sure he's OK.'

'Thanks, Dilys.'

He didn't exactly run, but he certainly had no time to lean on gateposts and admire the sheep either. Where the fuck was Sam?

He turned the corner, ran up the driveway. Sam was sitting on the tombstone step. He looked up.

'Dad? Where've you been?'

Where had *he* been?

'Well where've *you* been, Sam! Christ, I was worried about you!'

'Nowhere.'

Nowhere. Uh-hm.

'When did Dilys bring you back?'

'Oh, about an hour ago. I came in but you were asleep so I went for a walk.'

'Christ! How did you rip your jumper?'

Sam shrugged.

'Sam? How did you rip your jumper?'

'There was a tree. It had all sharp bits on it.'

'Have you had any breakfast?'

'The lady made me toast, with this funny marmalade. And cake. It was all crumbly.'

'Sam, you must *never* just run off by yourself. Haven't I told you?'

'But you were asleep.'

'Then you should have woken me *up*.'

Sam shrugged again, a damned-if-you-do-damned-if-you-don't shrug. He'd tried waking his dad up after a night out before.

'Shouldn't you?'

'Yes.'

Shouting at Sam again. Poor kid, he wasn't quite having the holiday he'd been expecting.

'Sam, until Mum comes back' (– six months, ninety years –) 'or we can sort something out, you're going to have to stay where I can keep an eye on you.' Dammit, why not put the little rascal on a

(lead?)

'I'm going to be doing some work on the house. Now I want you to stay inside and we'll go out for a walk later on. But you're not to go wandering off. All right? Sorry, chief.'

'Can I do painting?'

'Yes.'

'Can I have the radio on?'

'Yes.'

'OK.'

An hour later James was up a ladder with a heat gun, burning off paint from a window, the exciting, choking smell enshrouding him. The discoloured paint wrinkled and scorched, peeling off in brittle strips. Off with the old.

And the new? He'd never before considered how

absolutely impossible life was without Adèle. Purely on a mundane level, how was he going to work and keep an eye on Sam, short of tying him up.

(like a dog?)

Now, for instance: Sam was either downstairs painting in the kitchen, or he was somewhere else, falling off a cliff perhaps or starting a fire. An active seven-year-old, there was simply no limit to the perils he could encounter or engineer. And James could hardly be up and down a ladder all day, it just wasn't possible to work that way. So he'd have to hire a child-minder. Where in God's name did you get a child-minder? And how did you know you could trust them? He turned the idea of Dilys over in his mind. Perhaps if he offered to pay her she might do it, maybe just mornings. How much? Christ, how was he supposed to afford it? Sebastian's deal had been fair but no more than that. The rate for the job, no special favours, not even for family. We all have to stand on our own two feet, Jamie. Start offering people something for nothing, you undermine their spirit. Take me for instance. Blah fucking blah.

Even if he could have found the time, James knew that he and Sam would quickly come to blows if exposed to each other for prolonged periods. He was struck by the thought that Sam was someone he knew only in controlled bursts, like a favourite sit-com. A couple of hours in the evening if Sam wasn't out at Beavers or piano. Stories at night, infrequent nocturnal glancings-in (just to check you're still alive, chief, no sweat), hurried, ill-tempered encounters early in the morning (not the best time for either of them). Drives out at weekends. A week last year in a guesthouse in Cornwall. Incredibly, that was it. He had almost no idea what Sam actually *did* during the day. At eleven, at three o'clock. What? He'd always imagined him sitting at a big wooden desk scratching his name on the lid. But he couldn't do that all day. Did he have a nap in the afternoon? Or was it only much younger children who did that?

(and dogs)

What if Sam didn't like the child-minder? Had he liked Dilys? The cake had been all crumbly, which could be either good or bad, but he suspected from Sam's tone that it was bad. And anyway, how much did he know about Dilys? Adèle had spent one night with her and ended up having a panic attack in the secure room. God knew what stories Dilys had been telling her. If they were anything like Dave's or Lewyn's stories, it was no wonder that Adèle had gone

(barking mad?)

had had a breakdown, an episode as Dr Kavanagh had called it. A psychotic episode. Was a woman who gave people psychotic episodes the most appropriate person to look after his only surviving child? No, that was unfair, Adèle had simply succumbed to the strain and the delayed shock of losing Ruthie; Dilys couldn't possibly have pushed her over the edge in one night. (Surely.)

A girl from the town then, perhaps. Mind you, if the local people he'd met already were anything to go by, he'd be hard-pressed to find anyone even half-way suitable. (Had Adèle been suitable? The question wriggled out from under a secluded rock in his brain, and squirmed out of sight, ignominiously.)

He caught something out of the corner of his eye, and, twisting round, very nearly unseated the ladder, rocking hard to the left. Damn! The scraper fell to the ravaged concrete path, and James saw Lewyn standing in the field, carrying a large, still object in his arms.

sweet christ not Sam you murdering bastard!

'James? I think you'd better come down.'

Elvis. It was Elvis.

*   *   *

The two men regarded the sprawled heap of dripping, bloodied fur at their feet. Head bashed in. One eye put out. Rear left leg gone. James experienced a sudden swimming feeling, waves of unreality crashing and booming around him, and Lewyn's hand pressed on his shoulder, steadying him. The dog was recently dead, still bleeding warm red blood, and wet.

'He was down on the rocks, under the top field. He'd got lodged in a rock, otherwise he'd have been washed out.'

'Lewyn for Christ's sake,' James said weakly.

'I just saw this big brown blob, I couldn't think what he could be, so I went down to have a look. Not a pretty sight is he?'

'How—' How not to make it sound like an accusation?

'Lewyn, how could this have happened?'

Lewyn shook his head.

'Well you found him! You must have some fucking idea!' James felt as if he were drowning, foam and spray hissing around him, fingers clutching at the slick, shiny wet rocks, the demented abstract determination of the sea dragging and pounding him.

'Sorry. Sorry Lewyn.' Lewyn put a clumsy arm round James's shoulder and stared ahead, unable to look at James's twisted, working face.

'Let's go in and sit down.'

'No. We'd better get him out of sight. I don't want Sam to see this.' He crouched down and scooped up the sodden, heavy, inert animal. Foo-Foo. Shit-breath. Killer. Pity for the dog fighting against revulsion at the raw stump of flesh, he lifted Elvis up in both arms and, staggering slightly under the weight, carried him off in the direction of the cliff.

'James? Where are you going?'

Well, where indeed? Where do you hide a dead dog from an inquisitive child? He stopped, baffled. Then he said, 'Under the wall, in the corner. Cover him with branches. It'll have to do for now.' He reeled to the corner of the field, dropped the dog over the wall, and started tearing at a hawthorn bush growing nearby. Lewyn watched him, helplessly. James stood for a moment looking at the makeshift covering, then turned round and came back.

James sent Sam upstairs.

'Just *do* it, Sam. Don't give me a hard time now. I'll come up in a minute.'

James and Lewyn sat at the kitchen table, with Sam's painting things all around. Another burning building, James noted dimly. Smoke engulfing the whole of the top of the floor, the sky transformed from paper white to Rowenta black; something else to worry about. When he got the time.

'Tell me again, Lewyn.'

'Like I told you, James. I was up in the top field—'

'Why?'

'*Why?*'

'I'm sorry, Lewyn, I'm not really thinking. This is all so . . .'

'Tha's all right. I was up there and I was by the fence, and I saw your dog lying on the rocks. I went down the steps, you know, further along, and climbed over to him. Carried him up. He couldn't have been dead long, he was still, you know, he wasn't stiff or anything.'

'You didn't see anyone around?'

Lewyn hesitated, then shook his head.

'No. No-one. They must have been there before I got there.'

'They?'

'Whoever did this.'

'You mean you think a *person* did it?' Eye put out, leg missing.

'I'm sorry to say I do, yes. I can't see any animal taking out the eye. Can you?'

Well maybe not, but did that mean you could see a *person* doing it? What on God's green earth kind of person?

'Oh now come on, I can't, I refuse to believe that there's somebody roaming around in broad fucking daylight mutilating animals. People don't do that, he was just a *dog* for pity's sake!' James heard his voice trembling, and put his hand to his face. Lewyn watched him steadily.

'I think we have to believe it, James. There's no animal would do that.'

'Not another dog?'

'No.'

He thought of Adèle, eerie in her dressing gown on the wet cliff. *It wasn't me! (Click.)*

'What am I going to tell Sam?'

Bad break, chief. Elvis didn't make it.

Lewyn sat, uneasy but solid. James stood up, and went to the stairs.

'Sam? Would you come down here please?'

He supposed it was rather a lot to ask of a child to accept that his mother had gone away, for an unspecified reason and duration, and that his dog had been killed, all in forty-eight hours. But all the same something in Sam's response tripped off alarms in him.

'Oh.'

Yes, and? Sam sat and fidgeted, glancing at Lewyn and his father in turn.

'So he isn't going to come back?' The boy sounded, more than anything else, disappointed.

'No. Elvis is dead now, Sam.'

'The lady said dead people come back when Jesus calls them.' James had to think for a second to connect 'the lady' with Dilys: damn it, there was always someone ready with the Baby Jesus when your back was turned.

'She said that dogs can go to heaven as well, if they were good.'

'Look Sam, I don't care what Dilys has been telling you, I don't want you to think Elvis is going to come back. I don't want you to be disappointed.' And yet, wouldn't it be good for Sam to be able to believe that Elvis wasn't gone for ever? It might cushion the shock for him. Comforting lies. James was sometimes envious of those who could live in a world where no-one was ever gone for good and we'd all be reunited in a better place.

'But the lady said . . .'

'Sam!' Sam subsided, cowed, and Lewyn caught James's eye. James was ashamed, more than that he was sick and tired of himself. Increasingly he heard his father in his voice, silencing dissent, guillotining debate, shouting down. Everything would then be established and orderly and easy, and no-one would have to say anything, or indeed have anything to say. Was that how he wanted Sam to turn out?

Lewyn stood to leave.

'If you need a hand with – with—'

'OK. Thanks, Lewyn.'

Lewyn crossed the field; he was thinking that Sam hadn't wanted to know how Elvis had died, how he'd come to be found on the rocks. He went home and took off all his clothes and put them in to wash. Ninety degrees. He stood naked at the sink, scrubbed his hands with Swarfega. Small particles of dog seemed to have found their way on to every part of his body.

No, Sam had been more interested in the question of

a canine afterlife. Lewyn knew it was only in his dreams that dead things moved again, a kind of eviscerated resurrection shuffle, each part crawling and twitching towards its own ghastly transubstantiation.

He lay in the bath, ducked his head under, splashing vigorously. Inch-and-a-quarter-long black hairs floated around him.

soul: surviving after death, separated from the body.
    hearken: listen attentively.
    (attentively: listening carefully.)
Sam was finding this happened more and more. He would look up a word in the battered Penguin English Dictionary, and he'd find that he'd have to look up the words that explained what the first word meant. The shadowy intuition was beginning to form that the whole project had a curious circularity to it. Words meant other words, which meant further words; and they all seemed to mean each other.

He went back to the other book, the one that the people who couldn't spell properly had written a long time ago.

' "Oh LORD my God, let this childe's *soul* come into himm againe!" And the LORD *hearkened* to the voice of Elijah, and the soul of the childe came into him againe.'

Well, that was clear enough. Sam copied it into his red exercise book in neat writing.

13

Sheep

Sam swung his legs against the hard seat, singing faintly. He liked the shoe shop, it had a nice smell, dusty and cardboardy, and he liked the tall racks of shoeboxes, a wall completely covered in identical white containers, each with its own secret content of style, colour and size, nestling two by two. He had sensed that money was not, at the moment, the minefield it had been until recently. Previously if he needed new shoes or even flip-flops for the beach it had provoked tension and tight lips from his parents. Admittedly since Ruthie had gone away finances had eased somewhat, but even so the run-up to Christmas was a period of tight negotiation and some anxiety. Sam was a good bargainer, he knew just how far he could go without pushing his luck, a phrase that fell from his dad's lips like a curse. You're pushing your luck, Sam. He generally managed these days to stay on the right side of this invisible but decisive line. Elvis had died, and Sam was going to get new trainers, and they weren't his Christmas present, he would get something else for Christmas. Not in any likelihood the flashy electronic games system he'd opened the bidding with, but he was prepared for that.

James looked at his watch. Dammit, it was nearly ten. He was due to visit Adèle in Cardiff and Sam was going to stay with Lewyn for the day, and be very good. If Lewyn had even the smallest complaint, Sam sensed, it would knock off some fraction of the value of the Christmas present. Well, he'd just have to work round that. James fidgeted. It was all very well having a relaxed attitude to life, taking your time, moving at a slower pace, but dammit he had to get on!

The assistant reappeared with an armful of shoeboxes, and Sam began a meticulous inspection of some of them. Brand consciousness had recently awoken in him, and two of the boxes were examined purely for the sake of appearing thorough: he certainly had no real intention of walking round in Hi-Tecs or Dunlops.

James smiled up at the plump, balding assistant, and knew instantly that he wouldn't be getting out of here before 10.45, 10.30 at the earliest. He was going to have a conversation.

'What just visiting are you?'

James explained, he hoped not too tersely, what they were doing here, the assistant punctuating his account with expressions of interest and comprehension.

'So you're up by Dinas then? I haven't been up that way, oh not since a few years back now. Bit out of the way that, isn't he? Lovely area though, if you like him rugged. I had a sister lived up Brynhelwyn, but she moved down to Port Talbot a few years ago, her husband got promoted see; she don't like it though, Port Talbot people is very unfriendly evidently, but I tell her you've got to give him time, you can't just expect to settle in straight off . . .'

James smiled and nodded. Sam was having trouble lacing up the Reeboks, and the assistant took one off him and started to thread the lace through the innumerable eyes. James suspected that the more holes you got the more you paid, and cast a regretful eye on the clearly discarded Dunlops. The assistant fed the lace through with a nonchalant expertise. Slowly.

'. . . you must be pretty near Stumble Head then, you'll have seen the monument?'

James was caught off guard by the question; he'd been contemplating grabbing the shoe from the assistant's pudgy fingers and lacing it himself, no disrespect but *really* . . .

'Monument?'

'Aye. Can't be more than a half-mile up from you, up on the cliffs there. Worth a visit, I'd say. Quite a story, I'm surprised no-one's mentioned him to you. Well I say that, you'll find people who think the whole thing's best left and forgotten about. Neil – you know Neil at the Sailor's, do you? – his grandad was one of them. Neil won't talk about it though.'

James watched the sausage fingers fiddling with the lace, slowly, slower. Quite a story, eh? It sounded ominous. He revised his estimate upwards to 10.50. Call it 11.00. He writhed on the chair.

'1928. There's still one or two left who saw it, there's an old girl lives out somewhere near you, matter of fact, must be ninety-odd now. They interviewed her for the *Mercury*, back in the seventies, fifty years on you know, and she was seventy or so then. Come to think of it she may have departed by now. Yes. She saw it.'

He paused, his fingers merely turning the scaled-down replica of a training shoe now, all pretence at actually aiding the process of selling abandoned.

'Saw what?' James said, feeling that otherwise this fat fuck (well he was sorry but for God's *sake*!) would continue hinting delicately round the edges of whatever it was indefinitely. He was reminded of Uncle Seb's vulgar, tactless tactfulness and his endless bloody good-bloke chattiness.

'There was a meeting. They used to have them back then, big open-air meetings. New Connection they called it, some kind of Methodist splinter, they were very big round here. Don't see too much of them now of course.'

James suspected from his tone that he'd stepped into one of the innumerable factional debates that covered the whole area, like cracks on Tottenham Court Road. He'd expected when they first arrived to find an orderly community of Methodists, the valleys united in chapel song. And then he'd walked around Fishguard: Methodists, yes, but also Baptists, Congregationalists, Presbyterian, United Reformed, and that was just the English-speaking churches, the Church in Wales, Welsh Methodists, Independents, not to mention an astonishing number of Jehovah's Witnesses and Born Agains. A delicate fracturing of the people, as subtle and profound as the gradings of the middle class in Highgate, distributed along fault lines that were as much organizational as doctrinal. Protestant, but as much against each other as they were against the Catholics, who were nowhere to be seen.

'This was a big-deal meeting evidently, more or less everyone in the area across to Llanthietho who were in this New Connection went. Thousands, by all accounts.

'They had it on the cliff top, July I think it must have been, and they had a big preacher, one of the original New Connection men, I forget the name now, but he was an important man, oh yes.

'Well he was standing there on some kind of platform they'd built special, and he was whipping them up, lots of hellfire and shouting. People would come up on the platform and confess, you know, and he'd forgive them. Crying and wailing and God knows what. This old girl, she said that some of them started doing the old speaking-in-tongues routine when this preacher touched them. She was towards the back evidently, and she said she could feel it spreading through the crowd, people falling on the

221

ground and leaping about. Said she thought there was going to be trouble. She got herself out of the way, but she reckoned she could still feel it, like a 'lectric current or something, people were sobbing and holding on to each other, confessing, and there was the preacher calling out to heaven, calling on God to come down and save them.

'Then she said he shut up for a minute, waving his arms about, and she thought he was just getting inspired, but he wasn't, he was falling off the bloody platform wasn't he, stupid rickety thing was falling down. So of course everyone starts pushing forward, and the poor buggers at the front went flying off after him, they prob'ly thought it was Judgement Day or something. There were people trying to shout "Get back!" but no-one was taking any notice, they just kept shoving forward. She said that she couldn't be sure but she thought she saw people just jumping off, arms stretched up to heaven, just flinging themselves off like they thought they were going to fly away to Jesus.

'They didn't though, unlucky for them. Ended up in a big pile on the rocks, couple of hundred of 'em, stacked up like sandbags, with the big-deal preacher at the bottom. Lots of them got washed away, they were finding bodies all along there for weeks after. New Connection kept quiet after that, apart from collecting for the monument. I think it pretty much finished them off.

' "This Tablet erected to the Eternal Memory of those Pious Souls who joined the Heavenly Choristers in this Place, 1928." Tha's all he says, and a carving of Jesus surrounded by angels. They tried to pass it off as some kind of a miracle for a while, but no-one was having it really.

'The old girl says she never talked about it for years after. Said she felt ashamed to have been there, to have felt that current. She says she'll never forget seeing people just running off the cliff top, calling out to Jesus, stretching out their arms. Stumble Head, aye.'

The assistant gazed away, and James looked at Sam who was blinking up at him.

'Dad?' Sam whispered, 'I'll have the Reeboks. OK?'

The acute psychiatric ward at Cardiff Royal Infirmary was a busy, bright, efficient-looking place, nurses going confidently about their business, more male nurses than usual, with the patients in an extraordinary variety of moods and postures, moving amongst the staff with an air of uneasy helpfulness. There was a truce, but the threat of it breaking lurked in every clean, well-lit room. It seemed to James to be a very appropriate location for people whose sense of reality had been altered: it was an unreal place, nothing at all like the outside world. An asylum?

Adèle was in the Occupational Therapy room; there was an area at the back where the patients were able to paint. Dr Kavanagh had said that schizophrenics were often seized with the desire to paint and draw, even if before the onset of their illness they hadn't dipped a brush into water since school. Many were able to paint, competently, lucidly, when they could do little else. Of course with Adèle it wasn't so much occupational therapy as occupation: the art therapist who came in two afternoons a week had been struck by Adèle's businesslike routine. She'd asked Adèle if she could see any of her previous work – maybe James could bring in some slides? Adèle had denied that she'd painted before. Someone else had done them and falsely attributed them to her. The painting that she'd just finished was another of those. She was surprised that the therapist couldn't tell: she must be a fool. Adèle tolerated her interest, never certain that she wasn't really another patient. She humoured her, but disdainfully.

James had bought flowers at the stall in the car park, then dumped them in the rubbish bin by Reception. They seemed a sham, as falsely cheerful as the bunny rabbits and Mickey Mouses people papered nurseries with, as if they could keep terror and hallucination away. Spuriously optimistic charms to ward off dread and the awful icy isolation of dreams.

He gave the bag of Adèle's clothes and toiletries to the ward sister, then stood at the door of the day room; the television was on, but quietly, and for the most part unattended. One or two of the patients looked up at him, but didn't appear to register anything. Dr Kavanagh had spoken of a tapering of affect, the marked inexpressivity that schizophrenics sometimes withdrew into. The ultimate manifestation of this was a state that James had heard of before: catatonia, prolonged absence of any movement, not from paralysis, but from a seeming atrophy of the will to do anything, or from extreme, incapacitating fear of performing any action. She'd told James of patients locked into a posture, like a statue, which could be held for hours, days. Sometimes there would be something she'd called waxy flexibility: the patient would allow her or himself to be put into a position and would then retain it. (Dr Kavanagh, James thought grimly, certainly didn't pull any punches. She'd calmly described very regressed schizophrenics, unreachable ones, who would decorate their bodies with stamps, coins, matchboxes; others, incontinent, immobile or repeating a small repertoire of movements incessantly.)

But these were rare cases, extreme cases. Most patients were far more subtly affected, Dr Kavanagh had assured him. Adèle was a world away from those chilling, hidden, secret souls; and with luck and perseverance and hope (hope again, a word that Dr Kavanagh used as matter-of-factly as chlorpromazine, and as confidently of its effectiveness) she would never get that far. They would arrest her symptoms, relieve her of them, and they would *reach* her, persuade, cajole, draw her out; she would recover. Dr Kavanagh had explained that she believed some people needed to go through a schizophrenic period to release the unbearable tensions they'd had building up in them, perhaps from their earliest days. For some it was the only way, and the symptoms were equivalent to the itching of a wound as it healed. (She fell short of actually recommending it, however.)

Dr Kavanagh said. God, she'd better be right.

Adèle looked up from her work, smiled faintly, went back to it. He wasn't sure if she'd actually seen him or not. She was certainly not pleased to see him, nor displeased, nor surprised, nor any bloody thing he could identify.

'Adèle?' He spoke gently, absurdly anxious not to disturb her.

'I thought you weren't here,' she said, dabbing at the picture. 'But since you are, you ought to know. It wasn't me that did any of those things, it was you-know-who.' She gave him an understanding smile and, shockingly, a wink. 'I would never do anything like that.'

'Adèle?' He didn't know what to say, he had no words. 'Are they treating you OK? Del?'

She paused.

'They're treating me with treatments. What do you expect them to do? Treats. Ice-cream and black fruit, but it's all poisoned unfortunately.'

He wanted to touch her, hold her – if he touched her she might come back to him. He ached with his longing for her, but he was inhibited by the thought that perhaps touching wasn't allowed here, that a nurse would come and tell him off. He wondered fearfully how his touch might feel to her: repugnant, or worse, nothing at all. And how might she feel to him: waxy? His arm twitched futilely.

The picture was a landscape, small by Adèle's standards; she was using thick textured card instead of canvas, and water colours instead of oils. The sheep were there, wild-eyed now with terror, some seeming to try and rush out from the picture, others twisted round to look at something deep within the composition. And there was something he'd never before seen in any picture of hers: a human form. It was this figure that the sheep were turning to look at, were running from. A very indistinct shape, but unmistakably human. It seemed out of scale with the rest, though that could have been a trick of the perspective.

'Closer,' she said. 'I can almost see the face.' She wiped her hands on a cloth and threw it aside, one of the old familiar painting mannerisms. She was still there! The thought leapt about in his brain. Still there!

'So. How's the car running?'

So grotesquely inapt was the question that he laughed aloud, he couldn't help himself.

'Fine. I think the hand-brake cable's wearing a bit though.'

'Broken probably. None of the machines work properly round here, ask anyone.' She put her head on one side, reflecting, then continued.

'You see, everything's been broken and spilled out, but there's more to come, it'll all have to come out. Come out and pray, pray to be forgotten by all your sins. Do you see?'

'Adèle.'

'A secret dell, hidden in the branches. Is that where

226

you put it?' Elvis, covered in hawthorn boughs. He felt himself stiffening.

'A delicate flower, oh just thrown in the bin.'

Psychotic insight Dr Kavanagh had said, but she'd meant the implausible, nonsensical connections schizophrenics often began to see everywhere. This was real insight. Two lucky shots: would she try for a third?

'Adelts don't do that kind of thing.'

He relaxed again: just words, word salad Dr Kavanagh had called it. Words flung together, chiming meaninglessly like the door bell to a demolished house.

'Sampled the handwriting. Off the wall.'

She intangibly but quite definitely dismissed him, withdrew into the painting again. The window had closed.

James left the room. He sat in a chair in the corridor by the door, and when a nurse came smiling past he said, 'Excuse me,' and started to cry. She guided him to a small waiting room, held his hand. She arranged a cup of tea for him.

Lewyn crawled behind the sofa; Sam, blindfold, followed him on all fours.

'Baaaaaa!'

He doubled back, past the television, and out into the hall.

'Baaaaaa!'

Sam twisted his head round, locating the direction of the sound. It was a surprisingly good game, Lewyn decided, though rather hard on the knees and thigh muscles. The object was for the blindfold person to catch up and touch the other, following the sounds he made. Sam, being nimbler and having more recent experience of crawling than Lewyn, was finding it far easier and much less tiring.

James had left at ten o'clock and wasn't due back till

at least four. Six hours. Lewyn was realizing how exhausting it could be looking after an active child. Sam had wanted to see all the sheds and outhouses, with their curious cement roofs and bowed window lintels. Someone had recently asked Lewyn if he could buy them and turn them into what he described as an 'agricultural crafts museum experience', and had been greatly disappointed when Lewyn explained that he merely rented them, and all the land. His family had been in the area for generations, but suffered disaster in his grandmother's time and had to sell everything and lease it back.

Sam had had a ride in the red Massey Ferguson tractor and even held the wheel, a responsibility he had taken immensely seriously. He'd gone up the ladder into the hay loft, and been conducted round the sheds, wanting to know the names of all the objects, and what they were for. His capacity for inquisition seemed to know no bounds. His attention had been particularly engaged by a wood-handled implement hanging from a nail on the wall.

'What's that for?'

'That? He's a dibber, he's for making holes in the soil to plant things.' Sam examined the instrument, a thick shaft about eighteen inches long, pointed at one end with a crosspiece at the other to hold it with. The pointed end was sheathed with iron, studded with rivets. Sam had to use both hands to hold it.

'Baaaaaa!'

Lewyn was at the top of the stairs; Sam felt his way forward, found the bottom stair and laboriously heaved himself up.

Sam had been intrigued by the York multigym and had with Lewyn's assistance been just about able to drag down the pulley, though not with any weight on, grimacing and groaning like a power-builder. The workroom had also been thoroughly examined, every drawer and cupboard looked in, the nails and screws and drill bits named and explained. They'd played a little game where Lewyn put his hand in the vice and Sam tightened it, Lewyn pretending to be in agony.

'No no! No more. Aaaaagh!' Sam had giggled and given the handle an extra turn.

In between these technical discussions, Sam had quizzed Lewyn about Jesus and the Bible. Lewyn had been meticulously neutral in his explanations: he was prepared to say neither that it was all true nor that it was not. He felt, with Dave, that Dilys had been perhaps a touch over-zealous in her evangelism. He had confirmed that the Bible was very old and that a lot of people believed it, but beyond that he'd confined himself to don't knows and maybes.

The breadth of the child's knowledge astonished him: not just the things a seven-year-old could be expected to know, the Good Shepherd and the Sermon on the Mount, but the minor prophets, Chronicles, Kings. Sam seemed to have dipped in and out, extracting stories and names and events more or less at random, but a theme that returned several times was resurrection. Lewyn assumed this was an interest prompted by Elvis's sudden demise. If people, then why not dogs? If dogs then why not sheep, rabbits, fish? The child was perfectly innocently reducing the great revelation of life everlasting to a kind of repair shop where no form of existence was too humble to qualify for the divine treatment. Slugs? If animals, why not plants? What about grass? And if people and animals could come back *really*, with their bodies as well, then what about meat that people ate? Would it come out of their bodies and reform itself? Lewyn grew increasingly uneasy about this line of questioning and tried to steer Sam away.

'Baaaaa!' He let Sam catch him on the landing so they could swop over roles.

Sam didn't appear to be at all traumatized by his mother's abrupt departure, nor had he been upset by James's refusal to let him visit her. He placidly accepted that his mum needed a nice long rest all by herself, somewhere a long way away. He knew she was in a hospital, and that she might be there for quite some time. How long was quite some time? he'd enquired, and James had come close to an outright lie: she'd be back soon, maybe before Christmas. What was wrong with her? Another half-lie: James said the doctors didn't really know. (This was more or less true – Dr Kavanagh had been unable to say clearly what kind of disorder schizophrenia was.) James assured him that everyone would do everything they could to make her better.

Sam had not exhibited any particular distress, either, when they'd buried Elvis the previous evening. James had dug the hole, in the same corner where he'd temporarily hidden the corpse, and had wrapped Elvis in a blanket; then Sam had been allowed to watch as James covered the dog with earth. James had stood at the graveside and improvised a short speech.

'Elvis was a very good dog. He was brave and obedient and loyal. He had a good life.'

'And he never bit anyone,' Sam chipped in solemnly.

'No. Never bit anyone.'

James had been assailed by a memory of Elvis as a puppy; he'd been from a litter of nine and would have been put down if they hadn't taken him. He'd been rather undersized, and his removal from his mother at such an early age had left him shaken and suspicious. James had brought him home in a shoebox lined with an old jumper. Elvis had stood unsteadily by the hissing gas fire, trembling and groggy. The vet had given James a pipette and some vitamin solution, and he'd squeezed the fluid into the tiny, desperate mouth: he'd put a few drops on to his thumb and the sharp little teeth had closed over it, but not enough to hurt. He remembered the urgent wetness and warmth of Elvis's mouth, and, standing beside the low hummock of earth, closed his eyes. Sam watched him. James took some of the stones from the wall and put them over the grave, a low pile. Sam did the same. It seemed inadequate as a ceremony, and not for the first time James wished he could pray. Sadness rolled up in him. He took hold of Sam's hand and led him back to the house.

'Sam? It'd be OK to cry, chief.'

'Oh no it's all right,' Sam said, thinking of the Resurrection and the Life. Elvis would be back.

Lewyn allowed Sam to tie the blindfold on him, and then loosened it slightly; he watched until Sam had trundled away out of sight, arms and legs moving purposefully together. Cheating, admittedly, but there was no way on earth he was going to crawl around the house in the dark: the mere idea of it sent ripples of cold through him. He'd once woken screaming from a nightmare where he was trying to find the light switch to the workroom, feeling along the wall in total darkness, the switch gone, stumbling forward into an unknowable, endless corridor of nothing. He shuddered, reliving the annihilating, senseless, booming frenzy of that moment. After that he'd always left lights on in the hall and landing, and a lamp in his bedroom. Darkness was where the beast lived. He heard again his screams rolling through the dark, empty house, imagined hearing them from the attic, from the workroom, and his flesh tingled as he adjusted the blindfold.

'Baaaa!' Sam called, sounding some distance away, somewhere near the barn. Lewyn came after him.

*   *   *

James stopped at a Hungry Traveller. He wasn't hungry, but he felt the need to get out and walk about. Park the car. Buy something. Interact with the world on a simple, mundane level. He was in no rush to get back; the visit had been a great deal shorter than he'd anticipated, and he wasn't due to pick up Sam till four o'clock. He lingered amongst the overpriced sandwiches and cakes, ending up with a Chelsea bun and a prawn and salad roll. The woman at the checkout rang up the ludicrous prices, unblushingly asking for some outrageous sum of money, and giving him the change, without looking at him directly once. He thanked her and took the receipt: the numbers all added up in an exquisitely simple, arithmetical fashion, items and subtotal and amount tendered and change. There was no hyperbole or darkly imaginative rationalization. He folded the receipt and put it carefully into his wallet. It had become important to him to preserve such evidences of order and reason, like Galileo hugging his star charts to himself.

It wasn't just the nightmarish visit to the acute psychiatric ward that had undermined him. He reflected on the last four weeks, the bone excavation, Sam screaming, the revelations about Guy and Edith, Adèle's abrupt plunge into insanity, and then, most troubling of all, the death of Elvis.

Someone, rather than something, had killed Elvis, and it hadn't been Adèle. Not just killed him, but savaged him, blinded, mutilated him. James found it almost impossible to imagine any human being doing that to a dog. But someone had. The same person, presumably, who had performed those other monstrous violations on the sheep.

It wasn't me! James! (Click.)

He crumbled inwardly at the thought of how readily he

had believed that Adèle could have been responsible. Admittedly she had been at the scene, and she had certainly been in the grip of her insanity by then. But to accept unquestioningly that the woman he'd been living with, *sleeping* with (only hours before. Jesus!) the woman who was the mother of his children, was capable of ripping apart a living animal! What else should he have believed, though?

He could keep the thought away no longer; it bubbled up from where it had been lodged for weeks now, like marsh gas.

Lewyn.

Lewyn, who had known that James would find something buried near the septic tank, and had had that story ready about Raoul and his bonfire. Who had been struggling with Adèle on the cliffs with the still-warm carcass under his feet. Who had appeared at the house with Elvis's poor, dripping body in his arms.

Who was at this moment minding Sam.

He stood up, banging his knee against the moulded plastic table and sending a shock wave through the detritus piled on it. Hungry travellers looked up from their doughnuts and coffee and ashtrays as he barged through, a wild, unshaven man hunting frantically for the exit.

'Sam!'

Lewyn flung open the doors of sheds and outbuildings, squinting into the darkness inside. The secret, looming interiors glared back unco-operatively, as if angry at being invaded by the bright winter sunshine. He ran back to the house and searched it methodically from top to bottom, hesitating as always at the door to the basement before thrusting it open and, averting his eyes from the vanishing perspective of the stairs, fumbling blindly for the light switch.

He stood at the top of the stairs; there was nowhere for a child to hide, unless he was in a cupboard. Lewyn went down and opened them all. Nothing.

'Sam!'

He charged back up and out into the neat fenced front garden. Seventeen acres of fields, a main road, and then an unlimited expanse of cliff top. Stone walls, trees, stream beds, culverts, hedgerows. He tried to think. Sam was probably hiding as a joke, part of the game. He couldn't have got far – he was probably somewhere nearby, in one of the buildings. Lewyn returned to the barn, flicking on the dusty overhead lights one by one with the row of switches by the door. Even in full daylight the high small windows let in only a dim glow. It was a converted cowshed, still divided into stalls on both sides with a corridor between them. It had grown incrementally over a long period in an apparently ramshackle fashion, and there were numerous side rooms and additions. He examined each stall in turn with more than necessary thoroughness, kicking over impossibly small heaps of discarded and wrecked furniture. Somewhere at the back of his mind he knew that the heap of lumber was waiting for him. He was in no hurry to reach it.

'Sam! Where are you?'

His voice fell flat and dead in the rank, sunless building. He worked his way along the rows of empty and half-empty stalls, scanning methodically, furiously.

James accelerated into the stream of M4 traffic, pushing the twelve-year-old car to the limits of its capability. Every MOT it passed now was a bonus, borrowed time. Starting first go was a dim, distant memory, tinged with nostalgia and regret; the driver's door had to be lifted and levered and massaged into place, the clutch had developed a nasty, expensive-sounding grinding noise, like an old man getting his phlegm up. Reverse was sometimes, quite simply, not on the menu, not to be found however ingeniously the gearstick was manipulated. Nought to what? as the sticker said.

His understanding of a car engine was limited strictly to a kind of global overview, what part did what and how much it cost when it went wrong. Adèle had pretended to believe, only half jokingly, that the car was powered by a capricious spirit which could be placated and appeased by flattery and sweet talk, and James felt that this could almost be true.

'Come on,' he murmured furiously as the clutch coughed and ground, 'come on, you handsome, brilliant machine, you miracle of craftsmanship and high-tolerance engineering, come on you bastard!'

The lumber was stacked at the far end of one of the added-on rooms, a mighty heap of beams and boards and planks in various stages of soundness and decay. It had been there for as long as Lewyn could remember; clearing it had been one of those jobs that for various reasons got put off from one year to the next. His father had added to it every so often; it had eventually become a central repository for all the unused and unwanted timber on the farm, reaching up to the high, cobwebbed ceiling.

Lewyn could not recall a time when he had been unaware of it. It had been a part of his interior landscape, an unvisited part, for ever. Nor could he pinpoint a time when the beast had arrived and taken up residence there: it had assembled itself from the rotten, cracked heart of the pile, from the insidious, silvery threads of the dry rot, from the rough splintered surfaces. It had developed, filling up the shadowy spaces like an embryo in a womb, growing limbs that snaked up into the gaps between the pieces, growing eyes and ears. A mouth.

Lewyn leaned on the wall outside, away from it. In a minute, he told himself. I'll go in in a minute and look. Unconsciously he felt for his pulse, shifting his thumb around on his wrist, though he could feel the blood singing clearly enough in his neck and ears. It felt as if it would come spurting out at any moment, hot urgent licks from his eyes and nose.

'Sam!'

His voice was desperate, frightening in its need and hoarseness.

'Sam! Are you in there?'

His ears strained for any sound, anything at all, but all he could hear was the roaring in his sinuses and behind his eyes.

'You better come out now. I'm not kidding Sam, you could hurt yourself in there!' Hurt yourself, get your brain ripped out, be chewed into a ragged pulpy mess. His hand squeezed his groin rhythmically as he stared at the wall in front, with the knowledge that the pile was only two steps away, around the corner. He closed his eyes.

'*Sam!*'

The sound dropped at his feet; he pictured the beast sitting hunched over in the pile, his red glittering eyes flicking, grinning with his wet, raw mouth. Tired of sitting quietly, snatching the odd rabbit in the darkness, ready for juicier, tenderer meat. Listening to his frantic noises with gleeful anticipation.

In a minute, he told himself. In a minute I'll have done it and it'll be over. He counted backwards from sixty.

The two male orderlies held her arm as she shrieked and arched, writhing against them.

'I can see his face! I can see his face! I can . . .'

236

A nurse walked quickly into the day room, saw what was happening, and marched straight out again.

'. . . see his face! I can see his . . .'

The nurse returned, puncturing the seal on a small glass vial with a syringe. The two restraining the jerking, seething woman uttered small sounds, part comforting, part stern.

'Now you're fine, you'll be fine in a moment.'

'. . . FACE!'

The nurse smiled at the distraught woman, speaking loudly over her screams.

'Adèle? I'm going to give you something to make you feel better. Please try to relax.'

'No no no no no no no—'

One of the orderlies rolled up Adèle's sleeve and twisted the arm upwards. The nurse squirted the needle, expelling the air, then, holding the forearm steady, jabbed the needle into its muscle.

'Look at his face! Oh oh oh oh oh *o-o-o-o-o-h*,' the last sound a rising note composed purely of terror. Adèle's eyes were fixed on the painting in front of her, glittering pupils surrounded by bright, foamy pools of white.

The nurse held her hand, a thumb checking the pulse; she frowned at Adèle's frozen mask of fear, a rictus of desperation and horror. She slumped suddenly, held upright by the orderlies. The nurse scrutinized her, checking her eyes.

'I can see his face.'

Adèle tore her gaze away from the picture and looked pleadingly at the nurse.

'Can't you see who it is?'

The nurse smiled. She nodded at the orderlies who helped Adèle away. The nurse held her hand, talking quietly.

'You're fine now, nothing to worry about. There now.'

'. . . four, three, two, one.'

Lewyn braced himself against the wall.

'Sam?' His voice dropped to a conversational level, and the blood was dead in his veins, churning sluggishly like buttercream about to turn.

Baaaa.

He opened his eyes, feeling each individual hair stiffen on his legs in a wave. He thought his heart had stopped; his arm had adopted an absurdly unrealistic pose, slightly flexed in front of him. He tried to force all the life in him into his ears, focusing his eyes on the arm. Had he really heard it?

Baaaa. Baaaaa.

It was unmistakable, though very distant, coming from somewhere in the wide open world outside the barn. And it wasn't a child. It was sheep. Panicking.

He tore himself away from the wall and ran, imagining the creaking, splintering sound of rotten wood being clawed away as the beast, cheated of his victim, rose at last from his nest. Lewyn pounded down the length of the barn, reached the door, stumbled out into the fading daylight. He dropped the latch and sweat spilled out all over him, trickling cold behind his knees and over his stomach. He stood for a moment panting, swallowing.

Baaa.

It was coming from the top field, a faint high sound, many voices together. It was something he usually only heard in lambing season, when a dog or fox got in among the sheep. He ran down the lane, on to the road, then up across the fields. As he ran, he became aware of another sound, also high. It sounded like someone playing cowboys and Indians. A child.

* * *

James took the corners at reckless speed, sounding the horn. If anything was coming the other way it was in for a big surprise. The road twisted and wove like noodles in chop suey. And chop suey, thought James, would be an appropriate description of how he'd end up if there was anything unfortunate enough to cross his path.

He turned the last corner, horn blaring, braked, wrenched at the complaining driver's door which lurched and groaned under his clumsy hands. It wouldn't open. You couldn't open it like that. He took his hands away, clenched his fists, then gently, *gently* squeezed the handle and eased it up and over, just as he was always telling Adèle to do. Lifted it clear. The door clunked open, settling down half an inch, and he leapt out.

'Sam! Lewyn!'

He was unknowingly conscious of a commotion coming from somewhere nearby, and his legs moved in that direction, guided by something like a voice saying 'He's over there.' Instinct.

The steps down to the rocks were treacherous at the best of times, crumbling and uneven and overgrown with creeping plants. In fading light and with feet made uncertain by his hurry, Lewyn found that he was in danger of toppling over and ending up as a colourful splash on the rocks. He made himself slow down, holding on to the garish pink handrail, controlling his forward momentum. He could see the child clearly below him, struggling in the choppy dark green water.

'I'm coming!' he called. 'Hold on!' Something puzzled him for a moment, but he had no time to stop and think. He lowered himself down the zigzagging, precipitous steps until he could jump. The water was breathtakingly cold, swelling heavily, angry. He swam to where Sam was treading water, got hold of him and pulled, dragged,

239

wrenched him along, shoved him up and out, on to a rock, heaved him up, went under briefly, fought against the panic of the heavy black water. He surfaced again, shaking the tangy, sticky water out of his ears and hair, shoving some large floating shape out of his way. Sam was holding on to the rock, inching himself forward. Lewyn saw that he was safe and concentrated on getting himself out. He lay on the rock beside Sam and put his arm round him; he felt himself blacking out, then coming to, in no more than a few seconds. Sam had his eyes and his mouth clenched shut, he was breathing hard and fast. Had he swallowed much? Lewyn shouted over the booming, thundering surf:

'Sam? Are you all right?'

Sam nodded convulsively, his body going into a spasm of shock. Lewyn got a better foothold and shakily stood up, pulling Sam with him. He half dragged the boy along the rocks to the steps, then put him over his shoulder and pulled himself up one step at a time, his free arm wrenching at the handrail.

He was fifty yards across the field when James appeared, scrambling over the wall. Lewyn stood still, panting, and James landed, came forward a step, stopped dead.

14

Making Sense

There came a stage with many schizophrenics when 'they'
became 'he'. Before this they had been at the mercy of a
loose, ill-defined set of observers, plotters and arrangers,
an amorphous army who were at work everywhere setting
things up, organizing coincidences and chance events.
And then psychotic insight bloomed like a strange un-
gainly flower; the voices offstage crystallized into a single
entity, often one person, who was controlling the whole
mystifying spectacle. It was the sufferer's way of making
sense of what was happening, and could often be a good
sign. Far easier to challenge a single, coherent, if elabor-
ately structured, delusion than a chaotic hubbub of fears
and fantasies. Other less fortunate patients never reached
this stage, their beliefs becoming increasingly disordered,
often logically or physiologically impossible: their brains
had melted, for example, or their eyes belonged to
someone else.

In Adèle, Dr Kavanagh reflected, the delusive system
had become highly structured, focusing on the revelation
she'd seen in her paintings. The attack when she'd
had to be sedated had been the turning point and marked
a new phase in the course of her illness. It was Dr
Kavanagh's habit to keep a record of the patient's
statements as a narrative, from their point of view, as if
it were true. In this form the story could be examined and

the patient made aware of what was illogical or contradictory, or just downright implausible. Of course the patient had to be at a certain stage of recovery to be able to accept such an approach, and many never attained it. A badly hallucinated person, distracted by voices and accusations, often was simply unable to attend closely enough, the doctor's voice drowned out by the chorus of insinuations and whispered allegations. Adèle seemed to have been spared any overt hallucinations of this sort, though she appeared sometimes to be attending to something no-one else could hear: she would glaze over, frowning, twisting her head. Listening. Whether or not she perceived the sound to be external from her was unclear.

Dr Kavanagh reviewed her notes. So far Adèle's story ran something like this:

'I murdered my child (Ruthie) because my other child (Sam) wanted me to, as part of an experiment he was conducting. He wanted to know if he could bring someone back from the dead without killing them himself. The experiment was a failure: Ruthie didn't come back. Sam made me drown Ruthie by pressurizing me mentally. Not exactly as a voice, but I knew that was what he wanted me to do. I thought someone was shouting "drown, drown", and I interpreted that as referring to Ruthie.'

Nothing too unusual there, she reflected. A parent who had tried and failed to save her child from a fatal accident was certain to experience appalling guilt: that could often be the worst feature of the tragedy. Adèle was both accepting responsibility (she had drowned Ruthie) and blaming someone else (Sam). It was an elegant and clearly very useful mechanism.

'After we moved to Wales Sam continued his experiments. He killed a sheep, tearing off its back leg and part

242

of its hindquarters. I found the torn-off parts and hid them, in the freezer and in my studio.'

Also oddly plausible, at least the part about hiding the sheep flesh: what more logical place than a freezer? And in an artist what more characteristic response than to paint it?

'He killed the sheep to see if he could bring it back again. This also failed.

'One night I woke up and heard noises from the field. I went out and he was there with another mutilated sheep. He was trying to throw it over the cliff. He ran off when he saw me coming, and I tried to bury it for him, so that no-one would find it. But a neighbour came out and saw me. Everyone assumed that I'd done it. But it wasn't me.'

Adèle was presenting herself here as a protective, dutiful mother, sheltering her child from the consequences of his actions. She had managed to 'forget' this until she saw the child in one of her paintings, when it all came back.

There was nothing logically impossible here: there were no aliens from the centre of the earth or other unlikely agencies at work. The reasoning was – well, *reasonable*, given the outlandish premises. And, Dr Kavanagh knew from her interview with James, the mutilations had indeed occurred. Whether or not it was Adèle who had committed them was a matter for somebody else to determine; ultimately it would become a police problem. It was Adèle's interpretation of their meaning that was important here.

Adèle was due in five minutes. Dr Kavanagh closed the file and leaned back in her chair. She knew how important it was to be clear-headed and alert when talking to schizophrenics. Apart from the unreachables, the catatonics, they were characteristically highly animated and expressive, and she couldn't afford to miss any of the clues they threw out.

She cleared her head by picturing herself lying on a grassy bank with the sun shining down on her from a cloudless sky. Sheila Kavanagh, aged fifty-six, consultant psychiatrist. The other danger, and one which had tripped her up more times than she cared to acknowledge, was the sheer plausibility of much of what her patients told her. She knew of colleagues who had stumbled into the trap of entering into their patients' belief systems, finding them attractive, beguiling places, full of a kind of truth. A profoundly convinced patient could subtly undermine even the most experienced therapist, she knew. It was vital to be aware, consciously, fully, from minute to minute, of who was who. I am Sheila Kavanagh. I am fifty-six years old, a widow of ten years' standing, with a daughter who lives in Manchester. She has two children: I have their pictures here on my desk. I am a consultant psychiatrist, I work for South Glamorgan Area Health Authority. She heard herself repeating this ritual statement of self, and considered her schedule. She had a case conference at 1.15, a budget meeting at 4.00, a number of small, important chores to attend to before she drove home to her house where the toilet didn't flush properly and the stair carpet needed replacing. She dropped each item into a grey metal box, a neat row of them, and locked them all. She opened her eyes.

'Hello, Adèle. Please sit down.'

'Dr Kavanagh, it's extremely important that I go home right away. There are bad things happening there.'

Lucid, she noted. No obvious disorder of speech or thought. Appearance generally good, hair, make-up. An improvement.

'What are the bad things?'

'I know you don't believe me. I know I've been ill. But

244

I'm better now, and I've simply got to get back. Please sign the relief form or whatever you have to do. I'm ready to leave immediately.'

Relief form. Adèle was asking for help now, asking the doctor to relieve her of her suffering, make her ready to go back to her life. If there had been a relief form then Sheila Kavanagh would willingly, gladly, have signed it. If only life was like that. Adèle was presumably thinking of a release form, necessary for her to leave the custody of the hospital. A waiver of responsibility.

'I'm glad to hear you're feeling better. Won't you sit down?'

Adèle was standing by the chair, on the other side of the desk.

'Please?'

Adèle sat, clearly impatient at the waste of time involved.

'Dr Kavanagh . . .'

'You can call me Sheila if you like.'

'Yes all right, *Sheila*, you don't seem to understand. Something dreadful is about to happen, and I have to stop it.'

Impending catastrophe, the often crushing fear that some calamitous event was imminent. It could sometimes be a kind of retrospective acknowledgement of the appalling havoc the illness had brought into the patient's life. Or it could be indicative of the fear the patient had of going back to ordinary, mundane routine, after the florid protection of the illness had been removed. Either way it could be interpreted as a positive sign.

'What is it that's going to happen?'

'Oh, I've told you. Look, I know this must be hard for you to believe, but my son is extremely dangerous, he could kill somebody. I can stop him.'

The dangerous child. The part of the patient's mind

245

that had revolted, gone bad, was often perceived by what remained of their consciousness as an external thing, a person. A child, after all, was part of you in a way that no-one else could be.

'What's he going to do?'

'Well I can't be sure, but I think the next part of his experiment is going to be to kill a person himself, to see if he can bring them back. He thinks it's possible to do that, he believes it. I've told you.'

'The last time we spoke, you mentioned to me that he'd read something that bolstered that belief. Would you explain that again?'

Adèle sighed.

'There was a woman living in the house before us. She wrote something on the wall, I read part of it, it was about how her husband was killing people. I think Sam read it all, I think he's imitating what the husband was doing. He was killing people ritually, a kind of sacrifice.'

A woman locked in a room, writing on the wall of the wickedness of the world and her husband. A nearly perfect image of mental illness, Dr Kavanagh thought. *Mene Mene Tekel Upharsin*, the most significant part of which meant thou hast been weighed in the balance and found wanting. The writing by a divine hand that appeared on the wall at Belshazzar's feast. Found wanting. At the base of much mental disorder, she knew, was a poor self-image. In schizophrenics this low self-esteem had reached disastrous proportions, prompting the accusatory voices: spy, pervert, murderer.

'So this woman's husband was a murderer, and Sam is following in his footsteps? Is that right?'

'Don't you take that bloody tone with me! I'm telling you the truth for God's sake!'

The truth, the truth which no-one else could see but which was so compellingly clear to the schizophrenic.

'OK. Sorry. How are you going to stop him?'

'Well what do you think? I'll call the damn police.'

'And tell them what?'

Adèle, for the first time, paused. Sheila Kavanagh watched closely: a crack in the defence?

'I'll show them the paintings.'

She relaxed again. No, no chink of light there. Self-validating proofs were something that schizophrenics were rarely lacking.

'It's so *clear*! And the latest one – oh it's horrible. He's not going to be content with sheep for much longer, I'm sure of it. Please, please, I've got to get back.'

'Adèle, I want to ask you something. Why is Sam wanting to do all this? Why?'

'Isn't it obvious?'

'Not to me, I'm afraid, no.'

'Christ, you're supposed to be the fucking expert! Because he's *mad*!'

And there it was, that word so rarely uttered in mental institutions, that short, eloquent, painful word. If Adèle could conceive of her child as mad, then it might not be long before she could discard the projection on to her child, on to someone else's husband, and use it on herself. And if she could begin to see that it was she that was – well, 'mad' said it as clearly as any psychiatric textbook – then she would be truly recovering. Of course the realization would be agonizing, and the weight of shame and humiliation at what she had done and believed while ill would be worse than physical pain, but recovery could never be easy, not for the schizophrenic. Adèle would have to live with the memory of her insanity, her screaming, her fighting, her undignified, uncontrolled behaviour and monstrous accusations, for the rest of her life. But that was the price she would pay for her sanity. Adèle had become ill very suddenly and very intensively:

paradoxically that meant that her chances of a full recovery were better than average. It was the slow growing, slowly maturing schizophrenia – the oddly mis-named 'simple' type – that was more intractable, harder to reach. Adèle had simply dived, clean and deep, and she might even now be on her way back up to the surface.

'Tell me about your new painting.'

'Why? Are you going to let me go if I do?'

'Please. I'm interested. I understand you're preparing for an exhibition? That must be exciting.'

'You think I could exhibit those – those bloody *things*? They're sickening. Since you ask, this last one shows my son Sam dragging a sheep off to the cliff, the sheep's bleeding, the other sheep are going crazy. Oh Christ. There's someone else around now, I can't see who it is yet, but he's in terrible danger. Oh!'

'These are things that are really happening? Or about to happen?'

'Really happening, yes yes, I've *told* you.'

'I know this is hard for you, Adèle. Please be patient a while longer. How do you know these things are happening? After all you're not there, are you?'

'I don't know how I know,' said Adèle, and Dr Kavanagh detected a change in her posture, a touch of abstraction.

'Adèle? What's happening now?'

'Hold on . . .'

'Adèle?' Dr Kavanagh knew that a hallucination could sometimes be staved off if the patient's attention could be distracted out from herself, out into the real world.

'Adèle? What was your mother's maiden name?'

'Sheldon. Shhh . . .'

'What's your date of birth?'

'Birth?'

'What's your favourite food? Tell me.'

'Grass, glass, smash, crash, boom, underneath the wa-ter you shall push your daugh-ter, now she's here and now she's gone, now the devil's got his bone . . .'

'I can't understand you—'

'Tie the rocks around their feet, now the devil's got his meat, when you call their names aloud, they'll come out and join the crowd.'

Sheila stood up and knelt down in front of her, trying to catch her eye. Eye contact would sometimes bring a patient back from wherever they had gone: most schizophrenics avoided it as much as they could.

'Look at me.'

'I can't see you, I can't *breathe*, oh, oh.'

'I'm right here.'

'Oh, oh, oh, oh . . .' Adèle was panting, and Sheila took her hand and squeezed, moving her head to try to catch her attention. Adèle relaxed little by little, and Sheila felt her hand squeezing back. Gripping her. She was pulling herself out.

'Can you see me now?'

'Yes.'

'Try to relax. Breathe deeply.'

'Yes.'

'I'm going to let go of your hand now.'

'Yes. OK.'

She returned to her chair, and Adèle rubbed at her forehead, frowning.

'Have you got a headache?'

'No, not really.'

'Would you like a glass of water?'

'No thank you.' Adèle shook her head.

'OK. Just rest for a minute.'

Dr Kavanagh looked hard at the Perspex frame containing the photographs of her grandchildren, smiling, healthy children, passing exams, winning prizes at swimming galas, just discovering their strengths and talents. Self-doubt, guilt, panic – that was all unknown to them yet. Still to come.

'You know what kind of eyes he's got?'

She looked up to find Adèle's angry, knife-sharp concentration on her.

'Who?'

'You know who. Sheep's eyes, that's what he's got. The Devil's eyes. Eyes that can see in the dark. See in your head. Up here!' She tapped her temple. 'He knows all the right triggers. He's pretty advanced for seven.' There was a curious pride in her voice, the pride of a mother in her child's attainments, but mixed with dread at what those attainments were. Something rather different from cycling-proficiency certificates and grade two cello.

'He knows what he's doing. And so do I. I'm the only one who knows. If no-one stops him then he'll go on. Because he's evil.' Her voice was level and controlled now, rather flat.

'So you'd better write it all down in your file, Dr Kavanagh. Then when it's too late you can read it all and wonder why you didn't do anything about it. Some children are good, some are bad, some are mad. My child happens to be in the last category. I should know, shouldn't I? He's driven me here so I'll be out of his way, because he doesn't need me around any more. He'll probably try a different tack with James. I think he's got Lewyn fairly well in hand already. Covering all bases. It's perfect. Who would ever suspect a bright-eyed, please-and-thank-you, may-I-be-excused-please little boy?'

Dr Kavanagh studied her. How must it feel to believe, really, truly *believe* that your child was some kind of devil who controlled people's minds and tortured animals as an experiment? How could Adèle bear to believe it?

250

Again, it wasn't necessarily a bad thing: it would be so damaging, so appallingly, crushingly hard to sustain the certainty that the child you had borne, carried, fed, loved for all those years was a sadistic animal, a freak. Adèle wouldn't be able to hold on to this belief for very long. She would have to let go sooner or later, and when she did Sheila Kavanagh would be there to catch her. It would be a hard fall.

The wire had been stamped down, flattened, leaving a dip low and wide enough to step over. He'd have to replace it. There was half a roll in one of the sheds somewhere. There were tufts of wool caught on the barbs, coarse cream-coloured strands. He'd have plenty of time for mending fences now James and Sam were gone. Gone to his parents in Bristol.

'I'm sorry, Lewyn, but I just can't leave Sam here any longer. You can understand that, can't you?'

That was when he'd calmed down; Lewyn flinched from the memory of how he'd been when he arrived on the scene. Well, it was his child, you could understand it. All James knew was that his son had nearly been killed. Lewyn had been supposed to be looking after him, instead of which he'd damn nearly let him drown.

But that wasn't it. James in his rage had not hidden the fact that he believed Lewyn was involved in the incident in some way, if not directly responsible.

'I don't want to discuss it, Lewyn. I don't want to know. I'm taking him away from here, and that's it.'

'James please, listen . . .'

He clenched his eyes shut. His voice had sounded so weak, almost pleading. Had he been crying? He hadn't cried since that day in barracks, rocking back and forth with Dilys's letter crumpled in his fist, Steve Delaware sitting on his bunk with him. The end of the world.

The sheep edged around him, politely apprehensive, unconcerned at the death of three of their number the previous day. Knowing but silent, like a flock of spies or diplomats. Keeping secrets.

What had they seen? Lewyn observed them, trying to find some key to their coded impassivity. He watched for signs, for any deviation from their invariable, immemorial repertoire of behaviours. Sam had said they'd come running at him, frightened him, chased him off the cliff. Lewyn knew such a thing was impossible, and he knew that James knew it as well. Sheep didn't behave like that.

His father had kept a battered, board-bound book in the kitchen, an almanac of agricultural lore, not as a reference but as a kind of charm. It contained paragraphs on such matters as 'What tyme lambes shulde be wayned', and 'Blyndeness of shepe, and other dyseases, and remedies therefore'. Most of the remedies involved applying tar to various parts of the sheep and letting blood, and most of the symptoms, whether of 'maggottees in shepe', 'the blode in shepe', 'the pockes', or even of 'the woode evyll' were the same: hanging of the head, excitability and scratching and loss of appetite. Even in their disorders sheep were subject only to small variations from their eat-grass-and-then-go-over-there routine. 'The woode evyll' made them 'to halt, and to holde theyr necke awry'. 'The blode' caused them to 'stande stil, and hange downe the heed'. The outbreak of sturdie in his father's time had gone unnoticed for some time, simply because there again the early symptoms were barely discernible from the normal: a tendency to hold the head down and stand still. Only when the brain had been thoroughly eaten away by the flat, swollen-headed worms did they do anything at all interesting: they walked in circles and ran off cliffs.

Could it have come back then, the sturdie? He watched, looking for heads down or standing still, and saw it everywhere. That after all was what sheep did, it was their job.

As far as he was aware, sturdie was the only thing (short of demonic possession, as with the Gaderene swine) that would make a sheep run over a cliff. It was possible that the Tullians' dog had brought sturdie back, but he'd been wormed before he came and again at Lewyn's insistence after the first mutilation. The fields were harrowed and denshired in rotation, not that that necessarily prevented it: though Lewyn retained a primitive, almost druidic belief in the purifying qualities of fire, and the spectacle of a field of scorched grass and undergrowth was one from which he took great reassurance. At the end of each winter the sheep innocently licked up a phenothiazine and salt mixture from their feeding troughs: again, only a partial solution, but the best that could be managed on his budget.

In any case, he would know by now: the later stages of the infection were unmistakable. The sheep would struggle at being handled in what Mr Astley called a 'sturdie way'; their movements would become highly erratic, the inability to hold a straight course degenerating into increasingly tight circles, always in the same direction, until they fell, exhausted. They would become blind: Mr Astley had said he'd even seen them turn somersaults just before the end. The disease was also known as 'gid', for the reason that the sheep would appear to be drunken, staggering and lifting their feet high in stylized, almost dance-like steps. This 'giddiness' was also quite unmistakable.

Lewyn didn't keep a dog, primarily for the reason that however rigorous the worming you couldn't prevent the possibility of infection entirely, particularly when there was a history of parasites in the fields. Dogs would eat sheep droppings whatever you did: it was their nature. The scale of his operation in any case didn't require a dog – the sheep could be managed and moved about perfectly well by a man with a stick and an understanding of their ways. So cross-infection from a farm dog was not a possibility here.

Demons, then? His father's almanac made no mention of demonic possession, gave no indications of what to look for. He wondered what a sheep would do if possessed, and laughed. It would probably hold its neck awry and stand still. It might – perhaps – run at a young boy and drive him over a cliff, but Lewyn allowed himself to doubt it.

There was one other thing that would cause a sheep to run: fear. Fear was most marked at lambing when a ewe was quite capable of running long distances, and fast, if frightened: but she would run from, not towards, the menace to her lamb, keeping it galloping alongside her.

From, not towards.

The only explanation that made any sense was that the sheep had panicked: and if so, then they must have been panicked *by* something. Imagination was not one of the qualities for which sheep were noted. Unlike people, they didn't invent their own terrors.

Panicked then. By what?

Lewyn fingered the barbed wire, the clumps of wool slightly sticky on his fingers.

By a small boy running at them, shouting, waving a stick?

The picture came to him fully formed, Sam in his new trainers and baseball cap, whooping and charging, zig-zagging over the field, rounding them up like a show dog; they stamped, their ears up, they ran, from, not towards.

He chased them to the fence that he'd stamped down, he chased them over it, he lost his footing and fell with them. Lewyn remembered his puzzlement, that odd distraction, while he was rescuing Sam from the water: large, wet forms bobbing round near him, he'd pushed one of them away. Sheep. In the chaos of his desperation to save Sam he hadn't had time to take notice of them.

'James, it doesn't make any sense, can't you see that?'

But all James had been able to see was that his child had fallen into deep, dark, cold water and that it was Lewyn's fault. James must have believed that Lewyn had thrown him off and the sheep with him. He must think I'm a killer, Lewyn mused, fingering a discoloured, matted shred of wool, a madman. He wondered what else Sam had told him. Whose word did you take, your own child's or a comparative stranger's?

There was something else that Lewyn had wanted James to know: that he hadn't told him the whole truth when he'd said he hadn't seen anyone around at the time of Elvis's death on the rocks. Not seen: heard. Singing and chanting, a high, pure voice. A child's voice. It was this that brought him out to the top field. And a peculiar, evasive sound that he'd been only intermittently and dimly conscious of, but which now returned to him, a sound like an electricity pylon in a still field in summer. Humming.

'I don't want to hear any more, Lewyn. I think I've heard enough.'

'Listen to me, James . . .'

'*Enough*. For Christ's sake. No more.'

The look on James's face had been disgust, distaste, the look of a man who'd put his hand under a rock and found the soft, decaying, maggot-eaten body of a rabbit. The rabbit was Lewyn, a person capable of mutilating his own sheep, tearing a dog apart alive, throwing a little boy in new trainers off a cliff.

It hadn't occurred to James to question why this same man, this flyblown, sick, stinking, rotten animal, had risked his own life to save the child he had just tried to murder. James wasn't questioning, wasn't listening, wasn't thinking: he was just running, like a ewe with her lamb, from the devil. From? Lewyn thought, standing at the damaged fence. Or with?

The fuse like a lost earring in her hand, she had stood in the cold basement. The screwdriver had a red handle, with lateral ridges to make it easier to grip.

Adèle lay on her bed in the bright hospital room, staring up at the ceiling. She tried to find what preceded this scene, what had taken her first to James's toolkit and then to the freezer where the ragged, matted lump of flesh lay, damning, silent.

Silent. She fastened on the word, following a crack from the light fitting to the window. Dead things couldn't speak, couldn't make any sound, that was one of the ways you could tell they were dead. If a dead thing wanted to make itself known it would have to find another way. The light buzzed, but it wasn't going to explode now, she knew that. It was just buzzing quietly because it was full of electricity and electricity buzzed. Not even a buzz really, more of a hum.

Sam hummed. Was he full of electricity then? She dismissed the idea, finding it ridiculous. Where did such absurd notions come from? No, he hummed because he liked humming, he wasn't even aware he was doing it.

If a dead thing wanted to make itself known, wanted to be found, discovered, how would it do it? She examined this idea: also ridiculous. Dead things didn't want anything, they had gone beyond wanting. To be dead was to lie very still and not want anything. But I'm lying still and not wanting, and I'm not dead.

(If someone had hidden a dead thing but wanted it to be found . . .)

The crack disappeared at the window. She considered briefly that it might continue out into the open air outside. A crack in the air. It might be there but you wouldn't be able to see it, no-one would be able to, it would be invisible. Hidden. It could be there for ever and no-one would ever know because you couldn't see it or hear it or touch it . . .

(If someone hid a dead thing and wanted it found, how would they draw someone else's attention to it? What kind of invisible crack could you outline in the air to lead them to it?)

. . . or smell it . . .

(She blinked. She almost remembered. She'd hidden it because if anyone ever found it Sam would get into trouble. But she was disturbed by it, disgusted by it. Every time she opened the freezer to take something out she was nauseated by it. It was)

. . . or taste it.

(*sickening*)

At last she had it. You could let it rot so that someone would say, for God's sake what's the *hum* in here, it smells like something died in here, where's it coming from, well I never, look what I've found in the freezer.

And if that didn't work you could let it get so good and rotten that it spilled out its rottenness on to everything else, so that finally something you ate, something that had touched it, been touched by it, made you sick. That's what you could do.

She blinked again. That's what someone had done.

What she, in fact, had done. What she had forgotten about (it had just flitted away somehow).

Jesus. There were other cracks in the ceiling. What else had she forgotten?

She pondered.

15

Apples

They crossed the Severn Bridge, the astonishing audacity
of its design a revelation in the winter sun. It seemed to
be held up by force of will as much as anything, the great
pillars and wires merely a nod towards an appearance
of structural soundness. Wales fell away behind them,
separated by the broad expanse of water spanned by this
fragile, tenuous cage of steel and faith. James felt the
oppression of the last few weeks vanishing, as the low sun
flickered through the struts. He breathed more easily, and
something in his shoulders fell a bit further, relaxing after
weeks of being screwed up tight. Sam sat sullenly behind
him watching the cars: he liked spotting Beetles. James
tried not to think about what they were heading for.

The phone call to his mother had been short and
heavily loaded. He said merely that he and Sam would
be coming to visit, and that they might want to stay for a
while, maybe a few weeks. And Adèle? No, she wouldn't
be coming. A pause. Well it'll be tremendous to see you,
James. When should we expect you?

He'd also rung Sebastian: the work would be held up
for a while. Oh, sorry to hear that. How long? James had
shrugged down the phone. A few weeks? He had no idea
how he was going to finish it. He suspected he probably
wasn't going to. Nothing wrong I hope, Jamie? No no,
just a week or so, a break for Christmas. Work going well,

is it? Oh, oh yes, very well. A week or so away and then he'd be right back on it, finish well on schedule, maybe even early. He knew the final cheque wouldn't arrive until it was all done to Sebastian's satisfaction, which, by the look of things, would be never. Sebastian might even demand some of his advance back. Already spent.

('Beetle!' Sam yelled, forgetting his mood, as a car drew level with them, packed with people and children and dogs. The children made faces and screamed; Sam watched them with a disapproving tilt to his mouth.)

Ah well. What had gone had gone, what was to come was unknowable. But for the moment, suspended in the air between two countries, flying through the steel spider's web of someone else's genius for optimism, James was happy.

There was a moment of shock as the two old people coming down the drive turned into his mother and father. They were so small, so grey, so ancient! It had been only three years since he'd last seen them, but the picture he carried around in his mind had been taken at least a decade ago. It was then that he'd told them about Adèle, about the Ruthie that was soon to be; that there was to be no wedding.

Salad and cold meat in the kitchen. Sam politely but firmly declined the meat, and grated cheese was finally produced instead.

'You'll never get to be big and strong like your daddy if you don't eat your meat,' James's father admonished him, and his mother clucked her agreement. This vegetarian nonsense was doubtless one of Adèle's silly fads. Sam looked to James for support.

'Dad?'

'It's OK Sam. You don't have to eat it if you don't want it.'

'Go on Sam. Have a little taste. Just for your grandma.'

'He doesn't want it. Neither do I.' Solidarity, thought James.

'No wonder he's looking so pale. You're not looking so well either, Jamie. Human beings were designed for meat-eating, you know. I saw a programme.' His father's voice.

'Yes, and they were also designed to eat cheese!'

'Oh, James.' His mother shook her head.

Opening shots, James knew.

As soon as his plate was clear Sam asked to go to bed: it was early yet but he could legitimately claim to be tired from the drive. He had the tiny guest bedroom, the old nursery, at the front. It was too small. The light from the street shone in, and the curtains didn't quite close. He didn't like it.

James sat with his parents in the newly carpeted front room, watching the new 28-inch colour television. It had teletext and special speakers, the purpose of which were unclear to James, except that they made it louder. The chair he sat in, part of an immense suite including footstools and corner units, was limitlessly comfortable, deep and enveloping. Neo-gothic in design, it all but had flying buttresses. The arms ended in protuberant knobs the size of a baby's head, supported by scrolled and fluted columns. The suite was also new: Ray had taken an early retirement and a lump sum from the factory where he'd risen, over forty-two years, to the lonely eminence of Supervisor. Evie now worked part-time at a teashop in town: on her first day they'd put a mop in her hand and asked her to clean out the toilets – calmly, implacably, she had declined, and after the first week they dropped the subject. She was not a woman to be swayed.

James felt drowsy, as he always did after driving. The

heating was on, an ornate log-effect gas fire that he remembered from way back. One of the bars on the grille had been twisted when he'd thrown a tennis ball at it in sheer, white-hot frustration. It was still twisted.

One hot day in the university library, James had stumbled on a book of surrealist poetry, simple nonsense for the most part, but one line had stuck in his head:

'No-one said apples for nearly a minute.'

Well here they all were and no-one was saying apples, saying it in the clearest and loudest of voices. Evie had a striking clock – it struck all four quarters, based on Big Ben. It was a mournful, underwater sound, one that James had heard at odd times of the day and night all his young life. The chimes could be turned off with a switch on the face, and then the absence of them would become somehow even more disruptive; you grew tense waiting for them, you expected them at every moment. They were usually left on, even when next door hammered on the wall.

James sat waiting for the chimes, sinking further into the capacious maw of the scarlet and gold upholstery, thinking apples, apples, little green fucking apples.

'Hello little 'un,' Maurice Partridge called over the fence. Sam looked up and saw a white-bearded, white-haired man standing in the next-door garden.

'Who are you, then?' he asked, as Sam stood bashfully holding on to the washing-line prop.

'Sam Tullian,' said Sam, fiddling with the prop.

'Tam Sullian eh?'

'No. *Sam Tullian*,' Sam said, a little louder.

'Tha's what I said. Tam Sullian.'

Sam surveyed him seriously.

'Whatcha doing then, Tam?'

'Nothing.'

'Must be doing *something*.'

'Not really.'

'Oh. Wanna see a frog, do you?'

Sam shrugged. He'd already seen a frog.

Maurice Partridge lifted him over the fence and plonked him down in the middle of an ornamental forest of small shrubs and conifers. Everywhere he looked there were things growing, banked up along the fences and arranged in beds. A line of stepping stones snaked through the immaculate grass, disappearing behind a screen of roses on a trellis, still flowering, pink and yellow. The pond was at the far end of the garden, fringed with low climbing plants. Sam's shadow fell over the water, surmounted by the shadow of Maurice Partridge. Sam could see no frog.

Maurice said 'Wait a mo,' and retired to the shed behind the rockery: before he came back a fountain sprang into life in the centre of the pond, and a waterfall began to gather strength on a raised shelf, dribbling and then gushing. Sam was astonished.

'Maybe that'll wake him up,' said Maurice, returning to the pond. 'He likes a bit of a splash.'

Sam concentrated like crazy, but there was no frog.

'Ah well, maybe he's gone for a bit of a stroll,' Maurice said at last. 'Got a lot to do, frogs have. Never mind.'

'I better go back,' said Sam. 'My dad shouts if I go wandering off.'

'Quite right. You on your holidays are you?'

'No. I don't think so,' said Sam. 'We were but I don't think we are now.'

'Oh. Ah well, better get you back over that fence then, eh? Mind out for the plants now. They don't like people trampling all over them.'

'How do you know?'

'They told me.'

'Oh.'

Maurice lifted him up and lowered him over on to the cement path that ran up both sides of the desolate, scrubby turf on the other side of the fence.

'Tam. Tam Sullian,' said the bearded man, and went back to his gardening. There was something about that child: holding him was like holding a sackful of puppies. There was a lot going on in there. The fountain splashed on, suggesting hot days and leisurely afternoons.

Evie Tullian watched from the kitchen window. She hadn't spoken to Maurice or Joan Partridge for twelve years, and she wasn't about to start now. She'd have to have a word with James.

A week later James was ready to explode. His stomach was a clenched fist, his mouth was zipped tight shut, pulled up at one corner. His shoulders were aching again.

Incredibly, no-one had yet asked him where Adèle was. Conversation was strictly a matter of local affairs and table talk. You're never going to leave that lovely bit of ham? Finish it all up now Sam, just for me. There's a bit more if anyone wants it. You got to eat, James.

On Sunday evening Evie was driven by Ray to choir, and fetched back an hour and a half later: other than that the evenings were long and unbroken by any respite from the enormous television with the special speakers. Sam stayed mostly in his room writing in his exercise book, and James sat, deadened, aching, clamping his teeth amidst the suffocating, too-soft furnishings. Whoever cracks first it won't be me, he thought grimly. As sure as God made . . .

One day Sam sidled up to him, coyly, tugging at his sleeve. James followed him upstairs to the cupboard-sized room: Sam pointed to the bed. It was wet.

'Dad? When are we going back to Wales?' he whispered.

Back to Wales. Between the devil, James reflected, and the deep blue sea there was only a very fine line, a tenuous web of steel.

Sam had been in danger in Wales. James had felt it very strongly. Whatever, whoever it was that was carving up the animals had its eye on Sam too. Early on Adèle had said she'd felt something in the field, had asked him to stop digging. He'd laughed at her. Soon after Sam had had his fit in the trench. He'd been painting burning buildings, apocalyptic visions of peril and chaos. How much he'd been affected by Adèle's incipient madness was impossible to gauge: Dr Kavanagh assured him that schizophrenia was not genetically transmitted, there was no schizophrenic gene. True, children with two schizophrenic parents stood at greater risk of developing it than other children. But how much was nature, how much nurture? Dr Kavanagh had shaken her head. So little was known.

Something had got to Adèle, some unsettling tremor, triggering off her disorder. Could it have got to Sam also? (Lewyn, who had lived there all his life. Had it got to him?)

No, with a hundred and fifty miles of distance between them, James felt certain that Lewyn was not responsible for those gruesome, bestial mutilations. He didn't believe it, not any more. There must have been someone else wandering about, a local who'd been worked on by whatever it was Adèle had felt in the field. James pictured a slavering, semi-human form hunched over the still-warm corpse of a sheep, feeding.

If Lewyn had been right about Raoul Charpentier's bonfire, then Raoul had himself been such a creature, murdering wife, children, anyone who happened along.

Had he somehow returned? James shook his head. No. That was all a long time ago. Raoul was in another country now, or dead.

Who was that by the hole?

Could the sheep themselves have been somehow affected, driven mad, savage, murderous? Killer sheep from hell. Coming soon to a cinema near you. James laughed aloud.

Well whatever, whoever it had been, it hadn't been Lewyn. Lewyn had pulled Sam out of the sea, saved his life. How could it also have been Lewyn who'd caused him to fall? It didn't make sense. Lewyn had tried to tell him this before they left. James struggled with it, gave up. Maybe it was the devil. That was as good an explanation as any.

The Christmas tree was duly erected and decorated, exactly seven days before Christmas Day. It was the same tree and lights and balls that James remembered from his childhood. It was placed, as ever, on a low table behind the television, where it sat diffidently, inconspicuously, lit up only to check that the bulbs were working, then again for an hour on Christmas Eve. Its principal function seemed to be to reinforce Ray's belief that it was a fire hazard: he would glare at it nervously from time to time, as if expecting it at any moment to burst into flames. He checked before retiring for the night that it was un-plugged. He checked first thing in the morning. He sternly lectured Sam that he must never go near it. And he lectured James on the importance of keeping Sam away from it. All his life James had been frightened of fires at Christmas.

Walking down Park Street, James was considering what present was suitable for Adèle. He'd bought his parents his and hers bath towels, which would lie under the inflammable green plastic tree alongside Sam's present, a stripped-down budget version of the games system he wanted. It was the best he could do, and anyway he was in no frame of mind for Christmas shopping. The windows of every store were jammed solid with things that Sam needed – urgently – to examine for very short periods of time just in case he saw something better than what he was expecting to get. Gifts for wives, husbands, fathers in exuberant, costly profusion, but gifts for schizophrenics?

According to the (highly selective) reports from the hospital, Adèle was stable and responding well to her drug régime. The four daily injections of chlorpromazine were now reduced to one single dose, and the side effects were minimal. What Dr Kavanagh described as the extra-pyramidals, the EPSEs, were taking their toll, however, causing Adèle some stiffness in the joints, particularly in the wrists, which was obviously an impediment to her painting. Dr Kavanagh spoke of 'encouraging' results from the psychotherapeutic sessions, but was unable to predict when Adèle would be sufficiently recovered to resume her life.

James knew that he wasn't getting the full story here. Dr Kavanagh believed in maintaining close links between the patient and the family, but that didn't mean telling them everything. She had chosen to withhold Adèle's extraordinary accusations against Sam, believing that they wouldn't serve to make Adèle's return to her family (whenever that might be) any smoother. James was reluctant to visit her again, and ashamed of his reluctance. He had abandoned her, as much as she had abandoned him, and try as he might he couldn't think of going to see her as anything other than a distasteful chore to be put off for a while, like clearing out the back of the car. Besides, nothing very useful was to be hoped for from his visits, he felt: Adèle seemed only to be able to see him tangentially, obliquely. She slid away somehow, a chunk of ice shattering on a frozen pond.

But he had abandoned her, oh yes, he had handed her over to the approved social workers and the psychiatric nurses, to that curious, menacing tribe of professionals and semi-professionals who James thought of as feeding on the mentally ill like flies on meat. Even though he knew he couldn't manage her, he felt that he should have tried, tried harder, longer. Maybe he could have brought her round, snapped her out of it. He was harassed and made miserable by the thought that he could have done more. He knew her better, in all probability, than anyone else on earth. She was almost a part of him. And he'd prosaically signed the admission form, handed her over. She had been received as matter-of-factly as a registered-delivery parcel.

Betrayal. He wondered if he would ever feel the same about her now that he'd done that, if she would feel the same about him. Ten years, and then a flick of the pen on a hospital admission form. Here you go. She's all yours now. You try.

So what kind of Christmas present was applicable in these circumstances? Everything he saw in the crowded shops seemed designed for people whose lives were not hedged round with guilt, betrayals, unfathomable disorders of the heart and mind; there was nothing that was adequately serious.

They sat on a bench on College Green, watching the streams of people parading up and down Park Street. Sam, whose present was now bought, wrapped and ready to be positioned under the perilously combustible tree – though still nominally a secret – was taking only an academic interest. He would buy his mum some small, randomly selected item of marginal utility and low cost later on. He had other things on his mind.

James was very conscious of how much Sam hated Bristol. The bed-wetting was now a regular occurrence, and he'd noticed other things: a tendency to stay, alone, in his room, a habit of silentness, a general state of inactivity and lethargy. Sam, he knew, wanted to go back to Wales. Back to the fields and cliffs where some subhuman thing, some devil, drooled and gibbered over animal carcasses.

And, to his astonishment, James found that he did too.

He'd tried to speak to his parents the previous evening. The tag on the bath towels would have to say From James and Adèle, and the thought of that had set him off. Ten minutes into the Scene South-West News, over a piece about a sponsored abseil, he'd opened his mouth and spoken.

'Adèle's in hospital. In Cardiff. She's got schizophrenia.' It sounded ludicrously melodramatic, but he was damned if he was going to go hinting and suggesting, using the enormous vocabulary of euphemisms that surrounded the mentally ill, like the forest of thorns that grew round Sleeping Beauty's castle. Had some problems. Couldn't cope. Needed a rest. No, let's call an apple an apple here.

He was reminded of the way people had responded whenever Elvis had had wind (which had been often). Slight shifting motions, legs crossed the other way, throats cleared. Or the kinds of things people did between movements at a symphony concert. (Del had dragged him to Mahler's Fourth once, early in their courting. They'd both left after the second movement. Before the fat lady sang.)

His dad spoke up.

'We're very sorry to hear that, James. Very sorry indeed.' Oh you liars, James thought between clenched teeth. Wasn't it a validation of their dearly cherished, unshakable belief that Adèle was unsuitable? That he should have found someone more his own kind? He wanted to shock them further, provoke them into an honest reaction.

'She's on the acute psychiatric ward. Along with the killers and the psychos.' He was shaking.

'Oh Jamie.' His mother's voice; the one she used when he was fourteen and owned up to taking money out of her purse for fireworks, when he was seventeen (seventeen for God's sake!) and she'd found a *Mayfair* under the rug in his room. When he was twenty-two and told her he'd met someone, a girl . . .

'Oh Jamie.' After everything we've done for you, and this is how you repay us. We hoped for better.

'Schizophrenia? That's when you think you're two different people, isn't it?' Ray might easily have been discussing various grades of adhesive at the factory.

'I don't know. Not in Del's case, anyway.'

'Schizophrenia? Yes, you think you're two different people. I saw a programme on it.'

There it was, the guillotine. Ray had seen a programme. End of discussion.

'Oh Jamie.'

Haven't you got any knitting to do, he thought viciously.

'Incurable, isn't it?'

'Her doctor says people get over it sometimes.'

'Yes well *doctors*—'

'Why don't you say what you think, Dad? Why don't you say we knew all along, we warned you but you wouldn't listen. Why don't you say well I always thought it was a bit suspicious about Ruthie's accident, I always thought she wasn't a fit mother . . .'

'Hey, hey, I don't have to listen to this . . .'

'. . . and what about Sam, he must be mad as well, it's hereditary, I saw a fucking . . .'

270

'You just . . .'

'. . . *programme!*'

'. . . listen to *me* for a minute!'

The last word, always. James stood up, his face was twitching, his body was burning with adrenaline. Fight or flight: he flew.

''Tis the season to be jolly, tra-la-la-la-laaaa . . .' blared the speakers from the Rotary Club Christmas tree by the Watersheds.

'Dad?' Sam said, critically studying the plywood sleigh, and James's heart contracted.

'When are we going back to Wales?'

The next day was the day before Christmas Eve. James was sitting in the back garden with gloves and scarf. Sam sat beside him. That was another thing James had noticed: Sam, when he wasn't holed up in his room, was becoming increasingly dependent, almost clingy. They were playing I Spy, having to work hard at it because apart from 'g' (grass) and 'c' (cement) there was nothing very much *to* spy. And Sam didn't seem to be getting 'cement'.

'Something beginning with 's',' said James in frank desperation. He was thinking of 'sky'.

'Hello there!'

James looked up: a late-middle-aged man with a beard like Jehovah. Maurice Partridge.

'Jamie, isn't it? Well well well!'

'Hello Mr Partridge.'

'And the little 'un, I forget what he's called now . . .'

'Sam,' said Sam, carefully.

'Tha's 'ee. Tam. Tam Sullian.'

'No. *Sam.*' Sam couldn't understand why he kept getting it *wrong*.

'Long time no see, Jamie. How's it going?'

'Yeah, all right, not so bad you know.'

'Dad, can I go in now please?'

'Yes, off you go you little horror,' said Maurice, and Sam disappeared, with some dignity, into the house.

'You keeping well Jamie?'

'Fine.'

'And that scarlet woman you took up with? That Jezebel?' Maurice smiled. He had overheard enough to know all about 'James's woman'.

James laughed, then the laughter caught in his throat, he swallowed and blinked, his lower lip trembled.

'Yeah, she's . . .'

He hung his head as the tears ran over his face.

'. . . she's *fine*.'

'Oh son. Don't take on now.'

James approached him, wiping his nose with his gloved hand, feeling about eleven years old with his first dead hamster. Maurice put his arm over the fence and patted his head.

'Not gone and had a row, have you?'

'No, no . . .' James blubbered, snuffling indecorously.

'Not gone and left you, has she?'

'No.'

'Oh now. There now. Don't you take on.'

James heaved silently, resting his head on Maurice Partridge's arm.

'Can't be as bad as all that.'

'Don't know what to do!' James sobbed, and Maurice stroked his head, crooning as he'd always done in the past.

From the kitchen Evie watched, her face a mask of granite. Sam stood at the top of the stairs, eyes closed, humming.

'Whatever it is, you can't run away from it,' Maurice said; James, embarrassed and wet-nosed but steady again, shook hands over the fence, remembering only at the last minute that the glove he was proffering was besmeared with the slimy fruits of his grief. He laughed and, with some difficulty, they shook hands, right to left.

Evie turned suddenly, dropping a glass, ran to the stairs, screamed: James crashed into the house seconds later, and looked where she was looking. Sam lay in a heap at the bottom of the stairs, his limbs twisted awkwardly under him; he wasn't moving.

'Sam.' James whispered the word, breathed it as if with his final breath, and the boy stirred and opened his eyes. He sat up, and James approached him with the same nameless, inexplicable dread he'd felt that other time, when Sam had sat up on the kitchen table. *Who was that by the hole?*

'Did I fall down again?' Sam said, and James turned and looked at his mother.

'Do you know anything about this?'

Three hours later they were out of the house and driving, Sam once again asleep on the back seat; as they neared the toll for the bridge James realized that he'd left Sam's Christmas present under the deathtrap tree. He shrugged mentally. It could stay there for eternity for all he cared, and if it and the tree and the neo-gothic furniture burned to a fucking crisp then he for one would not be sorry. Whatever happened he would never return for it.

They were going back to Wales.

Something Missing

At eight-thirty the next morning James opened the front door to a healthy-looking girl of (he guessed) about seventeen; she wore jeans and a quilted jacket.

'Yes?'

'Pauline. Pauline Hughes. Mrs Parrish sent me over.'

'Who?'

'You are Mr Tullian, are you?'

'Yes.' No question about that one, even if it was a bleary eight-thirty a.m. on Christmas Eve. Then he remembered.

'Oh. Dilys's niece. Pauline.'

'Tha's it.' She smiled, with exaggerated patience.

'Shall I come in then?'

'Yes of course.'

He made her a cup of coffee and she cheerfully answered his questions. Twenty years old, student at Sheffield Poly, training to be a physiotherapist. Home for Christmas. Dilys had rung her late last night, straight after James's call from the phone box in Fishguard, and she'd agreed there and then. She hated Christmas, couldn't stand the thought of sitting in with her parents (amen to that, James thought); she'd looked after her two brothers and sister since she was twelve. Loved children, but she wanted to wait a while before she had any. She wanted to travel round America, and a young child would be a distinct liability. Besides, she hadn't met anyone yet who she thought was a realistic candidate for splashing about in the gene pool with. She was looking for someone intelligent, ferociously handsome, hairy and with a big nose.

'Oh and in case it was about to cross your mind, Mr Tullian, forget it. I'm not interested in older men.'

James was shocked for a moment, then laughed.

'Well, I'm not interested in fucking the baby-sitter either, if it comes to that. I've got enough to worry about as it is.'

'Yes, well I'm sure you'll sort it out,' she said, regarding him firmly. Whatever it is, please don't feel you have to burden *me* with it, her face said. This is business. Four pounds an hour, eighty-thirty till six.

'OK. I think you'll probably do.'

'Why *thank* you, Mr Tullian. Do you want to introduce me to your pride and joy? Oh and by the way, I don't cook.'

'Neither do I.'

'Tough.'

Half an hour later she was marching purposefully off along the cliffs, with Sam in her wake. If she knew anything about children it was that you tired them out before they got a chance to tire *you* out. Pre-emptive retaliation. She waved goodbye and disappeared around a corner.

Dilys had also rung Lewyn.

'Guess who's coming back to Ty-Gwyneth?'

Lewyn had had a strange moment of confusion – Edith was gone for good, surely?

'James Tullian that's who, and little Sam.'

'James? He's in Bristol.'

'Not any more my darling. He's come back. Couldn't

275

keep away from us 'parently. I think there might have been a spot of bother with his parents, but he's not saying. Anyway, back he is. I thought you might want to know.'

And so, when James came up the path the next morning, Lewyn was waiting for him.

'James.'

'Lewyn.'

Lewyn looked away and flicked his stick.

'Lewyn, I owe you an apology.'

'Nothing to 'pologize for James.' Lewyn's heart was beating, fast.

'Well let me say it anyway. I more or less accused you of trying to murder Sam. For Christ's sake! I was out of my mind, Lewyn, I wasn't thinking . . .'

'Understand that,' Lewyn mumbled, and felt the blood rising to his cheeks.

'It was inexcusable. I'm sorry.'

'Handsome of you to say it. No harm done.' Lewyn looked at him. 'Good to have you back, James.'

Now where have I seen that look before, James wondered, and was suddenly back in the university sports centre, staring at his reflection in the open glass door of a shower stall. A decade ago, before Adèle, before Ruthie or Sam, a sleek wet young man of twenty-one, smiling at something. And now he remembered what.

He'd been swimming, and when he came in to change, his wet feet slapping the tiled floor, he had the place to himself. He was abruptly taken with the idea of stripping off his Speedos and walking around naked. Usually he would have slipped into one of the changing cubicles, wrapped a towel discreetly round his waist, removing it in the stall and hanging it over the door. He wasn't generally speaking a man for public nudity.

He stood, irresolute, in the middle of the tiled room: then he pulled off the Speedos and walked to the sinks, very conscious of the weight and swing of his newly-liberated genitals. He danced in front of the mirror, raising his arms above his head, punching the air.

'Christ Almighty!'

He whirled round and standing in the doorway was a figure, a man, watching him. The man met his eye, flicked down his body and then met his eye again. Looked. James cupped his hand over his cock, and his hand registered the pulsing of the blood: he was semi-erect. The man leaned against the door post, completely at ease, unhurried.

James had thought: well, I could. I could smile, say hello, get chatting. I could arrange to meet later, have a drink, go back to his room. I could. The moment had stretched out, becoming eerie and unsustainable. The man in the doorway shifted his weight, then walked to one of the changing cubicles. James went to the shower, now decently veiled in his white towel, and the hot water massaged and caressed him, playing up and down his body.

And he smiled at the thought that his life could just then have taken a completely different turn, that he could have become a new person, a person different from anything he'd imagined before.

I could. Could I?

He met Lewyn's eye, seeing there a strong vigorous image of something, an image of a new James with a new set of ideas and imperatives, a new love, one that wasn't Adèle. Lewyn was close, reachable, warm: he was solid.

'How's the little 'un?' said Lewyn, to break the charged silence.

'Oh fine. He had a fall, but you know what children are like. He's pretty resilient.'

'James I don't know how to say this, so I'll just come out with it. I'm a bit worried about Sam.'

James stiffened. Lewyn ploughed on.

'There've been a couple of little things, nothing really I suppose, but it's been on my mind.' He gave a short, colourless description of the sounds he'd heard, the sounds that had brought him out to the top field to find Elvis splattered on the rocks. The game he'd seen Sam playing: throwing plastic animals off the cliff and calling them back. His feeling that Sam had deliberately given him the slip while they were playing Sheep: the impossibility of Sam's account of the sheep rushing him. James listened, pulling at his ear.

'Lewyn, there's obviously something around here, I don't know what it is. I would have thought you'd know more about it than I do. From what you've told me, there's been a lot of funny business in the area. Whatever it is, it started before we got here. Sam's a little boy, Lewyn: he's seven years old. You've never had any children, have you?'

'I think you know I haven't James.'

'Well, if you had, I don't think you'd be saying what you seem to be saying. Sam's mother has had a major breakdown. I think it would be surprising if he didn't show a few signs of stress. Don't you?' James worked hard at keeping his tone level. Lewyn looked away.

'Aye. I'm sure you're right James. I just thought I should mention it. No offence.'

'None taken. I know you can't afford to lose sheep, I know you've got a business to run here. But Sam isn't your problem. Believe me. And however it was he ended up in the sea, I'm here to make sure it doesn't happen again. I've got a job to finish, and I intend to finish it. Sam is going to be supervised every minute of every day until we leave, and whatever is trying to get him, it won't succeed. I'm his father.'

'Aye.' Lewyn smiled again. 'Well anyway, good to have you back, as I say.'

'Thanks, Lewyn. And if you feel like risking it, you could come over later and have your tea. I don't suppose my cooking can be any worse than what you've had before.'

'Aye. You may be right there.'

'In fact, come to think of it, what are you doing tomorrow? Christmas Day, in case you'd forgotten.'

Lewyn hadn't forgotten. He would usually go to Dilys and Dave's, and suffer Dilys's tortured vegetable version of Christmas dinner.

'Nothing too much.'

'Right then. Come round about seven. Mind you, seeing Sam at Christmas might just confirm your worst fears. He can become a bit of a monster!'

'Well, I'll take my chances.' They shook hands, and Lewyn watched him as he went down the path.

They walked for half a mile before Sam showed any signs of tiredness, and the Stumble Head monument seemed a good place to rest. Sam laboriously read it, then asked Pauline to explain it to him.

'This tablet, they mean stone, erected means put up, eternal memory, that means remember for ever; pious souls, pious means good, souls means—'

'I know what soul means.'

'OK. Those pious souls who joined the Heavenly Choristers: means dead people.'

'To remember for ever the good souls of the dead people?'

'Tha's it.'

'Oh.'

Pauline sat with her back to the stone and Sam, after a certain amount of fidgeting, sat beside her.

He looked around. This would do. In the next field were a flock of sheep, cropping diligently. There were a number of hay-feeders lying around. Yes, this would do fine.

'I want to play a game,' he said.

James returned to the house. He walked around, quietly, afraid somehow of disturbing the silence in it. His footsteps seemed loud, the boards creaking under his feet. He went from room to room, ending up in Adèle's studio. There was a canvas on the easel against the window, an unfinished landscape. He looked at it for a while, searching for clues. Adèle had been mad when she'd painted it, but it seemed so controlled, so sober. Almost banal, just fields and trees and sheep. He found himself studying one of the trees: there was something odd about it. He couldn't concentrate, it was too quiet. He gazed out of the window, distracted, thinking about Lewyn and the look he'd given him, like a surprising but long-expected Christmas present, something he'd always wanted but never known.

Sam's game was a simple one. The idea was to drag the hay-feeders, four of them, into a straight line along the cliff top. They were on wheels, and Pauline, having first extracted a promise from him that he'd help her put them back again afterwards, was happy to co-operate: Sam seemed as intent on exhausting himself as she was. The grass beneath was yellowed and flattened, and the wheels were rusty, stiff to begin with, but surprisingly easy to move when they'd cleared the weeds away from under them.

Once in place, Sam assigned the roles.

'I'm a fox. You're the shepherd. All the sheep are eating out of the hay things, and I'm trying to get them.

So you've got to chase me round. OK? And I keep hiding. OK?'

Pauline assented. In her experience a running-round game was always fixable so that it was the child who did all the running.

'OK fox. I'll give you ten seconds to hide. Then I'm coming after you.'

Sam waited until he was satisfied that her eyes were really shut, then ran behind the hay-feeders, on the cliff side, and hid. This would be a good game.

There was a patch on the wall of the small shed, the opposite of a shadow, because it was lighter than the surrounding wall. At the top of it there was a hook. It could have been the mark where a large crucifix had hung, a large rather crude crucifix. Lewyn looked at it: he'd never hung any crucifixes up, and certainly not in the sheds. He couldn't understand it. He traced the outline with his finger.

He went over to the barn, switched on the overheads, glanced around. Something was different, there was a quality to the dusty, shadowy interior that had never been there before. No, the other way round – there was something missing, an absence of something, like the paler patch where the cross had been in the shed. He walked through the barn, his feet taking him straight and sure to the room where stood the pile of lumber. The timbers seemed to have shifted, settled, collapsed.

Yes. It was as he'd suspected. The beast was loose.

'Gotcha!' She lunged at him and he ducked away, laughing harshly. He ran between two of the feeders, squeezed himself through and hid again. She would have to go all the way round. She sighed. Sam was a bit too good at this game for her liking: she felt like a veteran tennis player being given the run-around by a Californian upstart with a ponytail. Oh well, five minutes more and then she'd suggest another game, one you could play sitting down. Something a touch more cerebral. Like pretending to be asleep.

'Mrs Lucas tells me you've stopped painting,' said Dr Kavanagh, regarding the composed, alert figure in front of her. She had been conscious, as soon as Adèle had walked in, of a change. Something had been resolved, sorted out.

'Yes. I've finished now.'

'That seems rather a pity.'

'Oh, I'm going to carry on. But not until I get out of here. What I mean is, I'm finished for now.'

'I see.' Dr Kavanagh produced her lovely, brilliant smile. 'You're looking very well, Adèle. You look different somehow.'

'Do I? Well, I feel a lot better. You see I can remember now. Everything.'

'Would you care to tell me?'

'Certainly.'

Dr Kavanagh listened, hard, to the story. Adèle was fluent, unemotional but not flat, lucid. She spoke clearly and without hesitation. Were it not for the extraordinary nature of the subject matter, Dr Kavanagh would have had difficulty in finding any disorder of any kind. She sat back, attending.

Pauline looked around. Where was he, the little bugger? He'd wriggled back between the feeders, and by the time she'd got to the other side he was nowhere to be seen.

'Sam?'

The sheep in the next field jerked up their heads with one accord, as if on strings, as hands shot out from the hay and grabbed her hair and she screamed: then the hands yanked her head down on to the sharp, rusty edge of the metal dividing plate, yanked again. She slumped into the feeder bleeding from the forehead, and Sam fought his way out from beneath her. Damn. Another one ruined. The blood was running into her hair and over the hay. He tried to drag her out of the feeder but she was too heavy. Damn bloody damn, as his dad would say. Then he had an idea. He went round to the back of the feeder and, bracing himself, heaved with all his strength. The wheels were stuck fast. Damn. He heaved again, and this time the wheels shifted; another heave, and the thing was in motion. The grass in the field was cropped right down in the thorough-going manner of sheep, who finished off the last inch and a half or so of what the cows left, so there was no resistance. The feeder trundled squeakily along, with Sam grunting and groaning behind it, then the front wheels went over the edge: Pauline was towards the front and her weight overbalanced it after a moment of inertia. It toppled, crashing down the rocky slope, dragging a small avalanche of loose chippings behind it. It smacked the sea with a great reverberating boom; Sam peered over the edge, and was satisfied. The sheep blinked, then went back to work.

Sheila, alone again in her office, finished her account and sat back, looking at the pictures of her grandchildren. She picked up the papers and read them through.

'The first time he did it, he just left it on the cliff. I'd heard something, it had woken me up. I went out and found the carcass. There were parts missing, a leg and a piece of hindquarters. I knew I had to find the pieces, because if anyone else did he'd be in trouble. I ran along the wall, the dark branches waving in the wind, and went down the steps to the beach. The handrail is painted a very bright pink, and I think this lodged in my memory somehow.'

An eye for colour, even when she was basically sleep-walking.

'I scrambled around on the rocks, because I was certain he would have thrown the pieces down there. I found a syringe lodged in a crevice, above the high-water line: it must have been left over from one of Raoul Charpentier's parties. When I'd found the parts I brought them up and hid them. I intended to return and bury the rest of the carcass, but I must have forgotten and gone back to bed.'

Sheila already knew the next part, about the hiding places. Freezer and studio.

'I took the fuse out of the freezer plug, so that the meat would eventually rot and be found. It was the only way I could think of.'

Strange logic, but logic all the same. She'd had to find some way of resolving the conflict between protecting Sam and dealing with her disgust at his actions. Indirect, but logical, logical.

'The next time he did it I found him. He'd woken me up again and this time I knew exactly where to go. I told him to go in, I'd deal with it. He must have been making quite a bit of noise, because while I was burying it Lewyn (a neighbouring farmer, the owner of the sheep) came out. He thought I'd done it. I couldn't explain, because Sam would get into trouble. If anyone ever found out he was doing this they'd have put him away. I couldn't allow that. I'd already lost one child. I thought I could help him.'

Not just logical but understandable, human. If once you accepted that a seven-year-old boy had become deranged to the extent that he was capable of such actions, then these were the things that his mother would have to do if she was going to protect him. And in doing them she

284

would be beset by such conflicts, such guilt, that they could, in a person predisposed towards it, trigger off a psychotic episode. Exactly the kind of episode that Adèle had in fact undergone, and appeared now to be pulling herself out of.

Dr Kavanagh picked up the Perspex-framed photographs of her grandchildren. Smiling, confident. Some children are good, some children are bad. And some children are mad. The only thing needed for Adèle's story to be wholly credible was Sheila Kavanagh's belief that any child could be so – well, Adèle had said it perfectly.

Evil.

Coming out into the daylight, Lewyn squinted and blinked. Surely that couldn't be Sam coming up the path?

'Sam?'

Sam waved.

'I thought you were with Pauline?'

'Oh yes. I was. Then she felt sick so she had to go home. My dad said would it be all right if I came up here for an hour? He said he'll come and get me when he's finished what he's doing. He said he's right in the fucking middle of it. He said I wasn't to be any trouble.'

Lewyn was surprised, but also pleased. If James was prepared to entrust Sam to him again, then he must genuinely have got over his suspicions of him. And looking at Sam, a dishevelled, dirty, mucky-faced kid, Lewyn found it difficult to sustain his belief that he could really be the one who'd been tearing sheep and dogs apart, limb from limb. After all he had no evidence, it was just a hunch. But he'd certainly be keeping a close eye on him, that much was for sure. Sam smiled.

'Do you want to play a game?'

* * *

James meandered into Sam's room. The stuffed monkey grinned at him, oblivious to the fact that it had lost an arm. Bloody children and their bedrooms! The place was a tip. He picked Sam's clothes off the floor, dumping them on the bed. He stripped off the sheet, dislodging the pillow which fell to the floor with a clink.

Clink?

He walked round to the other side of the bed and picked up the pillow. Underneath it was a key.

It wasn't me! (Click.)

He held the key, the metal cold and sharp on his palm, like a sliver of ice. The key to the secure room. What was it doing under Sam's pillow? The monkey, dismembered but still grinning, was saying nothing.

He crossed the hall, turned the corner, climbed the two steps; then he released the bolts and inserted the key. The door swung open. This time he was taking no chances: he dragged the chair out of Sam's room and wedged it in the doorway.

In the full afternoon light the columns of writing were starkly visible, ranks of inelegant hieroglyphics, reaching from just below the ceiling to a foot or so above the floor. The tops and bottoms of the columns were distinctly less legible than the middles: hard to scratch cleanly when you were stretching up or crouching down. One of the columns was completely disordered, the lines wavering and the characters reduced to jagged scrawls. She had perhaps tried to write at night? Or she'd injured her right hand somehow – or someone else had injured it for her – and was trying her left? But the rest of it was clear. He started at the top of what he took to be the first column, the one nearest the door.

'–I-don't-know-how-long-Ive-been-here-it-seems-like-years-he-wont-let-me-out-anymore-not-after-I-saw-him-with-Celia-on-the-cliff-dear-god-how-will-I-save-the-girls-he-means-to-have-them-I-know-dear-god–'

James gritted his teeth and read on, doggedly.

'No more! Aaaaagh! No!'

They were in the workroom playing torture. Lewyn had
his hand in the big vice on the worktable, and Sam turned
the handle an inch at a time, until the jaws were pressing
just hard enough to hold his hand still.

Lewyn looked down at the grinning child and abruptly
thought: the dibber. A pale patch on the wall, cruciform.
Sam had been quite taken with it, he recalled. Had it been
there since then? He couldn't remember.

He opened his mouth to ask Sam, and Sam took the
handle in both hands and twisted it a full half turn, then
another.

'Sam! Christ, what the . . .'

He scrabbled at the handle with his left hand as Sam
ducked away from him and ran to the stairs. He ran to
the top, reached up over his head and turned off the light.
Blackness fell all over Lewyn and he clamped his eyes
shut.

'Sam!'

Lewyn could hear him scratching around, like a rat in
the dark cellar.

'Put that light on. It isn't funny Sam!'

He again tried to reach the vice handle, but the choking,
enveloping darkness drained him of his strength. The
dark smothered his face. If he kept his eyes shut, if he
couldn't see, then he wouldn't be able to see the darkness,
the panic would recede. His right hand was throbbing, the
knuckle joints bruised and tender against the cold iron of
the vice.

He forced the terror out of his mind, made himself
think. There was an Anglepoise lamp on the worktable.
The switch was off somewhere to the left. He reached his

left arm out, feeling a dreadful, crushing vulnerability. Anything could happen in the dark, any senseless, insane, appalling thing. The blood boomed in his ears; he could feel it backing up along his right arm, the veins swelling like a stream in spring. Bolts of pain were shooting out from his crushed hand, but the panic was worse, unbearable—

Think.

He worked his left hand over the wall, feeling his way along: no switch. Oh Christ oh Christ oh Christ oh

He could hear something bumping, then the sound of metal dragging along the floor. A freezing, incapacitating slow wave of terror broke in his mind, and he simultaneously broke sweat, little trickles of liquid fear crawling down from his armpits and knees, down his back, his stomach, like worms, cold, slithering worms—

Think.

Where was the switch? He should have reached it by now. He was stretched to his maximum, splayed out against the wall like an exhibit in a glass case, except that no-one could see him because it was so—

He screwed his eyes tighter, clenching muscles he'd never felt before in his face, muscles that no-one would ever use unless they were in extreme pain, or worse, extreme fear. He shook his head violently.

Think.

Then it came to him: lower down. The switch was nearer the ground. He fumbled his hand down the wall, twisting the left side of his body, pulling on the bruised, pulpy joints of his right hand: he knelt, his free hand writhing over the plaster, desperately trying to feel the contours of the switch.

Click.

Through his eyelids he sensed the return of light to the cellar, but now the thought of what he might see was almost worse than the terror of seeing nothing. His hand froze.

He opened his eyes.

Sam was hurtling towards him, holding the dibber out in front of him in both hands; the light glimmered dully on the iron sheath of the point. Sam opened his mouth and a shrill, crazed, primitive scream came from him, sickeningly loud in the dead acoustics of the cellar room.

'E-e-e-e-e-e-e-e!'

Lewyn just had time to yell out a single syllable –

'*Sam!*'

and then the dibber gouged into him, catching him squarely in the armpit. He looked up: Sam rammed it in further, turned it (quarter turn, clockwise) then let it go. It hung in the air, dropping slightly under its own weight. Sam watched him as his eyes misted over and a low gurgling sound emerged from his mouth: then he slumped forward, and his head drooped.

Sam stood for a moment; then, satisfied, he went up the stairs and out of the house. It would be dark in an hour or two and he had a lot to do. The folded red exercise book had fallen out of his back pocket and now lay on the floor, innocently, near the spreading pool of rich red blood coming from the crucified farmer.

'–if-you-wont-help-me-Ill-find-someone-who-will-youll-not-get-out-of-here-they-have-to-die-theyre-devils-Ill-make-it-painless-I-sed-if-I-cant-stop-you-god-will-he-laughed-its-gods-work-Im-doing-cant-you-see-that-Ill-burn-them-burn-all-the-devil-out-of-them-a-burnt-offering-is-pleasing-to-the-lord–

'Let-me-out-then-Ill-help-you-he-laughed-again-your-no-better-than-they-are-he-says-theyre-not-his-anyway-how-can-he-say-that-sweet-christ-hes-out-there-now-I-

289

smell-smoke-god-if-your-there-stop-him-if-you-exist-
there-is-no-god–'

He was three-quarters of the way down the second
column by now. The writing had taken on a cramped,
urgent quality, and several times he had to reread a line
to make sense of it. The gaps between the words occasionally disappeared altogether, and many of the letters
could only be inferred from the context. Punctuation was
entirely absent.

Why had Sam wanted the key to this room? What use
could he possibly have for the deranged, semi-coherent
ramblings of a madwoman? A chill stole over him at
the thought of Sam standing here, alone, painstakingly
deciphering the laborious scratches, decoding them.

Who was that by the hole?

Lewyn had seen a bonfire. He'd smelled burning meat.
He'd seen someone poking the fire with a stick. When he
was coming to from his fall amongst the bones, Sam had
said something about a man with a stick, trying to tell him
something.

James shook his head. Not possible. Sam had just had
a funny turn, that was all. There was no way Sam could
have spoken to Raoul Charpentier in the trench where
the

(midget? sheep?)

bones were.

(or children's?)

Maaaa!

The certainty flooded him that what he was reading
was no madwoman's fantasy, no psychotic hallucination.

It was true.

'–he-sed-its-done-now-the-lord-is-satisfied-with-my-
work-they-will-sin-no-more-I-have-purified-them-the-
police-will-come-I-sed-they-will-find-them-but-he-sed-
Ive-thought-of-that-youll-see-soon-enough-oh-god-he-

frightens-me-I-will-watch-he-will-not-have-me-like-
he-had-them-my-Briony-my-Jonquil–'

He'd killed the children, just as Lewyn had said, burned
the bodies, as some kind of a sacrifice.

Now she's sinking like a stone
Now the devil's got his bone.

He couldn't read most of the third column, apart from
one word, god, which stood out against the jumbled
scratches. He turned to the fourth column, the last one,
near the window.

'–burnt-my-hand-but-it-is-healing-now-he-sed-Ill-put-
a-stop-to-your-scratching-he-will-have-to-kill-me-first-
its-done-now-he-sed-but-the-sheep-must-die-too-they-
are-tainted-by-the-same-evil-as-those-children-but-I-
will-keep-their-bones-he-sed-and-use-them-what-for-I-
sed-he-laughed-youll-see-he-sed-he-has-given-me-no-
food-today-not-emptied-my-bucket-I-will-go-mad-if-I-
stay-here-any-longer-I-can't-breathe-there-is-no-air-no-
food-again-today-he-has-not-come-to-the-room-I-can-
hear-no- noise-in-the-house-has-he-gone-away-he-
couldnt-leave-me-here-to-die-I-will-go-mad-not-mad-
please-thats-what-he-tells-people-they-think-me-mad-I-
am-not-mad-please-jesus-not-today-I-heard-a-sound-
downstairs-he-has-come-back-oh-jesus-I-will-watch-he-
will-not-have-me–'

James looked up. Funny kind of time for someone to
be out on a powerboat. Nearly dark. Why would anyone be out in a powerboat or flying a model aircraft or
using electric power tools, sheep-shearing maybe, no, the
wrong season. And then he thought Christ, I know that
sound and jerked his head round just in time to see the
chair being whisked away and the door slammed shut. He
heard the bottom bolt slide into place, then a pause,
something scraping on the floor, creaking, then the top
bolt.

He stood at the window, immobile, finally believing what he'd really known all along but had suppressed, rejected, evaded.

The truth in madness.

Adelts don't do that kind of thing.

Could a child?

17

Heavenly Choristers

'Whoooo-oo-oooh! Whoo-ooo-ooo-ooooooh!'

Sam screamed and charged across the field, herding the stamping, bleating creatures towards the gate. There were about twenty-five of them, Sam estimated, so he needed about eight. A third. He managed to isolate a group of them from the rest and, after a great deal of trouble, got them through the gate; they dispersed round the field, instantly calm again. Ten. Oh well, that was close enough probably.

The hay-feeders were lined up along the cliff edge, apart from the one that had carried Pauline to her watery resting place. It was a shame she'd got spoiled, she wouldn't be any good now. But he'd had to think of something quickly: he hadn't counted on a new person coming along. They had to be perfect, unblemished, which meant without any damage, or they wouldn't work. Oh well.

He tramped back along the cliffs to the house. He needed petrol and matches, and maybe some wood, though he could probably do without the wood. The light was fading fast now.

A booming, battering noise greeted him at the house: his dad trying to get out. Sam ignored it. There was a can of petrol in the basement – it was to make the lawnmower work in the summer. It was very dangerous, because if you got it on yourself you could go on fire and if you drank it your insides would melt or something. It was one of the reasons he wasn't allowed to go in the basement. He'd have to be careful. He grasped the carrying handle on the tin and dragged it to the stairs. It was really heavy, but he lugged it up, step by step, the metal handle digging a weal into his fingers. He lumped it out through the kitchen and into the front room.

'Sam? Is that you? You'd better open this door *right now*! I mean it Sam. No kidding now.' His dad, yelling from the secure room. There was only one can of petrol so he'd have to go a bit easy.

Matches. His mum had probably left some in her room. She needed them for her cigarettes. He went up and rummaged around in her chest of drawers. He found an old box of 7-Eleven matches; she must have brought them with her from London. What a funny thing to do! She was always doing funny things, ever since he could remember. He counted the matches: seventeen. That ought to be enough.

He dragged the can over to the big scruffy couch. The sheep portrait gazed down at him unblinkingly. What did she want to paint sheep for? Sam liked painting too, but he didn't want to paint any boring old sheep. He liked painting houses. Houses on fire.

He poured some of the petrol on to the couch, balancing the can on the armrest and allowing it to tip over just enough for a slow trickle of the pale liquid to slop out. Not too much, though. He dragged the can out to the front step, carefully replacing the cap, then returned to the front room. The match flared, and Sam threw it at the couch: it went out before it landed. Damn! He tried another, with the same result. He pondered for a moment, then went up to his parents' room again. He wished his dad would shut up for a bit, all the noise was making it difficult to think properly. Again he rummaged in the drawers; near the back was a crumpled white and purple packet of Silk Cuts, the ones his mum liked best. She must have put them there in case she ran out in the middle of the night. Sam hated cigarettes: the smoke got into his throat and made him cough. But he could see how they might come in handy. There was a whole one and a half one.

'Sam! I promise I won't be angry but you've got to open this door right now. This isn't a good game, Sam. Right now, I mean it . . .'

Back at the couch Sam lit the half cigarette, then, glancing around furtively, took a quick puff. Uuugh. He wouldn't be doing that again. The smoke was disgusting and he coughed, his eyes watering, holding the horrible thing away from him. His dad said smoking was a very bad habit, but it was up to his mum if she wanted to: it was her funeral. Sam would never smoke.

He threw it on to the couch: it smouldered for a while, then there was a small 'whump' and the fabric began to scorch. Shoots of flame sprang up. He watched it for a moment to make sure it wasn't going to go out again; already the smoke was filling the room and curling up towards the stairs. The sheep gazed down, tranquil, alert, watchful.

'Sam! You're going to be in big trouble if you don't . . .' He turned and left the house, pulling the door shut behind him, took hold of the petrol can again and began the long, arduous journey back to Stumble Head.

James became conscious of the smoke by degrees. He was aware first of an irritation in his nostrils and a dryness around his eyes. Sam had come and gone, on God alone knew what business, but one thing was for certain: he wasn't going to open the door, which had been made well, fitting snugly into the surround, but not snugly enough to keep out the smoke. James coughed, and the word 'fire' went off in his brain, like a starting pistol.

He ran to the window, also beautifully made, but more importantly not locked. He opened it and the draught dragged in a small cloud of smoke from under the door. The window was higher than is usual, the lower end of it at shoulder height. There was a bar down the centre of the aperture, but there was enough clearance on either side to get out; he grabbed the bar and pulled himself up, wriggling his shoulder and head through. He looked down: it was quite a drop, and it would be hard to jump cleanly with the bar in the way. It would be more like a controlled fall – and the ratio of control to fall would be largely a matter of luck. He would be landing on the jagged rubble of the defunct concrete path that he hadn't got round to finishing yet: not the surface he would have chosen to land on, ideally. In an ideal world where he hadn't been locked in and set alight by his own fucking son . . . He shook his head. There was no time to think about that. The smoke was now a constant irritant in his throat; whatever he was going to do he'd have to do it soon.

He twisted himself, sideways, wedging his shoulder against the bar, and leaned out further, craning his neck upwards: the gutter was a mere two feet or so above the window lintel. This end of the house was two storeys only, clearly an addition to the three-storey main building. The roof sloped sharply up, double pitched; if he managed to keep his footing he could get up to the apex ridge and find a better place to jump, or even a downpipe. He didn't like the thought of trusting his weight to a rusty downpipe bracket, but it was a more attractive proposition than an optimistic leap on to rubble and hardcore. He stubbornly concentrated on his escape route, blotting out the reasons why it was necessary. If he allowed himself to think of that, he felt certain he'd end up sitting on the floor weeping while the smoke engulfed him. No, he'd deal with Sam once he was safely out. He'd cry later.

Sam rested halfway. It was nearly dark and the lights of Goodwick and Fishguard Bay were visible now; the trees and grass were losing their colour, fading out to an ashy grey.

It was a pity about Lewyn. If he could have kept him whole he would have done: as it was, he wouldn't be coming back. Still, that was what the book said. His arm should be wholly withered, which meant completely buggered (as his mum would have put it); admittedly it also said his right eye should be utterly blinded, but he hadn't had time for that. He'd done the best he could by turning the light off – he hadn't allowed for Lewyn's Anglepoise lamp. Oh well it'd have to do. Jesus would understand, he was sure. He'd kept his mum and dad unblemished anyway. That was the most important thing. They would live for ever now, though his mum wasn't exactly dead yet. Well, he'd see to that when he got time.

He regretted Elvis though. He'd tried to keep him whole, but the stupid animal had struggled so hard that Sam had had to subdue him. The eye had been a mistake – he'd been aiming for the throat. And then he'd broken his leg dragging him to the cliff: he couldn't allow Elvis to go over with a leg broken, so he'd hacked it off with the little Stanley knife. Better a clean stump than a broken leg, he was sure. Elvis had screamed: he hadn't understood what Sam was doing. Well he was only a dog after all. You couldn't expect him to understand everything. Sam was certain that even if Elvis didn't come back he'd go to heaven and live for ever up there. Maybe Jesus would give him a replacement leg. Would Jesus be able to fix his eye? Sam wasn't sure, but if Jesus could make a whole person come back when they were dead it'd surely be nothing much for him to give a dog a new eye. He hoped so anyway.

He was sorry too about the sheep, but they'd been so *difficult*, running about and bleating. And he hadn't realized just how heavy an adult sheep was, and how fragile their legs were. He hadn't known then about the unblemished rule: he'd thought that if you just got them over somehow, even in pieces, it'd work. Well he'd learned, and the day he'd been staying with Lewyn he'd perfected the technique of scaring them over. He was getting the hang of it, like when his dad showed him how to hammer nails. There was a knack, his dad said, you had to get the hang of it. But he obviously hadn't got it right yet: no-one was coming back, not Ruthie, no-one.

He'd taken quite a risk with Ruthie, but for a first attempt it hadn't been too bad. He'd always been able to make his mum do things: you just thought them at her and after a while she did them. It didn't work with his dad for some reason. In any case he wasn't that bothered about Ruthie – she wasn't exactly a lot of fun. He wasn't at all sure he *wanted* her to come back, come to think of it, if she was always going to be crying and clinging on to his mum.

No, the thing he was really excited about was the Stumble Head people, the Heavenly Choristers. Hundreds of them, the man in the shoe shop had said. All unblemished. If he could get *them* back, that'd really be something. Just imagine, a whole gang of people coming back and living for ever. And all thanks to him. His dad would be proud of him. He probably wouldn't mind about being locked in the room and set on fire. It'd be quite an achievement, just like when he'd come top in maths at school. Better even. His dad might buy him a bike. Sam briefly regretted the lost Christmas present, but it was worth it. It'd been hard to make himself fall down the stairs and it had really hurt his back, but it had certainly worked.

He would try to get the lady at the party and Edith and the girls back too, but that had all been rather a long time ago, and he wasn't sure Raoul had killed them right anyway. Raoul might not have known that they had to be unblemished, and he'd messed about with the girls' bones. When he'd talked to him before he fell in the hole, Raoul had said that they were all devils, even the sheep. Sam found this a bit hard to believe, and his confidence in Raoul had suffered accordingly. Then when he'd read the writing on the wall his estimation had risen again: Raoul knew all about sacrifices and fires and all that. Edith's account had become unreadable in places though, so he couldn't be sure. Raoul probably knew what he was doing, at least most of the time. Oh well, he'd give it a try. No harm in trying, that's what his dad said.

Almost dark now. He picked up his can and struggled on. Nearly there.

James had one hand on the gutter; the other was bent behind him, holding the bar. He hooked a leg up and wedged it against the window frame, then raised himself, slowly, carefully, pulling on the guttering. He had a queasy, vertiginous feeling that the gutter would come away at any moment, but it was surprisingly sound. He nerved himself for a second, then let go of the bar – for what seemed like a long time his hand reached above his head for the gutter, as he hung from one arm, secured only by the leg braced in the window, leaning precariously outwards. His fingers found the rough metal of the gutter and he grabbed on to it, rested.

Jesus!

He released his other hand, shaking the blood back into circulation. Then he gripped the gutter again and, closing his eyes, heaved. He was aware of his own noises, mutterings, grunts: he was distracted momentarily by the realization that this was exactly how he sounded when he was making love with Adèle.

'Easy now. Easy. Eeeeeea-sy-now.'

His arms shook uncontrollably with the exertion and his hands grew slimy with sweat. He was going to fall, he knew it! The water in his bladder tilted and lurched, tingling. He opened his eyes and stared at the sky. The muscles in his upper arms stretched, complaining loudly.

'Uuuuuuugh!'

A bit more, a bit more, just a – little bit – more!

He managed to lever his elbow into the gutter, and the extra purchase allowed him to pull up the other leg. He raised himself until he was standing on the window ledge, straddling the dividing bar, both forearms secure in the gutter.

Now for the last part. He counted backwards from five, then he forced his forearms down, kicking his leg up and round until his heel reached the gutter. He scrambled up over the loose slates, clawing at them, got his chest then his belly over the gutter and on to the roof. He kicked at the gutter, which began to give way under the pressure, but he was safe now, his legs dangling harmlessly as he inched his way up, until he was spreadeagled on the roof, panting, exhausted, victorious.

Digging his heels against the exposed battens, he mountaineered up the treacherous slates, finally reaching the ridge. He sat astride it, offering up incoherent prayers of thanks to a God he'd never believed in.

'Thank you Jesus. Thank you God. Thank you Jesus.'

He tilted his head back and drank in the night air.

300

* * *

The sheep edged round the dark field: one of them found the hay-feeders and began to chew the fibrous matter, looking up frequently as Sam poured carefully measured amounts of petrol into the hay, distributing it as evenly as he could.

The sky was almost black now, a shade of blue so deep as to seem darker than any blackness. There was no moon, and the stars gleamed fitfully, a long way away.

Sam finished with the can. He stood up on top of one of the hay-feeders. He cleared his throat.

'All the people in the sea
You must hearken unto me
Holy Mary, quite contrary,
Jesus and his holy dad,
If you're good or if you're bad
When I call your names aloud
Come back out and join the crowd.'

He stamped rhythmically to keep the time and the sheep watched him, startled, all ears, as his shrill voice sang out.

'When the sheep go falling in
You will have your go again
They go in and you come out
You will hear me when I shout
Jesus and his holy dad
We will bring the people back.'

Sam paused, aware of the ten pairs of black, suspicious eyes on him. He couldn't remember the next bit. He felt in his back pocket for his exercise book: not there. Damn! He must have dropped it somewhere. Bloody damn! He backtracked over the last few lines, frowning, muttering them under his breath. Oh yes.

'You will live forev-er
All come out togeth-er

Everybody in the deep
I will swop you for the sheep
People in the wa-ter
Like a cup and sau-cer
O-U-T spells
Out!'

He jumped down and struck a match: the hay caught immediately and he went on to the next trough. The sheep that had been feeding ducked away as the flames licked up. Within seconds all three feeders were blazing brightly, sparks and charred fragments floating down. The sheep stood, finally seeing something that astonished them, as the sudden light threw their long, dancing shadows across the field.

The little boy ran behind them, then took off his baseball cap and swung it round his head.

'Wooo-oo-oooo! Woooo-oo-oo-ooooh!'

He hit the ground running and raced in through the front door. A blast of smoke and heat gripped him at the throat; he took a deep breath of night air, then shouldered his way through to the kitchen. He reached the sink, smashed the window over it and again gasped in air. He found the light switch, then wet a tea towel and put it over his face. There was a hose somewhere, for cleaning out the cellar. He stumbled down the stairs, grabbed at it, dragged it back up.

The smoke gave way to steam as he played the water over the blazing couch, choking through the tea towel. The boards around it were charred, but there was nothing much else in there to burn: thank Christ they hadn't furnished the place yet! He flung open the windows and the smoke and steam churned about in great heavy slabs, then began to thin out. He left the hose running over the floor and fled.

Where to? James stopped on the grass outside the house, trying to slow down his overheated brain. Where would Sam be? He had absolutely no idea.

Never mind, get to a phone, call the police. He couldn't have gone far. He raced over the dewy grass towards Lewyn's house.

Drip drip.

The slow red drops oozed down the handle of the dibber and collected along the crosspiece where they fell, one by one, on to the floor.

Lewyn stared, filmy-eyed, at the pool of congealing blood around him. His left hand twitched. Not dead then, he thought cautiously. Not quite. He tried to lift the hand but it was a gargantuan thing, the size of a planet, miles and miles away. It was made of some dense, inert substance, like rock.

Try again.

Drip drip. My blood, he thought wearily. If I don't do something about it pretty soon all my blood will just drip drip drip away.

The hand twitched again, then dragged a little way along the floor, towards his body. It crawled up over his leg, sluggish, stupid, disobedient.

He contrived to wrap the grey, inflexible fingers around the crosspiece of the dibber. Now you must pull it out. Can't.

Try again.

The fingers curled round the wooden handle, and he forced himself to take an interest in their activity, tried to wrench his thoughts away from the slow, hypnotic dripping of his vital fluid. The angle was tricky, but he dislodged the thing, and heard himself give a mighty scream as the torn tissues, ragged, raw, were ripped apart again. The wooden implement clattered to the floor.

Didn't I have another hand somewhere, he thought idly, just out of curiosity, and painfully twisted his head to the right. He followed the line of the arm along until he reached a blackened, swollen glove on the end of it, trapped in a vice. Boxing glove? he wondered, and then the scream rang out again as he realized what it was.

'Lewyn! You in there?'

James smashed at the front door, kicking and shouldering until the panels splintered open. He reached in and twisted the handle.

'Lewyn!'

In the basement Lewyn heard the voice and tried to find one of his own, one that wasn't a simple scream of despair.

'James! Down here!'

The sheep screamed, terrified now, as the shrieking child charged and charged, turning them round, blocking their exits. They stamped, their heads high, calling out to each other in their high, harsh voices and restricted vocabularies. Between the devil and the deep blue sea was a wall of fire, brilliantly coloured flames dancing up into the sky.

'Wooooooo-oo-ooooh!'

They ran into the inferno, jumping clumsily over the burning hay, catching alight, screaming as they plunged over the other side and off the cliff. They tumbled down, transfigured, beautiful, incandescent forms sailing out, like the brightest of angels: Sam, alight also, also screaming, falling behind them, dimly aware that once again he'd got it wrong.

The sea received them with a hiss, like a great devouring snake.

It wasn't like doing Bronze Medal at school, Sam found

himself thinking as he plunged down into the deadly blackness. For one thing it was unbelievably cold, much colder than the swimming pool. It was colder than his body knew how to experience or express to him. And the water in the pool, he thought, it didn't slosh about the whole time. Also in the brilliantly lit swimming pool you could see right down to the wavering, glowing, ghostly pattern on the tiled floor. You had to pick up a brick with your pyjamas on: Sam remembered (his thoughts revolving lazily as shock took over his body) how odd his body had felt having his Count Duckulas stuck to him like another skin. His clothes now were much heavier of course, but apart from that it was the same thing really. The most important rule, the one that Mr Matthews said time and time again, until he had everyone imitating him and giggling, was:

Keep cool, keep calm.

You just had to hold your breath, not struggle, and you'd float. Because people, Mr Matthews explained in the booming, echoing acoustic of the pool, are naturally buoyant, that means they float. You could keep your eyes shut if you were frightened by how funny everything looked underwater (and Sam decided against taking a little experimental peek as his descent slowed down – the thought of all that black water all around him, above and below and for miles on every side).

Calm, said Mr Matthews. Cool. And Sam held the words in his head as great flows of terror and cold buffeted him, the freezing water no longer taking his heat but giving its own negative energy, covering him with the gentle, insistent breath of the dead, who showed no inclination at all to come out of the sea.

And suddenly Sam began to feel something he had no words to describe, no thoughts to imagine: a great, whispering, limitless, embracing *peacefulness*, a quiet, throbbing feeling of being drained of all worry and pain, an awareness that this was a good, tranquil place to be. Calm, but not in the way Mr Matthews had had in mind: this was the calm of shock and heat-loss, the calm of drowning. A good place to be, Sam thought as he began to rise again through the turbulent water. He thought he might like to stay here. For ever.

James helped Lewyn into the ambulance, holding his left hand.

'You'll be fine, you'll be all right, you'll—'

'James I . . .'

'You'll be—'

Lewyn pulled James's head down to his mouth, kissed him awkwardly on the neck.

'I love you,' he whispered.

Oh God, James thought, as if I didn't have enough love to deal with. Love for Adèle, love (incredibly, still) for Sam, and (neverendingly) for Ruthie, the love he felt trying to cram itself into his eyes and throat. Oh God please no more love.

And in any case, he thought abruptly, I don't know how. A lifetime of 'backs against the wall' had left him with only the most rudimentary notion of what a man might want with another man. And none of it seemed to have anything to do with the way he felt about the injured, possibly dying, Lewyn, whose breath had just stroked his ear, whose eyes had just met his.

James held Lewyn's hand in his and sensed the urgency, the heat, the passion of Lewyn's feeling.

Could I?

It was such a small, simple, unassuming question, like a shy animal breaking cover and then darting back out of sight. A shrew, perhaps, waiting for the age of the dinosaurs to come to an end so it could take over the world. If the answer was yes – James was unable to compute the consequences that might attend.

He recalled the smell of the day room at Cardiff Royal Infirmary, the scent of controlled desperation and leaking sphincters and forcibly-injected optimism. The day-in day-out compassion of the nurses, starched into their uniforms, the diffident, anxious collusion of the patients.

He held Lewyn's hand and felt an answer to Adèle's impalpable disconnection, her breath the air from another planet, the completeness of her ruination by the thing she loved most in the world, her strange, lethal child.

His child also. The fruit, as they said, of his loins. Of his love.

Could I?

But then it came to him: the question was superfluous because, he thought, I already do. Whatever it might mean and however he might try to feel about it, it had already happened: he and Lewyn were connected, and he was a different person now.

So could he ever again hold Adèle to him, aware of her unconscious vigilance concerning Sam's welfare? Could he ever again innocently, unthinkingly, love her, without restraint or limitation or question? The question that had now been posed by Lewyn's urgent hand and the flutter of his breath against James's ear.

'I love you,' Lewyn whispered, and James squeezed his hand back in answer as the paramedics guided him into the ambulance. He watched the lights flashing as the vehicle pulled away, the alarm rising up, an awakening beast crying into the night.

Fifty-nine, sixty, he was nearly asleep, rocked by the unending rhythm of the soft, murderous sea. Sixty-one, sixty-two – unknowingly, Sam's breath escaped him, bubbling up alongside him as he suddenly surfaced: he awoke with a start as the freezing wet air slapped him across the face and the surf boomed gigantically in his ears, no longer muffled by the depth of the water.

The paddling motions he'd been born with, refined by Mr Matthews's instruction, carried him back to the rocky beach. He clambered out of the breaking surf and crawled out on to land, like some antediluvian sea creature who had decided its evolutionary future lay beyond the sea. Or like a drowned soul called back from the deep by witchcraft. Sometimes, Sam thought, sometimes things do come back.

James returned to the cellar of Lewyn's house where three policemen were standing about, one of them filling in evidence slips for James to sign, the evidence itself already bagged up. They were waiting for someone from Forensics to come to collect tissue and fibre samples and to take pictures. There was certainly no shortage of blood to take samples from. After the pictures, some lucky sod would get to clean it all up. And after that the hunt would be on for a next of kin to notify, at this festive season.

They looked up as he came down the stairs to the room, and he was strongly aware of their interest in him. Professional interest. He doubted that they got much action in the usual course of things, and he felt unpleasantly certain that he was going to be the centre of attention for the next few hours at least. Would he have to make a statement? He sniffed the air, at first unable to place the smell. Then he identified it and closed his eyes. Blood.

He looked at the policemen, not knowing how to speak, what to say. He'd already reported Sam as missing: there was a search team on the way from Haverfordwest, coastguards, all sorts of people. Christmas Eve. He felt apologetic for causing so much trouble. It was going to be hard to shake off the old parental habit of assuming responsibility for Sam's misdemeanours, he thought, though Sam had certainly progressed from kicking balls through people's windows. Yes sirree.

One of the three approached him, a young officer with a full beard that was clearly his first attempt at the genre. He plucked nervously at it as he came towards James, and James could feel the hesitation in his manner.

'Mr Tullian? My name's PC Lodge, how d'you do,' he offered his hand, 'and this is PC Garner and PC Brophy. We're going to want to ask you some questions, but there's no hurry for any of that, see: we could maybe get you a cup of tea or something, you could sit down for five minutes. Bit of a shocker all this, eh?' James was at first surprised by the concern in the officer's tone. Then he thought: star witness. They need me in good condition. Only a witness – or maybe a suspect? There was, he realized, no good reason why they should accept his story about Sam. In fact it had seemed distinctly implausible to him as he'd told it. My son impaled this man against the wall, then locked me in a room and set fire to the house. Then he disappeared somewhere. How old is he? Oh, seven. Hm. It occurred to him that he should perhaps be careful what he said now, then realized that he had nothing to say in any case. He laughed, was shocked by the inappropriateness of the sound, mumbled an apology. The young officer turned to the other two, who shrugged eyebrows.

'Sir?'

'I'm OK, really,' James started to say, but stopped when he found his eye resting on the contents of one of the plastic evidence bags which were lying on the workbench. It was so familiar that it took him a moment to register it.

A red exercise book. Sylvine, feint and margin. And on the inside of the front cover, he knew, was written neatly Sam D. Tullian. The policeman stood aside as James walked past him towards the workbench. The exercise book had been transformed by the plastic envelope from a simple, innocent item of stationery into something more sinister: into evidence. He picked up the bag, the plastic cool and glossy, almost slimy. Lodge made as if to stop him handling it, and then, seeing the expression on James's face, backed down.

James withdrew the book from the bag, as if he were handling a snake, and opened it at random. As he read his awareness of the room and the high, alarming smell of Lewyn's blood, his consciousness of the predatory attentions of the police, all fell away. The world collapsed around him, like a disaster-movie set, as, for the first and last time, he entered the mind of his son.

Woe to my worthless shepherde!
Let his arm be wholly wither'd
His right eye utterly blynded!
  Woe: misfortune, sorrow.
  (misfortune: bad luck)

Sam's neat, deliberate handwriting covered the pages, definitions and quotations incongruously mixed in with maths problems and doodles, and what looked like attempts at a poem.

Strike the shepherde, that the sheepe
may be scattered
Two thirds shall be cut off and perish
And one thirde shall be lefte alyve
And I wille put this thirde into the fyre.
  Perish: die.

310

Bayonet: blade that fits on the muzzle of a rifle.
(rifle: a long-barrelled gun)
Pyre: a funeral mound, for burning the dead.
Sacrifice: offer to a deity.
(deity: a god)

six divided by three = two
If Mary has twelve oranges to share equally between
Harry, Bob and Bill, how many will each boy receive?
Four. One third of nine = three, two thirds of nine = six.

James flicked the pages over. He recognized some of
it as coming from the secure-room wall. (Sampled the
handwriting. Off the wall. Sam pulled the handwriting off
the wall.)

If he brynges a lamb as his offeryng, he shall
brynge a female without blemishe.
blemish: fault, flaw.
flaw: defect, fault, blemish.
(fault: defect)
(defect: imperfection)

And the priest shall offer the whole, and burne it on
the altar; it is a burnt offeryng, an offeryng by fyre, a
pleasing odour to the LORDE.
(odour: smell)

The second Angel blew his trumpet,
and something burning with fyre was
thrown into the sea.

James turned the page.

And the sea gave up the dead in it.

311

'Jesus Christ,' he said softly.

Stumble: fall, trip.

'Jesus Christ,' he said again, to the bearded policeman, 'I think I know where he is.'

They could see the glow as they drew up to the Stumble Head turn-off. One of the officers stayed in the car to contact Haverfordwest who would redirect the search team. James and the other two entered the field.

The hay-feeders were smouldering and flickering as they reached them. James regarded them, and was aware that he could *feel* Sam's recent presence here, as if he were a famous psychic brought in at the eleventh hour by a desperate police force. I haven't got a cravat or strangely penetrating eyes, he thought, and felt like a charlatan.

'Graham! Over here!'

PC Brophy was standing at the edge, shining his torch down on to the sea where a number of large forms were bobbing about. PC Lodge joined him and the two men scrambled down the side, the shale clattering as it accompanied them. They shone their torches over the heavy swell of the sea.

'Nothing. Just some sheep.'

They climbed back up, panting, and Lodge came across to where James was standing.

'Mr Tullian. I have to ask you. Do you know what's been going on here? If you know anything you'd best tell us now, see, and save us all nearly breaking our bloody necks on the bloody cliffs all night.'

James looked at him without expression.

'Mr Tullian?'

'He was here,' James said, then giggled at the melodramatic way it came out. 'And I think he's still around somewhere.' The officer began to move away, then turned back.

'Why would he come all the way out here? What for?' James shrugged.

PC Lodge tugged at his beard, and James stood, at a loss, in the dark, damp field, aware that this young policeman was finding him very odd indeed.

'Mr Tullian, once the rest of them get here, the frogmen and all and the Divisional lot, I'm going to have to tell 'em why you brought us all out here. Make a report, see. And if I just say, well Mr Tullian here, he had a feeling see, they're going to look at me daft. Everybody's going to want to know what you and your family have been up to out here. But I can't tell them unless you tell me, see? I'm supposed to know.' He smiled. 'They'll think I've not been doing my job right, see? You wouldn't want 'em to think that would you?'

Christ, James thought, he wants me to like him. All this lunacy, and he thinks that if he's charming enough I'll explain it all to him.

'I don't know what's been going on,' James said, trying not to sound indignant.

'Where's your boy, Mr Tullian?' asked PC Lodge, and James realized with a shock that this rural policeman wasn't the pushover he was pretending to be.

'I've told you, I don't know. But I think he's nearby.'

'Because of what was in the exercise book.'

'Yes, but also . . .' James stopped, shrugged, feeling as guilty as the most miserable sin. 'Sorry,' he added.

PC Lodge swung his flashlight around, along the walls, over the grass: a sheep, caught in the beam, stared back, its eyes perfectly blank, perfectly calm.

'What, he's somewhere here d'you think? Hiding maybe?'

James looked round helplessly.

'Or where?'

'In the sea?' said James. 'I don't know.' He didn't want to have to think about all the places Sam might be.

'Mr Tullian, I hate to say this but if your boy's down there in the sea then by the time the rescue team get here it's going to be too late. For God's sake if you know where he is . . .'

'I don't know! Christ how many more times!' James felt his eyes fill up and turned away to wipe his face with his sleeve. 'I don't know where he is,' he said, and Lodge, believing him, patted him on the shoulder and murmured, 'Sorry. This is my job.' He went over to the smouldering hay-feeders, pretending to search them, though it was obvious at a glance that Sam couldn't be there.

He didn't now believe that Sam was going to be found that night. So there was going to have to be a major missing-person search on Christmas Day, which was guaranteed to go down a storm. He sighed heavily, already regretting the big Christmas dinner and the long slouch in front of the telly.

And it would all be for nothing, he thought. Because although he was sure now that James Tullian was telling the truth, he was also, and more reluctantly, sure that Sam Tullian was already dead.

He stroked his newly acquired beard as the dim light from the smouldering hay fell on him, and listened to the sea raging against the cliffs far below. In the field behind him the sheep trod gently.

The O.T. room was freezing in the pre-dawn light of Christmas Day. Paper streamers and cardboard Father Christmases were hung about, jarring, incongruous.

She regarded her final painting. A field, this time at night. No sheep. No people. Not even any trees. Black

314

and dark green, relieved only by the stars, which were falling, reflected in the heaving ocean.

Luxury liner on maiden voyage hit by floating iceberg. Distress calls sent. Ship sinks. Most lost on board, some survivors in lifeboats return to tell the tale to a shocked and humbled world, who will never again believe that anything is unsinkable.

She remembered seeing a cartoon: a long queue of anxious relatives at the shipping-line office, and a man at the front with a polar bear asking, 'Any news of the iceberg?'

The stars were falling and so how would she ever find her way home? She had lost her way, but more than that, she'd lost her map of how to get back. Her home: it was a place not to be found on any chart, and there did not appear to be any roads to it. It had vanished as surely as the iceberg, and she was unsure that she even wanted to find it.

I have lost my place in the world, she thought, in the same way that I might lose my place in a book. The only thing to do was start again, from the beginning. Except that second time round, she felt sure it would all be different.

She turned off the lights and went back to bed.

The two little girls stood up in the water, their identical yellow dresses clinging to them. They smiled and waved.

It's all right, Lewyn called, you can come out now.

Edith stood beside him, the nail in her hand.

Is he dead? she asked.

Yes, Lewyn said, the beast is dead now.

Who killed him?

Lewyn pointed to a figure standing nearby: James.

He must love you very much, she said, and flung the nail away, far out to sea.

The machines hummed all around him, the saline and plasma drips, the heart-rate monitor.

The machines roared and boomed all around him, but Lewyn knew what to do: he walked along the assembly line until he reached the chute where the twitching, half-familiar hunks of flesh dropped down. He reached up and pushed a button.

Silence.

It was full daylight when the police brought James home. He was demented with shock and exhaustion, but the sharp, powerful smell of the burned upholstery and charred wood gave him the energy to turn off the still-running hose and crawl upstairs to his bed, blind to the wet footprints ahead of him on the bare wooden stairs.

He collapsed, staying awake just long enough to register the faintest, most elusive of sounds coming from the secure room. He twitched as he fell into sleep, thinking neon light, wasp, electric train.

He slept and the smell of the sea hung over his dreams, sharp, salty, nearby, tickling his nostrils. He dreamed of great fish leaping in the sea and making a gentle, strangely familiar sound, which, oddly, now seemed to be coming from somewhere in the house:

Hmmmmmmmmmmmmmmmmmmmmmmmmmmmmmm.

THE END

THE IMMACULATE
by Mark Morris

'Easily Mark Morris's best novel so far . . . a real contribution to the literature of the ghostly'
Ramsey Campbell

Jack Stone, outwardly shy and unremarkable, writes works of dark and tortured fantasy which have captured the public imagination. Despite his celebrity status, he is a lonely man whose smart London life is a form of exile. He has painful memories he does not wish to examine, roots he refuses to revisit – until he meets Gail, a beautiful emphatic girl who seems to sense the shadows that surround him.

When news arrives of a death in his family, Jack is forced to return to the horror that has coloured his nightmares for years: his childhood home. There he finds the terror and humiliation he remembers from his upbringing, but he discovers something else as well – a revelation more startling than he could have dreamed up in his wildest flights of fantasy . . .

'Fast gaining a reputation as the most stunningly original dark fantasist working in Britain today'
Starburst

'A skilfully constructed tale, topped off with a mind-boggling twist'
The Times

0 552 13971 8

HOOLET
by John McNeil

'THE SHORT-EARED OWL IS A SERIAL KILLER, SLAYING MERCILESSLY ON A MASSIVE SCALE . . .'

Sandy Douglas watches birds – the feathered kind mostly – especially birds of prey. When someone begins murdering women, killing them by night, ruthlessly, silently and totally without warning, it is Sandy who first gives the killer a name – The Hoolet – after an owl he has been writing about in his nature column for a London newspaper.

Called in by his editor to cover the investigation, Sandy becomes a creature of the dark, a lurker in the shadows, an anticipator of evil to come. While each successive killing baffles the police even more and increases the fear which holds the small Scottish town in its grip, Sandy seems always to be one step ahead. But how far can his word be trusted? How true are the newspaper reports he files every day? And why have the police suddenly started watching Sandy?

Told through Sandy's eyes, *Hoolet* unfolds into a mesmerising and gripping psychological thriller, full of startling and unsettling twists which build to a shattering and surprising denouement. With this powerful and disturbing novel of a serial killer loose on the banks of the Clyde, John McNeil has delivered a debut of chilling originality which marks him out as a new master of the genre.

0 552 13489 9

SOMEBODY COME AND PLAY
by Clare McNally

For thirty years there had been peace beside the waters of Lake Solaria except in the rambling mansion where Myrtle Hollenbeck paced up and down like a mad woman, waiting for the return of her children.

But Myrtle's waiting is soon over: one night she is found hanging from her daughter's skipping rope. Everyone believes Myrtle's death to be a case of routine suicide; everyone, that is, apart from Cassie Larchmont, the ten-year-old child, who witnessed Myrtle's death, and Robert Landers, an investigating police officer who hears from Cassie how a dark shadow stood by Myrtle's side that fearful night.

At the same time, Nicole Morgan comes into Cassie's life. Dark-haired, malevolent, dressed in quaint old-fashioned clothes popular decades before, Nicole seems bent on luring the other children into Myrtle's haunted mansion. The fabulous playroom they discover conceals untold horrors, while outside the terror that has lain quietly on the lake bed for thirty years rises slowly towards them. Only Landers can save them before that evil kills them all . . .

0 552 13033 8